STAR TIME

STAR TIME

Joseph Amiel

Crown Publishers, Inc., New York

Published by Crown Publishers, Inc.,
201 East 50th Street, New York, New York 10022.
Member of the Crown Publishing Group.

CROWN is a trademark of Crown Publishers, Inc.

Manufactured in the United States of America

To my sister, Linda

ACKNOWLEDGEMENTS

In the hope that my perceptions would be accurate and insightful, many people in the television industry gave liberally of their time and experience while I was engaged in doing the research for this book. Because I promised anonymity to many and might compromise others, I have chosen not to name anyone individually. Yet, each and every one of you who helped me with this book have my deepest gratitude.

I wish to offer particular thanks to a present and a recent senior executive with major networks who have both seen so much during their illustrious careers and generously imparted their wisdom to me, both in interviews and by reviewing the entire manuscript's first draft for errors. To the extent that there are any, the faults are solely mine, as of course are the viewpoints.

Special thanks should also go to those strangers—now friends—in news who kindly allowed me to observe their operations and to interview them despite their pressured schedules. Watching them in action deepened my respect for their profession.

Prologue

Greg Lyall lay in bed later than usual, reflecting on the turn of events that, yesterday, had placed him in command of the Federal Broadcasting System—its television network, its stations, everything—the prize that finally made his marriage and his other regrets worthwhile.

As if sensing that his thoughts touched on her, his wife stirred and opened her eyes, smiling at him for an instant, before turning over and returning to sleep. He slipped out of bed and padded softly into his dressing room. Closing the door behind him, he moved into his bathroom, a mausoleum of gleaming black and gray marble, and stepped into the shower.

At thirty-seven Greg's tall, trim body was still an athlete's and still suggested youthfulness. His manner had so often been described as charming that the characterization had become as much condemnation as compliment. Few people guessed how hard he had worked to master the amiability that precluded dislike, to suppress contrary impulses and desires in pursuit of his aspiration to head FBS. Greg was sure that the consensus within the company, probably within the entire television industry, was that he would quickly drown in his new post, leaving widening ripples in the shape of a smile to mark the spot. Other executives eager to displace him would count on it.

He dried himself, and while he shaved he flipped on the small TV set sunk into the wall beside the mirror. FBS's early-morning program came on. He considered it a dull, ill-produced offering. A fashion expert was discussing with the program's vapid hosts the current fall fashions being modeled by anorexic females swiveling by them. Greg frowned at the inappropriate booking. At this hour men dressing for work made up a large part of the audience; they would switch channels instantly. He did.

And his breath caught: Christine Paskins's blue eyes were staring at him. One of the country's most popular newscasters, she was a strikingly

1

beautiful blond with a lively on-screen personality that reflected the quick mind behind it. For the last two years, she had co-hosted her network's early-morning smorgasbord of entertainment, chit-chat, human interest, and snatches of news that was now challenging "Today" and "Good Morning, America" for the lead in ratings. Rumors were flying that despite being offered an annual salary of over a million dollars, she was balking at renewing her contract and wanted to return to hard news.

That was very much in character, Greg mused. Broadcast executives tended to capitalize on her fresh good looks and popularity with viewers and to ignore the astute, experienced newswoman behind them. But as Greg had first learned ten years before, broadcast journalism had been Chris Paskins's passion since childhood, and she was very good at it.

Suddenly, his admiration was quickened by an idea.

Although in a hurry now to get to his office, he stopped a moment at the end of the bed. The cover had fallen away, and his wife's sleeping figure was curled into protective serenity. She looked pretty asleep, he admitted, with her hair spread into a careless aureole on her pillow. He had no doubt that she inwardly believed herself responsible for his promotion. She might well be right.

Walking south on Fifth Avenue toward the FBS Building, Greg's thoughts turned to the problems facing him as the new chief of the tottering broadcast empire. FBS was in dire straits, and little time remained to save it. Ratings of its prime-time entertainment shows were scraping bottom, putting it far behind the other three major networks, in some weekend time periods even behind the new Fox network. That translated into dismal advertising revenues and the prospect of heavy losses. Unless he developed some hit shows by next season, eleven months from now, FBS might sink beyond saving and might even be seized by a corporate raider seeking its valuable stations.

FBS's second problem was excessive costs. He intended to prune away deadwood in the executive ranks and overstaffing everywhere, restructuring the operation to make it lean and fighting fit again.

Greg believed, though, that the third problem, the dismal ratings and quality of the foundering news division, could be attacked immediately.

What differentiates a network most visibly from competitors is its news anchorperson, who presents the news each night and is the focus of live coverage during important events. Each network's Dan Rather, Tom Brokaw, or Peter Jennings is its readily identifiable emblem, its herald who attempts to attract beneath the network's banner the largest audience for his news proclamations, and thus the largest amount of advertising revenue for the broadcast.

That morning, while shaving, Greg had become convinced that the

2

way to lift FBS News out of the cellar was to hire Christine Paskins as its permanent news anchor.

The floor director on the rim of the brightly lit set called out, "In five, four," marked the last three seconds silently with the appropriate number of fingers, and then pointed at Christine Paskins and her male co-host to indicate that the commercial break had ended and they were on.

"Welcome back to 'Starting the Day' on this crisp autumn morning," the male co-host read with practiced cheerfulness from the tele-prompter glass in front of the camera lens. "All over the Northeast the trees are turning gold and red, and in our final half hour, we'll show you how fall looks in several beautiful old New England towns this time of year."

Chris Paskins, beside him, dressed in a blue silk dress, remarked pleasantly, "We should have worn fall colors today."

She shifted her attention from her co-host to the camera. "But first, the President's recently unveiled drug-war plan has met with a good deal of opposition from Democrats in Washington. The Senate's majority and minority leaders will be with us from Washington to give us their views. That's after the latest news from Charles Hartnet. Charles?"

Everyone on the set relaxed. The news segment would take three minutes.

Chris began to leaf through her notes for the joint interview she would conduct with the senators via satellite. A voice in her earpiece stopped her.

"There's been a change, Chris." The speaker was the show's producer, Ron Skink. "Kathy Trowbridge will do the interview right from Washington."

Chris's gaze shot between cameras toward the control-room window in the rear of the studio. She could just about make out Skink's form in the darkened booth. He was standing up, but curled over the long counter to speak into the intercom mike. Her lapel mike would carry her own angry voice to him.

"Are you trying to tell me a couple of minutes before an interview I personally arranged and prepared questions for that you've shifted it to someone else?"

"Oh, didn't anyone let you know?" the unctuous control-room voice replied. "That's unforgivable. I'll get to the bottom of it, Chris."

"The question isn't whether I was told, but why you switched it without telling me."

"Well, because of your husband, it just made more sense. We didn't want viewers to think we were favoring either side in the debate."

3

"My husband's position never stood in my way before."

"Oh, I know, Chris, I know, I know. But this drug-war plan is so controversial, they insisted."

"*Who* insisted?"

He pointed upward. "The executives. I'm just a gofer in this."

"Right," she seethed.

At nine o'clock, as soon as the program concluded, Chris stormed into the control room, catching Skink just as he was trying to slip out.

Ron Skink was a small, frail-looking, callously spiteful man with overly long gray hair. A cigarette clenched between crooked, stained teeth invariably dripped ashes on a decades-out-of-style suit with bell-bottom pants. His unattractive appearance and his being married never inhibited him from propositioning every woman who crossed his path, rarely with success. What he *had* mastered, however, was the knack of deftly placing a knife between shoulder blades while blaming someone else for the deed and then commiserating over the death wound. Despite a history of failure at producing similar programs, he had somehow lulled the News Division's executives into forgetting that the morning show he claimed credit for turning into a hit became one only after he was fired.

Chris believed that Skink's advent as producer this year, her second on the program, had caused a marked decline in its quality. Out of a need to build a reputation and put his own stamp on an already popular show, he often acted illogically, arbitrarily, and even spitefully in picking stories and setting its tone. One of Chris's reasons for not wanting to renew her contract was her dislike of Skink. Unfortunately, network management considered him a loyal "pro" and felt that replacing him would be a sign of weakness that ceded her too much power.

A large company that manufactured heavy earth-moving equipment and sold cosmetics door-to-door had recently bought the network. One of its financial executives, an accountant, who knew a lot about numbers, but little about television, had been placed in charge. He had ordered his lieutenant overseeing the News Division to get tough about raising its income and lowering its costs. Although the network needed her to maintain the show's ratings, the News chief had refused to raise her salary, believing he had the upper hand in negotiations because her contract precluded her from moving to a similar show for two years. To increase the pressure on her to knuckle under, he had stalled the talks until less than a month was now left before her contract expired. Skink was convinced he had the man's strong backing.

"I'm really sorry about the interview," he intoned with practiced concern. "I wish there was something I could have done."

"Who did you claim took it away from me?"

4

He shrugged his widened shoulders, freeing some ashes from the suit. "You know I can't say," he told her in a voice that seemed to ache with concern for her.

"I'll just have to call your bosses one by one to find out."

Chris spun on her heel and strode down the corridor and up the stairs to her office. Skink was an untalented lowlife, but he was more of an annoyance to her than anything else. What she really hated was this morning program itself, filled with guests plugging their products, activists attacking others without providing practical solutions, psychologists hawking their books that claimed to repair the love lives of unhappy women or an emotional syndrome no one had until then ever noticed, and an endless procession of vacuous actors praising their films and TV shows, the latter usually on that network.

"It's nothing but a video fan magazine," she lamented in private. She desperately wanted to return to straight news, but her network's news programs and newscasters were flying high in the ratings, so no position she wanted was open. Her ambition had no flight path.

Skink had taken particular pleasure that morning in keeping her off the drug-war debate, flexing his power in a way that would demean her.

Chris's secretary was answering the phone at her desk as Chris charged toward her.

"It's someone named Greg Lyall," the woman announced, her hand covering the receiver's mouthpiece.

Chris stopped as quickly as if a door had suddenly swung closed in her face. She tried to clear her mind enough to make sense of the words.

"When I asked who he was, he said he was head of FBS," the woman continued. "But Barnett Roderick runs FBS."

"I'll take it in my office."

This was the second time in a few hours that Greg Lyall had shattered her composure. Stepping into the limousine that transported her to the studio, her gaze had fallen on the copy of *The New York Times* placed on the seat for her. The front-page story of his accession to the command of FBS caught her with the shock of a surprise punch. Embedded hurt and rage had welled up inside her, and she had quickly turned to the second section. Now, Greg was phoning her. The old anger stoked her present one into bitter fury. He could not have phoned at a better time.

"Hello," she snarled.

"You took my call. That's something."

"What the hell do you want?"

"Have you renewed your contract with your network yet?"

"It's no business of yours, but we're very close."

"I think we should talk before you do."

5

Chris was ready to hang up. "You have nothing to say I'd be interested in."

"What if I said that I wanted you to be the permanent anchor of FBS's nightly news, our prime newscaster. Election coverage. Summit meetings. Space shots. Catastrophes. Everything."

"Oh."

Probably nothing else he could have said would have halted her. For several seconds she thought of all the reasons not to be interested, all the reasons not to trust him.

"I take it you're tempted," he said, sensing it.

"I didn't say that."

"Enough to talk at least. How about tonight, over dinner?"

"I'll discuss it with my agent. If we're interested, he'll phone you."

She hung up and stared at the receiver. A knock at the door interrupted her thoughts.

"Come in," she said.

Ron Skink poked his head through the crack. "That interview with Prime Minister Bhutto? They want Sue Talbert to do that one."

"And just why?"

"Well, with your contract still up in the air, they seem to want to try out young reporters who might replace you."

"Don't they worry that I might get angry enough to leave the program and not look back?"

"Oh, I know, I know."

Skink managed to withdraw his nose an instant before the door slammed shut.

Chris had been thrown into a turmoil by Greg's phone call. Nearly nine years had passed since their last, bitter phone conversation. She had gradually hardened herself to what she viewed as his betrayal and had vowed never again to have anything to do with him. Even the offer of anchoring a network news program, of rising to a celestial sphere populated by so few, might not have tempted her if Ron Skink had not just added the last little bit of insult to his earlier injury.

She phoned her agent. He was excited by Greg's call. It would strengthen his hand when he met that morning with her network's president of News. He would try to meet later in the day with Greg.

Greg had no idea whether he could land Christine Paskins or not. At least she had not turned him down. That was probably more than he had any right to expect. He believed, though, that if he could just get her and her agent to listen to his offer, to his arguments, he might stand a chance.

Luring her to FBS would be the quick, bold initiative that would signal

6

to one and all that he was to be taken seriously, that he could restore FBS's luster and profitability. Her presence alone would guarantee half a point, maybe even a whole point more in the ratings. That jump would translate into higher prices for commercial time on the broadcast and immediately pump in perhaps an additional $30 million a year of income, even before the real revamping and improving of the broadcast began. More important, it would buy him breathing space and go a long way toward overturning the widespread impression that he was a lightweight to whom everything in life had been handed unearned on a silver platter: job, social position, and now power.

The problem was that Christine Paskins was the one person in the world who knew precisely what he had sacrificed to obtain those things. She knew he had sacrificed his soul.

Book One

LOCAL NEWS

JANUARY 1980

1

〰〰〰〰〰〰〰

I think a new reporter has been assigned to your corruption-trial story," a news writer informed Greg moments after he entered the KFBS-TV newsroom that Monday morning. Greg was the story's producer. "You'd better talk to Stew."

Stew Graushner, a bearded, rumpled man in his early thirties, was news director for the television station. Ordinarily, his office was one floor up, but a mass exodus of staff had recently forced him to occupy the executive producer's office on the periphery of the newsroom. Just before a Christmas vacation Stew had long promised his wife and daughter, his subordinate who supervised the station's nightly news programs had jumped ship to a rival station, taking with him a field producer and two reporters whose contracts were also expiring. Already overburdened, now left empty-handed, Stew had had to cancel his vacation in order to supervise the nightly news.

Greg leaned into the office. "I hear I've got a new reporter on my corruption-trial story."

Stew was a man whose pessimism reflected a funereal certainty that even good things happening to him were precursors to doom. Now, however, he brightened up. "Her name's Chris Paskins. I liked her reel. She's been working in Wichita."

"Wichita!" Greg muttered like a dirty word.

"If she doesn't pan out by the end of the month, we have the option to drop her. It's a no-lose deal." That seemed to be the part that had lightened Stew's spirits.

The only one who can lose is me, Greg commented to himself as he left to locate her.

Uncovering corruption in the city's water department had been Greg's story since he arrived in L.A. He had even tracked down a witness whom the prosecution had rushed to rely on. Now, four weeks into the trial, when the water commissioner's conviction seemed all but assured, the judge had scheduled a surprise hearing to reduce the charges. The scuttlebutt was that the defendant had cut some sort of deal with the DA.

At the assignment desk Greg learned that his new reporter had long since left for the courthouse to get an early jump on the story and would meet him there. Just what he needed, he thought, some overeager would-be Brenda Starr from the sticks who had neither asked him for background nor introduced herself, but who was already off and blindly running. Her trial at FBS promised to end quicker than the defendant's.

Stew Graushner emerged from his office. "You'll want to know what she looks like."

He handed Greg a black-and-white head shot of an arrestingly attractive young woman: large light-colored eyes, straight nose, small well-shaped mouth, blond hair with not a single strand out of place.

Greg observed cynically, "She can always do the weather."

The traffic was slug-slow and a parking place hard to come by. The hearing was already in progress when Greg squeezed into the courtroom. All the seats were taken, and standees were tightly packed into the rear and along the side wall. He spotted the young woman standing near the door.

"I'm Greg Lyall," he whispered to her.

She scowled. "Where have you been?"

He ignored her question. "What's happened so far?"

"They're still going through the preliminaries, but I've got it on good authority that Meachum's going to plead to a misdemeanor, no more than a year in prison. I already phoned that in. We made the ten A.M. news break."

"We what?" Greg felt as if he had been shot.

"Meachum's agreed to testify against some people," she went on, her gaze never leaving the action in front of the bench, "and I'm pretty sure who they are." She stuffed her writing pad and pen into his hands. "Take notes up here. The crew and I will catch him when he leaves."

Before Greg could stop her, she was out the door. With absolutely nothing to go on, this empty-headed idiot had put the most absurd rumor on the air. Visions of lawsuits and unemployment lines danced before his eyes. He did not dare leave for fear of missing the real adjudication. He had no idea what new sort of ruin she was creating downstairs for the station.

Ten minutes later, to Greg's stunned relief, the charges against the bribe-taking water commissioner were reduced to a single misdemeanor

12

that carried a sentence of no more than one year in prison. The defendant was released on his own recognizance. Court adjourned in an uproar with the dozens of reporters fighting to get out of the courtroom.

When Greg could finally push his way into an elevator and make it outside to the street, his crew—and his reporter—were nowhere in sight. He asked technicians from other stations if they had seen the KFBS crew, but none had. Greg's short-lived reprieve from disaster was about to be revoked.

Someone on the corner yelled, "There he is!"

The herd of newspeople toting video cameras, tape recorders, and microphones thundered around to the side of the building. Greg was caught in the middle of the pack and could not make out what was happening ahead of him until they were well down the block. Then, between people, he caught a glimpse of his camera and sound men standing shoulder to shoulder, wedging open the rear door of a black limousine.

A moment before the stampede reached them, the crew stepped back and let the limousine door slam shut. Revealed behind them was a blond young woman carrying a microphone. Her wide smile and blue eyes gleamed brightly in the morning sun. Reporters banged in vain on the limousine's sides as it pulled away, its darkened windows revealing nothing of its interior.

"Who the hell is she?" a reporter asked the others in a voice loud enough to be heard over the frustrated groans of his colleagues.

"Christine Paskins," Greg announced, guiding her away. "KFBS News."

"What did Meachum tell you?" someone demanded of her.

"His voice was too low for me to hear," she replied apologetically. "I won't know until we play back the sound bite in the editing room."

"Bitch!" the reporter closest to her sputtered enviously.

Greg hustled her into the mobile van. He would send people back later to pick up his and Chris's parked cars.

"Okay," Greg ordered, "what did Meachum say?"

"He's giving the DA Bronstein and McNulty."

Greg's mouth opened. They were the most powerful men on the city council. McNulty practically ran the local Democratic machine.

"And he confirmed that?"

"He was so surprised I knew the deal that he just said yes."

Greg glanced at the sound man, who patted the tape recorder in confirmation.

"Miss Paskins," Greg said incredulously, "welcome to KFBS News.

Did I ever underestimate Wichita! But don't you ever again go off on your own and put us on a limb like that."

"You were late," she reminded him.

Meachum stayed in hiding all that day and the lawyers involved refused all calls from the press. Greg had sworn everyone involved in the story to secrecy, and kept one of the desk assistants scanning wire-service reports and listening to an all-news radio station, hoping fervently that the facts behind the plea bargain would not leak out before airtime. All the while he was cutting the piece with the tape editor and writing, with Chris, the report she would record as narration.

As soon as her audio track was combined with the video, he summoned Stew Graushner into the editing room. So far, no one else had broken the story.

"Maybe our luck is changing," Stew exclaimed, instantly glancing heavenward with mock fear, as if expecting divine retaliation for expressing optimism. He returned his attention to Greg. "Let's do it as an anchor package. Quinn does an on-camera lead-in to his tracked piece and then an on-camera tag at the end."

That meant Chris Paskins's picture and voice would be cut out of the piece, and Quinn Harris, the anchorman, would introduce and end his own taped piece from the anchor desk. Except for Meachum's sound bite, the only narration would be Harris's voice describing the visual material outside the courthouse. The impression would be that Harris himself had gotten the story, thus enhancing his image as an investiga-tive journalist and ending for a while the phone-call complaints from his agent that his role needed to be expanded. Harris had an ego that was oversized even by anchorman standards.

"Stew, if you give Harris the story, you cut her feet out from under her on her very first day."

"There'll be other stories."

Greg pointed out the illogic of using the anchorman. "The key camera shot into the limousine shows her in one-quarter profile in the foreground asking the question and the commissioner looking right at her and answering. Harris is nowhere around."

Stew nodded in comprehension. "No way will it look like Harris's piece."

"It has to be her package. And it should be."

"You really think she's going to work out?"

Greg nodded. "I wish I could take the credit, but it was her scoop all the way." He allowed himself a smile. "She had me scared shitless."

Only to someone he had known as long and worked with as closely as

14

Stew would Greg make such an admission. Stew had hired him at a TV station in Pittsburgh four and a half years earlier, just after Greg was graduated from Yale. The station had been short a news writer. Greg had never considered news as a career. He had simply possessed a burning desire to get into television.

In the mournful manner Greg later discovered was habitual, Stew had opened the job interview by asking, "If viewers were really interested in what was happening in the world, would most of them be getting their news in minute-and-a-half chunks from the tube?"

He had released a puff of pipe smoke as regretfully as if it had been hope. "You probably have too good an education for this business. But maybe an English major from Yale can write and just maybe he's smart enough to know what he's getting into. Should I give you the benefit of the doubt?"

"How about if we flip for it?" Greg asked.

Stew thought the remark funny and confident enough to hire the young man to write news copy for the early evening broadcast.

Greg had learned quickly and was willing to work hard, and perhaps most important he thrived under the stress of deadlines as the clock hands moved toward six o'clock and the last edits and rewrites were feverishly locked into place. He was soon elevated to producer. No one suspected that Greg's determination camouflaged working-class desperation.

When Stew's success in Pittsburgh caused him to be hired to invigorate the news operation at FBS's Los Angeles station, he asked Greg to come along as senior producer. That was seven months earlier. Greg was twenty-six.

"We still have to work up ways to enhance Harris's image," Stew said, fingering his beard and eyeing Greg thoughtfully. "It might become your headache. Trying to do two jobs, I'm not doing either well. I have three options: The first is going outside for an executive producer. The second is promoting Bosworth."

"You don't sound convinced."

Stew nodded. "Bosworth is okay at producing the late news since it's mostly stories from the six o'clock, but he doesn't exactly inspire faith as a creative thinker."

"You said it might become my headache. I gather I'm the third option."

Stew shrugged. "I'm considering it. You're young. I don't know whether you're too inexperienced . . . or whether you have . . ." His voice trailed off in thought.

"What?"

"There's a fine line between what will grab an audience and

responsible journalism. I know you'll put together an entertaining broadcast—sexy story ideas, great visuals—but that's not the same as informing viewers about what's important to their lives."

"I think I understand the difference, Stew."

"Look, I'm not saying you have to be a fanatic, one of those types for whom news is some kind of a holy calling they'd die for. Put nine out of ten of those guys in charge of a broadcast and they *would* die . . . in the ratings. Sincere, but so boring nobody would watch. But you have to understand that with most people getting their news from us nowadays, we have a big responsibility, an obligation."

Greg knew that Stew liked to make a show of his commitment to journalism at a time when entertainment values were being emphasized in news production in order to attract viewers. But Greg also knew him to be a canny innovator who had livened the news presentation in Pittsburgh and again here in Los Angeles.

"If you're asking whether I have integrity," Greg replied, "I hope the answer is yes. If you're asking whether I'm interested in putting on a show people want to watch, the answer is also yes."

Stew's brow wrinkled with worry. "You said 'show,' not 'broadcast' or 'program.' "

"A slip of the tongue," Greg replied with a touch of embarrassment.

"One of those do-or-die news types would never have said 'show.' I wish I was as sure of your integrity as you are."

All afternoon word that News was working on a big story about the corruption trial spread around the station, although no one knew what it might be. As if driven there by a tornado warning, people gathered in the back of the darkened control room as airtime approached. The director faced a wall of TV monitors, his assistant director on one side, his technical director on the other.

At exactly six o'clock, animated graphics and music announced the early evening news, dissolving to a shot of anchorman Quinn Harris at the anchor desk.

"The corruption trial of city water commissioner Glenn R. Meachum," Harris began, "ended with dramatic suddenness this morning when he pleaded guilty to a misdemeanor. KFBS-TV has obtained an exclusive interview. Our reporter, Christine Paskins, is here with the facts behind this startling turn of events."

Harris swung smoothly to Chris, seated at the end of the desk.

"Camera Three, go in on her," the director instructed a cameraman through his headset microphone as Chris introduced her taped report.

"Ready tape on sixteen," the technical director alerted a technician at tape machine sixteen on another part of the floor.

16

Without needing to be concerned now about continuity or timing, Greg could concentrate for the first time on the face of the young woman replicated on monitors across the control-room wall. It was a fresh-scrubbed face, with the sort of American prettiness—honey blond hair flipped out below her ears, a soft roundness below high cheekbones the camera flattered, and well-formed features—that gets cheerleaders a close-up between plays during college football games. The eyes, though, were special; a translucent blue, they projected authority with a directness that transfixed Greg and a likability that evoked his trust. He remembered that he had glimpsed other qualities in them earlier in the day: self-confidence, a reporter's seasoned skepticism, and fierce pride. He had the feeling that one could know her for years and never probe through to all there was behind them.

She's got it, he thought. Whatever you call it—magnetism, charisma, star quality, sex appeal—it comes right through the camera at you.

"Roll tape," the director's voice sounded. The monitors displayed Chris's image at the entrance to the courthouse, and the story Greg had cut with her narration began to run.

After Harris shifted into the next story's intro, Greg slipped out of the control room to catch Chris.

"Was I okay?" she asked nervously.

"Terrific. Can I take you to dinner afterward to celebrate?"

For a minute Greg was afraid that Chris might misconstrue his attempt to welcome her to the station as a play for her. But her smile flashed with pleasure, and he relaxed.

A newcomer to the West Coast, Chris had never eaten Mexican food. Greg took her to his favorite Mexican restaurant. "They make the best margaritas," he told her, and ordered them. That was the sort of information he picked up automatically: the best steak house; the best tailor for the price; the best tailor regardless of price and thus to be noted for the future, when he could afford it; where to shop for shirts, for socks, for lighting, for antiques.

A handsome and personable young man who had finally grown into his long skinniness, Greg had regular, somewhat sharply formed facial features, dark hair, and dark eyes that drew an observer's attention. Instead of the casual, open-collar attire affected by nearly everyone working behind the television camera, especially in California, he invariably wore well-cut suits, albeit with the jacket usually hung on the back of his chair and his shirt cuffs rolled carefully back. He dressed for his aspirations, not his circumstances, having early decided that higher-ups were more likely to promote him if he already looked the part.

17

Chris shrugged off her own jacket before they were two steps inside the restaurant, as if her on-camera garb was a costume to her, not clothing. Greg noted that she was taller than average, slender, and lithe. The right sort of body for her, he thought, for a woman with her competitiveness.

During dinner they talked about the broadcast and how they might follow up with additional angles so as to keep this story KFBS's in the public's mind. She asked whether reporters at the station had regular beats or whether it was mostly general assignment.

"It's been so confused the last month or two that whoever is closest to the door usually gets sent out on a story." Greg explained about the recent defections. "So many people left last month, you'd think Payroll was sending out passports, not salary checks. We can use you."

He then asked her to fill him in on how she had gotten the scoop—events had been so rushed all day that this was their first chance to discuss it.

She had arrived at the newsroom around six to get an early start. The overnight assignment editor informed her that she was covering the hearing. She read through the file, viewed tapes of the last several pieces the station had done on the trial, and then drove to the courthouse to see what she could learn. Male court workers had jumped all over each other to be helpful to the newcomer with the innocent face.

"They told me about the plea bargain and even what door they were going to sneak Meachum through," she recalled with a smile, "so I wouldn't mess up on my first day."

Her campaign to land a job in Los Angeles had begun months earlier, when she sent tape reels of her work to every L.A. station. The others were fully staffed, but during a quick trip in for an interview, Graushner offered her a one-month tryout at KFBS-TV. Deciding to gamble, she gave notice in Wichita and last night was back in L.A. with her belongings.

Wichita was the fourth place she had worked; she was always moving to a bigger city, always able to show a better reel and more experience than before, always able to point to a ratings increase during her tenure.

"And each time there was a guy in charge who had a chip on his shoulder about women in news. A woman has to work twice as hard and be twice as good. That's just the way things are." Her words contained no conceit, but rather simply acknowledged prevailing attitudes.

During the last few months, she had become convinced that she was ready for a big city. "Not the network yet," she said. "That's still a few years away. And someday anchoring the network news."

She said it so matter-of-factly that Greg required a moment to detect the powerful ambition infusing the words. No hint of doubt invaded them. No self-deprecating smile was proffered to lessen them. This morning she had demonstrated that she was indeed willing to work harder and longer and maybe even better than other reporters to get where she was headed. And she knew exactly where that was.

Greg's own ambition motivated him as powerfully—he, too, was as hungry to be a winner—but he kept it to himself, locked behind a tactful, courteous manner that masked his aggressiveness. To observe a woman expose her ambition so nakedly startled him. Newswomen had been mouthing the slogans of equal opportunity for a decade now. Several had already become prominent, and some were even co-anchoring local news broadcasts. Barbara Walters had done so at the network level. But they had always seemed demure about their success, decorously surprised, as if they had been chosen by a lottery. Perhaps that attitude had been a pretense, he conjectured, but it certainly preserved what he considered to be their femininity. And yet, he noticed, the light in this young woman's eyes danced no less warmly for her admission. Her mouth seemed no less soft.

Greg learned that she was the youngest of three children. Her father, an inflexible, argumentative newspaperman who had accumulated many journalistic awards but been fired just as often for insubordination, seemed to have dominated her childhood. Although she idolized him and had taken his pugnacious virtue as a model for her own, Greg also sensed anger at him buried deep within her. Her mother and the rest of the family had paid a heavy price for his principled stubbornness, moving often as he changed jobs, until their last stop in a small town in Wyoming, a part of the West that still honored mavericks. There he had bought a marginal newspaper with a small down payment, became his own boss, and Chris was finally able to put down roots. She worked afternoons and weekends at the newspaper.

She had skipped a year in grade school and was graduated four years ago from the state university.

"Where you were probably homecoming queen," Greg guessed.

"I really didn't have time for any of that. I worked at a newspaper to help pay my way through."

Determined to break into television reporting after graduation, she had found herself confronted by ingrained prejudices against women in broadcasting. Stations offered to hire her only as a secretary, despite her credentials. She finally took a job at a tiny TV station in rural Montana, the only one that offered to hire her as a reporter. The husband and wife who owned it became a second family to her and

19

convinced the owner of a bigger station to take her on. By the time she left that second job, she was anchoring the local news broadcast, which rose to number one in its market. That had happened at her next stop as well and most recently in Wichita.

"Your father must be proud of you."

"He thinks television's a cartoon version of the news for the retarded," she replied ruefully. "He thinks I sold out. But then he's never taken me seriously. I could never overcome my first mistake where he was concerned—being born a girl. But I'll *make* him proud of me," she added with some vehemence.

"Is that what drives you?" Greg asked.

Flustered, she glanced away.

Surprised that inquiring about her drive had embarrassed her, when the fact of possessing it had not, he pressed her for an answer. "Why pick news? Just because your father's in it?"

A smile broke across her face. "It's lust, pure and simple—absolute, unreasoning obsession." Her voice was as vibrant as the smile. "It's like asking why I breathe or love. I read half a dozen papers a day and constantly scan the wire services. When I'm not at work, I'm always turning on news broadcasts or discussion shows or reading magazines or just talking about news."

She fell silent for a moment, trying to give expression to the commitment she felt. "I want to make sense of the world for people—or at least tell them why it doesn't make sense. I want them to know they can rely on me for the truth. We're the ones who have to guard the truth for people. If we let ourselves compromise on that, the whole system fails."

"Why TV? Newspapers do that, too."

"They're impersonal. Print reporters are just names hardly anyone notices under the headlines. People can skip over something in a newspaper, wrap their garbage in it."

Eyes wide, her face drawing close to his, her voice grew urgent with her ardor. "But in television I speak right to them. I'm the one—my words, my nuances, my tone—who makes them understand what's happening to them and why it's important." Her concluding words were spoken defiantly. "They can't ignore me."

Stubbornness, self-righteousness, and indignation were somehow all bound up in her with a demand for respect, Greg concluded. Maybe that's what a calling is, he speculated, thinking back to his conversation with Graushner that afternoon. At that moment he decided she was beautiful.

She interrupted his thoughts. "Tell me about yourself."

"There's not very much to tell." He was determined not to repay her confidences with his own.

"Are you married?"

"That sort of thing, you mean."

"Men who don't say much about their backgrounds often are." The words were straightforward, but he could sense wariness behind them.

"Not married. Never have been."

A luminous smile lit her face.

"I come from a small city in western Pennsylvania," he continued. "My dad raised me after my parents broke up. He died two years ago. My college education was paid for by a tennis scholarship, although the school would never admit it gave out sports scholarships. I worked at a TV station in Pittsburgh before I came here."

The brief biography hid more than it disclosed, but was more, though, than he usually allowed. Buried beneath the vague facts were years of childhood pain and of struggling to create what he had now become, ultimate secrets he entrusted to no one.

She gazed as intently as a prosecutor, intrigued by his discomfort. "It would have been a lot safer to stay put than to come to L.A. What drives *you*, Greg Lyall?"

He started to shrug and form an answer that would fend off the question, but her eyes appeared ready to mock such guardedness after her own candor.

"I don't want to be ordinary," he snapped before he could restrain himself, startled to find himself confiding a thought—a fear—that he never had before to anyone. "You know, someone life tosses around, someone in a small town who just tears the days off the calendar until he dies." He wanted her to understand. "Even more than the money and all the other things that go with making it to the top in TV, I want to sit in the driver's seat and be one of the guys who gets to steer the world."

She was serious now. "You sound like you really believe you can make it."

"Someday. If I want it enough."

She tried to sound casual. "Anyone special in your life right now?"

He shook his head. "I make it a policy not to date women who work at the station."

"That's not the question I asked."

"I thought it should be out in the open. Dating a coworker just leads to complications."

The long hours, the trips, and the camaraderie produced casual affairs in news departments as prodigiously as a microwave oven pops corn.

21

Stew Graushner forbade romances among staff members, believing they sowed divisiveness among a news team that must work closely together. Stew had early appreciated Greg's discretion, his sense of propriety in a sensitive profession. Greg had always taken care to reveal no secrets, keep his own counsel, and restrict his social life to women he met outside the office.

Chris tried to make light of the rejection. "Don't emotions enter into it? You know, the blistering heat of unbridled passion crushing your noble resolve?"

He laughed. "Complete with ripped bodices and full symphony orchestra during the steamy sections? Most people are a lot more calculating about relationships, don't you think?"

She did not answer, and silence closed in around them. When the waiter went by, Greg asked for the check. He rejected her offer to pay her share, reminding her that he had asked her to dinner. She smiled impishly.

"Then I guess you've just broken your rule about not dating someone from work."

He drove her back to the garage near the station where she had parked. Then her car followed behind his as he led her through the unfamiliar streets to the small hotel where she was staying. He waved good-bye through the open car window and drove to his apartment.

Late that Saturday afternoon, after his own tennis match had ended, Greg sat on the terrace of his date's country club watching her play the third set of a hard-fought match. In the distance small figures moved in carts along green fairways or clustered on the darker swatches at the ends.

The Los Angeles friends Greg had made at Yale and at tennis competitions had eased his move west, gladly inviting him to their houses and their country clubs, where he met others in their prosperous circles. College had been a true finishing school for Greg. The small-town boy's diligence in unlocking the metaphors of John Donne and the economics of Adam Smith was rivaled by his study of affluent, cosmopolitan classmates. His tennis success and ingratiating manner permitted a socializing that his provincial background might otherwise have denied him. He had grown up determined to own good things and live well. At college he learned to dress and carry himself with style; he saved every penny to buy just the right jacket, just the right sweater.

Friends were mystified when he announced at the end of his college years that he had chosen television for a career and not law or investment banking, where his new contacts could be of benefit. Now, however, his occupation endowed him with a certain glamor; he seemed wired to what was happening.

What set Greg apart from most other young men was a self-assurance that derived from his certainty about where he wanted to go and who he wanted to be. He had chiseled away what was extraneous to that identity to become the image of his aspirations. Not being able to afford the new Mercedes convertible he coveted, he bought an older model of a superior year, which provided a panache of its own. Because of its ocean view, he took the tiniest of one-bedroom apartments and furnished it with a few excellent pieces of furniture.

The last few days had been hectic ones for Greg. Now was really his first opportunity to consider Graushner's statement that his youth might prevent his being named executive producer. Greg was in a hurry and his sights were set very high. The executive producer's job would be a real step up in responsibility and prestige, and he wanted it badly. The increased salary was important, too, not only because he liked to live well, but to pay off the credit-card debt he had incurred to get a running start on the L.A. life-style—debt of any kind made him uncomfortable. But he could only sit and wait.

When his date's match ended, they and several friends moved into the lounge for drinks. The television set above the end of the bar remained on for the local news after an FBS sports event. Greg's eye kept wandering to the screen. Ten minutes into the news broadcast, Chris Paskins appeared, microphone in hand, a street intersection behind her. He moved to a stool at the bar. The story was about a child injured in a hit-and-run accident in the Valley.

"That your station?" A male friend had joined him at the bar.

"Yes."

The screen switched back to a shot of Chris at the intersection for her closing standup, her final on-camera comments.

The other young man studied her. "Is she that good-looking in person?"

"Better," Greg heard himself saying.

"Can you fix me up with her?"

"She's . . . She's going with someone."

"Shame."

The other young man moved away.

Greg was as angry at his friend as he was amazed at his own reaction. Another story came on, but Greg continued to gaze unseeing at the screen. Then, abruptly, he strode to the pay phone at the other end of the bar and called the newsroom.

The desk assistant who answered the call transferred it to Chris. "Hello," he heard her say.

"That piece . . . you did," he began, stumbling over the words, "the piece on the hit-and-run victim . . . I just wanted you to know I liked it."

"You saw it?" She sounded pleased. "I figured everyone in southern California would be out doing southern-California things on Saturday . . . you know, surfing or playing tennis or barbecuing."

"Look, I know this is short notice, but if you don't have any plans for tonight, maybe we could get together." Greg suddenly grew apprehensive. "I've had an idea for a story—maybe even stretch it over several nights—about the way the election races are shaping up in California this year. I thought we could talk about it over dinner."

"I'd love to." Her answer was swift, her tone elated.

"Great."

"The only thing is, I'm supposed to hang around here till nine in case another story breaks or my piece is recut for the eleven-o'clock and I have to record new narration."

"Tell the assignment desk you'll keep calling in. We'll have dinner nearby just in case. Pick you up outside the station at seven."

"Seven. My turn to treat."

Greg hung up and returned to the table. He fabricated an excuse to his date about a critical story suddenly breaking and his need to get to the newsroom.

"Can you meet us later?" she asked, trying to sound understanding.

"Doesn't look like it."

"You and I haven't seen each other in over a week," she reminded him.

"I'll call you in a couple of days."

He strode quickly toward the locker room to strip off his tennis clothes and take a shower. His skin felt as if it were on fire.

During dinner neither Greg nor Chris kept up the pretense that they were meeting to discuss work. Both were gripped by an intense attraction. The crumbling of Greg's resolve seemed to confirm to both that its force was irresistible. When nine o'clock passed with no phone call from the newsroom, he suggested they drive to the ocean, which Chris had never seen. "It's near my apartment," he said.

The moon, round and luminous as an electric coil, seemed to blow white heat at them across the water to their feet. She stood straight, he noticed, even in the sand, where she might be expected to flex her body against the unfamiliar unsteadiness; her will did not appear to recognize compromise.

She gazed at the vastness for a long time. She had never before seen water extend all the way to the sky and glanced at him to share her wonder. A silver sheen rolled down the curve of her cheek and along her neck. The silver splashed wide again beneath the hollow of her throat and was just climbing the roundness of her breast when it crept out of sight beneath the fold where her open blouse collar arched outward.

The thought of her breasts, cool and concealed beneath the fabric, stirred him. He leaned forward and kissed her, then took her into his arms. He was hard almost at once, insistent and uncomfortable against her leg. She surprised him with her boldness: opening her mouth to taste his tongue and shifting her body to fit him into the recess where her torso and legs met.

When he drew away to stare into her eyes, black disks now with a thin blue circumference, they met his forthrightly, not masking her desire. His hand slid from the small of her back and around her ribs until it cupped one breast beneath the blouse. Her breasts were small and high, needing no bra. He rolled her nipple gently between his thumb and forefinger. Her eyes closed, and her lips parted.

After a while her hand slid down his hip and across the front of his pants until her palm rested on the swelling trapped downward. She unlocked the zipper, drawing her knuckle down the rounded ridge as she did. Her hand slipped into the opening to grasp his penis and free it. A moment later her other hand moved down to cradle and gently stroke it between them.

"Let's go to my place," he said a moment later.

He picked up his jacket from the sand and draped it over an arm, hiding his exposed penis from view. That he did not self-consciously stuff it back into his pants seemed to her a successful test of his character.

Wordlessly, each with an arm around the other's waist, they trudged back over the uncertain footing to the street and across to his apartment house.

He undressed her slowly on the bed, wanting to see and caress each part of her body as it was revealed. He liked her naturalness about her nakedness and about sex, the pleasure she took in her own pleasure and his. When his finger dipped into the wetness folded between her thighs, her hips rose to meet it.

He moved to place himself above her, watching her face in the stripe of light across the pillow. She gripped his hips with her thighs as he filled her.

"It feels perfect," she sighed, after they had found a slow, rolling rhythm. "Everything feels perfect."

25

He did not reply, but he sensed something supernatural and glorious dancing out of the dark corners of the room and into the secret, darker places in their bodies, something that turned their nerve endings into fuses burning toward an ecstasy that eventually shook through them, first her and then him, and obliterated their minds.

For Greg and Chris nothing would ever be the same.

2

~~~~~~~~~~~~~~~

Greg gazed at Chris's naked profile supine beside him, a sinuous line of silver inlaid on black by the moonlight. The rise and fall of her breasts appeared too rapid for sleep.

"Are you awake?" he asked.

"Yes."

"What are you thinking?"

"That you felt good inside me. You?"

"That you're beautiful." He chuckled. "And how good it was. Not very profound, are we?"

"Sex has a wonderful way of reducing our intellectual posturing to the basics. It either feels good or it doesn't. You felt good."

"You sound like you didn't expect me to."

"I was a little afraid you'd be, well, unemotional." She rolled toward him, reaching up to brush a stray lock of hair away from his face. "Sometimes you seem sweet and giving. Other times you're purposely impenetrable."

Greg's expression was impassive, but inwardly he was flustered by how accurately she had read him. Once in a while he envisioned himself as being two separate people: the outer one larger, impregnable, within which the inner hid like the Wizard of Oz peering out of the other's eyes and manipulating his arms and legs; the outer Greg was the sentinel, careful, premeditated, censoring words of the too spontaneous inner man that he saw no advantage in revealing.

Chris was staring into his eyes. She frowned and quickly sat up on her side of the bed.

"You look as if you won't feel safe until I'm out of here. I'm going."

"Where to?"

"My hotel."

"It's"—he looked at the clock radio—"three forty-two in the morning."

27

"I don't want to overstay my welcome."

He reached out for her arm. "If I thought you were, I'd tell you."

She swung around to peer into his eyes again. "No, you might not. You might make me feel ill at ease, so I'd leave on my own and you wouldn't feel responsible."

Greg was discomfited. "You always say what you're thinking?"

"I try to. Do you?"

"No," he admitted, "not always. Sometimes, it can be hurtful . . . or counterproductive."

He pulled her gently back down to the bed. She did not resist him. He kissed her.

"I don't want to be impenetrable. I really don't." His smile bent into seductive invitation. "How about you?"

She laughed lightly. "That's the last thing I want to be right now."

The next kiss swiftly deepened into arousal that swept them away once more.

They stayed in bed making love, conversing, regretfully dozing, until well into Sunday afternoon. Greg was astonished at the zeal of her lovemaking. As a lover she was as intensely passionate as about everything else she cared about. Her ardor lifted his own beyond the possibility of a retreat to guardedness or a resort to calculated finesse, above thought or even wonder that thought was absent, into the realm of purest sensation.

At four in the afternoon, she borrowed his shirt and rolled-up jeans, and they went for a walk along the beach. She's precisely who she is, he realized as he glanced at her striding along beside him. She's the Westerner: candid, skeptical, self-reliant, no-nonsense through and through. And beneath that, unexpectedly, deeply passionate.

That observation assumed enormous proportions in his mind. Although she had glimpsed his tendency to remove himself, he believed that all the time he had been with her, he had been precisely who *he* was: singular, unified, instinctive, natural. He had been truly open to her and to the pungent, turbulent emotions she evoked. Words had been on his tongue before they had been on his mind.

On the way back to his apartment, Greg bought fried chicken and beer at a take-out restaurant. Just inside his building's doorway, he and Chris kissed, provoking anew appetites for each other that stifled physical hunger.

The food lay uneaten for hours. When they finally discovered that she liked white meat and he dark but that both liked to sip their beer from the bottle, in a silly way the rightness of their match seemed confirmed. She also insisted on handing him exactly one-half what the food had

cost; she was not yet ready for the assumptions implicit in taking m
from him than she gave.

Neither had ever been in love before, nor was either—for different
reasons—prepared to admit that love had seized them. Chris wisely
wanted time to know Greg better and comprehend what was happening
to her before dismissing the last sentries within. She was a young
woman who suspected exaggeration or excess of any kind, and what
she was feeling was exorbitant, luxuriant, blinding. For his part Greg
was unwilling to believe that an accidental liaison, completely unpre-
pared for, could rout a lifetime's careful planning.

Chris had fallen so quickly and so hard for Greg because he had
thoroughly disoriented her. Having no emotional ties in Wichita and
wanting none here, wanting only to work hard and succeed, she had
been confronted on her very first day with a man she had found
disturbingly attractive, a man with strength, intelligence, and apparently
character to match her own. His rejection of her at that first dinner had
mortified her, despite the humor with which she had coated the
moment. For all her frankness Chris was a woman who wounded easily
and rarely risked exposing her inner feelings to the possibility of hurt.
Consequently, the impact of Greg's return to her was magnified. Her
rampantly sexual response overwhelmed them both.

*For as long as she could remember, Christine Paskins had fought to
be taken seriously. Watching her father teach her older brothers to fish
and play ball and pushing them to achieve in school, Chris was galled to be
ignored in the guise of being cherished. To her parents' horror she insisted
on boys for playmates and gave no quarter in the roughest of games,
parading her skinned knees home like badges. Her parents might punish
her disobedience, but she refused to capitulate. She slaved over her homework in private and then dared them not to be proud of her when she ex-
celled.*

*Chris sensed her mother's discontent at being solely a wife and mother.
She saw a larger world for herself. As a result she grew up both angry at
those in authority who blocked her from her rightful place in it and
determined to gain the recognition she came to crave. In her adolescent
fantasies she always played the champion of everyone not granted a fair
chance in life.*

*One evening, during the summer before Chris was scheduled to go off
to the University of Wyoming, Sam Paskins came home with a copy of that
week's edition of his paper just off the press. Chris had written the cover
story, a searching analysis of the effect federal land policies were having on
the area's ranchers.*

"Molly," he exclaimed to his wife upon entering the kitchen, "I want you to read this. That girl's got the stuff to make it in newspapers."

He had not noticed his daughter at the kitchen table, clipping off the ends of the string beans they would eat for dinner. She was beaming, but unswayed.

"I've already told you. I'm going to be a TV reporter."

"But you're good enough for newspapers." Then, fearing she might grow swelled-headed with the praise, he immediately lessened it. "Or might be after you get some experience."

No reduction in the compliment could steal back the approval he had bestowed. She did not argue with him. She simply shook her head. Everyone in the family had long since learned that when Chris shook her head, bulldozers could not budge her resolve.

Molly Paskins laughed at her husband's exasperation. "You're too late by years, Sam."

"But my God, Molly, television!" He said it as if his daughter were considering a career in prostitution.

"She's a woman, Sam. When we women have news for the neighbors, we can't be bothered waiting for printing presses to roll it out and trucks to deliver it and people to get around to reading it. We want them to hear it right now and from us." Her glance at her daughter was full of pride. "And Chris won't let anyone stop her when she has something she wants to say."

Among the qualities that attracted Chris to Greg was that he really listened to her. He really liked women, and he really listened. She felt her feelings would be safe with a man like that.

On Monday, Greg drove Chris to her hotel for fresh clothing and then to the television station in the tower on the FBS lot. Along the way they decided that discretion about their new relationship was the wisest course—the only course, really. If he learned about their romance, Stew would certainly fire her to forestall staff jealousies and divisions. Her termination would separate the lovers, block Chris's career, and lessen Stew's faith in Greg.

All that first Monday morning, it took a lot of willpower for Chris's face not to register delight when her eyes happened to meet his or to keep a happy exclamation from spilling out of Greg when he happened to encounter her. The strain was especially hard on Chris, who had never acquired Greg's habit of self-protective concealment.

At an editorial staff meeting, they took care to sit on opposite sides of the room as Stew made some announcements. Secrecy bound them.

In the days that followed, dissimulation in public became a habit to which both adjusted. Occasionally, Chris went out to cover stories that Greg supervised as producer, but their paths usually crossed only in passing and in the afternoon, when they were back in the building readying pieces for the broadcast; they were both then too intent on their work to exchange more than a quick smile and a sentence or two. But even in those brief moments, joy at the unexpected encounter would leap within them like a puppy at the door. Whenever they were alone together, the passion that both had expected gradually to abate continued to overwhelm them. Increasingly, the realization became inescapable that they were in love.

One night toward the end of that first week, Chris's candor overcame her wariness. She inadvertently blurted out the words "I love you" while they were cooking supper. Abashed, worried that Greg's response might not be what she wanted to hear, she turned away so that he need not feel he had to respond.

"I love you, too," he had answered, amazed at the revelation; inner walls he had meticulously constructed since childhood were tumbling.

Exuberant at his admission, she impulsively pressed on. "You know when I first fell in love with you?"

He shook his head.

"Last Saturday night," she confessed, "when you phoned me in the newsroom for a date."

"Even before we went out that night?"

She nodded, her smile radiant at the recollection. "I had been wanting so badly for you to ask me out, ever since that first dinner together. But you told me you wouldn't date someone at work. You were always so totally cool and reserved, always saying and doing exactly the right thing. I thought of you like those Olympic speed skaters in their skintight outfits: all strength and sleekness, no pockets bulging with unsightly frailties or history, no needs begging to be noticed. I was intimidated."

"You?" He shook his head incredulously. "I was so nervous I could barely speak on the phone that night."

"That's just it! I could hear all that nervousness. It was like your stretch suit suddenly split up the rear. You were human. I melted."

"I never felt about anyone what I was feeling about you"—he corrected himself, willing to be honest because *she* had been—"what I *feel* about you."

For a long while they stared at each other in delighted amazement. Then, without another word spoken or their eyes unlocking, Greg began to unbutton her blouse.

*   *   *

Stew Graushner's gloomy nature was invariably directed not at grasping for happiness, which he considered beyond possibility, but at the more prudent task of avoiding outright sorrow. Anything more positive than disaster was invariably a surprise. After he canceled their vacation yet again, he had expected his wife to explode and to follow up with months of sullenness. Instead, Patty decided her life would always be composed of such disappointments if it depended on waiting for him for its satisfactions.

"It's you!" Patty declared derisively as he stepped through the front door one night. She stood before him, arms folded, face set in disapproval.

"Hi, honey. What's for dinner?"

Patty exploded. "That's just like you! Just like you! *Dinner!* From now on don't expect to count on me for your dinner!"

An argument between them seemed to have begun without him. Stew foresaw his night ending in a migraine and continued bewilderment as to the nature of his crime. He assumed a questioning expression, hoping that would prompt, without his risking speech again, an explanation of what he should not count on her for.

"My slavery is at an end!" she announced. "I've found out who I am."

"I'm really happy for you," he hurried to assure her, in case she was accusing him of withholding that information.

He soon found out what she was talking about. Next day she enrolled at a local university to gain the education an early marriage had denied her. Somewhat belatedly, Patty Graushner had made her way into the growing army of dissatisfied women seeking independent and equal opportunity.

From that moment on, few meals were made for him, the house was rarely clean, errands were left undone, and he saw her infrequently— she was always studying in the den, late into the night. Now his lunch hours were frequently dedicated to rushed visits to their seven-year-old daughter's school for teacher conferences or bake sales. Without fully understanding what had sparked this change in his once very comfortable life, like a modern Job he accepted his new circumstances and plodded on.

Stew and Patty had married in his last year at Penn State, her first. To make ends meet, she had quit school to work as a secretary, and he had taken a part-time job writing news at a local radio station. He had hoped, after graduation, to teach on the college level while writing and selling his first novel. Finding that teaching jobs were scarce and low paying, however, he switched into television news after graduation and speedily advanced. He eventually grew a beard and assumed a pipe as a signal to others and a reminder to himself that someday he would write the novels he was sure were burning somewhere deep within his soul.

Now, the combination of doing two jobs at the office and Patty's withdrawal from family life at home were wearing him down. He finally capitulated to his fatigue and recommended to Ev Carver, the station's general manager, that Greg be made executive producer. He set up a meeting for the three of them.

Greg entered Carver's office a step behind Stew. The curtains were drawn. A desk lamp provided the only illumination, lighting Ev's face demonically like a fire from below. Greg would later conclude that the effect was purposeful, a means of cowing underlings.

Ev Carver was a muscular, broad-shouldered man, just over six feet tall. His eyes were hard and dark, his hair a red fading to brown.

"Stew tells me you're sucking up to him to become executive producer."

Carver had a reputation for provoking people so as to force them off stride and gain insight into their poise under fire. Greg ignored the insult and considered what else he knew about Ev Carver.

Several anxious network executives had tried to slow his climb, but he seemed an inevitable force. Decisive, calculating, ruthless if that would get the job done, Carver drove his subordinates relentlessly. At thirty-three he had already turned around FBS's Chicago station before being moved to Los Angeles and given a free hand to revive that station's declining popularity. He got everyone's attention the first day by firing three top executives and scrapping a local morning talk program in favor of cheaper syndicated game shows. By week's end he had lured Stew Graushner from Pittsburgh to overhaul a struggling news operation. Anything like his Chicago success would make Ev Carver a surefire bet for the network's upper ranks.

Legs crossed, hands clasped on his lap, eyes locked on Greg's, Carver grilled him for an hour about his background and his approach to every aspect of the job. Greg answered deftly, while ambivalence grew toward his interrogator. Although he admired Carver's quick intelligence and potent personality, Greg thought he sensed coursing deep within the man, like vibrations almost below audibility, the rumblings of a primordial brutality.

"What do you think of Brett Winters?" Ev suddenly asked. Winters was an anchorman on a competing station. "If you look at the eighteen-to-thirty-four-year-old women's market, he's got the pussy in the audience by the short hairs."

33

"He's a good-looking model who can read the words off a tele-prompter. And he has trouble with the three-syllable ones. If you're thinking of hiring him, my opinion is he's going to hurt them badly when news breaks live. He won't last."

"You and I both know how much I could hike the ad rates with a stud like that."

Carver's tone, even more than the words, carried the disturbing assumption that he was familiar with Greg's most private thoughts, as if he were eavesdropping on a mental phone line. Toward the end of the interview, Greg made the point that a reputation for news excellence and other public service would prove important when KFBS next had to show the FCC it deserved a renewal of its broadcasting license, an ordeal that concerned most station managers. Ev lifted his boxer's hands from his lap and leaned forward.

"To hell with the FCC!" he snarled. "You think they're going to make good if News loses money? News is a pain in the ass! Only worth the trouble it causes me if it turns a decent profit and delivers the largest possible audience to my evening lineup. You'll have a lot of leeway to run your own shop, Lyall, but fuck up on either of those, and you're out on your ass. Deliver and you're golden. In the end the only thing that matters in television are the ratings. That's the way this business works." He smiled with an intimacy that alarmed Greg. "And that's why it's made for hustlers like you and me."

Only then did Greg understand that he had passed muster. Stew was ordered to keep a close watch. Greg's failure would be considered Stew's, and both would pay the penalty.

"One more thing," Ev added, his expression like a farmer's eyeing gypsies near his chicken coop. "I hired a consulting firm to analyze our news broadcasts, to tell us how to raise ratings. Their report should be coming in soon. I'm eager to see what they propose."

With that the newsmen were dismissed. Stew looked as if a close relative had died.

"The plague is about to strike one and all," he moaned when he and Greg were back in his office, "regardless of race, creed, or personal hygiene. These consultants all recommend the same superficial, plastic presentation. Matching jackets. A funny weatherman. Very brief news reports with lots of visuals. Keep it simple, very local. Fires. Violent crime. Accidents. Sex. Cuddly human interest and consumer stuff. Lots of smiling banter on the set. You know the routine."

"We all try to attract viewers with some of that. You were doing it in Pittsburgh when I was hired."

"Some, sure, but the consultants don't want you to do anything more. That's it. Nothing deep, nothing that runs more than a minute fifteen—forty-five seconds would be ideal. Structure every story as a confrontation, a drama. Go for the emotions. It's all a kind of entertainment. No ideas. No explanation. No exploring how the system might be failing people. As if anything the least bit complicated or abstract will send the poor viewer scurrying to another channel."

"Maybe this report will contain some useful ideas."

Stew scoffed. "You don't understand how a consultant works. He surveys viewers to learn what news they want and then advocates it. Not the news they need to know. How can you ask people what news they want if they don't know what the news is until it happens?"

Stew slumped down into his chair. "We're a nuisance to Carver. He's a salesman. The station's sales and profits are what he's judged on—the bottom line. The News Division can sometimes cut into that. Like when he warned me not to run stories that might throw a bad light on an advertiser." Stew reflected a moment. "There's another reason: He wants us to run scared."

Greg was informed when Chris's option was exercised, but Stew had early made up his mind as to her value. She rented a furnished studio apartment near Greg's. Most nights, they stayed at his place because it contained a double bed and he was phoned at odd hours by the assignment desk. Every morning at six-thirty an assignment editor called to consult with him on the preliminary rundown of the day's stories and which reporters to assign.

The couple's lives together began to assume a pattern. Chris would return to her own apartment each morning to change for work—earlier whenever Greg informed her that the assignment desk would be calling with an early assignment. She would drive to the station in her own car.

He spent the day supervising producers and reporters who were covering the day's stories, revising the broadcast's lineup, and preparing the way it would be presented on air. She went out to cover stories and then returned to edit them and write and record narration for them. After the nightly broadcast, if she was not scheduled for the occasional late shift, they would rendezvous back at Greg's. Whoever arrived first would begin to prepare supper. The other would join in soon after.

Greg had grown up doing a lot of the cooking for his father and himself. The ordered succession of acts cooking required and the small talk exchanged began the process of filtering out the day's concerns.

Over dinner the talk would continue about their work or the news in general or the ordinary matters couples discuss. Then they read or watched television and usually made love before falling asleep. For the first time each had a confidant to whom dreams and fears could be disclosed. Chris was far quicker to reveal secrets than Greg. Although he was surprised to realize that he enjoyed exploring the uncharted territory of life with another person—getting to know her, to care about her—and she whisked away the loneliness that had habitually propelled him to spend evenings and weekends out with friends, he was also far less used to the isolation that secrecy imposed on them.

Apart from appearing to run into each other on Saturday mornings at the local supermarket with their separate grocery lists, as might any two acquaintances living in the same neighborhood, they dared risk few joint activities away from their sanctuary, which made it also a kind of prison. Yet, however carefully correct they had to appear to colleagues, the joy that grew out of living together was inextricable from their joy at working closely with each other, each relationship heightening the intensity of the other. Knowing they might have to answer at night for their professional decisions kept them slightly higher on their toes during the day.

Once, during lunch in the commissary, another woman reporter advised Chris that she was hurting herself at the station by acting so coldly toward Greg. The woman insisted on inviting him over to their table. Afterward she expressed delight at having been the catalyst for the friendlier behavior the two had exhibited.

"And all the time I wanted to wring your neck over that piece of yours," Greg admitted, laughing, when they were back home, sipping beers from the bottle, feet up on the coffee table.

Her expression turned comically incredulous. "You couldn't be referring to the 'Gorgeous Bathrooms of Beverly Hills'?"

He nodded. "Not the piece itself, but those dumb sound bites from the contractor you fought me on. They should never have been in there to begin with."

Her expression heated. "*Assigning* that piece was the real mistake."

"People are interested in how the other half lives."

"Their *toilets?* You can't be serious."

"Viewers envy that kind of luxury. They can't get enough of those stories."

Chris was incredulous. "Those rich people are just mindless gluttons."

"I'd love to have a bathroom like the one where the shower came out of the swan's mouth."

"A shower is just something to wash yourself off in. Or have I been missing something all my life?"

"I'll bet we get more letters about that piece than anything we do all week." He smiled maliciously. "We ought to make it a weekly feature.

The high point each week would be a shot of you using one of L.A.'s most luxurious potties."

"I'll let someone else win an Emmy for that one." She reflected a moment. "Would you really like to live like that?"

Only to Chris and only lately had he felt trustful enough to divulge some of a past he had tried to eradicate. "I grew up as the poorest kid in the richest neighborhood in town. We lived in a dilapidated little house because my mother wanted us to be in the best school district. Every time there was a strike or layoffs at the steel mill, we went back into debt. I was always afraid one of my classmates would wander by and realize just how poor we were. But they already knew."

"You must have had friends."

"Enough, I guess, but I always felt they just tolerated me. We were the token working-class paupers." He grinned. "A lot of that changed when I got a regional tennis ranking. They thought I might become somebody and didn't want to be cut out."

"Did you feel inferior?"

"More like just an outsider, hungry to get in. I had the feeling the other fathers had mastered some trick or tactic my own father was inept at. I worked my tail off to make friends with their kids and learn it."

"Was it your father who wanted you to take tennis lessons?" She knew that Greg's father had turned down a minor-league-baseball contract in order to help support a widowed mother who died before Greg was born.

Greg shook his head. "Tennis wouldn't have occurred to him. No, that was my mother."

Chris grew thoughtful. "You know, you never talk about her."

"She died when I was young," Greg said, and abruptly stood up. "I think the roast must be ready by now."

At dinner Chris renewed her campaign for grittier, more significant stories at the station. Greg argued that he had to spread good assignments around to keep all the reporters happy. That answer failed to satisfy her.

Finally, when she refused to drop the topic, his voice rose. "When we're home, you can't lobby like this. It ends when we leave the office."

Chris shook her head. "I'm not about to hold it in and let it eat away at me. Uh-uh. Who else do I have to talk to?"

Like opposing tank drivers on a one-lane road, both prudently backed off and ended the discussion. But the issue remained unresolved in both their minds.

*   *   *

Greg had occasionally subbed for the executive producer, but the pressures on him when he took the job full-time were greater than he had anticipated.

Before, he had been a craftsman who shaped the story a superior had chosen for him or at the very least had approved. Now, although he had a daily meeting with his senior people to exchange ideas and set the rundown, Greg himself bore the ultimate responsibility for picking which events and trends occurring in the region—and if important enough, the world—KFBS-TV would inscribe on the awareness of much of southern California.

Greg's own strong viewpoint about what made an event newsworthy and how to report it operated under certain constraints. Newspapers needed only to tell the truth. In exchange for obtaining a government license to broadcast over public airwaves, however, radio and television stations were obligated to provide news as a public service and to do it in a way that demonstrated fairness to contrary opinions.

The financial constraints on Greg's news choices were even more daunting. Lead or major stories were self-evident: earthquake tremors downtown, a baby-sitter's gruesome rape and murder, the governor's latest tax proposal, the Americans held hostage in Iran. Choosing the other stories was more complicated; they had to be newsworthy, interesting to viewers, and cost-effective to shoot.

Investigative and enterprise journalism that expended days or weeks pursuing a story that might not materialize was too costly for television. A newspaper reporter could take a bus to an event and then write it up, but television needed to send out a truck carrying camera and sound people with their equipment and often a producer to make arrangements and oversee the shooting.

Consequently, most TV news coverage had to be planned ahead of time with certainty. Stories already reported in the morning newspaper were a reliable source, as were such near-ceremonial events as the mayor's press conference, the opening of a playground, and a dinner honoring a legendary film star. One person at the assignment desk even kept track of stories to be covered in the future. Between the rare investigative and the predominantly preplanned were the unexpected stories, the accidents and fires and personal tragedies that local news rushed to and was justified by.

Chris refused to acknowledge the limits Greg faced and continued to badger him to let her do more investigative pieces. "Tonight you ran that story about a car-insurance rate hike without looking into it," she pointed out one night.

"Higher car insurance is something people will want to know about," Greg replied.

"But we also ought to tell them whether the increase is just a windfall for the insurance companies or necessary to cover higher accident losses. Does anybody on the insurance board who voted for the increase have ties to the insurance companies? Is there—"

Greg interrupted her. "And you want the job of looking into all those questions."

"Somebody ought to," Chris said earnestly. "My insurance broker tells me something smells rotten there."

"All right, but for God's sake, keep it lively. Those numbers could put us all to sleep."

He was mindful that in her earnestness, she sometimes overlooked the production values that caught and held the audience's attention. But because like all executive producers Greg was concerned about maintaining viewer interest, he sometimes tended to flashy subject matter and presentations that might give complex or thoughtful material short shrift. Her expectations of him were a goad, as well as her reproach if depth or coverage slipped toward the superficial.

Although it might take her several days of digging, Greg would argue that his reason for approving Chris's assignment was pragmatic, not idealistic: If she did dig up some dirt, viewers might come away with the impression they were getting "better news" from KFBS. Over time, he believed, the audience would grow. A scandal about car-insurance overcharges could make a big splash and draw new viewers.

Yet, something more was at stake, he knew. Ambition for Greg had always been synonymous with advancement of some sort: originally academic or in a sport; afterward, progress up the career ladder—more money, more responsibility, being able to acquire a long-craved possession. Each advance had validated the climb and the climber. Attention to anything else would be a diversion. Yet, in his new position, Greg sometimes displayed a commitment to providing news that went well beyond how it might abet his career. He wanted to believe that he was motivated by principle. But whatever the cause, every small success registered by the newsroom—a minor scoop, a critic's pat on the back, a slight rise in the ratings—seemed amplified and purer to him as a result.

Greg's vision of the broadcast was threatened when the consultants' report finally arrived. Unexpectedly, so was his relationship with Chris.

Stew's original conception to fill KFBS's six-o'clock local news hour had been a well-defined magazine format: the usual segments for hard news (with periodic updates), the weather and sports for which most viewers tuned in, as well as segments denominated as Life-styles, Health, Arts, and People. Providing no surprises, the consultants advocated expanding the latter segments at the expense of news and lightening its treatment. They also praised Chris as an underutilized asset and strongly recommended employing her exclusively and more extensively in them. About the only part of the report with which Stew totally agreed was that one. After a long discussion Greg thought he had changed Stew's mind.

The two men had no doubt when they entered Ev Carver's dimly lit office that he was in favor of imposing all of the report's recommendations.

Greg presented their counterargument. "Too many other newsrooms in town have already adopted the consultants' 'happy talk' format. If KFBS did the same, we'd become just one more clone added to a group fighting with identical weapons to win a bigger slice of the same audience. We might even *lose* viewers."

A couple of the report's suggestions were useful, the newsmen agreed: a new set, more high-tech graphics to give a livelier look to the weather segment, and more interview features.

"But we shouldn't shortchange the news," Greg contended. He could hear Chris's voice in his head. "Trivializing the news gives viewers *less* reason, not more, to watch our broadcast."

Ev finally yielded to their arguments that they might lose market share.

As he and Greg were about to leave, Stew halted in the doorway. "Oh," he recalled, pulling on his beard, "there's one other recommendation I think we should implement. The consultants loved Chris Paskins. They especially raved about that piece she did on Beverly Hills bathrooms. They want her to concentrate on those Life-styles and People kinds of pieces. That makes a lot of sense."

Greg argued vigorously against the move, pointing to her excellent hard-news work. But prejudiced by her good looks and the authority of the report, his superiors ordered Greg to feature Chris exclusively doing soft news, like fashion reports and gossipy show-business interviews. They would promote her appearances with on-air and newspaper ads.

Chris was stunned when Greg described her new role that night. "They all thought I was a failure at hard news, right?"

"No, that never came up. They're making the change because they think you're very good—the report picked you out especially." He wanted her to understand that her new slot was a promotion. "They figure you'll get a lot more prominence doing Life-styles and People than you ever would with the usual news reports."

Chris hotly disputed the move. The controversy continued over dinner and then several cups of coffee. Chris could not convince him.

"All right," she finally conceded, "I'll do those softer pieces, but at least give me my fair share of hard news."

Greg could not. He had no leeway.

For several months Chris swam amidst the frothy news. She covered film premieres and interviewed actors and directors, often at their homes. She discussed new trends in recreational activities and restaurants and decorating. She reported on California's hottest clothes designers. Although she and Greg tried their best not to bring the discord home, she was growing increasingly disaffected—from her work and from him. He sought more hard-news opportunities for her.

When the entire reporting and production staff was pressed into service to cover California's presidential primary, Greg was able to assign her to follow Ted Kennedy's campaign. He was pleased by the results: incisive reporting and astute analyses of the candidate's political strengths and weaknesses. She did her homework and the diligence showed. At the June 3d victory celebration, she was able to obtain meaty interviews because of relationships cultivated with Kennedy's family and advisers and with several Hollywood celebrities who had supported the candidate.

That was what caught Stew's eye. "She's so good at that. I don't want to waste her on news."

Greg contended that she was a solid reporter who would draw more viewers if she were given serious assignments, but he made no headway. When Stew's resistance grew combative, Greg backed off, fearing his support for Chris might raise suspicions of personal motives. He felt as if he were walking on an oscillating tightrope.

When they returned to the apartment in the early-morning hours, both still too energized to sleep, Greg divulged to Chris his conversation with Graushner. She exploded.

"I can just bet how wholeheartedly you endorsed me," she charged sarcastically. "Why did you even have to consult him? You're the one responsible for assigning beats and stories. You're using him as an excuse. You can do it on your own if you want to."

Greg prided himself on self-control during an argument, convinced that it usually gave him the upper hand. But angered by her failure to acknowledge his powerlessness in the matter, he, too, exploded.

"You and your damned ambition never give up, do you? You're

relentless. I stick my neck out, and instead of thanks for trying, you blast me. You haven't got the slightest bit of sensitivity about how precarious the whole situation is for me."

Her eyes were aflame. "Always for you, for *your* career. If you really loved me, you wouldn't hold *my* career back with those flimsy excuses. The real trouble is I threaten your 'manhood.' You're frightened I might outshine you."

"Don't tar me, of all people, with that feminist brush that we're all male chauvinists at heart. I wouldn't have fought so hard for you if I were. What's really at the bottom of all this is that you're trying to use me and my position at the station to get ahead. I'm a stepladder to you. When I don't deliver, you blow up."

Chris started to storm out of the apartment, but halted at the door, her hand on the knob.

At that moment the realization struck Greg that during all the time he and Chris had been together, he had never once been lonely, that he had truly been happy. When they were apart, the knowledge that she would soon be with him was a source of anticipated pleasure, like a child's knowledge that his birthday gift was hidden away in his parents' closet.

"Don't go," he said.

That night they made love eagerly, contritely, desperate to erase the ugliness of what had just passed between them. As always, their sensuality was an ever-achievable, ever-surprising miracle. But neither had yielded, and both subconsciously understood that the differences caused by their single-minded, conflicting drives might be irreconcilable.

Although their infatuation remained as compelling as before, they grew touchier after that, less willing at times to paper over those differences. At work Chris fumed about the barriers placed across her career. While comprehending that the true cause was Stew Graushner and Ev Carver, she often focused her anger on Greg because he was closest and the messenger and a man. Some of that outrage sometimes slipped into her briefcase and came home with her at night, subtly contaminating her behavior toward him. He sometimes wondered if she truly loved him for himself or for what he could do for her career.

Secrecy and isolation, which had originally spiced their ardor, served at times to increase the friction abrading their relationship. Both were working long, pressure-filled days that summer and needed recreation, but they could not engage in much of it together. On the weekends Chris often went alone on long horseback rides in the hills to restore her serenity. Greg was not a rider. He missed the social activity he had delighted in upon coming to L.A. and had relinquished for her sake. He resumed playing tennis and sailing. Sometimes, he would dine or go to a party with friends he had made before meeting her—the sort of spirited, achieving, humorous people whose company he so enjoyed.

Chris had met a few of them. "They're boring and shallow."

"You're taking yourself too seriously. I have fun with them—no significance, just laughs and talk. And it's important to make contacts in this business."

"You and I have fun together," she pointed out somewhat defensively. She ignored his last remark. She disliked that sort of thinking, believing that one's work spoke for itself. "And we make each other laugh. Isn't it enough that we have each other's company?"

Actually, she would often have liked to join him out in public at social gatherings. But in a city that floated on a layer of gossip, an attractive TV correspondent's clandestine love affair would quickly have become common knowledge.

The secrecy was also bothering Chris in a different way. "I know it's foolish," she confessed after a long day alone with her thoughts, "but this skulking around makes what we feel toward each other seem squalid somehow. I feel dirty."

When Chris was sixteen, a girlfriend had told her own mother she was sleeping over at Chris's house when she was really with her boyfriend. She asked Chris to cover for her. Having been brought up to take responsibility for the consequences of her actions and to despise hypocrisy, Chris was bewildered by the other girl's predicament. If spending the night with a boy was acceptable, then you did it and felt no reluctance to tell your parents, regardless of their own views. If it was unacceptable, you did not do it. She herself did not do it only because she had not yet met the right boy.

She finally met him in Poli Sci during her first year at college and found sex an exhilarating delight. Her swift liberation unnerved and intimidated him. She discarded him after ascertaining that the cause of their mounting bickering was not, as he claimed, her aggressiveness in and out of bed, but his inability to cope with it.

Because she was so honest about her emotions and had only Greg for company, on whom her career depended as well, Chris tended to become more anxious when she thought things were not going well between them. As time passed, she confided a good deal about her early years and often read him her parents' letters or related bits of her phone conversations with them. She knew little about Greg, though. Recognizing that he was not the sort who spoke easily about himself, she accepted the vagueness with which he had sketched the past as a kind of affirmation that the major epoch in each of their histories had begun the day they met. But mystery offended the curiosity in Chris that made her a zealous reporter; like a tiny pebble in her shoe, the vagueness bothered her when she thought about it.

One night, when Greg had to leave her alone in the apartment for a short time, his telephone rang. His recorded voice on his answering machine asked the caller to leave a message. Chris heard a middle-aged woman's voice.

"Greg?" The voice was hesitant, anxious. "This . . . this is your mother."

3

~~~~~~~~~~~~~~~~~

A long pause ensued while the woman evidently hoped Greg
would lift the receiver. Then, resigned, she finally spoke
again, this time to record a message.

"You asked about the cemetery." She gave the name and address of
a cemetery and then halted again. Even more hesitant now, she stated
her phone number. "I hope you'll call me. Please."

When Greg returned home, Chris angrily confronted him. "You said
your mother was dead."

"She is."

Chris snapped on the answering machine to play back the message.
Greg's face was grim as he listened to it.

She pressed him again after the message ran its course. "You still say
your mother is dead?"

"She might as well be."

"I'm no psychic. But that's a very healthy woman's voice saying she's
your mother. I think I deserve a straight answer."

Greg bit his lower lip, and his face tilted upward. Anguish replaced his
customary self-possession.

"Tomorrow," he finally managed to say, "tomorrow . . . will be
fifteen years since my sister died."

Then, for the first time, Greg told Chris—told anybody, for that
matter—about his past.

*Greg's mother was born Esther Kaplowitz, in a small Pennsylvania city
near Pittsburgh, the only child of a Jewish haberdashery salesman and an
impoverished rabbi's younger daughter. When her parents balked at the
expense of sending her to college, Essie impulsively and perversely chose a
mate sure to distress them, but on whom she thought she could depend.*

45

Within nine months she had given birth to a boy and a year later, to a girl.

Her husband, Matthew Lyall, was an undemonstrative Protestant of Scotch extraction ten years older than she with no family left. Essie had mistaken his straightforward stolidity for strength. That the two were mismatched soon became evident, but both were determined to make the marriage succeed, she because of her children and her reluctance to admit defeat, he because he adored her.

Out of loyalty to her husband and perhaps as a final rebuke to her own parents, Essie gave her children the upstanding Anglo-Saxon names of Gregory and Margaret and saw to it that they celebrated Christian as well as Jewish holidays. Each year their small Christmas tree was topped by a Hanukkah menorah. She wanted them to feel comfortably Christian with outsiders, Jewish in private. She yearned for her children to be accepted into and get ahead in a world that had stymied her. That was why she had insisted on buying a tiny house in the best school district and why she scraped together the money each week for their music and tennis lessons. She drummed into them until it was a compulsion the need to excel in school and later on, in life. Riches and security and the freedom to do whatever they wished could be theirs if only they wanted it enough, worked hard enough. No sacrifice was too great to make. Success and family were the only things that mattered. Although she and her parents stopped speaking after her marriage, Essie insisted the children visit them most Sundays, if they could.

Essie was a magnet of joy in the house. Sometimes her humor would start everyone in the family laughing during dinner, even phlegmatic Matt, and keep them nearly helpless with laughter through the hurried cleanup afterward and as they watched TV. If a game show was on, she led them in their own game of aching for the luxury goods, as alluring as crown jewels, that were dispensed as prizes and exalted in commercials: for the Paris trips and the no-frost refrigerator-freezers and the futuristic automobiles to replace their shamefully battered and finless DeSoto.

"Someday we'll have that," she would often remark.

Greg had acquired his father's lean height and athletic grace and his mother's dark eyes and hair. The eyes were deeply set and sometimes disconcerting when they stared fixedly at other people's without blinking or appeared more reflective than a boy's his age should. Most of the time, though, they expressed a lively, gregarious nature and an eagerness to learn.

His sister, Meggy, younger than he, had lighter hair and large, somber eyes at the center of delicately boned features, which belied her tomboy nature and an athleticism similar to his own. The siblings were inseparable. She was Meggy and he Greggy, the closest of friends and playmates. The bond between them was sealed, though, in 1963, when Greg was ten years old, during the long strike at the plant where their father worked.

Essie brooded as the family's debts piled up. One night, finally, she confronted Matt after the children were in bed. She wanted him to find another job or try to start a little business that might give them the hope of a better future. Even if this strike ended, someday there would be another and eventually another and never would they be free of care.

Matt remained stubbornly silent.

"Don't you want to make something more of yourself?" she exclaimed with a sudden, incredulous awareness that guessed the fatal answer before the slow shake of her husband's head verified it.

"I'm a steelworker, Essie. That's what I do. That's what my father did. That's what I am."

Essie's voice chopped like a cleaver. "I can't rely on you, Matt. Ever. I can't let you drag me and my babies under."

Listening to the arguments and reproaches through the thin wall between their bedroom and the living room, Greg reached across the space separating his bed from Meggy's and gripped her hand. Like an incantation invoked to fend off evil, he swore they would never be parted from each other.

After that night Essie's dissatisfaction with her husband and his lack of ambition, with the bleak certainty that her life would never ease, became unbearable to her. She took a job during the day as a waitress in a luncheonette, widening the breach between them. Matt claimed she had done it to humiliate him.

Although she rarely allowed herself a new dress, Essie had always insisted on taking her seat in front of the television set well before the start of "To Tell the Truth," so that she would not miss envying what Kitty Carlisle was wearing. She ceased watching after that night, Greg noticed. He noticed, too, that there was a lot less laughter in the house.

Early the next year, his mother took Greg into the dining room, shutting the doors at either end. She wanted to talk to him like a grown-up, she said. The dining room was her favorite room in the house, the proof that they were a genteel family, she had often stated.

Greg waited for her to speak, but instead she gazed for a long while at the gleam dancing on the table and then at each carved-back wooden chair she had purchased over time, one by one. Greg suddenly understood that she was saying good-bye to objects she loved. He began to shake and staring at his knees, prayed that he was wrong.

"I'm leaving your father," she finally said, and then waited for Greg's head to lift and his eyes to meet hers. "I can't pretend any longer that

things will ever be better between us. I've decided to go to California. I've been told there are better-paying jobs for women out there, and people like me looking for a new start."

Greg could no longer keep his eyes on hers and shut them. But he could not shut out what she was saying.

"For the time being I can afford to take only one child with me . . . and even that will be hard. I love the two of you just the same, but a daughter needs a mother more than a boy, and so, I'm taking Meggy. When I'm settled and have some money saved up, I'll send for you." She leaned over and kissed the top of his head. "I love you, Greg."

"Then take me, too," he pleaded.

"I wish I could. But nothing here will really change for you," she promised. "You'll live with your father and go to school like you always have. You know how carefully we picked it for you."

"Don't separate me and Meggy." Having Meggy taken from him was even worse than his parents' separating, than being left behind by his mother, even than not being the child she chose to take with her.

"It's only for a little while," she said with her tone of finality that Greg recognized.

He had sworn to Meggy that they would always be together, that he would always take care of her, but they were being separated now and he could do nothing about it. The decision had already been made for him. He ran from the room before his mother could see he was crying.

When she left a few days later, Greg and Meggy had to be torn apart, sobbing. Matt said good-bye to his daughter at the door. He would not look at his wife or drive her to the bus station.

Sensing emptiness in the house, loneliness swiftly rushed in to appropriate the space Essie and Meggy no longer occupied, rebuffing all attempts at eviction; the other occupants were never rid of loneliness after that. Nor was Matt ever rid of anger at his wife's departure nor of his weighty sadness at his powerlessness to hold her. Taciturn before, he spoke even more rarely afterward. He allowed both his and Greg's lives to be ruled solely by the clock: time to wake, to eat, to work, to eat, to sleep, to wake again. He knew there were things he should do to comfort his son, but did not know what they were and would be incapable of doing them if he did know. They stopped eating in the dining room—it was too painful; loneliness appropriated all the empty, precious chairs and grabbed gluttonously at food for which they had no appetite.

Losing the two people who had always brought him happiness devastated Greg. Their departure gouged huge ruts along his heart, leaving a large tract of inner landscape scarred and barren. Wherever he went, their absence awaited him.

Greg's solace was the world that welcomed him from the television screen. Its population were the most dependable friends; they could never desert him. Its families were happy and their problems minor and always soluble. Its dining rooms were filled with carefree children and wise parents who never left them. He believed it to be the real world, everyone else's world; his own existence was a terrible, nightmarish mistake. He longed for a real family, like Ozzie and Harriet's, and imagined that their children were he and Meggy, not David and Ricky. He longed simultaneously for something even more inconceivable: for his mother to be there watching TV beside him as before.

His father sometimes watched with Greg, accepting whatever programs his son chose. Greg always avoided "To Tell the Truth." Occasionally they told each other how funny something was, but mostly they just sat together watching in the dark. Having his father there was better somehow, as if sharing their separate loneliness lessened it.

Greg scrutinized his mother's letters for word that he would soon be allowed to join her, refusing to let himself recognize that his father would then be left alone. He missed Meggy desperately and wrote to her with stories and drawings and with jokes he had heard on television. Writing was a difficult chore for his father, but each weekend he would set himself to the labor of writing a note to his daughter and ask Greg to include it with his.

As the second summer approached, his mother wrote that she and Meggy would be returning for a visit. Greg was sure she was coming for him. He began to make private choices: He would take his tennis racket, to be sure, and his baseball mitt, but not the bat, which was too heavy.

Only a few weeks before the scheduled arrival, very late at night, the phone rang. His father was holding it to his ear, listening, when Greg reached the living room.

"They're sure?" his father finally asked in a tone of utter desolation. And then he added, "I'll tell him myself."

His father slowly lowered the receiver. When he turned at last to Greg, his face was ashen.

"Meggy is very sick. She has a very bad disease: leukemia. The doctors don't know if she'll live."

Greg prayed fervently that night and every night afterward for his sister's recovery. He told God how much he loved her and missed her and how good she was. God would not let someone so young and wonderful die, he was sure.

Meggy died less than three weeks later. She was buried in California. Matt sent some money to help pay for the funeral, but none was left to travel there for it.

49

Greg was inconsolable. A silent father wrapped in his own grief was little comfort. Greg had trusted God, as he had been taught to do. Either God was a nonexistent hoax or a brutal monster to be despised. Greg was determined never again to place futile hopes in God. Or his mother. She had taught him that family was indispensable to her and must be to him. And then she had betrayed him.

The day after receiving the phone message, Greg and Chris drove out of the city to the cemetery. Greg had asked his grandmother, now a widow living in Florida, to find out its name and address. She and his mother had reconciled after Greg's grandfather died. The two women obviously hoped that the phone call would reconcile Greg with his mother, too.

To Greg's surprise the cemetery was Jewish. Having rejected God after Meggy's death, he had ceased to relate religion to his life and considered himself, if anything, Protestant because his father was. He parked the car, top up, on a knoll overlooking the meadow planted with rows of headstones where Meggy was buried. A small red Ford was parked on the road there, and a straight-backed woman in a blue dress stood before one of the gravestones. Her hair was short and dark.

"That's her, isn't it?" Chris asked quietly.

"Yes," he replied.

There was no doubt in his mind, although he had not seen her since that bleak December after Meggy died, when she had appeared without warning in the living room.

Greg's anger had been too quick for her. He ran off, stopping only long enough at the kitchen door to yell back, "You took Meggy away and killed her before I could get there. You knew I would try to save her if I came."

Next day, when he returned late from school after stopping to play basketball in the school yard, his mother was waiting on the porch steps for him. Head down, black hair cascading over the shoulders of a heavy black coat, white breath floating upward, she looked like a volcano in the dimming light. Beside her was a gift-wrapped box.

Hearing the front gate open and close, she looked up.

"Meggy would have died regardless," she said before he could run away again.

He did not want to believe that. "I would have kept her safe. I always protected her."

"I tried to, too," his mother said sadly. She then spoke so carefully he knew she had planned the words while waiting for him. "I truly had hoped

*that by now you and I and Meggy would have been together. Being
separated was only to be for a little while."*

He could perceive in her voice a plea for forgiveness for leaving him and
taking Meggy, that she would take him with her now if he gave her half a
chance—she had come back for that, he realized. But he would never
forgive her. If you truly love your child, you do not leave him, no matter
what. She had made her choice. Now he would make his.

Through the glass window in the storm door, he could see his father
sitting on the sofa in the lighted living room, watching them. Greg
marched up the porch steps past her and into the house to take the seat
beside his father. For the first time he could remember, his father placed
his hand on Greg's shoulder.

A few minutes later, his mother stood up and walked down the short
path to the sidewalk and then, turning onto it through the gate, headed
back to the bus station. Greg saw her for one final moment through the
living-room window. Her head pivoted, and he realized that she could see
him in the lighted room, so he looked away.

Someday he, too, would leave, he decided. Someday he would set out on
his quest for the success that would keep him safe. But the choice of where
and when would be his. Relying for happiness on someone he loved could
bring him grief, he had learned. To become important, to become a person
who mattered in the world and whom others had to take notice of, a person
who was rich and invulnerable and admired, that must be his goal.

Next morning the gift-wrapped box was gone from the porch. He
assumed his father had disposed of it.

Every Christmas after that, until he went off to college, his mother sent
Greg a card with a little note on it. He would read it and then make a point
of not saving it or the envelope that bore her address. He never answered
her, and she never returned.

After a long while Chris spoke again. "Isn't it time you forgave her?"

"Some things can never be forgiven," Greg quietly replied.

Chris wished she could understand what he was feeling behind the
impassive expression. It never changed and his eyes never wavered all
the time the woman stood at the grave until she finally drove away. Only
then did Greg start up the car and drive down to it.

He left the car and, picking his way the few feet up the narrow path
and then across two other graves, finally stood before the granite
marker that read: "Margaret H. Lyall." The *H* was for Henrietta, their
father's mother's name. Meggy had always hated it and made him swear
he would never tell a soul what it was. It made no difference now, but
he was sorry that his mother had placed it on the only permanent
reminder that Meggy had ever lived, of who she was. His gaze dropped

to the rectangle of myrtle at his feet. Somewhere beneath it Meggy lay, awaiting his good-bye all these long years. That thought broke the dam of tears behind his eyes, and he sobbed for all the years stolen from her and for how much during all those years he had missed her.

Much later, he noticed an old rabbi trudging along the sidewalk behind him and asked him to recite the Hebrew prayer for the dead for his sister, who had always believed in God. He wondered to himself if Meggy suspected at the end that God had forsaken her. He also paid the old man to say prayers for Grandfather Kaplowitz and for his father, even though his father had been a Presbyterian. The only reason he could give was that he did not wish to slight him in this episode of remembrance.

Chris drove back; Greg was too aggrieved. He seemed to have collapsed into himself. They had planned to stop for dinner at a picturesque inn tucked along a byway of the route, but Greg said he'd rather not, and they continued on into Los Angeles.

He fell asleep that night hugging Chris. All night, in his sleep, he pulled her tightly to him each time she shifted even a few inches farther away.

That episode breached the fortress Greg had erected around his feelings and allowed Chris, as no one else had been allowed since his childhood, to enter inside him. He no longer felt the need to present a perfect and impregnable facade to her. He could talk about his feelings and more significantly, about his fears. She lightened his heart.

Once he confided, "I'm so consumed by ambition, so driven, that sometimes I get afraid there's nothing else."

"There's love," she assured him. "And so much more. I know."

Changing viewing habits is a long process. As time slipped by and KFBS-TV news's rise was halted for a while or measurable only in tiny fractions of a point, the urgency intensified for a quicker improvement in the ratings. Stew grew more quick-tempered and capricious and put greater pressure on Greg. The ratings were still creeping up, but at an agonizingly sluggish pace as competing news programs struggled just as hard to fine-tune their presentations to attract viewers.

The previous executive producer had once been heard to remark, "If I didn't put it on the air, it never happened." But the job invoked neither cynicism nor self-importance in Greg. Rather, what exhilarated him was commanding the people and resources to transform his notions into pictures and words, to tame chaos like an unruly beast and make it dance to his tune in all those little boxes. This was the sort of authority he had hoped television would grant him, putting him into the pilot's seat

52

at the heart of the dogfight, while events darted furiously about him and decisions had to be made quickly, flawlessly. His deftness could enhance the broadcast, the station, and his career. An error could blow away all three. He loved the action, the responsibility. His desperation as a child to control a threatening universe had become an adult's desire for the power to make his wishes do his bidding.

Nevertheless, his frustrations and dissatisfactions were beginning to outweigh his rewards. He was irked that Stew's concern with the ratings dominated the man's judgement and narrowed it to shortsighted solutions.

"You keep asking me to give it some time," Stew asserted to Greg when the ratings had plateaued for a while. "As if Carver stomping all over my face to implement those recommendations in the report isn't bad enough, I get calls now directly from the network brass. You can hardly tell the vice presidents without a scorecard. I keep a list of them next to the phone, so I can figure out who the hell is calling. All they care about are the ratings that give them their audience flow into their network newscasts. They want results."

"Then tell Carver to schedule a hotter show as a lead-in to ours, so we don't start the hour at a disadvantage. Our game show is nothing. 'Donahue' across the street is killing us."

Enhancing the anchor's popularity remained one large area of contention between the men. Stew wanted Harris to converse cozily with other newscasters. Greg thought the hard-nosed, shirtsleeves journalist appeared uncomfortable.

"Viewers look to him for news, not comfort," Greg maintained. "That just isn't Quinn, and they can sense it."

Although Greg assured himself that the cause was not Chris's prodding, he was pondering moving Chris next to Harris at the anchor desk. She possessed the skills to hold her own, while her glamor would provide a good contrast and balance to Harris's muscular image. Greg knew better, however, than to suggest initially to Stew that she be co-anchor.

"Viewers really take to her—those consultants' polls showed it," Greg began. "They trust her. Maybe we ought to try her as an anchor on the weekend. You know, just as an experiment."

Stew regarded Greg as if he were insane. "No one would take her or the broadcast seriously. Every program needs a pinup. She's ours. I don't want to hear any more about it!"

This time Greg did not report the conversation to Chris; her anger would be directed toward him, not Stew. She would claim that his major preoccupation now was the cosmetic touches that could boost ratings and not the broadcast's substance.

One Saturday night they decided to risk dinner out at a restaurant and chose one they were sure was too obscure to attract people who might recognize him, even if they recognized her. But a young producer on the staff named Manny Ramirez came in with one of the secretaries and spotted them immediately. Manny was a bright, hardworking newsman originally hired to cover the rapidly growing Hispanic community, but Greg had found him too good to be pigeonholed. Both couples were embarrassed. To cover up, Greg invited the other couple to join him and Chris, who had "just gotten together to talk business anyway." Greg gathered that the young Latin had also intended a more private and romantic evening. An awkward time was had by all, but the other couple seemed to have been taken in.

Far more dangerous was an occurrence in September, when Greg and Chris were separately invited to a party given by producer Danny Vickers to celebrate the premiere of his newest TV series. It was a huge black-tie affair held at the Bel Air mansion he had recently bought. Greg had often played tennis with him. Chris had interviewed him for the broadcast's People segment. Vickers was a man who understood the need for maintaining good relations with the press. The party promised to be a stellar event, and invitations were coveted.

"Do you think we're compromising ourselves by going?" Chris asked stoically, prepared to forgo the event on moral grounds, but hoping Greg would agree that was unnecessary.

"We wouldn't treat him any differently, regardless of the invitation, right?"

"Right," she replied with relief, immediately moving on to consider the next problem: a formal dress. She had not owned one since she and her mother had made one for her senior prom.

Chris and Greg took separate cars to the party, finding their way there easily by driving toward the giant beams of light slicing through the sky above Bel Air.

Vickers was a high-school dropout who fast-talked his way onto a television-series set by claiming to be writing a paper for school. Once inside studio walls, he roved around to other productions until he was hired as a production assistant. Now, a dozen years later, several of his series had had prosperous runs on the air. One had lasted six years and earned millions for him in syndication. Danny Vickers could not direct or write scripts. He rarely even read one all the way through. He had been divorced twice and was rumored to be one of the town's spiffier cross-dressers. None of that mattered. A short, balding, kinetic man, at thirty-two Danny Vickers was already a Hollywood divinity: rich, catered to by the networks because of his "golden touch" in coming up with hit series, and lionized as the most beneficent of humanitarians by his publicity agents.

54

To welcome his guests, he had planted himself close by the French doors that opened onto the garden, where the party was being held. Having a poor memory for names, he listened closely as the butler announced them before turning away from the last guests and warmly welcoming the next, who were stepping out of the house. He had been conversing with Chris when, a couple of minutes later, Greg arrived.

"You didn't send a camera crew," was Vickers's hostile greeting to him.

Greg replied evenly, "After we got that tip about the demonstration, I held off to protect you."

"What demonstration?"

Greg's voice dropped to a whisper. "An informer tipped us off that if we sent over a crew to shoot the party, a group of militant black actors would demonstrate right outside your front gate. They're incensed that none of your series ever stars a black."

"Oh, shit." Vickers's belligerence had disintegrated into worry. "Did you tell them Redd Foxx once did a guest shot on 'The Darers'?"

"Window dressing, they said."

"Diahann Carroll and I are like this." He held up two fingers close together.

"I'd love to meet her."

"Hey, I could only fit three hundred people in here." Vickers regarded Greg anxiously. "These demonstrators, did you stop them?"

"Only by pulling the story and not sending out a crew. First of all, we don't cover stories that only happen because we showed up. But most of all, I didn't want your new show and you personally—a friend like you—hurt by a racial battle right at your front door."

Vickers was bursting with gratitude. His arms around their shoulders, he marched Chris and Greg around clumps of guests to the large stone fountain in the center of the garden that had been converted to spurt Dom Pérignon champagne. As he filled two glasses for them, he suddenly spied Burt Reynolds and Sally Field at the entrance.

"I owe you . . . Greg," he shouted back over his shoulder on the run, fumbling to remember Greg's name. "I don't forget those things."

"Did you really get a tip about a black demonstration?" Chris inquired suspiciously.

A smile flickered at a corner of Greg's lips before he gravely replied, "I promised my informant confidentiality."

Among so many guests, Greg and Chris decided no one would think it odd that coworkers were walking around together. Apart from the smattering of newspeople present, particularly from ABC, which was carrying Vickers's new series, the preponderance of guests were studio and network executives, well-known producers and directors, lawyer and agent power brokers, and the occasional politician and businessman. Liberally sprinkled among them were faces made famous by the large and small screens. To Chris's surprise she had become one of the latter and was approached by several people who recognized her. Shy about conversing with strangers when not in a reporter's role, she envied Greg's ease in such situations.

Greg and Arnold Mandel smiled in recognition as their paths crossed—they had met several times before and enjoyed the conversation. Greg introduced Chris, Mandel his wife, Nell.

Arnold Mandel was a reserved, slight man of about forty who usually had his hands in his pockets and rocked back and forth when he conversed, as had his rabbinic forebears. A sharp-edged film comedy he had written and produced was currently filling theaters across the country. Greg and Chris had found hilarious and worrisome the scathing view of modern marriage it presented and were relieved to be hedging their bet by living together before considering that treacherous step.

Arnold's wife, Nell, did not appear pleased by their praise for the film. "You wouldn't have enjoyed it half so much if it had been *your* marriage plastered thirty feet high on the screen."

Arnold tried to silence her. "Come on, it was fictitious. We've been over this. We don't need to bring it up in public."

Nell was still focused on Greg and Chris. "Remember the scene where the husband was caught with a stripper in the basement? In our case it was a starlet in the location trailer. Hooray for Hollywood."

Arnold shrugged apologetically to them. "My wife is under the delusion that if I go anywhere alone but to the bathroom I'm cheating on her."

She smiled humorlessly. "What I object to is being humiliated in front of millions of people."

Greg took Chris's arm. "I think we ought to move on."

Arnold glanced unhappily at his wife. "Say good-night, Graceless."

Greg remarked to Chris after they had stepped away, "He's a guy I really have a lot of respect for. She made him seem like a lowlife."

"They couldn't have started out like that. I don't think I ever heard my parents argue. I guess they must have."

"People end up growing apart."

"No!" she rejoined forcefully, gripping his hand, remembering that he had overheard the altercation between his parents that led to their breakup. "Not people who love each other enough."

Later in the evening, they went back into the house to view the furnishings. Vickers had let the world know the interior had cost a million and a half dollars, "not counting the artwork." They had expected the decor to be overdone: too much gilt, too much marble. Instead it was tasteful and restrained: spacious areas, softly gleaming woods, subtly colored fabrics, and a few superbly chosen objects. They were awed, Greg particularly. This was the sort of home in which his dreams had long resided.

Entering the living room, they noticed a small African statue on a side table. Made of ebony, it was a stocky male fertility figure with an immense penis held upright before it as proudly as a flagpole. Greg leaned toward Chris's ear.

"That only happened after you walked into the room."

They both laughed, their heads close together. Greg glanced up. Ev Carver was staring at them from the archway cut in the far wall, a sly smile spreading across his face. He had been too far away to hear Greg's remark, but had observed their easy familiarity.

"I didn't know you two were an item, as they say."

Greg hoped his shock did not show in a loss of composure. "As they also say, we're just good friends."

Chris excused herself to find the powder room. Ev gestured toward the hallway behind him. He was evidently waiting for a woman who was in there.

"Lyall, did Vickers hit you with something about a camera crew?" he asked as Chris walked past him and down the hallway.

Greg nodded. "I told him no."

"Good. He asked me for coverage on the phone the other day. I ignored him. Why the hell should we publicize an ABC show?"

Ev moved into the room. "That chick you're with, Christine Paskins . . ."

Greg nodded.

Ev searched Greg's eyes as he spoke, the sly smile reappearing. "She looks hot as a pistol."

"Could be," Greg replied matter-of-factly, unwilling to let himself be provoked.

"I wouldn't want to think you were using your position to get a little ass."

Greg fought to subdue his alarm. "We just work together."

Ev threw back his head and laughed. "I'd have said the same thing, Lyall."

Just then Sally Foster appeared in the archway behind Ev. She wore a black gown with a neckline that slashed a deep V of skin to her waist. Sally Foster was one of Hollywood's great beauties. Her career had been negligible until she won the role of an industrialist's wanton mistress in the series "Heritage Hall." Typecasting, many called it. The show was still going strong after five years.

"I'm ready," she called out to Ev.

"Her show's on FBS," the latter pointed out to Greg. Then he winked at him. "I guess we'll both be working late tonight on company business."

4

~~~~~~~~~~~~~~~~~~~

Chris's impatience at KFBS was rewarded after the national elections in November, when the station's action reporter left to take a public relations job with a chemical company accused of polluting the drinking water near several of its plants. The action reporter's beat covered consumer matters and viewer problems with local businesses or government: for example, mail-order goods that were not delivered as advertised or welfare checks lost in bureaucratic mazes.

Concerned that a reluctant Greg might obstruct her from becoming the replacement, she cornered Stew Graushner alone in the commissary and broached the idea, her manner suggesting that Greg had already given her the go-ahead. The idea appealed to the news director. This was not really hard news in his mind, just a kind of community service.

Chris then went to Greg and happily reported that Graushner had just approved her to become the new action reporter. She was sure, she asserted, that Greg was as pleased as she.

"Didn't I tell you that if you were patient," he said, "I'd arrange things for you?"

Chris might have gone for his throat if she had not noticed his wide grin. She did not think it funny.

What neither Stew nor Greg realized was that the abuses Chris now considered herself empowered to investigate would not be limited to tricky magazine-subscription ploys or poor nutritional value in suspect canned goods. By slowly and carefully widening her reach, she intended to make her role that of a thoroughgoing investigative reporter. She would have to do a lot of the digging on her own time, but once in a while, she might be able to sharpshoot at a really significant target. And those reports would make her name. As she had done all of her life, Chris had taken steps to determine her own future.

The only request Chris made that Greg turned down was assigning Manny Ramirez as her exclusive producer—Manny was too useful at taking on a variety of pieces. But Chris still hoped to be able to request him on important stories.

Chris fairly bubbled now at work and at home with Greg. So many obstacles in her life seemed suddenly to have been removed. She suggested to Greg that they begin pooling their paychecks and paying bills from a joint account instead of totaling up what each had spent and equalizing it. Greg thought it better to hold off on that leap of commitment for a while.

Greg should have been happy, too, but he was not. His own job had become a burden. Paradoxically, the full measure of his depression at work did not descend on him until shortly after the November sweeps, on the day the ratings service announced that KFBS-TV news had moved up into a clear second place in the L.A. market at six o'clock and was tied for second at eleven. Ironically, the consultants had played an unexpected part in KFBS's rise, although Greg was careful not to point that out. Having come across Brett Winters, the anchor for one of L.A.'s top-rated local news programs, when they were researching KFBS's market, the consultants recommended that a client station in Chicago hire him. It did so. Within weeks KFBS had climbed into his former station's ranking. The consultants would take credit for the success of both clients.

All Greg could see in Stew Graushner's eyes that morning was the relief of a man just reprieved from a date with the executioner.

"This came none too soon, Greg, none too soon," the news director confided. Then he added, "I just told Carver in no uncertain terms that he's got to give you at least another six months to climb into first, you know, by the second sweeps period."

Stew was positioning himself to cut Greg loose if blame threatened to fall; he and Carver would take credit for success and deflect it to Greg for failure.

At that moment the recognition of ratings' utter primacy finally penetrated into every nerve and muscle cell in Greg's body. Thoughtful, effective news coverage was laudable, but irrelevant. As Ev Carver had initially warned him, morality according to the gospel of television was the same as that of football: Winning was not the important thing, it was the only thing.

A vague sense of depression, of futility rewarding his triumph, settled on Greg, which he felt somewhat ashamed of. Once or twice he started to talk about it with Chris. Each time he held back, sensing that she, so focused on the significance of news, would not understand. Even if he was smart enough—and remained lucky enough—to guide his broadcasts to the very top, the best he could hope for was a move to another station that was looking for him to do there what he had managed to pull off here. Moving might earn him a higher salary, a better title, but never money on the lavish scale of his friends in television who were producing series or specials they developed or in finance who were reaping the rewards of their deal-making. Greg was dismayed to realize that he had no idea where five years of striving had gotten him.

Just as damaging to his spirit was his growing awareness that as the news broadcast's format had become increasingly fixed and he had fewer creative decisions to make, the work was becoming progressively less satisfying. What he had originally loved about it was that each day was an adventure in which he must always remain ready to take immediate action. Some days now he would have given a lot for a good old-fashioned catastrophe to disrupt the nearly preordained lineup. Once more he began to perceive the outer persona he presented at work as managing the tedium of each day apart from his inner self. And that inner self felt trapped.

In early January, Ev Carver called on Greg to handle a chore for him. The company's CEO, Barnett Roderick, would be arriving in Los Angeles for a general station review. His daughter would be with him. They would be coming from Reagan's inauguration in Washington and would continue on to Acapulco for a vacation. The other network executives arriving with them were going on to the San Francisco station. Ev had designated Greg to be the daughter's escort at the dinner that night.

"Why don't you just escort her yourself?" Greg asked.

"I'm bringing Sally Foster, for one reason. The network's thinking of spinning her off of 'Heritage Hall' to do a new series. The old man wants her there. Besides, Roderick once met my ex-wife. He wouldn't approve of a barely separated man dining with his daughter. He's protective as hell."

"But he's been married a couple of times himself."

Ev laughed. "Which means he knows better than to set his daughter up for more of the same." Ev's voice suddenly lowered to a near whisper; an order would follow, Greg knew, that would be perilous to ignore. "Putting you at the table is business, Lyall, pure and simple. If she's happy at dinner, the old man is happy. Just sit there, smile at her a lot, and keep your mouth and your fly closed. Understand?"

Greg nodded, ambivalent as he left Ev Carver's office. Although eager to meet the head of the company, Greg was not looking forward to being propped up like a department-store mannequin beside the daughter, who was doubtless so lumpish that station managers had to shanghai companionship for her. He also had no desire to explain to

61

Chris that he was going out to dinner with another woman—she would grow jealous and demand that he decline the invitation. Conversely, he could not reveal to his superiors that the reason for declining was that he was virtually living with Christine Paskins, whom he had recently named action reporter. He eventually decided on a truncated version of the truth: that Ev Carver had asked him to sit in on a dinner meeting with Barnett Roderick.

"Was Graushner invited?" Chris naturally wanted to know.

"I don't think so. Roderick likes to meet young up-and-coming executives. Carver's chosen me."

Chris was pleased for him and hoped the recognition might reduce the stress he had been under.

Ev was at the airport when the Gulfstream II landed with Barnett Roderick, his daughter, and several high-ranking network executives. Two limousines transported the executives to the KFBS building. Another transported Diane Roderick and the luggage to the Beverly Hills Hotel. She was told that someone would pick her up at six-thirty and bring her to Chasen's to join her father and Ev Carver for dinner.

The senior network executives convened in KFBS's conference room to hear the previous year's results and the business plan for the next. Ev had rehearsed his finance and sales directors for two days. Having done well for the company was not enough, Ev knew. You then had to sell what you'd done to those who mattered.

He had performed superbly in Chicago and instead of being moved up, had been shifted to L.A. Now, he had come through for them here, too. The station's profits and ratings were up, and he was delivering nearly ten percent more L.A. viewers than before to the network's nighttime schedule, which meant higher network ratings and profits as well. This time they had better move him up into senior management in New York or risk losing him to a rival. It was now or never.

The eldest of five children, Everett Carver was born Eduardo Victorio Carvalho, Jr., in one of the tougher sections of Chicago. His father was a Portuguese with a mechanical bent who emigrated to the United States and eventually opened an auto-repair garage.

The son, known then as E.V. to differentiate him from his father with the same name, was conscripted to work after school in the garage and hated it. He detested the disrespect the black grease on his hands and the blue uniform engendered in the rich men who brought their cars in to be fixed. But observing them taught him that wealth lay in their direction, not among his immigrant father's wrenches and murky lubricants.

E.V. chafed under the subservience his father exacted. The elder Carvalho tried to beat the wildness and rebellion out of his son. The day he was graduated from high school, E.V. pummeled his father unconscious and walked out the door of their home. He never looked back.

He bounced around from job to job, until he landed at a boiler-room securities operation, where he sold overpriced, often worthless stock to unsuspecting prospects over the phone. His nerve and glib salesman's tongue brought the nineteen-year-old big money. He quickly rose to vice president of sales. He wore custom-made suits now and bedded beautiful women he took to the city's most expensive restaurants and clubs—until the day the SEC and the Justice Department raided the crooked securities firm, arresting him and everyone else on the premises.

He and the president of the firm were sentenced to prison for what the judge termed "flagrant and vicious securities fraud" and were forbidden from ever dealing in securities again. Because of his age, the prison sentence was reduced to a year's probation. E.V. had learned a valuable lesson: Dealing dishonestly was a foolish risk because a smart man with a talent for selling could safely make a lot more money honestly.

Although he remained known to the probation officer as E. V. Carvalho, with the sleight of hand a new social-security card provided, he became Everett Carver at the college where he registered and at the ad agency where he had talked his way into a job. At the company Christmas party, he met the daughter of one of the agency's partners and began dating her. Within weeks they eloped. The name "Everett Carver" went on his marriage certificate and eventually on his college diploma. In many ways he had transformed himself into a new man.

From media buyer for the ad agency, he went over to sales at FBS's Chicago TV station, where he quickly rose to head the department. Made station manager, he drove people to turn a sloppily run operation into a money machine for the network. When he was offered the Los Angeles station instead of the job on the network level for which he had been hoping, he knew that he had to say yes and prove himself once again.

Inexhaustibly aggressive, Ev considered himself the embodiment of the American ethic that those who weren't winners were automatically losers. And he was willing to do whatever it took to win.

After less than a month in Los Angeles, he decided that life there would offer more to him without an unsophisticated wife who began to question his frequent late nights out.

"This city's a cocksman's candy store," he had marveled to a friend.

He opted for bachelorhood the night she surprised him with the news that she was pregnant. She eventually had to cave in to his terms: the *support payments she needed to live on in exchange for a divorce and an abortion.*

Greg watched the first few minutes of the six-o'clock broadcast and then drove out to Beverly Hills. Leaving the car with the hotel doorman, he entered the lobby and asked the man at the front desk to phone Diane Roderick for him.

"I'm Diane Roderick," a voice behind him called out.

Greg spun around to find an attractive young woman laden with shopping bags and boxes. She had evidently just returned from shopping.

"Could you give me a hand?"

She handed him the boxes, barely glancing at him, and obtained her key from the front-desk attendant. Then she headed out of the lobby.

Taken aback by her curtness, Greg regarded her departing figure for a moment, then shrugged and followed her into the garden behind the hotel. She was average-sized, he noted, her hair a chestnut-brown color worn shoulder length. From what he could tell from the rear, she had a well-proportioned figure and good legs. Her patterned dress was chic and highly styled. He tried to remember her face. Sleekly elegant, he recalled, the features well-formed on fine bones. He thought he remembered her eyes as gray. Her expression had been faintly imperious. That's how the really rich should look, he quipped to himself. Makes you feel they deserve it.

She unlocked the door to a bungalow set amid tropical flora and entered.

"Put them over there," she ordered, and pointed to a table on the side of the living room. Again before Greg could introduce himself, she disappeared into one of the bedrooms.

He deposited the packages and turned on the television set to watch his news broadcast. A few minutes later, when she emerged from the bedroom in a different dress, she appeared miffed to find him seated at the set.

"I'd have appreciated being asked before you decided to watch television," she remarked brusquely.

"I didn't see the need."

She stopped to look at him for the first time. "Have you worked at FBS long?"

"About a year and a half."

"They should have taught you better manners by now."

Her arrogance grated on him, but he spoke softly. "Look, Ms. Roderick, I didn't volunteer for this assignment."

"What's the phone number at KFBS?" she snapped, and reached for the telephone.

Greg told her.

She began dialing. "I'm going to lodge a complaint with your superior and have him send out someone else right away."

He was dumbfounded by her presumption. "You really believe that we all have nothing better to do than drive you around?"

Her stare was incredulous.

He motioned toward the television screen. "I should be supervising that broadcast right now. Anyone else hauled out here to replace me would also have to drop work to accommodate you."

She started to speak, but began to laugh so hard she could not.

He was growing angry. "Your idea of humor and mine are very different."

Her head was nodding, but she was still laughing too hard to speak. He stared at her, waiting. Finally, she regained control of herself.

"All right," he wanted to know. "Exactly what was so funny?"

She dabbed the tears of laughter from her mascara. "They said someone from the station was being sent to pick me up at six-thirty, so I naturally thought you worked there as a driver."

Greg began to laugh now, too.

"Look, I'm sorry," she added, her laughing face far from contrite, "I must have sounded like a shrew."

"Let's start again. My name's Greg Lyall. I'm executive producer of that news broadcast."

"And you drew the short straw and have to take the boss's daughter to dinner. Would you rather I went by taxi and told them I asked you not to bother?"

Quite apart from Ev Carver's irritation with him if she arrived unescorted, Greg did not want to lose the opportunity to make personal contact with her father.

"No, I'd enjoy taking you to dinner."

As he opened the door for her, she got her first good look at him. "You're young to be executive producer."

Greg placed a faint frown on his face. "I was a few decades younger when I took the job."

Sally Foster arrived at Chasen's a couple of minutes late, only to find none of the others had yet arrived. This dinner was important to her. She would go crazy if she had to stay another year in "Heritage Hall." Although the TV series was still popular, her career was on hold, she being only one of half a dozen actors sharing the show's limelight.

The role had been the dark-haired, sultry beauty's big chance, the

65

godsend she had prayed for when she was struggling for a break, even the slightest of bit parts, and living off the occasional modeling assignment and some light hooking when she was short on the rent that month. Those years of struggle after arriving from Alabama were terrible, as she was always scrambling for money, always rejected for the part. That was five years ago. Now she was a star. But her career was stagnating. No decent theatrical film roles had come her way and only one forgettable TV movie. Her next move would have to be to a TV series of her own. That would be an important step up; it would put her on a different level in town. She was earning twenty-five thousand dollars an episode, over half a million dollars a year, but she could be making three or four times that on her own show and have a piece of it, too.

A hot writer-producer had come up with a new television series idea he had talked to her about and she was wild to do. He had submitted it to FBS, where he had good contacts. But FBS's Programming Department was sifting through hundreds of proposals now and would finance pilots for only twenty-five or so this year. Everyone knew that Barnett Roderick made the final decision at FBS as to what shows would go on the air and when. For weeks Ev Carver had hinted that he would soon be having dinner with Roderick. She had screwed Ev's brains out, enduring his occasional cruelty, in order to coax him into taking her. She was hoping to dazzle Barnett at dinner and convince him she could carry a show of her own. If he seemed interested in something more from her to clinch it, she would have to figure out how to arrange that without Ev's catching on. Ev Carver was a very shrewd man.

Sitting at the large table alone, everyone watching her, knowing who she was, Sally felt like a beggar until Barnett Roderick arrived a few minutes later and took a seat right beside her. Everyone there in the business must have recognized him and been green with envy, she told herself. He immediately complimented her work in "Heritage Hall" and asked what her plans were for the future. That gave her the opportunity to mention the show FBS was considering for her. She was careful to sound interested, but not eager.

"Of course, I'm always open to new opportunities, but I'm very happy in 'Heritage Hall,' she said.

"We're very happy with your contribution to it," he replied in a courtly manner.

Sally decided not to push further, that she had said enough to get Barnett Roderick thinking about the show for her. Ev and Barnett began talking business, and she sat back to assess Barnett's companion. The woman was a West Coast newspaper publisher's widow in her fifties named Babs McAuliffe, who was prominent in her own right. She was slim and attractive. Her eyes were no higher at the corners and her chin line clean. It's a good job, Sally conceded, and wondered if men could spot surgery as easily as women or cared. Babs was worth tens of millions and Sally knew, from reading Suzy, inhabited the same elite social class as Roderick.

Greg was also in the process of assessing Barnett Roderick. FBS's founder and dominant figure appeared taller to Greg than in his photos, perhaps six foot one and still straight-backed and good-looking. His hair was dark with striations of gray only at the temples and full for a man in his early sixties. What was unique was his attitude of sovereignty, of unquestioned mastery of his surroundings. Without raising his voice or violating a gracious tone, every statement landed with the force of a command, every question with the import of a cross-examination, the total effect conveying some element of reproach for which the other person must strive to make amends.

Barnett had paid little attention to Greg until, during a lull in the conversation, he turned to him and said, "You've come into the news department during a fortunate time."

Greg did not know whether Roderick meant that the point-plus rise in news ratings during the past year had resulted from luck or that Greg was lucky to be hired at a time when the pendulum was swinging back of its own accord or perhaps fortunate because Ev Carver had taken measures that had raised the ratings. All of the possible meanings belittled Greg.

"I'd like to believe, Mr. Roderick, that I was instrumental in creating any good fortune our news broadcasts have had."

As if he had not heard the reply, Barnett turned back to Ev to continue their prior conversation.

Rather than being annoyed, Greg was impressed and somewhat amused by the older man's style. He sure doesn't leave any doubt who owns the ball we're all playing with, Greg thought, and glanced over at Ev Carver. KFBS's general manager was a touch more respectful than in his own lair, but not at all submissive. He knows his worth, Greg reasoned, and wants Roderick to know it, too. He always plays from strength, as if he's holding winning cards. Greg decided that just getting a chance to watch these pros made attending worthwhile.

Diane caught her father's eye. "Greg's news program is very good, Dad," she said. "I was watching it when he picked me up."

She flicked a look at Greg, allowing a smile imperceptible to the others to signal the small private joke.

"I hired Overmeyer-Hotchkiss to advise us," Ev pointed out.

"They help?" Barnett asked Greg.

Greg did not want to be caught between the two men. "A few things to think about," he allowed. He could not be sure whether the slight elevation of Barnett's eyebrow indicated amusement or skepticism and whether it was directed at his own or at Ev's remark.

When the entrées arrived, Barnett ceased to discuss business and turned to include Babs in the conversation. Sally was used to the usual Hollywood gossip at dinner: who had just made what deal or bought which house for how much or filled his or her bed with whom. The network head and the newspaper publisher began to discuss acquaintances and political figures who were all rich or powerful, as far as Sally could guess, but few of whose names she recognized. She placed her smile at the ready in case Barnett Roderick glanced at her, but she knew better than to speak.

Dinner ended early. Outside, waiting for their cars, Barnett told the others that he and Babs were meeting friends.

"I hope I'll see you again soon. I really enjoyed it," Sally said to him too quickly after he had spoken, she realized.

"Keep an open mind about a new series," he replied. And then as if the idea had just occurred to him, he added, "Why don't I look into it when I get back to New York?"

Sally beamed at him all the radiance she could generate. "Coming from you, a new series would be hard to resist."

Barnett nodded at her in the courtly way she had noted earlier, no more than that, but no less either, and turned to his daughter. "Do you two have any plans?"

"Greg promised to take me to a disco," Diane told him.

Greg smiled obligingly. He sensed the warning from Ev's eyes sear him. Worse, he observed what appeared to be a glint of distrust in Barnett's.

Diane noticed it, too, and added brightly, "It's my idea. I'm after his body."

Greg felt himself gagging. Diane was watching him, a smile slowly curling her mouth.

"There must be some really terrific place we can go," she said as she slipped into the passenger seat of Greg's car.

"You're going back to your hotel," Greg declared.

She laughed. "You're angry over what I said back there."

"My very short career flashed before my eyes. My career might be a joke to you, but it's damned important to me."

"Nothing will happen."

"I wouldn't put a bet right now on my job's extending past first thing tomorrow morning."

She laughed. "Daddy knows if I were being serious, I would never have said a word. For God's sake, he's my father. Now, what's the hot club?"

Greg edged the car into traffic, a forbidding firmness to his mouth. "I'm dropping you off at your hotel."

"No, you're *not!*" she replied in a tone that verged on dictatorial. "Office hours are over."

Her voice softened. "I really do want to go out somewhere with you. It's better I don't show up at the hotel if Dad and Babs have gone back there. Not just the embarrassment, although there's that." She turned in her seat to face him as he drove. "How well do you know Babs?"

"Not at all."

"Well, she's just lost fifteen pounds and had a face-lift. She's got the look of a woman on the hunt for big game. My father would make a perfect next husband. He's attractive, prominent, and wouldn't need her money or be marrying up."

"And you don't like the idea."

Her expression and tone hardened once more. "It's really none of your business."

"You were trying to give me a good reason not to bring you back to the hotel."

She glanced sharply at him, unused to being challenged. "All right, if you must know, I've always had trouble with the women who were serious about him, especially when I was younger. They start out trying to make friends with me because they think that will win him over. They end up trying to undermine me because they think he'll love them more if he loves me less."

"Does it work?"

She thought about that. "No, but it causes trouble."

"Did your mother do that, too?"

"He was crazy about my mother," she said tersely. She clearly wanted to end this line of discussion. "Nice car. You really keep it in great shape."

Greg reflected for a while. "Thanks for mentioning my news broadcast at dinner."

"Carver didn't seem thrilled when I did. There's something scary about him."

"Is that your opinion or your father's?"

"Mine. My father doesn't discuss business with me. He wants to shield me from that sort of thing. But that might change when I come into my trust fund. A lot of it is in FBS stock."

Neither spoke for a while.

"I'm enjoying myself with you," she finally said. "I really don't want the evening to end yet."

Greg yielded. "There's a little club that's very in right now."

Greg did not like the idea of being seen out with Diane. He debated how to tell Chris and decided there was no need unless word actually got back to her and she asked him about it.

The club was crowded. A few people wandered in and out of the pool room and the bar, but most had squeezed into the main room, where the band was trying to thump out enough decibels to deafen listeners to its mediocrity. He recognized a few people and waved hello, but none of them so far as he was aware knew Chris. Diane was acquainted with lots of others. It occurred to him as she swept through the overcrowded room that she moved with a flair that was very like the impression she made speaking: sophisticated, self-assured, provocative, forceful.

A couple of times they managed to push onto the dance floor. In between they shouted conversation at each other. Later, they went out to shoot pool and converse. She was better at the game than he expected. The caretaker at their country place had taught her as a child, she explained.

Alone in the pool room, they began to relax with each other for the first time. She was amusing company, Greg found. She seemed to think the same of him.

They left the club after about two hours and drove back to her hotel. Both admitted they had had a good time. Out of courtesy, he walked her to the bungalow. She unlocked and opened the door. Barnett was seated in the living room reading some documents. Glancing up, he noticed Greg standing outside behind his daughter.

"You kept her out late," he said.

"We had a good time."

Barnett studied Greg's face for a moment and then lifted the papers he held. "I like what's been happening with the news."

He did not say who he thought was responsible for what he liked, but Greg decided that was as close to praise as the man was likely to come, and he'd better claim it.

"Thank you," Greg replied.

"Good-night, young man."

"Good-night, sir."

Barnett closed the door.

5

〰〰〰〰〰〰〰

Nearly a month later, in late February of 1981, when the evening with Barnett Roderick had long been slipped into a bottom drawer of his memory, Greg received a phone call from Chuck Mason, the network's head of Human Resources, that summoned him to New York. He told Chris about the call, although Mason had told him not to tell anyone.

She felt a sudden churning in her stomach.

"Is it a sure thing the job would be at the network? In New York?"

Greg shrugged. His guess was that he was being considered as one of the producers on network news.

"Maybe they're looking for a new executive producer."

"Not directly from local. There are a lot more experienced guys already standing in line there to run network news."

"You must really have impressed Roderick that night. What did you two talk about?"

Greg repeated their brief exchanges.

"I'm proud of you," she said. "We've always known that either of us could get a great offer that might separate us for a while. It won't change anything."

Greg flew cross-country that night and met with Mason first thing in the morning. The man was vague about the job Greg was being considered for. Greg wondered whether Mason himself knew. The interview did not so much end as trail off, with Mason stating that others would want to see Greg as well.

Greg read magazines in an empty office most of the day and wondered what he was doing there. At four-twelve in the afternoon, Mason's secretary rushed in to tell him that Mr. Roderick would see him at four-fifteen.

The FBS Building sprouted among the row of towers on the Avenue

71

of the Americas that included the headquarters of all the other networks. At that moment in technological history, that short half-dozen blocks in the center of Manhattan comprised the nexus of American television.

Individuality had been banished from the other offices Greg had seen that day; all were brightly lit and contained identical window blinds, beige carpeting, and steel and plastic-laminate desks and cabinets colored beige and brown. The chairs, too, were identical. Barnett Roderick's office, which occupied a top-floor corner of the building, was totally different. Sheer curtains admitted a dusky light. The cabinets and tables were fine wood antiques. Sumptuous fabrics covered the sofa and chairs. Several abstract paintings were lit from recesses in the ceiling.

The phone rang as Greg entered. Barnett leaned forward to pick up the receiver. Only when he concluded the phone conversation did the corporate chief look up at Greg, who was standing just inside the doorway.

"Are you married to the news?" Barnett finally asked.

"I'm married to television."

Greg hoped that was the right answer; the discovery that it was also the truth struck him simultaneously. He walked to the desk, but did not take a seat.

Barnett spoke again. "I take it that means you've learned by now that news can be a dead end for getting ahead in everything but news."

Startled by the other man's prescience, Greg indicated that he had.

"Good." Barnett opened a manila folder before him and examined a sheet of paper. "People you've worked with say you're capable and ambitious. Your record shows the ability, but one can only guess at the ambition."

Barnett leaned back into the shadows beyond the light cast by his desk lamp. A small smile played on his mouth. "Are you ambitious, Greg? I mean truly ambitious? Ambitious for responsibilities and rewards that other men can barely imagine? Willing to take the risks, endure the dangers that ambition on that scale might demand?"

"Yes."

Barnett did not want the question taken lightly. His gaze seemed to probe Greg's soul. "Ambition like that is far rarer than one might think."

"Yes, I am."

Barnett nodded. Greg understood that that point at least, whatever it had meant, had been settled favorably.

When Barnett spoke again, everything had been decided. "I'm starting you in sales. You have news experience. Good. That means you know about product and production. But to rise in television, you

72

need experience where the revenue comes in, in knowing what it takes to make money—any fool can spend it. Working in sales will give you that. It will also introduce you to important players in this business: advertisers and their agencies."

Barnett referred to the paper in the open folder again. "You'll get a twenty-thousand-dollar raise. That should allow a single man to live quite well in New York. Mason will help you find an apartment. The company pays all moving expenses from the Coast. Three weeks should be sufficient time to arrange for someone to replace you in local news."

Greg sensed that Barnett did not expect an answer, that the confidence placed in him would have been shattered by the slightest hesitation, even by a question, and that the merest display of reluctance would have foreclosed this extraordinary opportunity forever.

"Thank you," Greg said with a firmness he hoped demonstrated his determination, his hunger, to succeed, and he left.

"Sales? You gave up news to be a salesman?" Chris was aghast. She had tried to sound selfless when the promotion first came up, even proud of him for advancing, but he was putting a continent's separation between them for what she considered the most mundane of occupations. "It seems to me you've gotten a real jump on your new sales job by selling out."

"Starting there is a means to an end."

"And justifies it, no doubt."

"To you news *is* the end. You love it for its own sake . . . for all the right, idealistic reasons. News is important, sure, but news isn't what turns me on about television. When Roderick asked me whether I was married to the news, it was suddenly crystal clear to me that I wasn't."

"I suppose what excites you is selling thirty-second spots and arranging barter deals."

Greg was intent on making her understand. "What hooked me as a kid was television *itself,* and I'm still hooked on it. I didn't know the difference between sales and programming or finance and operations. I just knew that I wanted someday to be the guy who pulls all the levers and makes piles of money doing it, who decides that "All in the Family" has had it or to buy more miniseries or that sophisticated comedy will be next year's key to high ratings after ten—or even that we should do more news documentaries."

An antic smile broke through Greg's beclouded face. "What I really want is to be the magician in the center of the largest control room in the whole damned network."

"Greg, you're not a child, and television isn't magic. It's a form of communication."

Greg laughed. "Don't try to convince me that little figures moving and talking behind a glass window aren't magic. Ever since I was a boy, like some sorcerer, I've longed for them to leap to my commands and bring me money and honor and power. Just snap my fingers and have all my wishes obeyed and everything become beautiful and safe. I'm going to make that happen."

Bitterness and hatred were Greg's initial responses to the fracture with his mother. Yet, very quickly, others rose up inside him to dispute for supremacy: Despite having remained with his father in their little house, he felt homeless, abandoned, dislocated, powerless against the battering of forces he could not evade. And lonely, always lonely. Television was his sanctuary, companion, comfort, and hope. Like the picture postcards of an earlier age, the set was the enchanted looking glass through which he glimpsed a life in which he was no longer alone or full of care, a life lambent with opportunity. His thoughts escaped into dreams of happy endings and loving, cohesive families that never were poor or broken apart or threatened by death or debt—the twin monsters with one face that lurked in the dark around his bed when he turned in each night. He was determined that his body someday escape as well.

Tennis, he hoped, would gain him a college education. By twelve he was winning local junior tournaments and by fifteen he was nationally ranked. Whenever he had saved enough, he traveled to a tournament out of the state. Other players might have more talent and ultimately go further in the sport, but few wanted as much to win, still fewer tried as hard. When he was losing and needed every ounce of grit to come back, he would exhort himself with the warning, "Lose this match, Lyall, and it's the steel mills."

Because his schoolmates possessed money and status, the lack of which had torn his family apart, Greg perceived, rightly or wrongly, that they also possessed the inner security he craved. He examined their clothing and belongings, and when he was invited, the furnishings in their homes, emulating as well as he could the conduct and speech he observed there. He was always scrupulously well-behaved, always careful not to afford their parents an excuse to deny him future entrance. His friends emphasized his high grades to their parents, hoping that would stanch the odor of his family's lowliness and that his studiousness would enhance them in their parents' eyes.

When Greg was fourteen, Debby Stimson's parents grounded her for two months because of her wild behavior and poor marks. Greg arranged to tutor her in Math and English after school in an empty office in the rear of the library. The second hour was invariably devoted to Copulation, a lab course new to him that Debby was highly qualified and eager to teach.

Television, however, was Greg Lyall's most reliable mentor and temptress. The colorful shadows lured his youthful longings as seductively as prostitutes in a red-lit window. He lusted after the beautiful women and envied the assured men with fine clothes and sleek cars who dazzled them. Although he was young, he understood that buried somewhere between the men's poise and the education he strove for in school was the secret tunnel from his own world into theirs. Television heightened his boyish yearnings into a craving to climb someday behind the glass and seek there the wealth that would keep him safe and the status that would prove his worth. All the while, it was also teaching him how to hide in plain sight, how to be anyone.

He read TV Guide voraciously: about the new shows planned for the fall and the executives whose careers were riding on their success, about performers from Nebraska or Iowa or anywhere whose sharp wit or attractive style or the luck of a producer's notice had lifted from obscurity and adversity to stardom. Those people became friends he had not yet met and confirmed the faith he had placed in television. Out there behind the kaleidoscope on the screen, out there in the blackness where the bright images were mysteriously born, were scarcely imaginable opportunities; infinite success awaited those with the ambition to dare to seize them.

The dissension between Chris and Greg dragged on through most of that day and the next and ended only after Greg promised to return to Los Angeles every other weekend. His job would bring him there at least once a month, his boss had told him, and he assured Chris he would come out on his own at least once more.

He took her in his arms. "I'll miss you every moment we're apart. It's just that this might be the one great chance to get what I want in life. I couldn't say no."

She nodded, holding back tears. "I guess if someone promoted me to White House correspondent or something incredible like that, I'd be the one trying to justify the move."

"If we can find a job in the East for you, this whole thing might just work out better for both of us."

She looked up at him. "I really want to believe it."

"Of course it will." He kissed her tenderly. "We love each other. That's all that matters."

* * *

75

The three weeks left to Greg and Chris rushed by like refugees trying to escape the onslaught of the coming separation. The couple continued to tell each other that the separation would change nothing because they loved each other. The apartment would continue to be their home together. Greg signed the lease over to Chris and shipped some of his furniture to New York. She would vacate her little studio at the end of the month and move her own furniture over.

This did not seem to either of them an appropriate time to examine concerns that had slowly risen to the surface like rocks in a cultivated field: whether his hunger for material success might clash with her idealism, his need for greater socializing become bored by hers for greater solitude, his penchant for fitting in and sliding through to gain his ends conflict with hers for head-on confrontation. Neither wanted to risk crippling the stronger attachments they both believed would allow their love to form a line of defense capable of stretching a country's width without breaking.

They focused instead on how much they loved each other and on the qualities in the other that brought them happiness, all the while concurring in little vows: "We'll telephone at least once a day." "We'll pick romantic places to spend our weekends together." "We'll take care never to argue when we're together."

No matter how tired they were, they made love each night and struggled to stay awake afterward to snuggle and talk a bit.

Stew Graushner's immediate reaction to Greg's transfer was soul-searching despair.

"Why is God doing this to me?"

"He's not, I am," Greg pointed out.

"You're just a front man."

Stew asked Greg to spend his remaining days defining long-term directions for the broadcasts and training his replacement as executive producer. Greg thought he would have to fight hard for Manny Ramirez as his choice, but Stew concurred immediately.

"He's ready," was all Stew said.

Greg immediately gave Chris the go-ahead on a political investigation he might normally have considered too costly ·or far-reaching. He recognized that he might either be compensating for guilt pent up by a failure to advance her more effectively or be satisfying an impulse for integrity he would not be here to take the blame for.

It was an open secret in California broadcasting that Ev Carver was exploring other possibilities in the event FBS failed to reward him with a significant job at the network. Greg suspected that might be the reason Ev did not review the Ramirez appointment, as he always did major decisions. Greg pondered how to inform Ev diplomatically that their dinner at Chasen's had resulted in he himself being the one called to New York. He did not intend to reveal, of course, his conviction that Barnett Roderick had singled him out for fast-track training and promotion.

Ev phoned Greg first.

"Human Resources just sent me your transfer papers. Chuck Mason there assumed I knew all about it. But we know I didn't."

"He told me not to say anything."

"Exactly how did this miracle occur."

"Roderick mentioned me to him."

Anger and admiration were audible in Ev's voice. "I was right about you, Lyall. You really are a tricky bastard."

"Nothing tricky about it. I was a lot more surprised than you when Mason called me."

"Maybe I ought to ask you to put in a good word for me. For all I know you've got the old man believing you're my ventriloquist."

"I'm going there at a very low level, Ev."

"But damn it, you're going."

A week later Ev Carver was made vice president in charge of FBS's owned-and-operated television and radio stations.

"Shogun" and "Hill Street Blues" would win Emmys that year and so would "Barney Miller" and actors in "Taxi" and "M*A*S*H." Prince Charles and Lady Diana's wedding would be broadcast and the miniseries "East of Eden" and "TV's Censored Bloopers."

During his first days on the new job in New York, Greg realized that he had to learn to look at broadcasting differently. Like Chris, newspeople usually considered television a medium of communicating information. Those in programming were likely to call it an entertainment medium, with the Sports Department jumping up and down to make sure their form of entertainment was not ignored. But the top executives at networks and stations never forgot that television was an advertising medium, a way of peddling viewers to advertisers to produce the largest possible revenue, which is what those executives were judged on. The worst of them might have wished they could broadcast only commercials, but knew that to lure viewers, they had to pay for programming to fill the airtime between them.

The broadcasting network itself was simply an organization that distributed the programs containing commercials over the air at regularly specified times to affiliated stations, usually some two hundred of them (plus a small number of stations owned by the network, which were located in major markets). The stations received compensation from the network for broadcasting its programs, but earned the bulk of their income from ads they sold during their own local programming and between the network shows.

Toward the end of his first week at the network, when Greg was dizzy with trying to master the intricacies of selling airtime to advertisers, he received a telephone call from Barnett Roderick's secretary.

"Mr. Roderick," she said, "would like to know if you're free to have dinner at his home tonight at seven-thirty."

Astonished, Greg mumbled an acceptance.

"You might come five or ten minutes early," she advised. "Mr. Roderick always dines on time."

Invitations to Barnett Roderick's apartment were prized. Legend had it that few, if any, top FBS executives had ever been invited there at all, much less to a private dinner. It was clear to Greg that Barnett Roderick had truly chosen him.

He immediately tracked down the shoeshine man working his way through the offices in the building, to be sure the man did not skip him. He asked a spiffily dressed associate for the names of the best haberdasheries and went to several after work. Nothing was wrong with the necktie he had on, but wearing a new one made him feel less nervous.

He then went home to shower and shave and put on fresh clothes. The one-bedroom apartment overlooking the East River was costing him nearly fifteen hundred dollars a month, but was the sort of place he had hoped to find in New York in precisely the right neighborhood.

At exactly seven-twenty, as he pushed the doorbell in the hallway outside the Roderick penthouse apartment, Greg was revisited by the same anxiety that had suddenly wrenched his insides as a boy when he had arrived at Billy Franklin's house for a Saturday-afternoon date. Billy's father was the ominous figure he had never seen who managed the steel mill where his own father worked.

The door swung back. Greg relaxed. Diane stood there, a broad smile on her face. A maid hovered in the background to take his coat.

"Welcome to New York," she said cheerily. "I've drawn the thankless job of being *your* escort at dinner."

Greg was pleased to see her. He had enjoyed her company that night in Los Angeles. She was as striking as he remembered: large gray eyes circled by long lashes, reddish-brown hair pulled back on one side, a green silk dress gathered on the same side.

They chatted about his impressions of New York as she led him down the long picture-gallery foyer, which was as wide as most rooms, with a high ceiling. The floor was marble and the walls covered in a deep blue brocade that set off the paintings.

"Would I recognize any of the artists from my art history course?" he asked.

She motioned toward one.

"A Picasso?"

"And there's a Degas. The one over there's a Vuillard Dad doesn't like very much and might sell. He's got his eye on a Matisse he wants to put in the living room. The paintings in the dining room are all nineteenth-century American with a water theme. You might recognize some of those."

The foyer gave onto an immense living room. Through the windows at the far end, he could see tall buildings in the distance, across Central Park. The living room lights were low, and the dark wood furniture appeared to glow from within.

Diane turned aside just before the entrance and led him off the foyer into a much cozier room, paneled in mahogany. Bookshelves above cabinets covered one wall. Barnett was seated in the largest of the armchairs watching FBS's network news program on a television screen recessed into one of the cabinets. Below it, with the sound off, other networks' news broadcasts could be seen on smaller television screens.

"Greg," he acknowledged perfunctorily, and his eyes swept back to the largest screen.

President Reagan was announcing that thirty-seven thousand federal jobs would be cut over the next two years, which would save an estimated $1.3 billion. Another report followed, a human-interest piece about an American ballerina trying to "defect," as the reporter cutely phrased it, to the Soviet Union, at least long enough to train with the Kirov ballet in Leningrad. Then anchorman Ray Strock gave his customary sign-off: "Good-night and hoping for good news tomorrow."

"What's your opinion of our news program?" Barnett asked him.

Greg did not have to deliberate on the question. This program followed his at KFBS, and he had watched it dozens of times. "It tends to be a headline service. It doesn't give viewers any more than the others and often less. Take that story about federal job cuts. We saw Reagan making the announcement and then a graphic of the figures. They could have explained and personalized the story, told us whether it was just fast accounting pencil work or real cuts. They might have interviewed worried federal employees in several parts of the country, so viewers could see that their own neighbors might lose their jobs."

Without any sign as to whether he agreed, Barnett stood up and guided him to the dining room. Greg took care to compliment his host on his home.

Dinner was an elegant affair with several courses. The maid who had taken his coat fluttered silently behind them with serving trays and a wine bottle. To his host and hostess, however, Greg gathered, this was an ordinary meal.

Initially, the conversation focused on Greg. Barnett inquired about his first week in sales and his impressions of various aspects of broadcasting and the company. But then father and daughter fell into a personal dialogue, and a remarkable transformation came over Barnett. Up until then, even toward his daughter in public, he had appeared autocratic, impersonal, but now that the two were in private, their enormous fondness for each other revealed itself in warmth and openness.

Barnett wanted to know about her day and how a fund-raising event she was organizing was coming along. He then asked about an art seminar she had been taking at the Met and was delighted to learn that one of his paintings had been mentioned by the curator teaching it. He teased her affectionately about the clothing bills she had run up that month, and she laughingly maintained that they had to be a mistake—she shopped only at K Mart.

When the meal concluded, Diane invited Greg to accompany her to a party.

"Go with her," Barnett advised. "You ought to start meeting people here. Diane knows everyone. I'll be dropping by later."

"I'd love to go," Greg told her.

The party was being given by the parents of Diane's friend Libby Dexter, whose most prominent features seemed to be long blond hair and a grandfather who started out with a small-town drugstore and left the family a billion-dollar pharmaceutical company. Libby took a long look at Greg and then pronounced her approval to Diane.

While strolling with him into the next room, Diane explained, "I told her I might be bringing someone."

"She seemed to know something about me."

Diane smiled coyly. "That you're tall, dark, and handsome."

Greg recognized a lot of names and even some faces she introduced him to. Many were well-known in business or philanthropy or descended from fabled founders of American industry. Several had accents and European titles. A few ballet stars, painters, and theater actors seemed to have been added for spice. All mingled sociably. At twenty-three Diane was one of the youngest. The purpose of the party was to honor a member of their crowd who had just returned from a stint as secretary of the Treasury with the outgoing Carter administration and who was assuming the chairmanship of a major international bank.

To his relief Greg knew two of the male guests. One was a highly ranked professional tennis player he had competed against in the juniors. The other was an acquaintance from Yale named Tim Jeffers, who had gone into his family's century-old investment bank upon graduation. Greg and Jeffers had been members of the same exclusive senior society and had always gotten along, but Greg had imagined the disparity in their backgrounds as being too great for friendship. Despite his belief that he had been tolerated solely because of his tennis prowess, Tim seemed genuinely pleased to see him. Greg wondered if his gawky, awkward college self had been more personable then than he had been confident enough to suppose. Diane and Tim were old friends.

"Yale and Skull and Bones," she remarked to Greg as they moved on. "I'm impressed."

"I even know which knife to use with fish."

"No fork?" She clucked her tongue.

"You seem surprised I didn't attend Wossamatter U."

"I know very little about you. The night we met I babbled on about myself, which I still feel a little chagrined about. Probably bored you to death, but you were too much the gentleman to say so."

Greg observed her disquiet at the recollection, but also that having once allowed him a glimpse beneath her perfectly charming, perfectly correct social surface, she felt they had formed some sort of bond.

"California, I admit, was one reason for my surprise," she continued. "The people I usually meet out there seem to have been created spontaneously; they suddenly just appear: no background, no family, no values."

"Why is it that people from other places always think that about California?" Chris had thought that, too, he recalled.

"Because the people you meet there all just had a hit series or started a company that makes some brilliant new computer part. You get the feeling they could disappear with the first bit of adversity. It's not the same in New York."

Although the sole talent of many around him had doubtless been to be born into the right families, Greg had himself been concluding that a good many others, whether renowned for pedigree or achievement, seemed to possess solid virtues from which their own or their families' stature had arisen and which would continue to support that renown. Even the most rapacious of the newly rich among the guests appeared to appreciate that acceptance within this ultimate clique required compliance with its etiquette and just as important, simulating accord with its enduring morality. Greg now comprehended why the people here had long been considered the Establishment.

Diane took his arm. "I want Uncle Bill to meet you." She led him over to the ex-secretary of the Treasury, and they all chatted awhile.

"You seemed quite impressed," she remarked afterward, her tone disapproving.

"The man was secretary of the Treasury."

"Well and good, but no need to show it."

All the while she was reproaching his enthusiasm, she was smiling and staring intently at his face. He knew she was attracted to him.

Book Two

PRIME
ACCESS

MARCH 1981

6

~~~~~~~~~~~~~~~~

W hen Greg joined Network Sales in March of 1981, FBS was riding a long crest of popularity that had put it at the top of the national ratings and, thus, able to command the highest prices from advertisers for its commercial time. Several months remained before June, when the "upfront" selling would begin. That was when advertising agencies, after examining the new shows and schedules, would negotiate to buy commercial time for their clients during the next viewing year, which would commence in September. Nearly three-quarters of FBS's prime-time inventory and half of its other time periods would be sold during the upfronts.

The prices a network charged advertisers for commercial time were based on the purchasing habits of the particular audience attracted to specific programs and viewing periods. Advertisers wishing to sell beer and pickup trucks to men would have to pay more for popular weekend football games; those seeking to sell feminine hygiene and beauty products to women might buy time during daytime soap operas. The broadcaster guaranteed the size of each show's target audience in the package of shows the advertiser bought. If the actual ratings turned out to be lower, the network would "make good" by running additional commercials for the advertiser free of charge. If ratings ran higher, commercial time not yet sold or held back as possible make-goods could be priced high, producing greater network revenue.

Greg was assigned to sell the advertising spots on daytime programming that remained unsold in the weeks just before airtime, the so-called "scatter" or "spot" sales, where audience size was not guaranteed. Unfortunately, daytime was the only part of the day when FBS lagged in the ratings, and a lot of commercial time was still unsold. It was feared that scatter prices would soon have to be dropped. Greg decided that his best prospects as buyers at the established prices would be new advertisers, not the old standbys cannily holding back their orders in anticipation that prices would drop. But how to find them?

If Greg had been more experienced, he would probably simply have relied on the written material that the Sales Planning people put together from the Research Department's analyses of the Nielsen and Arbitron ratings reports. But because he was very inexperienced, Greg went downstairs to Research's offices to find someone who could explain the figures to him in more detail.

The department head was tied up, so he moved down the corridor until he came upon an open door. A thin oriental man about his own age, his shirtsleeves rolled up, was perusing a wide ribbon of computer paper that ran in pleats off his desk and along the floor to where the printer cranked it out.

Greg stuck his head in. "Excuse me, would you know anything about the daytime demographics?"

The young man looked up. His eyes appeared enlarged in the disks of his spectacles. A wide forelock dropped across the top of the lenses like a valance.

"Sure," he said with a slight accent. "I do the analyses."

They shook hands. His left arm was held at an odd angle, the result of a stray mortar shell when he was growing up in South Vietnam. The young man's name was Jimmy Minh.

After he and his family emigrated, he won a scholarship to study math at MIT. He had a gift for statistics, and they entranced him. To him the demographics had personalities that eagerly whispered their secrets; they were men eighteen to thirty-five jauntily striding out to the home-improvement center because fewer would buy new homes this year; or they were higher-income retirement couples happily furnishing their new empty-nests in the Sun Belt.

Greg admitted he was a novice and asked for a lesson in deciphering the nuances. Jimmy beamed; he was delighted. Reflecting the personality of its leader, FBS was a highly structured corporation run along traditional, hierarchical, organization-chart lines. No one had ever come down to Jimmy's office to inquire about the numbers personally.

Jimmy labored in obscurity and was forced to keep much of the intelligence he divined from the numbers to himself. His superior insisted the department's reports be kept free of what he considered "guessing" or "bias." Yet, the boss seemed to have a bias of his own against displaying to the rest of the company his reliance on the skills of an Asian with a physical deformity.

Greg became amazed that so much information could be discerned from the audience samplings. When he noticed that a higher daytime viewership seemed to exist than could be accounted for in the individual adult age groups, Jimmy grew excited.

"You saw that, did you? My boss wouldn't let me explain it." He drew an arrow between two numbers. "Our daytime shows skew young and urban, much more so than the other networks. You can see we're very high among young adult women in cities. I'm positive that also means we're pulling higher numbers among urban teenagers than show up."

Greg was not nearly so enthused. "Teenagers aren't consumers."

"But they are. A lot of them are latchkey children or older teenagers who stop off to buy the family groceries on their way home from school. They help out and maybe even cook the family supper because their mothers are working. Here, look at the correlation to households with working women."

Greg immediately grasped the import. "And the teenagers probably pick up more of certain items at the store than older shoppers would. Snack foods, say, or soft drinks."

"Exactly."

Now, Greg, too, was excited—and impressed. "Could you write up something for me right away?"

"If you gave my boss a written request," Jimmy replied with a conspiratorial smile, "I'd have to."

Greg leaped to his feet, his own smile as wide. "As fast as I can put it on paper. You've just given me something to sell."

Marian Marcus could scarcely breathe as she entered the newsroom for her first afternoon as an intern in the News Department at KFBS. The job paid nothing and would last only three months, until she was graduated from UCLA, but she considered it her ticket into television, an industry that exuded all the glamor she craved—and personally lacked.

She was tall, but bent at the shoulders with the subconscious stoop of someone trying not to tower above shorter friends she had long ago shot past in height. Her face contained gray-brown eyes that were too small, an overly large nose that matched only an equally overlarge mouth. Her hair was the same gray-brown as her eyes. Her enthusiasm, not her appearance, had won her the internship, that and the intelligence demonstrated by her high marks. Vastly overweight, she refused to wear makeup and chose her bohemian clothing to make a statement about her nonconformity. Doubtless as a defense mechanism, Marian was militant about her plainness. She often looked like nothing so much as a colorful, giant balloon bobbing down Broadway toward Macy's on Thanksgiving Day.

The young woman's mind was fixed on only two things: her career and Derek Peters.

She had first encountered him on a day that her exuberance proved too great for her agility. As she bumped heavily into someone and turned to apologize, she found herself gazing at the handsomest face she had ever seen. Disconcerted by her clumsiness and his beauty, she dropped her eyes. When they rose, he had already disappeared into the crowd pressing through the doorway. But from that moment on, Marian Marcus was unalterably and unrequitedly in love with Derek Peters. Friends in the Dean's Office tipped her off to the courses he was taking, and she managed to transfer into another of them, which met on different days, so that, now, during four mornings every week, she was assured of being able to stare at Derek Peters. And at the many women who flocked about him. She never summoned the courage to say a word to him.

Marian stared about her in wonderment at the back of the newsroom, waiting for someone to take charge of her, afraid no one would.

Chris walked by at that moment and inquired if Marian was looking for anyone. Marian stared at her in awe. She was actually being spoken to by Christine Paskins, the woman who, night after night, stood up against landlords and other bullies. Marian explained that she had been hired as an intern, but no one seemed to have anything for her to do. Chris invited Marian to join her at the commissary for a quick lunch.

In need of research help and finding that Marian possessed a lively intelligence and an endearing manner, Chris appropriated the eager newcomer as her research assistant.

In every way but one, Marian was an astute and mature young woman. That exception filled the first ten minutes after her arrival every afternoon; they were devoted to what Derek Peters did or did not do that morning. Only once had Marian exchanged words with her fellow student. One morning they happened to be leaving the lecture hall at the same moment, and she became so flustered that she dropped a book and he picked it up. She somehow emitted, "Thank you." He answered, "You're welcome."

"He said I was welcome," Marian gushed to Chris, exhibiting a breathless exorbitance in her idolatry, both of Chris and of Derek, the incongruous innocence of a grown woman trying to hold on to the doorframe leading out of adolescence and into adult complexity. She ached for him. " 'Welcome!' If I could really be sure of that, I'd . . . Do you think he'd be interested if he knew I was saving myself for him? Oh, Derek!"

Chris's own sadness seemed lighter after beholding one of Marian's paroxysms over a fixation that swung wildly between poignant and ludicrous, so comical in fact that Marian herself began to joke about it. The younger woman pretended to be developing a plan to switch to a seat directly in front of Derek, which would block his view of the blackboard, so he would have to recognize her presence. When Chris induced her to go on a diet and her weight began coming down, Marian remarked that Derek's marks would now improve because he'd be able to see the blackboard again.

One day, Marian lamented that if only she had Chris's looks, she could have any man she wanted, Derek would be begging her for a date, she would be a happy woman. Chris confided what she had told no one else, that she had been living with someone she loved who had moved away to take a job elsewhere and she missed him desperately.

Marian did not inquire more deeply. From that moment on, however, she understood that her own playing at having a childish "crush" on someone she had never even met was now unseemly. As if she had been awaiting a reason to let go of the doorframe, Marian stepped fully into the murkiness of womanhood, within which lurked adult responsibility and loss. She never again mentioned Derek unless Chris brought him up, and then only with an adult's wry self-mockery. She began to care about her appearance and to dress better. The two women began to seem more nearly contemporaries. A real friendship began to grow.

Diane could not get Greg out of her mind. Claiming that her original escort had become ill, she invited Greg to accompany her and her father to a ball to raise funds for a major ballet company and was overjoyed when he accepted. She then immediately withdrew that other young man's invitation with the excuse that her father had insisted she accompany an important business associate.

Diane was not ready when Greg arrived at the apartment, so Barnett chatted with him about television for several minutes, primarily about prospects for the upfronts. She looked lovely when she appeared, in a blue gown with large sapphire and diamond earrings, necklace, and bracelet. The jewelry had been her mother's, she later told Greg, and now was hers.

In the limousine she briefed the men on the current season of the ballet company, one of the city's most prestigious cultural organizations. Socialites and philanthropists competed for the expensive honor of sitting on its board. As current head of the Junior Committee, Diane could expect to be asked to serve on the full board in a year or two. She viewed her many fund-raising endeavors as a necessary task in maintaining and enhancing her social position.

Once inside the hotel where the ball was being held, Diane drew Greg aside. She seemed nervous. Her tone became harsher, her manner demanding.

"Please exercise more restraint. That remark you made in the car."

"Your father seemed to find it funny."

"I'm sure he was being polite. And when you're asked what you do, simply say that you're an executive. You don't need to add anything."

"Not mention FBS?"

"I don't want people to think my father had to find me an escort."

"Instead they'll think I'm either out of work or with the CIA," he remarked irritably. "Anything else?"

"Well, I wasn't going to mention it because there's nothing we can do about it now, but I wish you hadn't worn a tuxedo with a shawl collar. You look like a band leader."

He was angry now. "Would you rather I left?"

A warm smile dissolved the icy expression. "Of course not. I'm really happy you came." But her expression quickly hardened again. "I just want you to be careful what you do and say."

Diane squared her shoulders, lifted her chin, and moved smartly toward the tables at which the young women on her committee were checking guests' names as they entered.

Greg was awed by the impressive company at the Rodericks' table. With them were the secretary general of the United Nations and his wife, the British ambassador and his wife, and a very tall couple whose horse had just won an important race in Florida and who had flown straight back on their private jet so as not to miss the ball. Greg became tongue-tied when he realized why the family name of the man, who was descended from a nineteenth-century tycoon, was the same as the steel corporation's for which his own father had labored.

Just pretend you're one of them, and you will be, Greg kept telling himself. And keep asking them questions so they can't ask about you. After a while, he realized he could hold his own, and his ease returned. Diane smiled at him encouragingly to convey how ably she thought he was conducting himself.

"It went well," she allowed herself to remark about the ball after it ended, when she and Greg were leaving for a disco. "No mistakes."

At the nightclub, too, she seemed to know everyone and introduced him. She was like a genie who could open any door for him, Greg decided. They danced and talked. She seemed more relaxed than at the ball and indeed, happy to be with him. And he realized that although he had considered the evening an opportunity to advance his career as the protégé of Barnett Roderick and the friend of his daughter, he was enjoying himself. He realized that the depression that had gripped him in the last months at KFBS-TV had disappeared as this new road of opportunity had opened before him. He just had to be careful not to do anything to offend the Rodericks.

Well after three in the morning, Greg asked the waiter for the check. Before Greg knew what she was doing, Diane handed her credit card to the waiter, who disappeared with it. Greg was furious, but it was too late to stop the man.

Greg stared out the side window as the limousine drove across town. Diane's eyes were closed, her head back tipped against the black leather upholstery.

"You're angry," she finally acknowledged, opening her eyes to look at him.

"I'm not a gigolo. I can pay for our drinks."

"You were my guest. Let's not ruin a lovely evening."

The limousine stopped in front of the entrance to his apartment house.

"Thanks for inviting me," he said.

Her hand on his arm halted him. "I've really had a good time with you tonight. I thought you were enjoying it, too."

Apologizing was not something she did easily, but she sensed that the moment required it. "Greg, I'm sorry if I insulted you. I handled it badly."

She leaned forward and kissed him on the lips. "Please don't leave angry."

"Apology accepted." He smiled. "I had a wonderful evening."

He stepped onto the sidewalk and watched her smiling back at him through the side window, until the car was well down the street. Was she just being friendly or did she intend something more? He let himself consider what a more involved relationship could mean to his career—and immediately felt guilty. He was in love with Chris. He walked toward the building's entrance and tried to put the calculating thoughts out of his mind.

Greg flew out to Los Angeles the following weekend with white roses, which Chris loved. He missed her very much. They had agreed to act as if he had simply come home after an overly long day at the office; they seemed to believe that refusing to acknowledge the distance between them would make the facts compliantly follow. They were giddy all the way back to the apartment, laughing and touching each other and kissing whenever the car stopped for a red light.

On Saturday morning the assignment desk phoned to advise Chris that a crew had been freed up for her that afternoon to shoot one of her stories. Greg arranged to play tennis with friends. They met up again for supper at a restaurant they doubted acquaintances would frequent.

Too little time had passed since Greg's departure for them to reveal the true nature of their relationship—colleagues would rightly suspect it had commenced far earlier. Secrecy was safer and besides, had become a habit with which they had grown comfortable.

During their long phone calls, Greg had told Chris all about his new job. At dinner what she wanted most to discuss was a complicated investigation of an influential real estate developer in which she was immersed. Her field producer was less of a thinker than a technician, and she truly missed Greg's advice. Greg felt the evidence was still not conclusive that the man had acted illegally. He cautioned her to step carefully and keep digging.

"Unless you have him dead to rights, he'll sue you and FBS for libel just to make it look like he's not guilty. This isn't just another little Hollywood gossip story. This guy has a reputation to protect."

"Getting stuck with the gossip stories wasn't exactly my idea," she replied sharply. Chris's anger at having been sidetracked so long on marginal assignments still lurked near the surface.

"I did as much as I could."

"I'm sorry," she offered contritely. "We have so little time together. The last thing in the world I want is for us to argue."

"That's the last thing I want, too. We promised each other we wouldn't."

Impulsively, Greg ordered a bottle of champagne. As the glasses were being poured, Arnold Mandel walked into the restaurant. The news of the movie producer's separation from his wife, Nell, had hit the papers that day. He looked so forlorn that they asked him to join them.

Arnold eyed the champagne. "You two are celebrating something," he guessed. "I'd only put a damper on things."

"I'm just celebrating being back on the Coast." Greg replied. "I'm out here on business, and Chris was nice enough to share a dinner with me."

Arnold took a seat. The anguish had been walled in within him for days. He was grateful for their company and for a chance to vent his grief.

"She was always so jealous—without any cause. You remember, always accusing me of cheating on her. Well, two days ago I spilled something on my shirt at lunch and went home to change it. I found her in bed with my lawyer. It turned out they had been lovers for five years." His voice caught and he tried to make light of it. "He's the busiest divorce lawyer in town. Now I know why."

He had to pause for a moment.

"You know," he went on, a sad smile torturing his mouth, "when she and I first met, the sex was incredible. I knew she was wrong for me—how critical she could act, for one thing—and that the sex would someday simmer down, but I almost couldn't help myself. It was as if I couldn't think rationally about her faults. After a while, the faults were all that were left."

When Chris and Greg returned to the apartment, they were eager to make love and escape the gloom Mandel's confessions had rained on them.

They would not have to wait long to see each other again. Next weekend they would both fly to Wyoming. Chris was excited. Greg would meet her family for the first time.

Greg found a message from Diane on his answering machine when he arrived back at his New York apartment on Sunday night. She had phoned the day before to ask whether he would be interested in visiting the Museum of Modern Art, "something every immigrant New Yorker should see."

Phoning her back, he told her that he had spent the weekend in Los Angeles. She seemed to want to ask him about it, but refrained, sensing he might grow irritated at her prying into his private life.

"I have tickets for a new play that's opening tonight," she said cheerfully. "We can drop into the opening-night party afterward. Do you want to join me?"

He was pleased that she wanted to invite him places he could never go and introduce him to people he could never meet on his own, but he did not like the dependence always being her guest also implied.

"Only if I can take you to dinner first," he insisted.

Barnett was out when Greg arrived to pick up Diane. He sat leafing through magazines in the study until, twenty minutes late getting dressed, she appeared. From what he could gather, she had changed her outfit twice and was still not pleased with how she looked. Barnett had taken the limousine, and they had trouble finding a cab and would have to rush through dinner at the restaurant he had carefully chosen to repay her hospitality. She was still out of sorts when they arrived and remarked that only tourists came here anymore. She cheered up when several people she knew stopped at their table.

For the rest of the meal, she did her best to defuse his annoyance with her. She was amusing and lively, and soon, he was as well.

Greg was thrilled to be at a Broadway opening night and to be one of the in people at the party afterward: chatting with the cast and backers who anxiously awaited the early newspaper editions, assuring them that

93

he had really liked the show and that it would be a hit. When the reviews turned out to be good, he felt elated for his new friends and at being where the city's excitement was occurring.

"This is really what New York is supposed to be like!" he whispered to Diane. "This is incredible!"

Two days later, Greg was scanning the *Times* and came across a photo taken the night before of Diane dancing at a charity event. Her jewelry was different from what she had worn at the charity ball, but no less lavish. Her partner on the dance floor was turned away from the camera, so Greg could not make out his face, but the caption identified him as Craig Watkins Putnam.

Greg felt as thoughtlessly disposed of as an empty plastic cigarette lighter. He had believed she was attracted to him, a foolish, conceited notion, he now concluded. She must have lists of men she called upon to escort her to all the events she attended, men on her own social level. Not that he wanted to get involved with her, he assured himself, but he had hoped to turn her fondness for him into the sort of long-term friendship that would afford him periodic access to Barnett. Otherwise, with so much on his mind, the CEO might forget about him.

Greg spent the next night at home. Without company, he grew increasingly bored. He watched television for a while and tried to reach Chris, but then remembered her telling him she had plans for the evening. He did not know what they were. Guilty at not divulging his evenings with Diane, he had been reluctant to inquire any further. Now, he was growing resentful and self-righteous. Because of the time difference, when she finally came home, he would long have been asleep.

His phone rang, and he jumped for it.

"Hi."

"Hi." The voice was Diane's. She spoke tentatively. "Are you all right?"

"Fine."

"Do you have something against me?" She sounded hurt.

"Of course not."

"Then why do you always expect me to be the one to phone?"

Greg was surprised. "I didn't know you expected anything. Besides, I thought you were probably busy. You're out a lot. Who's Craig Watkins Putnam?" he asked after a beat, trying to sound casual.

"Oh, the *Times* picture."

"What kind of guy insists people call him with three names?"

Greg heard a peal of laughter.

"You're jealous," she said.

"I just wanted to know who he was," Greg replied, annoyed at the trace of indignation he heard beneath his words.

"You are jealous!" she noted in disbelief. "You, who have all this incredible confidence."

Diane was delighted by the turnabout. She had stared at the phone all night, willing herself to wait Greg out, then castigating herself for crumbling, had dialed him. Now she realized that although he might not be willing to admit it, probably not even to himself, Greg really liked her.

"So as not to lose my alluring aura of mystery," she joked, "I'll just say he's one of my better lovers." Her laughter sounded full and rich. "All right, I'll make it up to you. I'm giving a small party for my dad this weekend. It's his birthday. Will you come?" Diane realized that she was holding her breath. When Greg did not accept right away, she became cross. "If being with me is that much of a burden to you—"

"It sounds like a private family get-together."

"My father asked me to invite you."

"I'd love to."

When Greg reached Chris on the telephone, he told her he would have to cancel the upcoming weekend with her and her family in Wyoming. He had to remain in New York for Barnett Roderick's birthday party.

Chris was disappointed. "That isn't a command, I gather. Just send him a necktie and tell him you have a prior engagement. This is important, too."

"I can't. You have no idea how extraordinary it is to be invited. No one from the company is ever invited to his private social affairs."

"Greg, we've lived together for over a year and my mother and father haven't once set eyes on you. This isn't fair to me."

"I just can't. I'll make it up to you. The week after."

"Mother will be at her sister's in Phoenix, and my father will join her there the week after that."

Greg was silent. This time Chris was the one who yielded, realizing that he would not. "I guess I'm not being fair, either. It is pretty amazing that Roderick's taking such an interest in you." Her voice brightened. "How about if I fly to New York to see *you* for the weekend? We'd have all Saturday and Sunday. I've never been to New York. Perhaps we could both go to the party."

"I'm sorry, honey," he said contritely. "The party's very small. The invitation was strictly for one."

"I understand. Some other time."

"I'll miss you. I'll be out to see you the weekend after. I promise."

"I'll miss you, too."

Fewer than fifty people were at the party, and only Greg was employed by FBS. Most of the guests were Barnett's contemporaries and came from socially prominent families. Feeling out of place, Greg spent the evening on the fringe of groups, observing Barnett circulate among them, exuding power. He had read somewhere that Barnett's aspiration had always been to gain entrance into their midst. To Greg the man appeared to be a giant among pygmies.

At one point Barnett noticed Greg watching him, and smiling, he walked over.

"I've had good reports on the headway you're making in daytime sales," he said.

"Thanks. Thanks very much. Happy birthday." Greg was overwhelmed at Barnett Roderick's interest in him.

"How are you getting along with Bill Jorgenson?"

"Just fine," Greg said. The head of Sales was several layers above Greg; they had exchanged nods twice.

"You could learn a lot from Bill. We'll talk later," Barnett assured him, and then added, before turning back to other guests, "There are a couple of things I'd like your opinion on."

Greg could barely believe what was happening to him. Here I am in Barnett Roderick's incredible apartment . . . on his birthday . . . with people I dreamed of meeting someday in only my most outlandish fantasies . . . and he invites me here and tells me he wants to know my opinion. Greg had only sipped at his drink, but he felt intoxicated. Even so, a small voice of doubt called a warning to him from somewhere in the back of his brain.

"Having a good time?" Diane asked. She had had to leave him alone most of the evening in order to act as hostess.

"Great. Terrific party." He glanced at Barnett, who stood just a few feet past her, conversing with "Uncle Bill." "Let me ask you something, Diane. Why on earth would your father care the slightest bit about my opinion on anything?"

"Because he knows that *I* care about you."

She stared up at Greg. Down to the gray depths of her eyes, he suddenly saw her love for him. At that moment he could have been truthful. He could have told her that he was in love with another woman or that he did not feel the same way about her. He could have, but he did not. Instead, he smiled gently and did what he thought would be the smartest thing, which was to say nothing. He sensed that Barnett, behind her, was watching.

96

Greg had hoped to observe the upfronts when they began, even if he did not take an active role, a way of edging into prime-time sales, where the action was. Early indications were that he and two other newcomers to Sales were considered too inexperienced to sit in.

Happening upon Bill Jorgenson when they were both awaiting the elevator, Greg said, "I was speaking to the Chairman the other night. He asked whether I was going to get the chance to participate in the upfronts. He said I could learn a lot from you."

Barnett had indeed made both those statements to Greg, but by putting them together, Greg gave the impression that the Chairman, as Barnett was known, had specifically intended Greg to observe the upfronts beside Jorgenson.

A large, heavyset man with a salesman's jovial manner, the senior vice president had not forgotten that Greg had originally been sent to the department on Barnett Roderick's recommendation. He had subtly accorded Greg favored treatment and had once been able to inform Barnett that Greg was well liked and showing a lot of initiative with scatter sales.

"The upfronts would be great training for you," Jorgenson told him. "I'd like you to be involved."

In the weeks that followed, Greg and Diane saw each other frequently. If she sensed that another woman awaited him in Los Angeles, she did not bring the subject up. She tried to accept his failure to phone as often as she did and his keeping his feelings so closely to himself that she could not be sure how he felt about her. Men had work and career concerns that she did not, she knew. But she spent large parts of each day thinking about him and worrying away the time until he would be free to see her. She forced herself not to quiz him or suggest too often that he do things her way—although he was quick to correct those matters she did raise, such as the new tuxedo he bought. He seemed to understand her concern that every little detail be just right in order to maintain the right image.

Diane had never felt so contented with a man as she did with Greg. She had always ended up dominating the men she dated for any length of time—and dissatisfied by the one-sided relationships. Greg was too strong to be dominated, which made her feel safe and allowed her affectionate side to emerge.

Her attachment deepened after he met her at the hospital. That was the one cause Diane felt so strongly about that she devoted at least three afternoons each week to the children's ward as a volunteer. She was devoted to its work and to the children. Many were there for

97

corrective surgery for orthopedic defects. Many to be cured of disease. But some could never be healed—some were there to die. She played with them all, helped them, took them for X rays or physical therapy, encouraged them.

Diane had first worked at the hospital when she was in high school, as a community-service requirement. The first day she had spent more time crying than helping. Each time she left, she was sure she would be unable to return. But at the allotted hour, she would appear again, her body suffering with their pain. The children were waiting for her. And their need for her—for as long as they might live—superseded her despair.

Diane had not told Greg what to expect when he arrived at the hospital to pick her up for an early supper that night, but waited to observe his reaction. He pushed open the doors to the ward, and his insides went weak. Children in bandages, in wheelchairs, feebly in bed. The greatest sorrow in his life, his sister's fatal illness, was here replicated the length of the room.

Greg played with the children and ended up reading to a sad-eyed little girl until she fell asleep. He and Diane missed supper and made it to the screening only minutes before the film began.

Occasionally, though, Diane sensed a detachment in Greg that also, contrarily, served to magnify her infatuation and his desirability. He was cordial, humorous, even affectionate in a companionable way, but displayed nothing like the love that, every day, she was feeling more deeply for him. Diane feared that if she did not entice him with invitations to interesting events, he might not wish to see her. Often the invitation came from Barnett and could not be refused.

Occasionally, a colleague at work would mention to Greg having heard that he had been seen out with the boss's daughter. Greg would minimize the matter, claiming he was just one of a number of escorts she called upon for her many social obligations. The answer seemed appropriate, and the rumors died down.

Greg skipped several weekends in Los Angeles and lied to Chris about the reasons. Although he had been absolutely correct in his behavior toward Diane, he was troubled by their relationship and the questions surrounding it and guilty about his duplicity toward both women.

One night, toward the end of a week in which he was scheduled to fly to Los Angeles, after he and Diane had dined at an East Side restaurant and were walking up Third Avenue under a warm sky, Greg could no longer let the question that most disturbed him go unanswered. He did not want to fool himself.

"Diane, was it your father's idea or yours that I come to New York?"

"He thinks a lot of you, Greg."

Greg refused to be put off. He halted and turned to face her. "Whose idea was it?"

Her eyes dropped; he was so insistent. "I think I suggested it. But he was all for it."

The pavement had suddenly opened beneath Greg's feet. "Why?"

"I told you. He was impressed by you."

"Was that all?"

"And he saw how happy I was that night you took me out in Los Angeles."

Greg had always told himself that Barnett Roderick had promoted him after detecting singular talents, that the relationship with Diane was simply a pleasant, chance friendship on which he was skillfully capitalizing, that he could always back away gracefully if it grew too enmeshing. At that moment he suddenly understood that if he were to part from Diane, his career would be crippled, probably destroyed for good.

"You *still* make me happy," she ventured to tell him. "I love you, Greg."

He took a moment to reply. "I'm very honored."

Her eyes recoiled as if he had raised a hand to strike her. "That isn't what I had hoped to hear."

Greg understood that he could not waver. He quickly took her in his arms and kissed her. Before, their kisses had been chaste, short good-byes. Now, Greg could feel the full extent of her need for him. Simultaneously, he was assailed by a confusion of emotions: ambition foremost and then, tumbling one upon the other, feelings of being fortunate and trapped and guilty and fearful and aroused. He did not know how to separate the feelings rapidly or reconcile them with self-interest. Nor did he want to. Thinking too long might jeopardize him. He pulled Diane against him more tightly, kissing her more deeply, his mouth opening hers, his tongue greeting hers.

"My apartment is near here," he said, arousal reinforcing ambition. "You've never seen it."

"I'd like to."

Her voice expressed pleasure and relief. She had become increasingly worried by Greg's propriety toward her, as if he feared her father's wrath or worse, as if he were not attracted to her, as if he did not love her.

He drew her into the crook of an elbow and began to guide her down the street. He nuzzled her hair for a moment, as he was sure she would like him to, refusing to let himself think about Chris. But he did not flinch from the truth about what he was doing. Making love to Diane Roderick, he recognized, was an act of the purest and most necessary self-interest.

And when he did make love to her, he made sure that he was very good.

All the way out to Los Angeles, random thoughts about his suddenly dangerous situation occurred to Greg, but his mind seemed clogged, and he could not think clearly enough to pursue the thoughts to conclusions. Making love to Diane had not been so much a choice as a quick, strategic escape from peril, which had served only to entangle him more. Keeping from Chris any knowledge of Diane, he saw now, had been an act of similar expediency, an attempt to evade making an unalterable decision.

The closer the airplane approached Los Angeles, the guiltier he felt toward Chris and the more he missed her. As it circled the airport and Greg put away papers he had brought from the office and barely skimmed, he finally acknowledged that sometime during this weekend he must choose one woman and renounce the other.

Chris was waiting at the gate to pick him up. She was overjoyed to see him after so long and had arranged to take the entire weekend off. They were to drive up to San Ysidro Ranch near Santa Barbara.

Greg was just edging the car onto an access ramp of the freeway when the police radio in Chris's car reported a shooting at a car dealership nearby. The briefest of glances passed between them. He swung the car wide to get back on the boulevard while she radioed the assignment desk that she was racing to the scene. A KFBS News crew was nearby and would be diverted immediately. For a few lucky reporters, such as Chris, Greg knew, stories seemed to materialize for their benefit, as if their presence were a catalyst.

Police were still cordoning off the street and ambulances were still arriving as Chris jumped out of the car and rushed forward, Greg only a step behind. She flashed her press credentials, but two policemen refused to admit them.

"Our crew will be here in three minutes," Greg threatened. "The first pictures they'll shoot is of you two telling us you don't want the people of California to know what happened here."

The policemen glanced sheepishly at each other and reluctantly, stepped back to admit the two broadcasters.

Seven people had been shot to death. Three others were badly wounded. Among the dead was the small car-dealership's manager, a nationalized Mexican. The killer was also a Mexican émigré. That morning U.S. Immigration and Naturalization authorities had denied his application for permanent residency and ordered his deportation back to Mexico within thirty days. Frantic, he blamed the manager for sabotaging his application and several coworkers as well. With two pistols he had bought, he walked through the premises, starting in the showroom and proceeding to the service center in the rear, calmly shooting down those he believed to be his enemies, among them several customers he had never before seen. He counted aloud the bullets remaining each time he fired. With one left, he committed suicide.

Greg withdrew to Chris's car when he saw the KFBS-TV remote news van pull up, before the crew could glimpse him. He observed her through the showroom's glass facade, deftly taking advantage of this lucky break Stew Graushner could not deny her. Totally intent on her report, she interviewed witnesses and then had the cameraman retrace the killer's steps as she described what had happened at each moment. Finally, she did a stand-up close. Not a word had been wasted, not a motion was extraneous. A regular late-shift reporter had been dispatched to the hospital to do follow-ups for the late-evening news program.

About an hour up the California coast, Greg pulled off the highway to find a tavern with a television set. KFBS-TV's news broadcast was about to begin. He and Chris ordered supper while sitting at the bar. KFBS led with the story and was the only station that had arrived in time to get pictures.

The couple ate leisurely while talking and watching the rest of the broadcast. They were preparing to leave when they heard the grave voice of FBS's network anchorman, Ray Strock, announce "a tragic scene in Los Angeles. Reporter Christine Paskins has the story with the first pictures from the scene."

Chris's eyes glittered in the dim light as she watched her report being rebroadcast, this time across the entire country. As soon as it ended, she took Greg's face between her hands and kissed him passionately.

"How fast can we get to Santa Barbara?" she whispered.

Greg realized once more that Chris was a single, unified whole. Her exhilaration over her success had excited her as fully sexually as it had intellectually. The love he felt rose up in flight toward her like a flock of songbirds, exciting him as well.

"We'll be inside our cottage in twenty minutes," he whispered back. "I'll be inside you five seconds after that. Count on it."

Her body trembled at the thought. He knew he could never love another woman the way he loved Chris.

Their clothing began to fall from them the instant they stepped through the cottage door, smiling at the great secret of sex they shared.

He lifted her onto his hardness without waiting to reach the bed. Wet and open, she wrapped her legs around him, feeling her as surely within him as he was physically within her. Sighs escaped them both as sensation and sanctuary conjoined.

The next morning, as soon as they began to stir awake, they made love again.

The rest of the day was spent horseback riding, Greg precariously; playing tennis, with Chris trying to make up in tenacity what she lacked in skill; walking in the woods; and reading by the pool. They ate too much at lunch and again at dinner.

They made love for hours that night. Only later, when she was asleep and curled naked and deeply content against him, did he finally force himself to wrestle with the anguish of choosing between two women. He had never been so torn in his life—between love and all his dearest objectives.

He loved Chris and she made him happy, but Diane would provide access to everything he had ever coveted, endowing him with the power and freedom he had always craved, propelling his ambition to the farthest reaches of the universe, to where his dreams awaited. All the gaping wants of his childhood would be filled. Banished forever would be the worries of poverty and exclusion that had harried him. The poor steel-worker's son would vanish and only the confident young Yale man Diane had chosen to marry, Barnett Roderick's heir apparent, would remain. He would become a member of America's aristocracy. Security, indeed wealth, would sit as confidently in his pocket as had his jackknife as a boy. The devoted home life ripped from him back then would be restored. But most important, his aspirations would be limitless. At last he would walk upon the stars.

Greg genuinely enjoyed Diane's company and believed the union would bring him contentment. She was attractive and gracious, a sophisticated and amiable companion. Capable of affection and humor, in private she was quick to hug and kiss and take his hand. She was as social as he. People, in fact, comprised her major interest in life—her father, the children at the hospital, friends. She loved children, as he did. Diane knew how much he wanted a large family, and she wanted one, too, she had assured him.

On the minus side of the ledger, he remembered how emphatic she could be to get her own way and how very testy when she did not. She had rushed to be the one to pay at a disco and earlier that same night, had warned him about his behavior. Occasionally, as then, she seemed overeager to be in control and uncomfortable when she was not. Or was he exaggerating her attitude in retrospect? Were their brief, minor disagreements an indication of greater disagreements still to come or merely a normal means of adjusting to each other?

Greg decided that his negative characterization of Diane's behavior was unfair, that those irksome attitudes had doubtless been caused by her nervousness at not yet knowing him well enough to be completely relaxed.

Greg found a reason to ignore or downplay every possible shortcoming. When he became troubled that she evoked no infinite tenderness in him, as Chris invariably did, he justified that by recalling his own conscious avoidance of tenderness toward *her*, so as not to show disloyalty. But focusing on tenderness forced him to consider the largest of her deficits compared to Chris, one he could not ignore: that he felt little passion for her. The desire Chris ignited could consume him.

But passion was only part of what he felt for Chris. He could talk to her as to no one else he had ever known. She was the only person he had ever let see the sometimes apprehensive inner man, hidden since childhood, who operated the limbs and voice of the Greg he had erected around himself. He loved her prodigiously, deeply. And because of that, he was tortured.

Greg looked down along Chris's naked body, remembering the first time he had lain beside her, in the little apartment by the sea. A great sadness overcame him. If he chose Diane, he would be losing the love that flowed abundantly, joyously, from her, and he would be plunging torment deep into her heart.

Yet, she, too, had faults, he reminded himself. She was as career driven as he and could become self-absorbed and reclusive. Their fights could be ferocious. So often their lives seemed separate, their aspirations parallel or contrary rather than shared; at times they were united only in that amazing passion. And passion, like any fever, he told himself, might pass. It had for Arnold Mandel and his wife. It had for his parents. Yet, always, he had to admit, towering over every other consideration that arose in his mind, was that his passion for success—for winning at the game of life—far exceeded his passion for anything else, even for Chris.

He could not lie to himself that he loved Diane. He might never feel about her as he did about Chris. But he gradually and logically convinced himself that love for her would grow over time. A hazy image of their lives in ten years illuminated the darkness above the bed. He could see an older Barnett offering Greg his own chair at the pinnacle of FBS. And as if in a painting, a smiling Diane amid their children in a palatial home gazing worshipfully at the viewer, at him. He could feel intimations of

103

the power he would wield, of the freedom to do and have everything he had ever desired, lifting him upward into that reverie. The grief he felt now would be replaced by satisfactions he could not yet begin to imagine. It all seemed so much more than he would be losing.

Determining finally that he must seize this opportunity to realize his destiny or risk having it pass him by forever, Greg decided that he would ask Diane to marry him. If she said yes, he would break off with Chris.

He knew Chris would be devastated because she loved him, but it never occurred to him that his greatest loss might be the love *he* felt for *her*: that his feelings for her, which had brought him such happiness, might embody his essence and his integrity as a human being. During all of that dark night, he never saw that what he might have exchanged to gain Diane was, in fact, his soul.

7

~~~~~~~~~~~~~~~~~~~~

Greg's hours on the airplane trip back to New York the following day were spent planning his proposal of marriage to Diane. As he said good-bye to Chris, his face had revealed none of the misery he was feeling. He had refused to allow himself doubts. His future was at stake. For all his calculation when making the choice, he took marriage and his commitment to Diane seriously. He wanted the moment to be romantic, and she would expect that. He tried to think where a man suitable to a woman like Diane would propose.

He decided he would take her to dinner tonight at La Caravelle, if he could get a reservation. Superb food. Restrained surroundings. Long-established. He did not have time to buy a ring and was reluctant to incur the debt until after she said yes. Besides, any ring he could afford would probably just embarrass her.

With dessert the waiter set down a bottle of champagne before them.

"I'm hoping we'll have a reason to celebrate," Greg explained. He paused. He wanted her to hear how sincerely he wanted her. "Will you marry me?"

"Do you love me, Greg? You've never told me."

"I love you," he said, eyes shining. "What kept me from saying it before, what almost frightened me away tonight, was that you might think I was a fortune hunter."

He leaned forward and kissed her, seeking both to convince her to marry him and from her silent lips, to provoke her answer.

"Yes. Yes," she finally said aloud when they pulled apart.

Greg felt himself zooming through the magic window and into the glamorous future he had always yearned for.

He took her back to his apartment and made love to her, sealing her acceptance. The experience was again enjoyable for them both, and he was sure that it would doubtless grow more so as they grew better acquainted with each other's likes. Greg had no illusions that it would ever approach what he had just chosen to discard.

At five-thirty that morning, Diane awoke, remembering that her father, who would soon be up and exercising, would become concerned upon discovering that she was not yet home.

Greg accompanied her in a cab, intending to continue on to his office to get a head start on the day. She prevailed on him, instead, to come upstairs with her and then and there ask for her father's permission to marry her.

"Daddy won't object if it's what I want."

Greg had hoped to delay the confrontation for a variety of reasons, not least among them the inferences Barnett would draw about the cause of his daughter's lateness. Greg wanted time to think through the right approach and for Barnett to convey back through Diane his response to the new turn of events. But because he suspected she might doubt his ardor if he delayed, he accompanied her upstairs.

Just as Greg was no longer under the illusion that Barnett, unaided, had singled him out for advancement, he could not lie to himself that he had seduced a guileless Diane into becoming his mate. On the contrary, he fully understood now that Diane had done the singling out and that Barnett had been the seducer. Although Greg was sure that Barnett would have preferred her choosing someone from her own class, someone substantial, he desired her happiness most of all and had acted to fulfill her wishes. He had offered up to Greg a foretaste of all the earthly delights that might be his if he were chosen, and if, in turn, he chose. And Greg had hungered for them all.

They found the Chairman in a large room Greg had not yet seen in the back of the apartment: a gymnasium with weights and exercise equipment around the periphery and in the center, a full-scale boxing ring. Barnett wore only shiny black trunks and high leather shoes. His hands were encased in boxing gloves, his head in a padded headguard. He was attacking the heavy bag. Despite his sixty-one years, he looked fit and trim. He finally glanced over at the young couple, who stood to one side watching.

"This is no hour to be coming home."

"We had a lot to talk about, Dad," Diane interjected. "Greg has something to ask you."

"Mr. Roderick," Greg began uncertainly, "I know this may sound sudden, and I guess it is, but Diane and I love each other. I would like your permission to marry her."

"My boxing coach has the flu," Barnett remarked, apparently oblivious of what had just been said. "I need a sparring partner."

Diane understood and was alarmed. "Daddy, Greg's not a boxer."

"Have you ever had the gloves on?" Barnett asked him.

"Once or twice in a Phys Ed class as a kid," Greg replied with a chuckle.

"You're certainly man enough to defend yourself—I hope."

Greg thought he detected malice in the tone. "Well, yes, but—"

"And love my daughter enough to fight for her."

"Of course, I do."

"Then take off your shirt and put on the gloves."

Greg thought the joke had gone too far and tried to beg off. "I'm a lot younger than you—"

The older man's eyes narrowed; the difference in age was a goad, not an obstacle. The challenge could not be refused. The extent of Greg's desire for Diane Roderick—and for all that went with her—was about to be tested.

Greg smiled tightly at Diane, trying to display fearlessness. As he started to remove his jacket, the sleeve caught on one of his cuff links. Unfastening it took an embarrassingly long time. He was grateful for every second. Proving his commitment and worth by fighting his father-in-law-to-be seemed insane to him, a throwback to some sort of primeval tribal ritual. He would lose no matter which way the fight turned out—and he had no doubt, despite his youth, what that would be. He glumly stripped off his shirt and tie and slipped his hands into the boxing gloves lying on the ring apron. Diane anxiously tied the laces.

"How long have you been boxing?" Greg asked Barnett.

"All my life."

"What about a headguard for him?" Diane asked.

"He's too much of a man to need it at his age."

Oh, God, Greg thought.

Diane fastened the other headguard on Greg, who then followed the older man up the wooden steps and between the red-velvet-covered ropes.

In the center of the ring, Greg lifted his fists into what he remembered to be the standard fighter's posture and waited for the massacre. Jabs swifter than he had anticipated snapped back his head. He tried to respond in kind and found himself pawing to keep Barnett away. The older man was dancing and circling, throwing an occasional jab, but obviously seeking an opening for a hard right hand. Greg, too, then began circling, to get away from it. A left hook staggered him from the other side. And then he caught a right that cleared his head.

He decided that he might as well try to do something and shot his own right out. It did no damage—Barnett was too shifty to hit solidly—but the fact that it actually brushed against something buoyed his spirits a little. Until the next right caught him watching out for another left hook.

He noticed blood on one of his gloves. The momentary satisfaction disappeared after he realized it was dripping from a cut somewhere on his face.

"Want to stop?" Barnett called out.

Greg swung angrily at him and was rewarded when the punch grazed a cheek. He began swinging wildly, hoping something would land. A hard uppercut rocked his mouth shut and lifted him off his feet. The ropes saved him from going down. And the bell. "That's more than enough," Diane called out, climbing into the ring.

"Do you want to stop?" Barnett asked him.

"I want to knock your sadistic head off!" Greg rejoined hotly. Actually, at that moment, all Greg wanted was a thick mattress under him in a darkened room.

Barnett smiled. "We'll shower and talk in the library."

Fifteen minutes later, with Diane sitting beside him and his face aching and continuing to puff up beneath a large Band-Aid, Greg asked her father for her hand in marriage.

Barnett replied circumspectly. "Normally, I would ask about your prospects in life."

Greg wanted no misunderstanding. This was the crux of the pact to which his ambition was about to bind him. "You know my prospects better than I. What do you think?"

The older man stared into the younger's eyes for a very long time, trying to plumb their sincerity. Then his gaze shifted to his daughter, eagerness evident in hers and apprehension about his answer and bountiful love for her young man.

Finally, he gave his answer, which was as much a pledge. "You have my solemn assurance that there's no limit to how far you can go at FBS."

Her arm thrust through Greg's, Diane hugged it upon hearing that.

"But Greg," he went on, "I want *your* assurance that you'll love and care for my daughter as well and faithfully . . . as truly as I do."

Greg did not hesitate. His decision had been a lifetime forming. He was resolved. "I want to—and will."

A smile snaked onto Barnett's face bright enough to illuminate the bowels of the earth. He leaned forward and shook Greg's hand.

"You have my blessing."

"You're a very lucky young man," the heavyset banker advised him. "She's a wonderful girl. I hope you realize that."

"Yes, sir, I do," Greg replied politely, and smiled at Diane.

"I think I'm pretty lucky, too," she said to the man, but with her eyes on Greg.

The party Barnett gave at his club to announce the engagement had been arranged quickly, but nearly everyone invited had come. Diane had just introduced Greg to the last of the guests. He excused himself to go to the men's room.

As Greg was walking back into the darkly paneled room, he was startled by the sight of a blond young woman who might have been Chris. She turned, and he saw she was a friend of Diane he had met earlier in the evening. Greg rushed to the window, trying to divert the excited onrush of memory. Looking out over Park Avenue, he wondered how long it would take before he would be able to forget her.

On the Sunday night Diane agreed to marry him, he had considered flying out to California the next day to tell Chris in person, but had remembered what she had once told him. "If one of us ever decides to end it, we'll just say good-bye, we won't drag it out. Quick and clean. I'd hate a lingering death."

Finally, late on that second night, after putting off the call all day and rehearsing what he would say, he phoned her.

"This isn't easy to tell you," he began, "but I've decided to end our relationship."

He thought she might have disconnected because she took so long to reply, but then her voice, quiet, halting, asked, "What made you decide now, so suddenly . . . especially after last weekend?"

"I needed time away from you to think. I've been doing that."

Chris's voice turned as sharp as her hurt. "You must have gotten a better offer. Who is she?"

Greg told her.

"You bastard! You scheming bastard!"

Greg did not reply.

"I guess last weekend was your bachelor party," she snapped. "One last, grand fuck. Living with me was kind of a detour for you on the way up, wasn't it? I should feel honored I was worth that much of your time."

"I loved you, Chris."

Sarcasm flowed over the edges of her words. "And now you don't?"

The abrupt click saved him from having to answer. More than a week had passed since then, but the click still resounded within the hollow center of his thoughts.

A woman's voice roused him from his musing. "Well, well, well, here's the lucky bridegroom-to-be."

Greg turned from the window and smiled, accepting her congratulations.

"I'm a very lucky man indeed," he once again agreed.

No loss in her life had ever struck so hard at Chris as losing Greg. She had warily opened her heart only to have it ransacked. She had trusted Greg and had loved him totally, and he had betrayed her totally.

I can't believe he could treat me this way, she silently keened over and over. I can't believe he didn't love me.

Wallowing in troughs of depression, she floundered from one reason for his desertion to another: Did he love this Diane Roderick more or was he marrying her only because she could offer him more? The latter, Chris reasoned contemptuously, but could not let herself completely believe it. At times she despised Greg because he had left her despite having loved her, and at other times because she was convinced he had lied about loving her and had used her from the very first. Sometimes, though, she told herself he had fled because he had found nothing in her worth loving. That was when she despised herself.

She reached out to a few women friends for companionship, but became so submerged in her despondency that she forgot a lunch she had scheduled with one and an appointment with another. Abjectly apologetic each time, she begged their forgiveness on the phone and ran out to purchase lavish gifts to be delivered immediately.

Only to Marian Marcus, though, did Chris open up to confide her grief and the reason for it. She had assumed, she told Marian, that she and Greg would spend their lives together—she had *wanted* to spend her life with him. Living together, she had always believed, was a prelude to marriage. They had argued, but always because their work put pressures on the relationship, never because of what they felt for each other. The one thing she had always been sure about was that Greg loved her.

She had feared his going to New York because it would separate them, not because she ever thought he might desert her. Never once had he mentioned the other woman, only her father. Remembering now all the canceled trips, Chris suspected that he had been seeing this Diane for months and had lied about his reasons for postponing trips back to L.A. Although knowing that she valued honesty above all other values, he had lied to her. Had he been lying right from the beginning, when he said that he loved her?

During those harrowing days, Marian ceased to be Chris's assistant and truly became a friend who cared about her, listening for hours and offering solace as Chris talked out her feelings of sorrow, often sleeping over on the sofa at her apartment just so Chris would not be alone. The friendship that had begun with Marian's outlandish confidences became cemented for life during that bleak time.

That first weekend, Marian insisted Chris accompany her to dinner and a movie. Chris was too preoccupied with her loss to concentrate on the film, and instead they drove for hours and talked. She rode horseback alone in the hills for hours the next day. Behind every tree and in every gully lurked her sorrow.

Soon, however, Chris began to fight the despondency by losing herself in her work, the only lover she still trusted not to betray her. A workaholic and ambitious before, she quickly became possessed; reporting became her only faith and ascension in her profession her hope for salvation from despair, to be achieved by enduring endless, penitential toil. Much of what used to be her free time was spent perusing stacks of photocopied public records and tracking down potential informers who might be more willing away from their offices to give her leads.

Chris even welcomed the outrage that abandonment by Greg aroused in her because it allowed her to close off her mind and heart to everything but her work. She yearned to hurt Greg as painfully as she had been hurt and felt purified by the rawness of her hatred. But her feelings flowed deeper and wider than retaliation against one man. Not only would her determination to succeed bring her personal fulfillment, but also vindication against everyone throughout her life who had ever tried to deny her her rightful opportunity. Her influence would increase with her popularity, she knew, and would safeguard her independence.

She was as zealous to safeguard her emotions. Never again would she expose them to the ravages that dependence on another's love could cause.

The day after the engagement party, the announcement appeared prominently in the *New York Times*. Already reports had appeared in newspaper columns and chatter about it had been flashing around the company: lots of calls to colleagues in Sales and at KFBS to find out more about this Gregory Lyall who was marrying the Chairman's daughter. Greg perceived in the congratulations a new caution and deference and from some, envy.

He was leaving the FBS Building at lunchtime when he encountered Ev Carver in the lobby. Ev halted, his red head cocked to one side, his mouth widening into a knowing smile.

"Opportunism, Lyall," he inquired, "or cowardice?"

By the end of the month, Greg was given a new title and responsibility for a small area of sales. He was by then working closely
with Bill Jorgenson. A sizable increase appeared unannounced in his
paycheck. He was prepared to use it for a down payment on an
engagement ring, but Barnett offered the couple the ring Diane's
mother had worn.

Ossie Krieger slumped dejectedly out of the office tower at the FBS
lot in Los Angeles. He had just met with a group of executives in
network programming, the department that chose, developed, and
scheduled the shows that went on the air.

Back on the day the new series were announced for the fall, they had
told him they loved the pilot show he had written and produced. They
had ordered thirteen episodes for the new fall season. Loved it? They
were delirious. He had come through again, they enthused, and fought
to get their own into the tangle of hands shaking his.

Now, just when he was about to start production, the network
refused to approve his scripts and insisted he shoot some new scenes
for the pilot. The woman character is too tough, they had claimed.
Audiences are turned off.

"But she's a cop. If she were soft, she'd get her head shot off three
times before lunch."

A programmer named Raoul Clampton came as close to articulating
the group's consensus as it seemed capable of doing. "There's tough
. . . and then there's *tough*. The problem is that she's *tough*. You
see?"

He didn't.

Paraphrased to him were surveys of viewer groups, psychological
profiles, and most telling, a memo from a vice president that quoted a
different vice president as having thought he overheard Barnett
Roderick wondering why the woman character didn't have a husband—
at least the man thought Barnett was referring to this show.

"That's when we did some hurry-up viewer focus groups—you know
how brilliant the old man's gut is." The Programming head turned to a
young man in new-show research for a report.

"Roderick was absolutely on target. Viewers said they liked soft, not
hard women." He nodded vigorously in agreement with his superior.
"The man is brilliant."

"That's why we have to give her a husband," said the Programming
chief.

Ossie was appalled by the new directive. "But she's a detective on
the streets. Half the attraction of the show is that the men she meets

are attracted to her and there's always the possibility of a love affair. Do you want a married woman having love affairs?"

No, they didn't want that. They put their collective heads together to brainstorm.

What had induced Ossie Krieger to leave the production company for which he had written his last hit show was the chance to go independent and own his own series. If it was successful, he would become rich. Not just salary-rich, but really rich, as episodes piled up that the studio backing him could someday sell as reruns to local stations after each episode appeared twice on network. Most important, FBS had promised him complete creative freedom. Ossie believed his ulcer had resulted from wrangling with network executives who directed him to make ill-conceived changes.

"What happened to my complete creative freedom?" Ossie wanted to know.

"You have it, completely," the head of Programming assured him. We're responsible to our stations. We can't let just *anything* go out over the air. It might be obscene or really crazy. So we need to approve scripts, right?"

"And casting," added Raoul Clampton, who was directly in charge of Dramatic Series Development. "But our hands are strictly off this baby. That's why we brought in a genius like you."

The dispute went on for two hours. When it was over, Ossie found he had little alternative to a compromise if he wanted the show to get on the air. The woman cop would be separated, but devoted to her estranged husband and hoping to get back together with him. He would be a straight, mainstream guy who can't understand why the sweet woman he loves and married wants to be a cop. She can't quite explain it herself, but her daddy was a cop and it's in her blood.

Ossie hated the changes. They were phony and diluted the woman's flinty, pungent character. His best hope, he decided, was to write her strongly enough to overcome the problems and maybe, just maybe, sneak by the network an early script that split husband and wife up for good. Maybe he could do better than that, he thought. Maybe he could have a robber kill the civilian husband, who is buying something in a store at the time, which would show that you can't hide from the problems of crime in this country. She could then track the killer down. Or was he just kidding himself that he could eventually change the network's mind?

Now, though, he had the unpleasant task of informing Sally Foster that the fierce, biting role for which she had left the successful series "Heritage Hall" had just had its teeth filed down. As a matter of fact, tonight he would have to sit down and write new scenes to be inserted into the pilot, and Sally would have to shoot them, so that her character would be softened in the very first episode. If she objected, he and the network would hire someone else to play the woman cop and would then reshoot *all* her scenes in the pilot.

But, of course, before any reshooting could be done, his pilot-script revisions would have to be approved by the network.

Greg's life quickly began to assume a kind of permanence he had never experienced with Chris. Diane depended on him for companionship far more than Chris had. She spent her days busily, he knew, shopping or lunching with her friends and doing volunteer work. Still, it seemed to him that except when she was at the children's ward, she marked time without him. Half-orphaned at birth and an only child, she had waited all her life for a mate and missed Greg terribly when apart from him, even if he was only at the office. Things she wanted to say to him filled her up to overflowing by day's end. She was lively and funny when she regaled him from her font of anecdotes and commentary, and he looked forward to the time together as much as she did.

The hectic upfront selling period had just commenced, and he was putting in long hours. One night, she kept phoning his office until very late, leaving a new message each time for him to call her.

The meetings broke well after midnight, and he arrived back at his apartment just before two in the morning. His phone rang five minutes later.

"You didn't call me back," she said as soon as he picked up.

"I just got home."

"I've been trying you every few minutes."

"The meeting ended so late I was sure you'd be asleep."

"I'd never go to sleep before you called."

Diane spoke the last line with an adamance that suggested she considered herself in competition with the network for his allegiance and attention, as she had always considered herself for her father's. She did not intend to share Greg.

Marian Marcus started in FBS's Programming Department on the same day that she was graduated from UCLA and took her last, regretful glance at Derek Peters. Chris had introduced her to someone who had ultimately hired her.

News was too factual for Marian. Her affinity for weaving fantasies about her personal life was a part of a larger interest in fiction. She loved entertainment and stories and thought she could sense what made them good and whether other people would want to watch them on television.

114

She was a fan at heart, dazzled by the glittering images on the little screen. Half-consciously, she hoped proximity would compensate for her own persistent plainness.

The other young people in the department, she found, were all good-looking and clever, "hotshots," she called them in her thoughts. Ironically, her plainness proved to be an effective means of deflecting the jealousies and ambitions that pulsed like sine waves through the department. Hotshots rose and fell. Marian would slowly climb.

Her first task was to read scripts and comment on them. She worked under Raoul Clampton in Dramatic Series Development. He did not seem much older than she, but he was definitely a hotshot: clean features, good clothes, great smile. He was nervous around superiors and toadied to them, but could be callous to subordinates and others he could dominate. Now, he wanted to know what she thought of the scripts she had read.

"We have high hopes for Danny Vickers's new show," he told her. "Anything that man touches is gold."

"Well, the script seemed an awful lot like 'The A-Team.'"

"It was supposed to."

"Won't people get bored with a show that's just like a show they already watch?"

"In television people can never get enough of a good thing. What did you think of Ossie Krieger's script?"

She handed him the report she had written up. He skimmed it and turned white.

"The son of a bitch killed off the husband!"

Marian nodded. "It was very powerful. You really care about the wife after that and can understand why she's a cop and so tough."

"Tough? What kind of tough?"

"Well, tough."

"Oh, God, *that* kind of tough."

Raoul grabbed for the phone receiver and immediately called his boss.

"Chad, we've got a problem. I just read Ossie Krieger's new script. He killed our husband." Raoul paused to listen, then spoke. "You're absolutely right. He's testing us. That's the trouble with geniuses, they think they're smarter than other people."

Raoul glanced at Marian for confirmation of his observation.

"Absolutely," he spoke into the receiver. "The husband stays. What's the point of taking meetings otherwise. Let him kill off somebody else's husband. The sister's." Raoul paused again. "Well, we'll *give* her a sister, maybe married to a really rich guy. Great clothes. You know, the 'Dynasty' look. The sisters could spend a lot of time together. How about lunch?" Raoul sensed confusion. "No, you and me."

They took several minutes to decide where to eat lunch. Then Raoul phoned Ossie Krieger and told him that the woman cop now had a sister she spends a lot of time with. The two husbands are really close. It's the sister's husband who gets killed. Everybody is really devastated. The sister turns out to be as tough in her own way as the woman cop is in hers.

"But a different tough, you dig? And naturally she's now really rich in her own right, head of her husband's conglomerate, big budget for clothes." His gaze was fixed on the clouds filling the upper half of his window, above the Hollywood Hills. "Oss baby, this is just off the top of my head, you understand, but maybe the rich sister's really a bitch, always trying to seduce the good sister's husband. I picture them kind of like Joan and Jackie Collins."

Marian gave back the admiring nod Raoul seemed to expect and wondered if the Sally Foster character was still a cop.

Greg lifted Diane's veil, and they kissed with deep commitment. Then, buoyant, they turned to face the expanse of affluent and illustrious wedding guests, parted straight down the middle like the Red Sea to permit the couple's passage out to their life together. Greg was one of their number now. He and Diane glanced happily at each other. He squeezed her hand. They would live happily ever after.

At the end of the year, when her contract expired, Stew Graushner offered Chris a top salary and the job of co-anchor with Quinn Harris if she would stay on.

"No." She was adamant.

"You're doing this to me because of that fight we had during sweeps weeks—"

"No, I'm not, Stew."

"—when I wanted to hypo the ratings by having you do a series on the great bidets of Hollywood, right? That's it, isn't it?"

"No, Stew, it has nothing to do with you. I just want to get away from this station and start fresh."

"But we all love you here. Think of it: co-anchor. The top-rated news program in Los Angeles."

"I'm not staying."

"This morning," he reflected gloomily, "when my medical exam turned up a clean EKG, I knew that something really terrible would have to happen today."

"Stew, I'm not leaving because of you. I'm just leaving."

He shook his head, grief battering his brow. "Greg Lyall was smart to get out of here when the going was good. Nine months later look at us. We're number one! Shit! Nowhere to go but down."

Chris vainly tried to comfort the inconsolable news director. Certain that he could not change her mind, he asked about her plans.

"I'll talk to other stations in town, I guess. See if any want me."

"They'll want you, all right. You'll bring ratings with you. Who's your agent?"

Chris was bewildered by the question. She was in news, not show biz.

"We all have agents," Stew informed her. "Usually not the same ones who represent actors though. Local news is becoming big business."

"The idea repels me."

"Most of us find an agent helps."

"How much do you pay them?"

"Usually they work on a ten-percent commission."

"Ten percent of what I earn? Just to make a deal I could make on my own?"

Stew said she was being shortsighted and gave her the name of a very good agent based in New York. She said she would think about it. But having someone negotiate for her offended her frontier directness; it violated her preconception of two people shaking hands over an honest bargain honestly arrived at.

She approached another network-owned station as the year drew to a close and was offered a hundred thousand dollars to co-anchor its local news broadcast. On an impulse, before she accepted, she telephoned Carl Green, the agent Stew Graushner had recommended.

The other end of the phone line erupted in an outpouring of friendly New York accent as soon as she gave her name. "Mass killing at a car dealership, maybe nine, ten months ago, right? Mexican guy. FBS. You're the hot reporter in L.A."

"I am?"

Green assured her that she was and that he was glad she had phoned. He had wanted to call *her* for a long while. "You're going to be a star."

"Don't say that. I'm a journalist."

"Stars are the ones who attract the viewers. That's the way the executives who hire you think. That's who they pay the big money to."

"You make the news sound like just another form of entertainment."

"Don't kid yourself. Everybody with any kind of fire burning in his belly wants to be a star. From the guy working his way up at IBM to the one who's an agent for newscasters . . ." He chuckled.

"Andy Warhol's fifteen minutes of fame?"

"I mean real stardom: money, power, adoration, immortality. The whole piñata. Be honest with yourself: Why else did you decide to go on camera?"

Chris changed the subject. "You said you'd been thinking of calling."

"A few months back I asked Stew Graushner if you had representation. He claimed you had another year and a half to go on your contract."

"How could he do that? My contract's expiring."

"He figured your new contract would cost him a lot more if I was your agent."

"I'm not staying with FBS. I have a very good offer to anchor at another station here in L.A. I'm sure I don't need an agent."

"How much?"

Reluctantly, she told him her salary and named the station. She did not like to talk about her money, especially such a large amount. It sounded like bragging.

"Give me till the end of the day to better it."

"What?"

"If I can't get you a lot more than a hundred thousand dollars by the end of the day, then you're right, you don't need an agent."

Intrigued, Chris agreed. Her only condition: Under no circumstances would she stay with FBS.

Carl Green phoned her back in less than an hour. She could take her pick. A local network-owned station had offered her a quarter of a million dollars to co-anchor. The station that had already offered her a hundred thousand had now doubled that figure, and he thought he could get them to stretch to two fifty also. Did she want him to try?

Chris was dumbfounded. "That's two hundred and fifty thousand dollars *each year?*"

"I know what the market is paying. You don't," he explained. "And I got one station to bid against the other."

"That kind of money is obscene. In his best year my father probably never made a fifth of that."

"Can he anchor?" Green asked cynically.

The agent briefly outlined the rest of the terms he had negotiated for her, points she had never considered. He had insisted any contract be for only two years—he wanted her to be free to move up to a network after that.

"You stick to reporting. Leave the negotiating to me. Like it or not, you've got what it takes to be a star."

Chris told him which of the two stations she wanted to go with. "I guess I have myself an agent," she concluded.

"Easiest fifty thousand I ever made."

"For an hour's work."

"Less."

"You sound very smug about it."

"You're going to love me."

8

B arnett's wedding present to his daughter and her husband was a twelve-room apartment on Fifth Avenue, several blocks north of his own. He released to her the first portion of her trust fund, which contained her mother's fortune and a large block of FBS stock. The rest of the principal and stock would be distributed to her over the coming years until, at age thirty, all would be under her control. The added wealth did not contribute significantly to her life-style—she had been receiving the trust's income since reaching twenty-one. During the months the apartment was under construction, she and Greg resided at the Carlyle Hotel.

Diane and Greg soon came to be considered one of society's glamorous young couples. She had gained her place in the upper class by reason of birth and what was still considered accomplishment among their women. Rich and chic, her taste in clothing was impeccable, and she possessed a valued ability to attract money and luminaries to charity affairs she ran with enviable organization.

Greg was proud of the way people gravitated toward Diane at social events. She worked hard, he saw, to insure that they did. She presented an exquisite image in public, her erect carriage showing off her designer outfits, her red-brown hair perfectly coiffed, her pretty face alive with expectations of the moment. She always said just the right thing.

In one sense, he soon recognized, she and Chris both sought the same goal: recognition. Chris wanted it professionally, Diane socially. Beneath Diane's facade, he sensed the parts of a more complex woman than he knew—she was dedicated to the children at the hospital, astute in dealing with people, and far savvier about money than she let on—but he could not comprehend the whole those hidden parts composed.

Greg sensed Diane was as proud of him as he was of her. Although he had won admission to the upper class by marrying one of its citizens, his other credentials did not dishonor her: He was satisfactorily educated, well mannered, charming, and fun to be with. His self-training had paid off; he fully epitomized the sophisticated males after whom he had patterned himself. No one, including Diane, suspected that his father had been a steelworker or that his mother was Jewish and alive. Diane declined to probe his hazily sketched parentage so as to circumvent awkward questions from others and wearisome obligations to his family. In both their minds, he had entered fully into *her* family.

Yet, when he stood among the shimmering people, Greg sometimes glimpsed eyes that tended to dismiss him for traveling on his wife's social passport. At such moments he felt as hungry for acceptance among them as he had as a boy. He was surprised to discover that his father-in-law had won acceptance the same way.

Barnett Roderick was thirty-three on the late-summer afternoon in Newport that he met and fell irrevocably in love with Dorothy Mayfield. Beautiful and gracious, she was among the most sought-after of society's young women, occupying a social position miles above his. The Mayfields had been members of American aristocracy since before the Revolution. A nineteenth-century shipping fortune had made them rich enough to support in fine style through many generations genteel descendants with discreetly small families.

Barnett Roderick had always considered women an easy commodity to obtain. Those who did not overtly pursue him invariably yielded to him quite easily. But Dorothy Mayfield was different from other women. He courted her with a shameless lack of what had once been his pride. Finally, her resistance melted, and she fell in love with the persistent suitor.

Acceptance into the elite class that had always rebuffed his eagerness to enter was the least of the wedding gifts she brought. Foremost was inexpressible happiness: She lifted the mourning from him that he had worn since a car accident killed his parents several years before. Sweetness, intelligence, and gaiety lit her and everything around her like a following spotlight. Barnett indulged her with every luxury she might wish for.

When she became pregnant, he was both thrilled and worried. She was so small-boned, so fragile. He had good cause for worry. She became gravely ill with gestation diabetes during pregnancy. Despite doctors' warnings, she insisted on continuing to term. Dorothy died giving birth to Diane. She was twenty-seven years old.

All the love he had lavished on his wife Barnett transferred to the daughter she had wanted more than life itself. Diane was raised by a

121

succession of competent nannies, who could not help but be pale imitations
of the loving mother she craved and needed. Barnett spent time with her
each morning and if he was home from the office in time, at night.

He remarried twice, the first time when Diane was fourteen. Both wives
were well-born women whom he thought he knew thoroughly and whom he
hoped would become mothers to Diane. She had been so close to her father
all her life that the entrance of each new woman into the family frightened
her; she feared he was abandoning her. But neither woman was able to fill
for Barnett or Diane the gap that Dorothy had left, and he quickly tired of
them. After each marital breakup, father and daughter drew still closer,
and his recollection of Dorothy floated higher toward saintliness.

Barnett's rarest talent was an uncanny ability to divine other people's
desires, to foresee precisely what it would take to get his way. As a
broadcasting executive the talent manifested itself as an intuition about the
public's tastes in new shows that, by the late seventies, made FBS the
industry's dominant giant and its founder a legend. As a devoted parent,
the talent had compelled him to add to his daughter's own natural
inducements whatever he sensed would win over the young man she had
set her heart on. He was as determined as with her mother that she not
want for anything.

Greg and Diane did not know each other well when they married. His
looks and poise had impressed her, but the way he stood up to her initial
bullying was what captured her respect and as a result, her interest.
Her imagined ideal had been shaped in the image of her father. Greg
was one of the few young men she had met with comparable inner
strength and intelligence.

For his part Greg admired a lot about Diane. She knew how to live life
graciously and taught him much of what he did not yet know about doing
so. He found he enjoyed being with her most at the extremes of their
social life: when they were out at an event and he could admire her style
and take pleasure in having such a wife, and when they were alone, just
the two of them, over one of their rare suppers home or watching
television or reading and making occasional comments to each other.
She could be warm and playful with him, even endearing.

As with most newly married couples, the frictions in their relationship
began to arise from what they had not yet discovered about each other.

One night Greg returned home very tired. By then he had been
moved to Station Relations and had spent all day alternately imploring
and browbeating executives at balky affiliates to clear their schedules
for network offerings. Several large stations were refusing to broadcast
a prime-time news special on American foreign policy and wanted to

preempt it in favor of their own entertainment programming; local sports or a movie would bring them higher ratings and more advertising income than they would lose in network compensation. Fewer stations would reduce the network's potential audience and the ad revenues.

The butler had laid out his dress clothes, but Greg sat down on the end of the bed.

"Look, instead of going to this charity dinner or whatever it is we've got on tap tonight, how about we stay home and take it easy or maybe ask some friends over?"

Diane frowned. "Everyone we know will be there. Don't be silly."

"Don't you sometimes just want to get off the merry-go-round for a while? No Peter Duchin Band or raffles at the door or kissing at the air so makeup won't get messed up."

"You really picked a terrific time to start this."

"Well, don't you?"

"Would you like me to insult Holly by not showing up?" Unspoken was Diane's belief that attendance was an obligation that maintained their standing in society and society's standing in the American hierarchy.

"If you could invite someone over, I don't know, just to play rummy or something, who would it be?"

"I've been looking forward to this all day. Of all the times—" Diane's eyes were blazing. "In exactly five minutes, I am going downstairs, getting into the car, and going to the St. Regis. You'll be ready by then unless it's your intention to embarrass both of us."

He stood up with tired resignation. "I wouldn't want to do that."

He began to dress. While he did, he mused over the unexpected firmness and inflexibility of Diane's will. Apparently, as he, she had been on her good behavior since before they married, compliant in order to avoid disputes that might end in a rupture. Only now had enough provocation arisen and was she sure enough of him for her anger to surface.

A few weeks later, Diane suddenly informed Greg that she wanted him to fly with her to Paris the following week on a shopping trip. For years, she explained, she had always gone to Paris this time of year to buy her spring wardrobe.

"There are important things coming up at work next week," he argued incredulously. "Besides, we've already decided how we'll use my vacation time this year."

"Daddy knows I always go to Paris this time of year. Sometimes he used to go with me."

Greg's anger was visible now. "You're not going to mention any of this to your father. You're never to say a word to him ever about my work."

"This would just be about taking a few days off."

"No!"

Having gotten married so they could do things together, she was exasperated by his stubbornness. "You're just like I am to him now."

Greg discerned that their marriage had not shifted Diane's primary allegiance. Her father was still the bulwark defending her inner security. How could Greg, a stranger with nothing, ever protect her like her father did? To her way of thinking, the only change marriage had brought was that her father now took care of them both.

She and Greg argued awhile longer, neither yielding.

Next day, Greg was leaving the FBS Building for a lunch meeting at the same time that Barnett was entering. They stopped to exchange a word or two.

"You look a little tired," the older man observed. "Maybe a few days away would do you good."

"Did Diane say anything to you?" Greg asked sharply.

Barnett regarded Greg closely, then shook his head.

"It's a very busy time," Greg told him.

The older man peered at him a moment longer, then nodded and walked on.

That night Greg was angrily explicit. "I don't know what you said to your father about wanting me to go to Paris, but you are never to mention to him what goes on between us."

Diane appeared taken aback by Greg's vehemence. "If you think I said anything to him—"

"I don't know. But I expect it will never happen again."

"Understand, Greg," she replied tartly, "I want nothing to do with your work or the damned company. My father and I don't talk about it. If it were up to me—"

She did not finish the sentence. Instead, she spun angrily away and departed the room.

Greg seethed all the while that Diane was in Paris shopping with her friend Libby. When she returned, she was vivacious and affectionate, delighted to see him, and eager to show off her purchases. His anger melted.

She had bought him neckties at Gucci and Hermès, dozens of them she thought he would like. She had missed him enormously, she confessed. It wasn't nearly as much fun without him; she had bored Libby silly at dinner by continuously bleating how much she missed him.

From now on, she vowed, she would discuss her plans early with Greg, and they would try to agree on everything.

Sally Foster was informed that FBS had canceled her new show just after shooting on the tenth episode ended. Her agent phoned her in her dressing room with the bad news.

FBS had introduced the series at midseason, delayed from the fall because of the network's refusal to approve writer-producer Ossie Krieger's scripts until he made their changes. The show's premiere had pulled a rating of 21 percent of all households with TV sets and a 34 percent share of the sets actually in use. Instead of rising as the show became better known, its ratings slid downward. By the previous night's viewing, the sixth week, they were down to an abysmal 11 rating and a 16 share and were crippling the entire night's lineup on FBS. Critics had been merciless in their attacks. Sally's personal reviews had not been bad, but those would be buried in the show's total collapse.

"Get me anything," she demanded of her agent. "A role in a miniseries, a movie of the week, anything."

She was stained now and had to wipe it off fast.

"I'll do my best, baby," her agent replied, trying to keep the discouragement from his voice. "This happens to everyone. This is just a little setback."

Not much was out there right now, he knew, particularly for an actress whose show had died as if it had had the black death. People in the industry would wonder if the fault lay with the series or with her ability to draw an audience.

Her friend Annette Valletta had found out the bad news somehow and phoned almost immediately afterward. The sincerity of her sympathy was even harder for Sally to take. Annette's new comedy series, also on FBS, had been an instant hit. Within a month it was in the top ten and was now a consistent first or second.

Sally went looking for the little Japanese lacquer box she kept in the dressing-table drawer. She fished around in back and then remembered she had taken it home and finished the last of the grass with friends the other night.

Oh, Jesus, what a time to run out! She had always gotten her supply from a stuntman with whom she worked on her previous series, but he was out of town now.

I just need something to calm me down, make me feel a little better right now, she thought. She racked her brain for anyone who might have some or might know a dealer.

She heard a knock and opened the door. Ossie Krieger was standing in the doorway, a sad look elongating his round face.

"Did you hear the bad news?" he asked.

She nodded and ushered him into the dressing room.

"We tried. God knows, we tried," he exclaimed. He slumped down into an armchair. "You were great in it."

"This is just a little setback," she repeated with a confidence she did not feel.

People probably said the same thing when they spotted the first flames on the *Hindenburg.*" Ossie's gaze lifted. "You aren't busy right now? I'm not interrupting anything?"

"Just a good long cry."

"Mind if we share it."

She shook her head. "You wouldn't happen to have any grass, would you?"

"I've got better than that." He jumped to his feet. "I'll be right back."

His absence was brief. Ossie locked the dressing-room door when he returned and sat down beside the glass coffee table. From a small envelope he began to pour a white powder onto the glass in parallel lines.

"You're going to be crazy about this stuff," he assured her.

He turned out to be right.

The news that one of the other men in the department was taking over his job in Station Relations shocked Greg profoundly. He thought he had been doing well as the point man who cleared the toughest affiliates for the network. Just the right amount of diplomacy, just the right amount of muscle. He had never failed at anything in his life. He was badly shaken. He immediately strode down the hall to see the department head.

An old-timer who had been with the company for forty years, the man had been recruited to join the fledgling TV network at its birth, out of the chain of Midwestern radio stations Barnett had inherited from his father. He had survived this long, it was rumored, by having a bloodhound's nose for corporate politics and an astute insight into how Barnett Roderick thought. He could smell trouble wafting on the slightest breeze. He was also one of the few men the Chairman was said to trust enough to confide in occasionally.

"I thought I'd been doing well," Greg declared. "You yourself told me that."

"You are," the older man admitted.

"Then why demote me."

"They have something else in mind for you, I hear. It will just take some time to materialize."

126

"What does that mean? Who are 'they'?"

The older man did not bother to answer the question, which was as good as announcing that the change had been ordered by Barnett personally.

"Level with me," Greg asked. "It will go no further."

The older man considered Greg's trustworthiness and then nodded. "They hadn't realized that your job was sensitive. If you mess up—a whole bunch of stations refusing to clear and really killing the night for us—someone might have to be blamed. They couldn't afford it to be you."

"So I'm getting penalized now for marrying his daughter."

"If you want to look at it that way. If I were you, though, I wouldn't look a gift horse in the mouth. Just sit tight. They'll find something a hell of a lot better for you."

"Without any responsibility."

"With less risk."

"I'd at least like a chance to discuss this with him."

"Don't," the older man cautioned. "He's not going to change his mind, Greg. Trust me when it comes to this. You'll only antagonize him. He does nothing without a purpose."

"So I just sit back and let it happen?" Greg had always gone zealously after his goals; he was not used to waiting for them to come to him.

"When it suits *his* purpose, not *yours,* he'll act. And not a moment sooner."

"Damn it, I intend to make something of my life."

"Ride with it, Greg, don't fight it. That'll take you a lot further."

The older man stood up. That was all he was prepared to say.

Several weeks later, Greg was promoted into a different department. By then he had reconciled himself to the fact that he would not necessarily rise because he performed well, but because he did not screw up, did not make mistakes, handled himself judiciously.

Anticipating the jealousy others must feel about his privileged status within the company, Greg took greater care to be liked and not to be controversial. He emphasized his charm and modesty.

Chris's high salary anchoring local news turned out to be a cheap investment. Within six months her new station had leapfrogged over KFBS-TV in the ratings. By then Stew and several others at that station had already moved elsewhere. Manny Ramirez, for one, transferred to the network's Buenos Aires bureau, which covered all of South America, on the promise that he would eventually be moved to network news in New York.

A lot of newscasters in Los Angeles were capable reporters and could speak well. Some even had Chris's tenacity and capacity for hard work. But her looks and personality elevated her above the almost undifferentiable multitude crowding the channels at news time. The beauty was inviting—fresh and wholesome—engaging both men and women viewers. She seemed an intelligent, honest friend in their living rooms. Audiences liked and remembered her.

Less than a year had passed on her contract when Carl Green opened up negotiations. He gave the network a choice. Either move her from local now at an increase or she'd move to another network on her own when the contract expired next year. They quickly agreed to make her the head network reporter in the Los Angeles bureau.

"What exactly does that mean, Carl?"

"An extra hundred thousand a year. You'll be the main person doing L.A. and West Coast pieces for the network's evening news."

"They've already got Tim Wiggens doing that."

"As far as they're concerned, Wiggens is already history. But I've got ABC hot to grab him."

"And you end up with *two* commissions."

"Enough with the commissions. Deep down you're still a little girl from Idaho—"

"Wyoming."

"—wherever, who's counting pennies. What's important is how much more *you're* making, not me."

Chris was confused. "Wiggens is good. Why did the network choose me?"

"Your Q-rating."

"What's a Q-rating?"

"They used to hook electrodes up to people. The more electricity popped out of their skin when you were shown on a screen, the higher viewer appeal they thought you had. Now they use questionnaires. Wiggens had high negatives. You didn't."

Chris was incensed. "What does that have to do with my professional skills: my writing, the hard work I've put in, my—"

"Not a damned thing. But without them, you'd fall flat on your ass and no Q-rating in the world could save it."

"Somehow I don't feel the joy at moving up to network I thought I would. It feels like I just won a beauty contest."

"Just think how you'd feel if you were the fifth runner-up applauding for the winner."

Chris fumed for days over the reason for her promotion. Newspeople were being judged like entertainers: not on whether they reported the news well, but on whether they delivered ratings and profits and audiences. Viewers simply assumed that anchors reading from a teleprompter were good reporters. News executives did not seem to care. The Greg Lyalls of the world were clearly the wave of the future.

"I can't wait to show it to you," Diane crowed. "It's just what we need."

That morning at her hairdresser's she had been skimming the latest *Town & Country* that a friend had informed her contained a good photo of her and Greg at a recent charity event. At the back of the magazine, she had come across an ad for a handsome country house for sale in nearby Connecticut. She phoned the broker right from the chair. As soon as she was combed out, she had her car and driver take her up to view the house. She immediately put down a binder and was back by afternoon.

To Diane's surprise, Greg was furious. "Why didn't you let me know?"

"Someone else had already made a bid and was about to sign a contract, but was too cautious about putting money down."

"The seller would have waited till the weekend or even till tonight so I could see it."

She was hurt by his attack. "But I knew you'd like it. I made sure it has a great tennis court and swimming pool for you."

"Diane, I'm sure I'll like it. San Simeon probably looks like subsidized housing next to it. That isn't the point."

She was now annoyed at his ingratitude. "After saving you all the bother of running around with brokers, I expected you'd be pleased."

"It's a decision we should have made together."

"I liked it. I bought it."

What both of them left unspoken was that she was paying.

Her impulsive purchase finally laid bare many of the conflicts inherent in their marriage.

Diane could be very determined about getting her way. The hospital's directors found that out after appointing her to the board in the mistaken hope she would be appeased and would weaken her campaigns to win more funds for the children's wing. Even her strong-willed father indulged her. Her determination naturally carried over into her marriage. She took for granted that her overwhelming financial contribution to the marriage automatically endowed her with greater authority to make decisions affecting her and Greg jointly. To reduce that authority, in fact, would have threatened her.

Although Greg saw only her strengths, Diane was actually a woman with many fears. As if listening to an internal shortwave radio, she was always reacting to voices and apprehensions he could not hear. She was afraid that Greg, whom she had pursued and whose inner strength she

129

now leaned on, might have married her for advantage, without truly loving her, and might leave her. She was afraid of losing her father's love—he was growing older; he might die. She was afraid that despite her family's social rank, some slip might suddenly cause the exclusion her father had originally experienced. And she was afraid to have children, afraid of the pain and of the changes childbearing would bring to her body and to her very contented life; that never having had a mother, she would not know how to be one; and most of all that childbirth was waiting to slaughter her, too, and leave her own children, in their turn, motherless. She lavished her maternal affection on children in the hospital and came safely home afterward.

Diane kept her fears to herself, particularly her aversion to having children. Greg was eager for a large family. She knew enough about his past to know there were chairs around his heart waiting to be occupied by sons and daughters who would return many times the love that was torn from him as a child.

All her fears, at bottom, were of abandonment or of death, which were one and the same. She fended them off with money—wealth and vigilance provided security. Greg made an excellent salary and contributed a good deal to their household expenses, but nowhere near what she could. He saved for expensive items and developed priorities. Never having wanted for money, she spent it freely. She could afford to be impulsive about her purchases and to gain her satisfactions immediately.

Greg had grown increasingly resentful of how casually Diane flaunted her monetary power. It demeaned him and provoked his deepest anxieties: the memory of his father's earning inadequacy destroying his parents' marriage. He needed to feel that he was, if not master, at least an equal partner. But his employment at FBS, his lack of resources, and the close bond between father and daughter made that impossible; Barnett assumed an unseen dominance in their home, he was a ghost always lingering, like the phosphors on a picture tube that never quite fade away after the set is turned off. The benefits Greg had sought through marriage were growing into a bramble bush of discontent between them.

The night they argued over her purchase of the country house Greg was already in bed reading when Diane entered from her dressing room. She had put on her most alluring nightgown, really a bit sexier than she felt comfortable with, black and mostly open work lace on top, deeply cut. But Greg never glanced up. He turned out the light moments later and went right to sleep.

That weekend, when she took Greg up to see the house for the first time, he found parked in the driveway the red Lamborghini he had once admired when they passed a showroom and she had denigrated as being much too flamboyant. When he turned to her in astonishment, he saw how anxious she was that the gift please him.

"I'm stunned," he assured her. "It's magnificent. Thank you."

She threw her arms around him. "And you'll love the house just as much. I know you will."

Greg usually drove the car at night, and only on back country roads. He treasured it almost as much as he felt belittled by it.

Chris bought a small house in the Brentwood hills and turned the little apartment on the beach over to Marian Marcus. The two women remained close and spent a lot of their free time together. Marian had little opportunity to date and Chris little inclination. Occasionally, however, Chris met a man who interested her, sometimes even enough to enter into a brief affair, but a deeper relationship never grew. None of the men could rival her career for her affections or provide more than transient pleasure—never inducing the consistent rush that infused her while digging into a tough story or reporting a late-breaking one. And certainly not what she had felt with Greg.

One or two big stories can catapult a TV reporter to prominence. Dan Rather was with the local CBS affiliate in Houston until Hurricane Carla hit the Texas coast and the nation watched him brave the storm's devastating force to report on it. Later, as a network reporter, he was in Dallas when President Kennedy was shot. But sometimes, those promoted because of an appealing on-camera presence lack the training or talent to produce quality work. Sooner or later, their facades crack and their inadequacies become conspicuous, first to their colleagues and eventually to the public. The collapse can be tragic.

Jessica Savitch's on-screen image endeared her to millions of viewers, but her journalistic shortcomings were already apparent to colleagues and superiors when a probable addiction fostered by private terrors suddenly made them evident to the entire nation during a ghastly two-minute newsbreak on prime time. As she began to read the brief headlines, her speech slurred badly and a haunted look invaded her eyes. The camera she craved and had always believed adored her had turned on her. Apart from commercials, her appearance lasted only forty-three seconds, but to those watching they were endless and agonizing. Whispers of drug use and professional incompetence could no longer be contained within the newsroom. Her career died that night. Only three weeks later, the rest of her followed. She and a companion were accidentally killed when their car plunged into a Pennsylvania canal in the dark.

Chris, on the contrary, had served a long apprenticeship. Experienced, talented, she was ready to make the most of her big opportunity, and she was a workhorse. She also had the preternatural luck or gift that often placed her in the path of news.

That was the case the morning she arrived early at L.A. International to catch a midday plane to Phoenix where she would shoot a story. She had not eaten that morning and went to the cafeteria for a sandwich. Seated in the booth behind her was a group of airline employees. Before she understood their whispered words, she sensed a tremor of apprehension in the tone. She interrupted them and asked if something had happened. A woman who recognized her as a television reporter confided that a plane en route to Hawaii had suddenly turned back with engine trouble and would try to make an emergency landing within the hour. Chris raced to the phone.

She was the only reporter on the scene. Her crew shot the only pictures of the 747 as it approached the runway on just two of its four engines, suddenly dropped the last ten feet into a crash landing that flattened the landing gear, and then skidded along the ground, spraying sparks.

Her network led with the crash story that night.

"Three people were killed," the anchorman led into it, "and dozens hurt when a charter-airline jumbo jet made an emergency landing just past noon today at Los Angeles International Airport. Our own Christine Paskins was at the scene for this exclusive report."

Chris's opening showed her standing in front of the still-smoldering wreckage. "Less than two hours ago, this Pan-Pacific Airlines 747 was on its way to Honolulu filled with happy vacationers . . ."

Chris's face and name became engraved on a lot of memories that night.

That impression was deepened a month later. She was out with a crew in downtown L.A. when a high-rise fire began in the area. Again her story became the broadcast's lead. She was bemused to note that little had changed from her days in local—a good fire with great visuals could always get you the top of the broadcast.

One envious competitor swore that Chris must have been causing the disasters to get to the scenes so fast. From then on, Christine Paskins was remembered by viewers and somewhere in their unconscious, instinctively trusted.

The L.A. bureau chief and his superior, the program's executive producer in New York, soon came to depend on her to be tossed any assignment and produce good work. Because of her sense of humor, that was frequently the end piece.

Often, the closing segment on a news broadcast is a light one, maybe featuring an animal or describing an act of individual spunk. The purpose is to leave the viewer in an "up" mood and wanting to tune in again tomorrow, rather than "down" and reluctant to chance another encounter with gloom. With California a kind of laboratory for avant-garde behavior, network broadcasts had gotten into the habit of frequently closing with wryly derisive pieces about some far-out bit of California activity: some new guru or therapy or article of dress viewers could laugh at. Chris usually found the stories fun to do. But she dug in her heels and revealed a stubbornly resolute character when she was assigned to report on the Surfing Swami.

"That's the bottom of the barrel, Hal. The guy's got a following of maybe two lifeguards and a swimsuit model. His theology is limited to 'Catch a gnarly big one.' I don't do any more California kook stories unless they have a point."

"Hey, this shows a new religious trend in the country. Bringing the Lord to leisure time."

"If this had happened in Kansas or Ohio, would you be doing the piece?"

"That would be big news. The eastern half of the country would be underwater."

"You know what I'm talking about. This is just a way to get a reflex laugh because it's California."

Figuring she was probably right, he dropped the story.

Greg became the youngest corporate vice president at the Federal Broadcasting System when he was named to head a new department for long-range planning, called Corporate Planning and Development. He had been moved around the company a good deal, but Barnett had never taken Greg under his wing as Greg had hoped he would and seemed to keep tabs on his son-in-law's performance only to be sure he was not being embarrassed by him. Greg hoped that this new post would grant him real responsibility at last.

He and a small staff of financial and business analysts worked six months to fashion a vision of where the network should be in ten years and a strategy to get there. Satellites were changing television. FBS should be investing abroad now, linking up with networks in other countries. Cable was quietly becoming a giant, gaining viewers and revenue at the expense of the over-the-air broadcasters. FBS should be investing in cable networks.

Greg futilely tried for two months to gain a spot on Barnett's schedule to present the plan. Finally, he demanded that Barnett's secretary carve two hours out of her boss's schedule for him.

*　*　*

"So you can see," Greg concluded, "if we continue to limit our thinking to over-the-air broadcasting in the United States, FBS and the other broadcasters will share a shrinking audience and stagnant revenues. But if we think of ourselves as a worldwide service for communicating entertainment and news—by cable, by satellite, by videocassette, and every other means—our market is vast and growing."

"Interesting," Barnett commented. "I'll think about it."

With that Greg and the plan were dismissed. Barnett Roderick was not a man given to long-range thinking, Greg reluctantly concluded, particularly other people's, and he did not like to be pushed. His strong suit was reaction: to the showing of a pilot, to a business opportunity on which the company could quickly capitalize, or to a problem that it faced.

Dispirited, Greg recognized that once more he had been moved into an undemanding position with an impressive title and salary because his failure in a critical role would be too visible. Other people who failed could be dismissed, but not Barnett Roderick's son-in-law, who would then have to be kept on—to FBS's detriment and to derision behind both their backs. Greg wore the trappings and reaped the rewards of some authority at FBS, but he merely went through the motions of accomplishment.

Once, when he approached his father-in-law with a request for more responsibility, Barnett told him flatly, "You've still got a lot to learn."

The subject was closed.

Like a film of dust, a vague depression began to settle on everything in Greg's life as he became increasingly conscious of owning almost nothing in it and controlling even less. He had set out from western Pennsylvania intent on making his mark and gaining admiration. But Diane and her father had actually provided the mark, which denied him that admiration. Even from her he now occasionally sensed an unconscious lessening of the respect that had originally attracted her.

134

9

The common wisdom among women in news that they had to work twice as hard as men to gain half the credit was never truer for Chris than after she was shifted to London.

Chris had lobbied for a year with the network brass to get posted to a foreign bureau. Considered important for a correspondent who hoped to make it to the top, a stint abroad provided direct exposure to world events, as well as the personal polish that could transform a small-town boy into a dashing "broadcast journalist" in Saville Row tailoring. Jennings and Rather had both been prepped for the anchor chair in a London post.

The tradition started during World War II when London was the headquarters for Edward R. Murrow and the daring young men and for only a short time, women reporters that he and William L. Shirer recruited—among them Eric Sevareid and Charles Collingwood. On the basis of absolutely no evidence, women's voices were assumed to be too high to sound authoritative to listeners. Four decades went by before market research disproved the sexist myth.

Chris's reports from Great Britain, Ireland, and the European continent were a staple of the nightly news. Her coverage of foreign affairs rapidly enlarged her stature. But the workload was crushing.

Even after a second reporter joined her, she still routinely put in fourteen- to sixteen-hour days six or seven days a week and had a scant personal life. If she *had* met an interesting man, she would scarcely have had the time to recognize him. She was always racing to the next interview or back to the office to write up her narration for a piece. When covering a breaking story, she stayed on duty until after the program in New York had transmitted all its feeds to the various time zones, so as to be available to insert last-minute updates via satellite. She lived out of a suitcase and did much of her sleeping on airplanes streaking across Europe to the latest news eruption.

In odd moments of leisure, she realized she was lonely. A feeling resembling regret occasionally struck her then: How narrow her existence had become and how alone she was. Her life consisted of doing a different solo trapeze act every day or two. Cameras recorded her feat for replay before millions of people. But there was no one to catch her if she fell or even to care if she did. And no one waited to embrace her each night when she finally reached safety.

Greg often compared his own career with Ev Carver's. Ev had climbed quickly and high by succeeding at the tough tasks he was handed. He had collected greater power and more departments, while flattening obstacles and people in his path. The force of his personality, the rumors of his success with women inside the company and out, added to his mystique as an irresistible force.

At a brainstorming meeting to develop a selling strategy to the ad agencies for the new season, Ev proposed a scheme that might have left the network open to antitrust charges. Greg was the only one willing to attack Ev's idea.

Ev laughed at him. "There are no rules, Lyall. You know that: You married the boss's daughter. All you have to do is keep your nose clean and your ass wiped."

Ev and the others simply went on as if Greg's comment had never been made. Each time Greg brought up a point, he noticed the same thing happened: courtesy, but no heed. To them he was as transparent as a man made of glass. They were careful around him because the Chairman had been the one to place him on display, occasionally changing the title on his pedestal. But to everyone he was familiarly known and dismissed as "The Son-in-law."

In 1986, after America's off-year elections, a reshuffling of assignments brought Chris to Washington in the prestigious post of head White House correspondent. She had not had to fight or lobby for the job. They had beseeched her to take it.

Again, Carl Green, her agent, would only agree to a two-year contract. Her stock was rising too fast to let her be locked in. She was now earning seven hundred thousand dollars a year.

The career advancement Greg had expected to procure by marrying Diane became more elusive and illusory as he appeared to climb higher at FBS, but never into formidable jobs. One particularly demeaning day someone forgot to inform him that the time had been moved up two hours for a meeting about the new fall schedule he and other senior executives were to have with Barnett and Raoul Clampton, the new head of Programming. The meeting had already ended when Greg arrived.

That night he joined Diane at a dinner party where he hoped pleasant company would lift his depression. That possibility ended when the hostess raised her glass to toast her husband. He had just been elevated to managing director of a large investment bank where he had gone after business school instead of entering his father-in-law's firm. Greg felt that everyone there who glanced at him was condemning him as a failure and a parasite.

During the three-block walk home to their apartment, Greg told Diane about the slight at the office that day and how badly he felt when their host's promotion was announced. She advised him to have her father fire the person who had forgotten to inform him of the time change.

Greg was aghast. "What would that solve?"

"It will get you some respect."

"The wrong kind. I'd like to earn it and respect myself instead."

In Diane's astronomy, people like her father who had the talent made it, the others didn't. Greg might well be deluding himself. He had everything so easy, and yet he seemed chronically dissatisfied. She grew short-tempered.

"Perhaps you weren't cut out for that sort of thing. Some people aren't."

Greg did not know whether Diane was purposely trying to insult him or rather, to ease his adjustment to failure. In either case no adequate rejoinder was possible.

He stewed over her remark for days, worrying that it might have originated with her father, during one of their daily phone conversations. All his life he had thought of himself as a winner, self-assured, capable, certain of his objectives. Yet, even he wondered whether it might not be true.

Diane's love for Greg had not diminished over time, but she had become edgier with him, less accommodating. She had chosen a man who, regardless of his physical attractiveness, his strong-mindedness, his magnetism, was below her social station, had no independent prospects, possessed only the salary her father gave him, and who needed her for all those reasons.

At a time when she might have reduced the growing tension between them by bending somewhat, she grew less respectful of his worth and less willing to do so, and all the while she was afraid that unless she maintained her control over him, she would lose him. Greg refused to bend on his side because his steadfastness was all he really possessed that was his own.

*   *   *

The worldly woman who strode into the White House's subterranean press room, put there during the earlier Nixon era in place of the Roosevelt swimming pool, appeared greatly changed by her years abroad. Chris Paskins dressed with style and could converse urbanely over a confit of duck or salmon en croûte while commenting comfortably on the St.-Émilion. She had a broad, sure knowledge of international crosscurrents and a far greater skepticism about people and their motives than the ingenue who had arrived in California from Wichita and had immediately fallen in love. She was also less volatile and more self-possessed. That was because little had changed on the inside. Confident then, she was more so now, but with her combative instinct kept under better control; she had learned that so long as she trusted no one, she need only do her work to the best of her ability to get along just fine.

Covering the Reagan White House was different from any previous assignment. With stories cascading down from the pinnacle of government, she was assured of getting on the air nearly every night, usually doing her stand-up in front of the White House portico. She was flooded with press releases, was briefed by press aides, and had almost no access to the President. Ronald Reagan's aides had perfected the art of gaining airtime for the President without the danger of exposing him to an encounter with reporters, where he might make gaffes and appear misinformed. She sometimes felt like a scribe indentured to the emperor with no clothes.

Refusing to take on faith what the White House press office was trying to sell her, she worked hard to track down the facts behind the stories and gradually developed contacts throughout the government—the Defense Department, Agriculture, State, the Treasury, Capitol Hill.

At first she resisted joining the herd making the rounds of cocktail parties and receptions and dinner parties, as she had resisted most of the social whirl in Los Angeles and for which she had been too busy in London. But she soon realized that so much could be learned after hours in Washington, so many useful relationships developed with the powerful in government, that she began to accept the invitations.

Hosts and hostesses considered Chris a prime catch: a TV celebrity to whom their other guests sought access, very attractive, single.

For the first time in a long while, Chris began to settle into something akin to a normal life.

Diane and Greg always spent a week in the winter at their house in Aspen. She was an excellent skier, having learned when she was young. Greg started skiing after they married, but as a good athlete he had quickly improved. No sport he had ever tried provided the sense of personal freedom that downhill skiing did—you swooped and glided and dipped wherever you pointed your skis. No ski resort was more congenial than the Aspen area, with its four skiing mountains, good restaurants, and shops full of the newest equipment and lavish clothing; and with its slopes, streets, and houses full of friends, many from the West Coast, whom he got to see no other time of the year. Aspen had the air of a perpetual party. Greg and Diane had spent some of the happiest times of their marriage in Aspen.

The second day of their vacation that February, they skied with a group of friends on the mountain that formed one side of the city. Longtime visitors still insisted on calling the mountain Ajax, so as to demonstrate that they were not among the glitz-ridden newcomers easily taken in by the fancy marketing technique of renaming it Aspen Mountain. Among the group was a friend's exuberant eight-year-old son, whose developing skill displayed enormous delight in unknotting the restraints of gravity. Being with the boy so much of the day caused Greg to feel keenly the absence of children in his life. He was in his midthirties already. It was long past the time that he and Diane began their own family.

They had fallen into the habit of bathing in the hot tub when they returned to their house on Red Mountain after a day on the slopes, and then, because they were already naked and their muscles felt warm and stretched and nicely tired, they would often make love and then sleep until eight at night, when they dressed and went out. Aspen was an interlude of unaccustomed eroticism between them.

"Don't put your diaphragm in this time," he said as they walked to the bedroom in thick cotton bathrobes.

She looked uncomprehendingly at him for an instant, then realized what he wanted. "Please, Greg, don't start that again. You know I'm not ready to have children yet."

"You'll be thirty soon."

"I'll think about it then."

She slipped into the bathroom and was out quickly. She found him sitting up against the headboard, arms crossed, his expression angry. She lay down beside him and put her head on his shoulder, trying to melt the coolness.

"It's a very big step, Greg, and it worries me."

"Before we married you swore you wanted children. Do you just keep saying you do to put me off?"

"I guess I want them," she hedged, "but not just yet."

"By now you should know. That's supposed to be the point of being a family."

"It scares me," she confessed.

"You're wonderful with kids. You'll be a fine mother."

"The responsibility is just part of it. There's the pain." She seemed to be feeling it.

"They can give you an anesthetic."

"Greg," she confessed, "giving birth can kill me. I'm frightened that I'll have the same problem as my mother and that it will kill me. The doctors tell me it can happen."

This was the first time she had admitted the truth. The assurance that she wanted children had been so important to him.

Greg lifted her face to look at his. "So, where does that leave us?"

"I need more time to think about it."

"Would you adopt?"

"Would you?"

"Someday maybe," he said, "if we had tried and failed to have our own. All my life I've felt as if I'm owed my own family back. You?"

"You know I love the kids in the hospital."

"That's easy to do. They're not your own."

"Adopting children is so precarious. I don't know how some of those mothers take it. Some have adopted kids with diseases no one expected. And no biological histories. The doctors try everything for them, but sometimes just don't know enough about them." Talking so long about the object of her fears was alarming her. "It's enough for now that we have each other."

She moved up to kiss Greg. He did not respond. She kissed him again, trying to arouse him, hoping to bury these thoughts under ecstatic sensation.

"Is that all there is for us?" he asked. "For the rest of our lives?"

"What do you mean?"

"Two people not really satisfied with each other . . . a little more selfish and a little less satisfied each day."

"I'm satisfied," she objected.

"No, you're just willing to accept less. How could you be satisfied with me when I'm not satisfied with myself?"

She sat up. "I've never heard you talk this way. We have a wonderful life. Look around you."

"None of it is *mine*," he said with sharp bitterness.

She put her head back down on his shoulder. "And you resent that it's mine."

Chris's initial thought upon finding herself seated next to Sen. Kenneth V. Chandler at dinner was discouragement. Although she had never met him, the bachelor senator from New York was known as much for his gossip-column dating life as for his legislative skill. She expected to find him drunkenly leaning against her by dessert and his hand groping for her knee long before that. Worse, he looked exactly as a senator was supposed to: a full head of wavy hair turning gray, full eyebrows over thoughtfully self-assured eyes, straight features, and the jaw of a gladiator. He might have won the job on the basis of an eight-by-ten glossy. The advent of television campaigning had produced a bumper crop of the type. He was forty-two years old, a dozen years older than she, had been in the Senate eight years, divorced ten, and in politics twenty.

"I asked our hostess to seat me next to you," he said upon meeting her.

"That's flattering," she replied, seized by an impulse to flee the dinner party immediately.

"I hope you'll be more flattered when I tell you the reason: I'm in love with you."

Chris was not even mildly amused by his flirting. "Do you really score in Washington with a line like that?"

"I've never used it before. But then a lot of years have passed since I was in love with anyone."

"Senator Chandler—" she began.

"Please call me Ken."

"Senator Ken," she said tartly, not about to assume familiarity, "according to well-founded rumor, you have taken up temporary residence in every bed between New York and Guam. One would expect that falling in love was something you did as often as showing up on the Senate floor for roll calls. Or am I overestimating your professional diligence?"

His expression remained serious. "I said I'd never been in love before. I didn't say I'd never been in bed with anyone."

"So we've all heard." She did not smile. "I'm offended, really, that you would use the line."

"I meant it."

"Even if that's true, it's foolish. All you know about me is the professional image I project on your TV screen. I'm only a small part of that person."

"Then imagine how much more I'll love you when I get to know the rest of you."

"Have you been drinking?"

"I don't drink. It used to be a problem for me."

"I'd heard that, too." The private frailties of its movers and shakers was as casually discussed in Washington as a john's tastes was by call girls—usually for the same reasons.

"You see," he pointed out, "we both have reputations that don't begin

141

to exhibit our true characters. For one thing I'm not the playboy you seem to believe I am. I'm really a little bit shy."

"Senator Ken, please spare me your stab at appealing boyishness. Offhand I'd say you usually have better luck when you play the man of power who says he's looking for a woman he can be just plain Ken with, can shed a tear with. You know, commanding, but sensitive. They tell me that's big nowadays."

"I don't know how much command I have, but the rest of it's true."

Chris frowned. "That material probably plays better with wide-eyed administrative aides and upstate campaign workers."

"I think you should be more open-minded. I intend to marry you."

Chris instantly turned to people on her other side and ignored him the rest of the evening.

Greg's anger flared. Increasingly, only a small provocation could ignite his and Diane's vexation with each other. Sometimes, like now, a single question was enough to do it.

"No," he replied crossly, "I will not spend my summer vacation with your father. We have him over for dinner. We go out to events with him. I work for him. My vacation time is my own." Greg had long since given up hoping that spending time with his father-in-law would improve his chances for promotion. Since the marriage, Barnett had talked very little with him about FBS. Greg suspected the reason was to keep from raising his expectations unreasonably.

Seated in the rear of the limousine, the sound barrier up, Greg and Diane were on their way downtown to a formal gala at the glass-enclosed Winter Garden in Battery Park City. She had just informed him that her father was renting a large house in Cap Ferrat for the summer and had invited her and Greg to join him. She was excited by the prospect.

"Oh, Greg, I know the house. It's wonderful, very big and right on the water. We'd have our own suite. And the French Riviera is such great fun in August. Everyone will be there."

"A couple of months ago I mentioned maybe going up to the woods in Canada, just the two of us and a guide. A cabin on a lake, fishing, hiking."

Diane was laughing. "I'm sure I didn't agree to anything like that."

"It would be a chance for us to get away from all this. To be alone together and really get to know each other again."

Diane had become serious. "Greg, if you want to take a weekend and go hiking somewhere, that's fine, but it isn't something I'd really be comfortable doing. Cap Ferrat would be for all of August."

"I can't take off that long. Two weeks is the limit. That and one week in the winter. That's what I get."

"Daddy wants to have a lot of parties and asked me to be his hostess. He wants both of us there," she concluded with a firmness that must originally have been communicated by her father.

The Chairman wanted his daughter with him for the month of August, Greg supposed, but was reconciled to having to take the husband part of the time as well.

For Barnett the world outside his home was divided into two groups of people: employees and those he needed. Greg slopped messily over into both categories. As far as Greg could tell, Barnett had never worked out how to treat him or how to value him and continually refused to take him seriously, except as a potential problem to be contained.

"I'm going to vacation in Canada," Greg repeated to Diane. "I want you with me."

"Don't start trying to give me orders."

"You can do whatever you want, you usually do. I'm going to Canada."

"What do you expect me to tell my father?"

"Tell him the truth, that we fight all the time and are resentful in between."

"I wouldn't want to upset him. And it isn't as bad as you make it sound."

"At least nothing that money wouldn't cure, right?"

"You seemed very happy with my money when we first got married."

"I like your money very much. It frees our lives from all the material care nearly everyone else in the world is bent over double by."

"It's just me you don't like?"

Greg stared at her in the shifting light cast through the car's darkened windows.

"No, I like you, Diane," he admitted. "What I don't like is either the person you want to turn me into . . . or the person I've become." A slight smile invaded the gravity of his expression. "I never understood before that Prince Philip had the hardest job in England."

"What is it that you want?" She was as exasperated as she was concerned.

"Equality. Emancipation. The vote."

Her anger now showed itself. "I am not about to give you control over my money."

"That's what it always comes down to for you," he said sadly. "All I want is what I've always wanted: for us to make the important decisions together."

"You can make all decisions yourself that you're prepared to pay for," she snapped. "And I'll make mine."

More than the financial imbalance was irreconcilable between them. He wanted so much from her that had no price or status, things she

143

would not or could not provide. Above all, he realized, he wanted very much to want her. And he didn't.

The car came to a stop. Diane looked out the side window. "We're here."

A moment later the chauffeur opened the rear door for her.

"Why is it," Greg asked her, "that our most important conversations are always slipped in while we're going somewhere?"

"Because that's the only time we're forced to talk to each other."

She stepped out onto the sidewalk. Greg stopped her as the limousine drove off to the parking area.

"I'm going to Canada for a vacation," he told her once more. "I expect my wife to go with her husband, not with her father."

He took her arm and led her toward the Winter Garden entrance. Diane hated it when Greg gave ultimatums. He sometimes acted as if he and her father were rivals. They could both be so difficult, so stubbornly self-centered, at times.

Barnett had already arrived at the reception and was speaking to people when they entered. Greg drew him aside.

"Barnett," he said, "thank you for inviting us to the Riviera. But we had plans to go fishing in Canada."

Barnett glanced pointedly at his daughter.

"Just for the first week of Greg's vacation," she said lightly, "and then I'll join you in Cap Ferrat."

Her gaze shifted to Greg, waiting to know whether he would yield as she had.

Greg finally turned to his father-in-law. "Yes, we're looking forward to it."

Diane's relief showed instantly. She hugged her father's arm and kissed him on the cheek. "We'll have a wonderful time. We always do in Cap Ferrat."

During the three weeks since the dinner party, Chris had refused to take Ken Chandler's phone calls and had overlooked his messages. Several times, she had dated a news producer employed by a different network. No sparks, but they had had fun together.

One afternoon a male reporter with whom she was friendly passed by Chris's desk in the press room and handed her an envelope printed with the return address of Chandler's Senate office. Chris was about to toss it away when the man stopped her.

"I promised not to leave until you read it."

"Do you know this guy?" she asked.

The other reporter nodded.

"Well?"

144

"As far as I can tell, he's a straight guy."

"For a politician, you mean."

The man nodded. No group was more scornful of politicians' morality than the reporters who covered them, interpreting officeholders' every act and statement solely in light of their desire to win votes.

Chris tore open the envelope and read the handwritten note within.

Dear Chris,

Doesn't a good reporter check out the facts before making up her mind?

Ken Chandler

He had guessed correctly that appealing to her professionalism as a journalist would probably move her to evaluate her prejudices. With less work facing her than usual for the next few days, she launched a full investigation of the Honorable Kenneth V. Chandler, Republican senator from the State of New York, graduate of Cornell University and Columbia Law School, summer volunteer to register black voters in the South, former assistant district attorney, state assemblyman, and then a congressional representative.

What began to turn up—and what she had a hard time believing—was that in spite of his being an astute and ambitious politician, every source confirmed his sincerity. He was a man who kept his word, a thoughtful, reliable man, and not the playboy he was portrayed as being. His divorce seemed to have resulted from incompatibility and not infidelity on his part. Since then he had dated well-known and not-so-well-known women, but usually discreetly. When a famous actress he was dating leaked a steamy story to the press for publicity, his reputation as a Casanova snowballed. Yet, so far as Chris could determine, he was not a man who made extravagant promises to women.

Marian had been urging Chris in their phone conversations to go out with "Senator Ken," as they had fallen into the habit of calling him. Now, she was insistent.

"You owe it to the man, Chris."

"But if he's not a phony, then he's crazy. Nobody in his right mind tells a woman he barely knows that he loves her and intends to marry her."

"You've been a reporter too long. Think of it as romantic. A man sees a woman on television or 'across a crowded room' "—she sang that part—"and falls in love at first sight. Besides, crazies do not get elected senator."

"Want to bet?"

145

"All right, I take that back. But admit you misjudged him. I think you owe it to him to go out with him at least once."

Chris paused to think about it. No doubt her false assumptions had caused her to treat him rudely when they met. "Okay, once. That's all."

Chris phoned Ken's office and invited him to dinner the next weekend at Sans Souci. The dessert, she assured him, would be humble pie.

"No," he said.

"You've been asking me out for a month."

"If it means letting you buy me dinner, I won't do it. I wouldn't feel comfortable."

"Tell you what, we'll have a picnic on the Potomac. It'll be fun. I'll bring the picnic. You bring the cherry blossoms."

"Fine."

For some reason Chris could not fathom, her buying the food for a picnic was acceptable to him, her buying the meal at a restaurant was not. He would bring wine and dessert.

Annette Valletta's previous series had been successful, but the large-eyed comedienne had been turned into a superstar by her zany TV comedy series "I Love Luba." In it she played a red-haired Russian immigrant married to an American rock-star band leader, whose TV show she was always trying to get on, usually with the connivance of her next-door neighbor Edna. Within weeks after premiering, the FBS show had shot to number one in the ratings, which allowed the network to dominate Friday nights.

Annette had known Sally Foster since both were struggling to make it in Hollywood, and she was the most loyal of friends. Sally had been invited over to have dinner with Annette and her new husband, Johnny. Sally had introduced the couple. When rehearsals for her sitcom ended late that afternoon, Annette began phoning Sally Foster's house. No one answered and the answering machine was turned off. Sally never arrived. Annette grew worried. Sally had become increasingly forgetful lately; she seemed to be at loose ends.

Finding herself unable to sleep because of her concern, at two in the morning Annette dressed, left a note to tell Johnny where she had gone, and drove over to Sally's house.

Since the demise of her own series, Sally had appeared in several made-for-television movies and three pilots that the networks turned down. She entered into a marriage that was canceled faster than her series and took up some hobbies. One was self-pity. Another was untrustworthy men. A third was rumored to be cocaine.

Annette had attempted to talk to Sally about the problem several times. Sally swore that she had only tried coke once or twice and had not used it for years. Annette wanted to believe her and used her influence to find Sally acting jobs, to little avail. Even when she was hired, she was often late, unreliable in front of the camera, and quickly fired. Sally always had a good reason why it had not been her fault. Studios grew leery of hiring her.

All the lights were on in Sally's house when Annette arrived, the front door was open, and loud music boomed from within.

She entered to find the house a mess, empty bottles and food on the carpet. A young man lay on the living room sofa with his eyes closed, listening to heavy-metal rock music on the stereo.

"Where's Sally?" Annette shouted over the music.

The young man opened his eyes. "Oh, wow, man! It's Luba! 'Oh, Luba . . . I'm home,' " he crooned in imitation of the husband's greeting on her show.

Annette flipped off the music. "Where's Sally?"

He shrugged. "Want some coke? On me." He pointed to an end table.

Annette went searching through the house and found Sally passed out naked on the floor of the bathroom. Her nose was white. Annette tried to wake her, but Sally appeared comatose.

Frightened, Annette yelled for the young man to give her a hand and threw a blanket over Sally.

He appeared in the bathroom doorway.

"Help me lift her," asked Annette.

"She probably needs the rest."

"Damn you!" Annette yelled. "Help me lift her!"

Wrapping her in a bathrobe, Annette strapped Sally into the car's safety harness and drove straight to a hospital. She feared her friend might be about to die from an overdose.

Several hours later, when Sally had come to and been dismissed by the hospital, Annette drove her south to a well-known rehab clinic and signed her in.

In addition to arranging for the cherry trees to be in luxuriant blossom, Ken Chandler had brought a violin case to the picnic.

"We going after Capone's boys?" Chris asked.

A machine gun would not have surprised her more than the violin he took out and the feeling and skill with which he played several pieces for her.

He admitted, "I'm trying to impress you and change your image of me."

"You're succeeding."

Ken's mother was a music teacher in Manhattan, his father a shopkeeper with a small lamp store. Playing the violin had gotten him a good education at New York City's High School of Music and Art. But he had always envisioned himself in public office, not one of twenty violinists in an orchestra pit. As soon as he could, he ran for the State Assembly and began his political career.

As she listened to him, Chris began to believe that Ken Chandler was that rare creature in public life, a decent man.

When a rain squall suddenly hit, they ran back to his car, each holding the picnic supplies with one hand and a corner of the tablecloth overhead with the other. Once inside the car, he asked, "Where to?"

"This is fine," she told him.

They watched the rain spatter on the windshield and distort the dappling river and the pink fringe of cherry blossoms beyond. Gradually, it came to Chris that she enjoyed being alone with this good man who felt comfortable with silences as she did, who did not mistake them for voids or endings but knew them as the ebb of life's natural rhythm. A man like that was a man you could depend on, a man who would be there for you. When the two did finally begin to converse again, they seemed to have known each other a long time.

Chris soon acknowledged that she loved Ken, but was hesitant to get married. The step seemed so final to her. She came from a home where divorce was unthinkable. Only after Ken promised her that if she ever fell out of love with him, she could end it did she say yes.

Chris and Ken were married early the next year in her hometown in Wyoming. Her parents liked him, which surprised her because her father distrusted politicians and could not abide most Republican ones.

The print and broadcast media had a field day profiling the celebrity couple, recounting how he had fallen in love with her before they had ever met, had instinctively known when he saw her broadcasting from London that they would someday marry. The public prominence of each heightened the other's stature. Chris's wide recognition and popularity reflected a luster on Ken that no amount of political accomplishment ever could.

Nineteen eighty-eight was also Ronald Reagan's final year in office, a presidential election year, and the year of the Iran-contra controversy, which rocked the administration and occupied many minutes on the news each night, much of that time Chris's. Her new husband was understanding, both about her long hours and about her on-air revelations and sharp commentary that sometimes embarrassed his party. Such annoyances were small blemishes on the vast happiness Chris had brought him.

With the Bush administration coming in, the executives supervising

Chris's news organization decided a reshuffling of reporters would be in order. Again, Carl Green struck pay dirt.

At a million-dollar-a-year salary, Chris agreed to become co-host of the network's New York–based morning news-and-talk program. That simplified her life. She could move to New York City, where Ken lived when he was not in Washington, and work regular hours, albeit starting very early each day; for the first time in many years she would have a homelife.

She and Ken took a large apartment on Central Park West. Her neighbors, used to and considerate of celebrities, bothered them relatively little as they shopped for food and strolled through the Upper West Side. Within a year her morning program's ratings climbed into neck-and-neck parity with the "Today" show's. As its only new element, she received much of the credit.

Chris settled easily into married life. She had been so burned by the end of her long affair with Greg that she had forgotten how much she liked the predictability, the close companionship, and the mutual reliance of living with someone she loved. She felt comfortable with Ken and admired his character. Intelligent and steadfast, he was not dynamic, but was always dependable. She was almost relieved not to feel with him the great, destructive storm surge of passion she once had with Greg.

If his career had been flourishing, Greg might have endured the growing acrimony in his homelife. But he could foresee no greater ascension at the network, only continued incarceration in a plushly padded limbo where sharp tools were taken from him, so he could not hurt himself or anyone else. At home he and Diane never yelled or threw things or called each other names—both were too well-mannered—but the atmosphere in the apartment was glacial and promised to remain so: just the two of them, alone while together, gradually growing more selfish. His increasing lack of contentment with the two halves of his life, divided neatly into day and night, but tainted by the same original sin, became too much for him to endure.

Greg and Diane barely spoke to each other anymore and rarely made love. When they did speak, every sentence was a reproachful accusation aimed at the other's flaws. Arguments were instant and vicious. The rest of the time, they silently endured each other's presence, but were worn out by the ordeal; they had no refuge.

Greg began to consider the possibility that had tortured him as a child: divorce. The prospect plagued him with guilt and worry. He had lied to Diane about loving her when they married, hoping love would grow, and had been determined to make the lie up to her by keeping her happy as long as they both should live. Divorce would evidence his failure. It would bring him loneliness and self-recrimination. He did not doubt that it would also strip him of his job—and every other now-corroded treasure he had married for.

"I want a divorce," he finally said when they were in the study after dinner. Those were the first words they had spoken to each other all day because of an angry exchange the night before.

Diane burst into tears. "I don't," she cried, and ran into her dressing room and locked the door.

Losing Greg was too disheartening for her to consider. She still loved him, although differently from the uncritical way she had before. And she still had hopes that the pleasures she once knew with him would someday return. They were a couple. She could not bear to think of herself alone. Losing him would rob her of much of the security that sustained her. However, so would the wrenching alteration of roles he asserted was essential to improving their relationship, but that she considered an excuse for his own feelings of inferiority. She would also have to agree to have children, which she feared might be a death sentence.

No matter how she tried to avoid the issue, however, Greg knew that he was reaching the point where divorce might be the only way to save what was left of his life.

10

~~~~~~~~~~

The late eighties were a trying time for the television broadcast industry. By the end of the decade, the network share of those watching television had shrunk from 90 percent to 67 percent and at times, lower. Cable now wired more than half the nation, and a proliferation of programming was available to viewers, including recent movies, twenty-four-hour news, sports events, and even first-run series. Most viewers now had VCRs and could rent movies on videocassette, ignoring network offerings. Independent broadcast stations now provided competition by running first-run syndicated programs. Some had even been linked into a fledgling network, Fox, that competed against the majors.

FBS had fared far worse than the other established networks. Its vaunted skill at picking the hot new shows seemed to falter. Some said the Chairman was getting on and had lost his touch. Ratings had spiraled downward, until FBS was badly trailing the other networks. Because advertisers paid for the number of viewers they reached, smaller audiences meant less revenue to FBS. Yet, network costs and staffing remained as lavish as before, as if this downturn were merely an aberration that would quickly reverse itself.

Barnett Roderick had created FBS and dominated the company. He had run it with an iron hand for over forty years and still approved all major decisions. He and his daughter together owned the largest block of stock. But now the long-docile outside directors on its board were suggesting that some changes might be in order, including a succession plan to prepare for his eventual retirement. Barnett had resisted talk of an heir apparent for years. And he saw no reason yet for the panic that wholesale changes implied. Just a few hit shows, and things would turn around. They always had. They would again. The very idea of picking a successor aggravated him; it was like arranging his own funeral.

By the spring of 1989, however, the woeful condition of the company's finances and rumors of corporate raiders interested in launching a take-over were forcing him to consider a shake-up in top management and at least, the show of a succession plan. Since the retirement of his second-in-command who had long watched over FBS's day-to-day operations, he had more or less ignored its growing problems. He would have to address them now.

Those problems weighed heavily on Barnett Roderick's mind when he arrived at the Lyalls' apartment for dinner. Diane invited him for dinner once or twice a month. Tonight she arrived home incensed by an incident at the hospital and she devoted most of the initial dinner conversation to it.

A child had died. Diane had held the parents' hands and told them nothing could have been done, but fervently believed that their child's chances to survive were drastically reduced because the hospital's resources were overweighted to adult services and it had no specialists in pediatric cancer.

"If we had a children's hospital, just for children and their diseases, we could attract the best experts in pediatric oncology, cardiology, all the specialties. This was a real tragedy. It has to end. And I'm going to do it."

"How?" Greg asked.

"I'm going to raise money for a separate building as part of the hospital. Kids from anywhere could come and be treated, regardless of whether they can pay. The hospital could certainly use the space we'd give up once we moved into our own building."

"That's an awfully big job to take on."

"I won't let anything stand in my way."

"You never do," Greg said.

He had hoped the comment would sound supportive and encouraging, but an undertone of reproach reached Barnett's ears. He began to listen more closely to the couple's conversation. Although it was amicable on the surface, Barnett sensed discord smoldering beneath like an ember under ashes. Not wanting to trouble Diane with what might have been a false impression, when he was alone with Greg in the study, Barnett confronted him.

Greg poured brandies for them both. Then, taking the armchair across from Barnett's, he confided the truth.

"Our marriage is near the breaking point. Diane wants us to stay

152

together—she wants it very much—but I'm tired of being her lap dog. I want children and so much more from her than she's willing to give. To give to *me*. Not to some damned institution."

Circumstances were so far gone that Greg no longer felt the need to hide his career frustrations either. "I'm also tired of being a parasite at work. You've been good about paying me well, but I haven't had a job in years that was more than shuffling papers."

Barnett was worried: Diane's happiness was threatened. His immediate response was to do whatever appeared necessary to keep the marriage together. That seemed to be to restore Greg's self-esteem.

"Please forgive me!" Barnett cried out, grasping Greg's hand—words and an act so unexpected and uncharacteristic that Greg jumped. "I'm to blame. You know how highly I think of you. The sky's the limit for your career. I told you that once and I meant it. But I should have foreseen that all this training to widen your experience would make you think I was holding you back. It's my fault. Of course, you're disheartened. Why wouldn't you be? Say you'll forgive me."

Not knowing how else to react to the startling outburst, Greg nodded.

"Thank you," Barnett responded gratefully. "As it is, I've held off too long announcing the reorganization."

"Reorganization?"

"That was what I'd been planning to talk to you about tonight. If I had any idea you felt overlooked, I would have put it in place long before this, but what with one thing and another . . ." His head swung sadly from side to side. "And all this while, you've been blaming yourself that you haven't gotten the promotion you deserve, letting it hurt your marriage . . ."

Barnett did not finish the sentence. He was thinking. Shielding Greg from responsibility—and from failure—had become a greater risk to Barnett's priorities than giving it to him. Greg would have to be cut loose to fend for himself. He was certainly bright and capable, but how bright and how capable were mysteries because, as Greg himself had pointed out, he had never been entrusted with a job carrying enough responsibility to test his talents.

Barnett mentally leafed through some departments that were important, but not critical to the company's success, departments that could be aggregated into one division under Greg in some rational way. The Finance vice president was nearing retirement. Moving Greg into his slot and adding the company's administrative operations to the financial ones under him would make some sense. The Broadcast Division would stay under Carver, who had recently been moved up to repair its problems, principally to develop better programming. All the rest of the company, including Publishing, Records, and the other nonbroadcast operations, could be consolidated under Bill Jorgenson, who ran most of that anyway. The logical assumption would be, Barnett was sure, that the three were candidates to be his successor; and their performance would decide the winner. The plan made operational sense and would placate the directors. Barnett did not concern himself with the many executives who would be angered or disheartened when Greg was jumped over them.

"Greg, I'm dividing the company into three groups and naming three group presidents. Just three. The three most capable men in the company. You're sure as hell one of them. I want you as my head of Finance and Administration, reporting directly to me. The salary would be four hundred thousand dollars a year." He listed the departments in Greg's new group.

Greg was flabbergasted. Until seconds before he had been nearly superfluous.

"Say you'll take it," Barnett implored him. "These are difficult times for FBS. You're a man I can count on."

"I had no idea."

Barnett appeared astonished. "But you had my solemn word."

He sat back. "Now that that's out of the way, it seems to me that you and Diane should be able to smooth out those bumps in your marriage."

"I'd like to," Greg answered honestly, his mind's eye filled by the heaping platter Barnett had just set down before him.

"Good."

Barnett went to the door. "Diane!" he called out.

Putting an arm around his daughter when she appeared and winking at Greg, he said to her, "Diane, honey, would you please help me convince this stubborn husband of yours to take the group presidency I'm offering him? He's quite a man you married."

Stew Graushner had spent his life waiting for catastrophes to batter him. For the most part he had been pleasantly surprised by their absence—until this year. God had simply been waiting until this year, he lamented, to ambush him, suddenly sending an avalanche of misfortunes careering downhill at him one right after another, as if Stew were a video-game victim.

He had departed KFBS soon after Chris, not wanting to be around when the ratings dropped. Burned out, he had left TV news to pursue his dream of teaching and writing. A local university had welcomed him.

154

Half his teaching schedule comprised courses in broadcast journalism, the other half creative writing courses in a two-man department. His pipe and elbow-patched tweed jackets finally felt appropriate, despite the southern-California warmth. His salary was drastically reduced in academia, but the university did not charge his wife, Patty, the cost of tuition for her four years of college and her subsequent three years at the law school.

By this spring he had finally felt optimistic about matters. His teaching career seemed to be going well, even tenure was a possibility; and Patty was now firmly established in a law practice. All their sacrifices now seemed worthwhile.

One night Stew brought home flowers and announced to her that he thought the two of them should consider a second honeymoon, maybe the trip to Europe they had never been able to take. Patty told him she didn't think that was a good idea because she had decided to divorce him.

She drew from her briefcase the separation agreement she had drawn up. She would get the house, where she and their daughter, Wendy, would continue to live. What little was in the bank would be hers as well, in lieu of child support. He would be responsible for Wendy's college tuition, though that was not really a problem because she would be attending his university and tuition for her would be free.

Bewildered, hurt, not wanting to stay where he wasn't wanted, Stew signed the document and left with his personal possessions. He stowed them in the old Dodge's trunk and drove off to a motel.

Next morning, as he was walking among the university's buildings toward his classroom, the head of their two-man Creative Writing Department approached him with more bad news. The department's budget had been cut back and one man would have to be let go.

"Nothing personal," the other man sympathized, "but since I'm the one who gets to choose, you're the one who leaves. And since the Journalism Department also has to cut someone, we kill two birds with one stone. Firing you works out quite neatly, don't you agree?"

Stew Graushner stared up at the mocking, malevolent heavens and trudged on, refusing to be beaten down. Still employed through summer school, he would use his time to start writing that novel. By the fall he would have enough chapters to find a publisher. He would rise again.

He spent most of the summer session trying unsuccessfully both to find a teaching job for the fall and to make headway on a novel. After weeks of staring at his typewriter, he began to bang out something he knew was superficial and that bored even him. If he had been grading the work, he would have given it maybe a C—for effort and clean

155

typing. Much of newswriting is collegial, one person bouncing words and ideas off another. He found that he hated writing alone and was awful at it.

His energy and attention drained quickly. He was always going out for ice cream. He gained ten pounds and had no novel to sell.

He began looking for work in television news. He had been out of the industry for seven years. Potential employers regarded him as an academician. They wanted hard-nosed, rolled-up-shirtsleeves-style newsmen, not bearded professors who theorized about TV news. Or *would* have wanted such people if budgets were not being cut in every newsroom in America.

By September he was desperate, as low as he thought possible without a terminal disease. He was broke, borrowed up to his nostrils, his rent overdue, and had no prospects. He decided God was holding back on a terminal disease only out of spite—because a hospital would then have to take him in as a charity case and put a roof over his head for free. He thought things could not possibly get any worse.

But then the phone call came from his wife. She was furious. Their daughter had not been allowed to register at the university because he had failed to pay the tuition.

Oh, no! He had lost the right to free tuition as soon as he finished teaching his last class.

With great trepidation, Stew dragged himself back to the campus and into the Bursar's Office. The woman in charge had always disliked him, and now he would have to rely on her dubious mercy. She was a burly woman, with a mole on her chin that had three hairs growing from it. He imagined a mole like that to be the last sight the children baked into gingerbread had before the oven door closed on them.

As he had expected, the terms were harsh: fifteen hundred dollars by the end of the day and two thousand more in a month. He almost looked down at his hands as he left her office to see if they had turned into gingerbread.

He drove the Dodge to a used-car lot and sold it for twenty-one hundred dollars. That left him six hundred. By sneaking out of his apartment late tonight without paying his rent, he might be able to stretch that until October. Of course, without a car, he would have to carry his belongings in suitcases and shopping bags.

He walked the two miles back to the Bursar's Office, paid her the fifteen hundred, and began walking across town to his apartment. He tried to look at the positive side. This was God's way of slimming him back down.

*   *   *

That same week FBS's much-vaunted new prime-time lineup premiered. It soon proved to be an even greater flop than the previous season's. Leery of FBS's new shows from the start, advertisers had done far less upfront buying than usual the previous spring. The company had hoped higher ratings would raise prices for the unsold or available scatter spots, the "avails." But with audience size way below what FBS had guaranteed the advertisers, free make-good commercials threatened to absorb much of the inventory of avails. The company faced the prospect of staggering losses in the coming year.

The final blow came in October when Barnett Roderick was felled by a heart attack and rushed to the hospital.

By chance Diane was in the children's ward. She rushed to Intensive Care. Near hysteria, she insisted all of the hospital's top cardiologists convene at the bedside—and even called in two associated with other hospitals for their opinions. She refused to leave her father's side, ferociously interrogating every doctor and nurse before she would allow a procedure to be performed.

"What would I do without you?" she kept muttering to him.

By morning his condition had stabilized, and it was clear he would pull through. A full recovery would take many months, however. Barnett knew he would have to pick someone to replace him as FBS's chief executive officer. He could remain chairman of the board and would doubtless continue to control it, but that post was largely ceremonial, simply the director who chaired the meetings. FBS's situation was too critical for the company to be without a CEO at such a dangerous time. Jorgenson knew every inch of the company and had a good mind, but he was over sixty and his energy was now suspect. That left Ev Carver and Greg.

Ev was the logical choice. He had a record of success, was the most experienced, and already possessed the most authority as head of all broadcast activities, which included the TV and radio networks and the owned stations. The stations, which had long been under his supervision, were far and away the most profitable part of the company. However, although perhaps not a fair test, the new programming developed this first year under his aegis had not set the world on fire.

Greg had shown to advantage in the short time since the reorganization, although the company's most important business determinations were being made in the other two divisions. He could be shrewd and pragmatic. The mystery was what he possessed beneath those qualities. Was he tough enough to make the hard decisions that faced the man at the top? Did he have the judgement and intuition to pick the new shows that would propel the network back upward in the ratings and to revamp operations in ways that would cut costs without harming efficiency? Greg had held a lot of midlevel posts that were affected by the programming and scheduling decisions others made, but he himself had never developed new programs or scheduled their placement in the lineup.

Yet Barnett's doubts were balanced by one intangible that only he would have valued or even sensed: Only Greg among the three understood that FBS had been the leader in broadcasting because it stood for something worthwhile that had since leaked out of television. What finally swayed Barnett to Greg, however, was his belief that even while recuperating, he could trust Greg to defer to his counsel and not to try to oust him; Barnett had every confidence his son-in-law could be controlled.

Even so, Barnett wanted experienced people under Greg and a fall back position. Although reporting now to Greg, Ev Carver would remain in place as head of his group and Jorgenson would stay in his slot as well. In case Greg failed, Ev could then replace him.

During Greg's visit to the hospital two days later, Barnett asked to see him alone. Greg assumed he wanted to be briefed on news from the office and started to fill him in.

Barnett interrupted. He took a deep breath, summoning his strength. "What I'm about to tell you is absolutely confidential. I'm resigning as FBS's chief executive. I intend to call an emergency directors meeting and name you in my place."

Greg was stunned. He had expected Barnett to make some kind of move, but kept away from real authority for so long he had been reluctant to anticipate being chosen. He had no enemies at FBS, but no zealous supporters either. Everyone liked him, but he knew that over the years the impression had arisen that little substance lay beneath the handsome facade, little accomplishment was produced by all that show of energy; he seemed to be a man who slid between the raindrops, never getting wet, who left no footprints.

When he finally replied, it was to say confidently, "I appreciate your belief in me. I'll try my best to justify it."

"Your best not only better be good, it better be fast. I figure you have a year to turn the company around—before the board or some raider takes it out of your hands."

"That's impossible. You know that." A year was an instant in broadcasting, a star's twinkle, hardly any time at all. It would take at least two or three years to put the company solidly into contention for the top spot.

"You might be able to stop the hemorrhaging in a year. If you can't, we might not get any more time."

"Look, it's possible," Greg conceded. "But even that would require a miracle."

The Chairman did not disagree.

Greg would have taken this job no matter how great the odds against him. The one advantage the crisis gave him, he reasoned, was the leverage to drive a hard bargain.

"There are a couple of things we have to talk about first."

The six-hundred-thousand-dollar annual salary Barnett offered was high enough, but Greg was more concerned about what he would gain if he met that one-year deadline and made the company profitable again with his operational changes and his own lineup of shows next fall. The two men agreed that in that instance, Greg would receive a large block of FBS stock, a five-year contract at two million dollars a year in salary, and additional bonuses and stock options based on profits each year.

Barnett's sole stipulation was that Carver and Jorgenson be kept in place for the first year. Greg sensed the older man's subconscious need to keep from him the last slice of the absolute power he had wielded for four decades. Yet, the demand was perfectly reasonable given Greg's relative inexperience.

"One thing, though," Greg declared. "I need a free hand to make changes in their operations and the final say over anything that's going out over the air."

Barnett nodded. "It will be your ball game to win or lose."

Barnett believed he had now fully redeemed the pledge given Greg some eight years before. He had relinquished to him command over one of the two things in the world he loved most.

But the happiness of the other was still in question: From what he could tell, Greg and Diane's marriage still remained shaky. Barnett considered an unwritten condition of the upcoming contract to be that Greg keep his own pledge that had been made in exchange for Barnett's all those years ago. Barnett knew how spoiled and difficult his daughter could be. He knew, too, that Greg had a tendency to withdraw mentally from situations he disliked, presenting an unreadable facade that concealed his departure and could make reconciliation difficult.

"I want your word," he said, "that you'll commit yourself as fully and faithfully to rebuilding your marriage as you will to rebuilding FBS."

Greg displayed no hesitancy. "You have it."

Barnett lay back on the hospital pillow. As he had on that earlier day, he now felt content. Greg's fidelity had been purchased on every front.

A company director to whom Ev Carver was close confidentially informed him that the directors would secretly be meeting to choose a new CEO. Ev was the logical choice to replace Barnett. His only gray mark was the discouraging prime-time ratings.

Ev's political instincts told him that he had to take action right away to appear decisive in meeting the programming crisis. He phoned Raoul Clampton, the head of the Programming Department. Because of the man's experience and allegiance, Ev decided to retain him. He would insist, though, on changes in the department he could immediately announce.

"Clampton," he declared, dispensing with preliminaries, "we're shuffling the deck in your department. Some heads have to roll. Ax whoever was in charge of new comedies and dramas. Give me two new names. I want this press release out by eleven."

Clampton, relieved that he was being spared in the bloodbath, thought quickly about whom to promote. "Hank Newton for dramas. Marian Marcus for comedies."

"A woman. That's good. We need to show one or two."

Ev paused to appraise the two names he had written down. "This doesn't look decisive enough. Give me more names. Ax miniseries, too." He listened for a moment. "I don't give a fuck if he's only been there a month. Fire the putz."

Barnett Roderick insisted on returning home from the hospital after his heart attack earlier than his doctors would have liked. He wanted to reassure the directors by holding the secret meeting at his apartment. No need for undue alarm or for us to get involved, he wanted them to think; the old man is still strong and in control. Just elect his new CEO and leave things to them.

Greg was the first to arrive and found Barnett awaiting him in the living room. The chief executive had set the stage carefully: the soft lighting to reduce his pallor, the famous Matisse behind him, the tall chair to support a back that otherwise might slump from fatigue. Barnett's expression was pensive.

"I never thought a day like this would ever come," he said.

"Just go on and on. Never retire and never die?"

"Seems a bit foolish when you put it that way. It just never crossed my mind."

Barnett's gaze focused sharply on Greg. "One thing I've always wanted to know. Did you have all this planned right from the beginning? Taking over for me like this? I could never be sure."

Greg did not reply.

As expected, the directors ratified Barnett's choice and voted unanimously to name Greg the company's chief executive officer and to confirm his one-year contract, which was to be kept confidential except for major financial terms that the law required be publicly disclosed. Attached to it was the bountiful five-year contract that would come into existence on the sole condition that Greg rescue the drowning company from the depths of red ink in one year. The unspoken question on all the directors' minds was whether he was up to the job or had been selected by his father-in-law out of nepotism.

Greg stayed behind to thank Barnett after the directors left. He assumed that was expected of him, but it was something he wanted to do. In their strange relationship, more than employer and employee, but less than relatives, tides of respect and concession warily ebbed and flowed between them in rhythm with the power each possessed over the other at a particular moment. Yet, behind the self each chose to present, they were unknown to each other, opposing forces barely glimpsed along a battlefront, the main body hidden behind trenches and barbed wire and artillery.

The Barnett Greg encountered after the nurse had helped her patient into bed was a tired and shrunken relic of the patriarch who had ruled the meeting.

"I wanted to thank you and to make sure you were all right," Greg told him.

"I'll get used to it." Barnett let his gaze wander up to the ceiling. "I've always wondered about those old, scarred lions you see on the African plains who've been beaten out by younger males. Sometimes they have a fresh wound that's not healing too well from an animal they've grown too slow or weak to kill cleanly. Life has to be harder for them than for others because they remember what it used to be like. Now all they have ahead of them is to shamble on toward death."

There was a knock on the open door, and Diane entered, her forehead bunched with worry for her father. "Are you all right?" she asked him.

He nodded. "Greg is now CEO."

Greg thought he descried in her brief glance at him the enmity accorded a usurper. And perhaps confusion, too, not knowing what feelings were appropriate toward each man, what could be said. The circumstance of Greg's accession was not a happy one.

161

"Are you going to be here all day?" Greg asked.

She nodded.

"We're having dinner at the Blakes," he reminded her.

"If Dad's all right."

"He'll be fine," Greg said firmly. "Tom Blake's a director and his bank is essential to us. I'll be here to pick you up at six."

Within minutes after the directors meeting ended, the Communications Department released the secretly prepared proclamation that a new CEO had been named. Within minutes it had started dropping into in-boxes and was being faxed along phone wires.

Greg had also placed a phone call, and Carver and Jorgenson were waiting for him in his new corner office when he arrived.

"This company is in a perilous condition," he began. "One way or another, I'm going to turn it around. I won't have time to stand on ceremony or attend a lot of committee meetings or always go through the proper channels. If something needs to be changed, I'll charge right in and change it. Costs are going to be cut, deadwood will be chopped off, new ideas and procedures will be introduced, and most important, new shows will be developed."

Saving money would not be enough, Greg knew. The network desperately needed some hit prime-time shows. A top half-hour sitcom could earn $3.2 million for the network's four minutes of commercial time—four hundred thousand dollars for every thirty-second commercial. Over the course of a year that hit could be worth fifty to a hundred million dollars more a year than a flop. The prime-time schedule contained forty-four half hours—or twenty-two hours—of programming a week. FBS was lagging behind in nearly all of them.

"I intend by next fall to have this company back on the road to health," Greg concluded. "If either of you disagree, I'll be glad to accept your resignation and offer a generous severance package."

He had studied the men while he was speaking. Bill Jorgenson, heavyset and over sixty, seemed to have overcome the shock of seeing his former trainee become his boss and knowing that with only a few years left until retirement, he had lost forever the race he had run all his life. His calculated jocularity would take a while to resurface. Now he was nodding his head vigorously.

"I'm with you all the way, Greg," he said.

Greg turned to Ev. By all rights the man should have been nervous. No love had ever been lost between them. On the contrary, since the earliest days each had recognized in the other a potential rival. Ev should have been expecting now to be fired, replaced by a man loyal to Greg. Greg had hoped Ev would construe the severance offer as a

162

graceful means of exit from an untenable position and choose to leave. But Ev seemed to exude a kind of smug patience.

"I guess if the directors thought it was important for us to stay on," Ev declared, "then we should."

Ev had somehow learned of his one-year protection under the confidential terms of Greg's contract. All he had to do was wait for Greg to fall, perhaps after an unseen push to send him tumbling.

Greg smiled, as if the decision to retain both men had been his. "I'm delighted. I couldn't want better men alongside me. Now, let's get to work. Next year's budget has got to be cut by fifteen percent, and I want to reorganize a lot of our operations. We'll do a lot of this as we go along, but I'm moving Hurley up to my old job as head of the Finance and Administration Group. This afternoon he and I will put together a rough reorganization plan to cut costs and streamline operations. His Budget people will work with you and your departments to implement it. I'm calling a senior staff meeting tomorrow afternoon to give a pep talk to FBS officers, but also to let them know they can expect changes. Over the next week I'll meet *alone* with every department head and their key people to examine their operations."

Part of Greg's reorganization would be to unpry Ev's fingers from around the company's throat. The man had placed loyal subordinates in critical executive positions throughout the company and spies elsewhere. His followers were mostly employees who were set in their ways, fearful of change, who often sought to climb upward by dint of an abject obedience that could substitute for competence. Greg wanted people who were committed to the company's rebirth and to his own vision of its future.

He nodded and both men rose. Ev hung behind as Jorgenson departed, a wickedly sly smile widening across his face.

"I guess, like they say, Lyall, blood can be thicker than talent. One thing though, you can't hide anymore."

Greg's own smile emerged. "Ev, there isn't any *need* for me to hide anymore."

Just before six, Greg picked up Diane at her father's apartment. Barnett was asleep.

When they were walking up Fifth to their own apartment, Diane spoke. "I'm proud he picked you, Greg." Until now she had not congratulated him. "But it feels strange that you're getting ahead because he's sick."

"I understand."

"Do you? I never wanted this for you, you know. I never wanted to share you."

"It's what I *always* wanted."

She glanced sharply at him, but refrained from probing more deeply.

They did not leave for the Blakes until after Ray Strock, FBS's longtime anchorman, briefly reported on the network news that Greg had been named to head the company.

"He sounds like he's announcing my death," Greg remarked with displeasure at the slow, deep-voiced delivery.

"Dad always liked that sense of dignity. He personally picked Strock for the job."

"A lot of his generation like Strock. But we've lost the younger viewers. He's dragging us down."

Diane grew concerned. "I don't think Dad's strong enough for you to discuss it with him right now."

"I don't intend to."

Greg was in a jubilant mood at the dinner party, accepting the others' good wishes on his new post. He noticed the heightened respect even in something so small as their facing him directly now when they spoke and having to turn to include Diane.

He was eager to make love to Diane that night and to demonstrate his eagerness to rebuild their marriage, as he had promised Barnett. She could not partake emotionally, but was glad that he seemed satisfied.

Greg lay awake a long while afterward rethinking the day's events and planning tomorrow's. He had wanted this promotion, this opportunity, this authority, for so long that only now did it strike him fully how difficult the job would be. This was his time in the spotlight at last, his time at the controls, with everyone watching enviously.

Greg's few career successes so far seemed so puny—nothing of a magnitude that would justify naming him CEO. Nearly a decade before, he had lifted a local news show from third to second in the ratings and sold some daytime spots for more than expected; and a few months ago, he had arranged an advantageous loan to pay production costs during pilot season. Hunger for success, self-confidence, the adoption of a sleek facade, might all indicate ambition, but certainly not capability.

What if his confidence was fatuous self-delusion? he wondered. Probably half the loony bins in the Western world contained a fully convinced messiah. Was his self-image any more realistic? Barnett had probably chosen him in the hope of retaining some control, not because he thought Greg the most qualified candidate.

If Greg did fail—and the chances were great that he would—what kind of life would be left to him: continuing to hope for his father-in-law's charity, anxious servility to placate his wife's contempt, always fearful that she might abandon him without money or hope? He had sacrificed so much to get his dearest wish, and now it might be about to topple and crush him beneath it.

Greg hadn't prayed since childhood and didn't now, but he remembered again why people did.

Book Three

NETWORK NEWS

OCTOBER 1989

11

～～～～～～～～～

C hris had just slammed the door on Ron Skink, the morning
show's producer, and spoken to her agent, Carl Green, about
the unexpected phone call and offer from Greg. She needed to
talk it over with her closest friend, Marian Marcus.

She stared at the clock. Nine-fifteen in the morning in New York, it
was only six-fifteen in California. The two women had spoken for over
an hour the night before, mostly about Marian's recent promotion to
director of Comedy Series Development. Marian would probably be up
exercising before going to work. Chris decided to chance making the
call.

"Guess who just phoned me?" Chris began as soon as the other voice
answered with a husky vibrancy that indicated she was already awake.

Marian was on her exercise bike; having lost twenty pounds the year
before and being terrified of regaining it, she had become a fanatic about
fitness.

"Who phoned you?" Marian repeated. "Let's see. I know, Jack
Kennedy. Had to be collect. You ought to trace it. There's a story
there."

"Be serious."

"Yasir Arafat wants to go on your show to plug his new deal with
Gillette. With every razor, the company will give away a free dinner
napkin to wear on your head."

"Someone in my life you're not going to believe."

"Greg Lyall."

"You've got a good memory."

"He's the only person in your life I wouldn't believe. He wants to hire
you?"

Chris indicated that he did, as nightly news anchor.

"He's moving fast," Marian observed.

169

"What do you think?"

"For him it's a smart move, smarter than most people here give him credit for. You'll hypo the news ratings and draw younger demographics."

"And for me?"

"Anchor is the glamor job in TV news. We both know that. And you're not happy where you are. But if you're asking me whether you should work for Greg Lyall, I can't help you. I've never even met him. All I know is the scuttlebutt around the network."

"Which is?"

"That he's never done much. I hope you don't mind my putting it this way," Marian said, chuckling, "but what he seems to be best at is being a son-in-law."

"He's smart. I can tell you that. And you can't trust him farther than you can throw a safe."

"Perfect credentials for success in television. Chris, I'd love for us to be working at the same network, but you sound very negative."

"I don't want that man within ten blocks of me." Chris paused to consider. "If it were anything but anchor . . ." She left the last word hanging in the air as well as in her own mind.

The conversation quickly ended. A little while later Carl Green called Chris back to confirm a private dinner at his apartment tonight with Greg Lyall. He had wanted to meet the man alone, but Lyall had insisted she be there.

Marian spent half an hour doing aerobics to a videotape and then some calisthenics before dashing through the shower, running a brush through her hair and a swipe of lipstick across her mouth. She grabbed a comfortable blouse and slacks and was out of her house and into her car on the way to work by seven-thirty. She might be older and slimmer now, but she was almost as heedless of her tall, slouching appearance as she had been at school.

Marian waved at the guard and guided her car into the basement garage in the tower at the FBS Television Studios, the company's several-acre complex. As always, she was sure the guard would not remember her and would ask for her ID. It was almost as if the size of her presence in her own mind had diminished with her girth.

Marian had held half a dozen jobs as she gained experience in Programming. Her rise in the department had come about, she knew, because she did not threaten her boss, Raoul Clampton. Her deferential manner, the mousiness of her looks despite her imposing height, her almost nonexistent social life, which allowed for long hours at her job, and her swiftness at reading the pile of scripts she took home each night all reassured him of her loyalty.

Survival in the Programming Department, she had early learned, depended on not standing out. She saw how others there had mastered the art of saying no to innovative projects. Saying yes put one out on a limb, exposed one to blame for their failure. Because so many more shows failed than succeeded, it was far safer to say no to innovation and to choose shows that copied the formats of previously successful shows. Marian hated that self-serving technique. No wonder so many shows failed. The concepts were tired and the viewers bored.

Programming's corridors were still dark when she entered her office. Two proposals for series that she had found intriguing and passed on to Clampton were back on her desk, doubtless dropped there late last night by his secretary. She recognized Clampton's red-ink scribble on the note clipped atop them. "Rejected." No reason for the rejection. Raoul Clampton was not the sort of man who left himself at risk by putting his reasons into writing. If the show proved successful at a different network, the wrong reason for rejection at FBS might prove embarrassing.

Marian's chin sunk onto the backs of her interlocked hands lying flat on her desk. She stared at the rejected proposals a couple of inches in front of her. Despite the lesson that should have been learned from this season's disastrous failure, the company seemed once again headed down the same old road that led over the same old bluff. Marian felt helpless. She had been trying for years with her well-practiced tactfulness to point out better routes, but the guy driving the bus still refused to listen.

Greg charged through his first day as CEO, aware that all those who caught the merest glimpse of him would be evaluating even that small snatch of performance against their skepticism. He had looked forward to the senior staff meeting as a kind of formal coronation in front of those who had ignored and undervalued him after the private investiture by the directors.

But as he stood peering at the sea of dark suits—few women had managed to penetrate television's upper management—he realized how ordinary was the kernel of self he had always believed distinguished him. Those watching him were also ambitious, had also sacrificed and struggled to reach the top, and hated him for having been handed the ultimate post they themselves coveted. Unless Greg demonstrated true achievement by steering the company back to profitability, his promotion would turn out to be as undeserved and nepotistic as all of them believed it to be.

Greg spoke well, trying to evoke a sense of team spirit in his listeners, but he could sense their fear. The word was already out that he was planning to cut staff.

The upcoming meeting with Chris remained on his mind all day, like the start of a long-delayed trial. A truce, however uneasy, would first have to be called between them if he was to have any chance of inducing her to consider his proposal. He had put several people to the task of contacting associates at Chris's network to learn clandestinely the exact status of her negotiations.

Almost as ticklish as making the original phone call had been the question of where to meet with her. A restaurant was too visible for a network head and a well-known newscaster; her own network could hear about it and would immediately pull out all the stops to sign her. Besides, there was something too friendly, too reminiscent of old times, about getting together at a restaurant; it was sure to alienate her. His office was neutral and businesslike, but she might be spotted entering the building. Her home would have been awkward and suggesting it an imposition. His, out of the question. Her agent, who sounded unacquainted with the couple's past history, had inadvertently solved the problem by inviting Chris and Greg to his apartment for dinner.

Chris was just zipping up the black silk dress she had chosen to wear when her husband arrived home. The Senate had adjourned earlier than usual for the weekend, and he had jumped on the first shuttle back to New York, hoping they could have a quiet dinner.

"I would much rather be with you," she told him frankly as they kissed hello, "but I have to go to Carl's. A meeting with a network head who wants me to anchor their nightly news."

She was already turning back to the mirror and did not notice the concern that appeared for an instant on his brow. He tried to brighten for her sake.

"That sounds like what you've been looking for."

She frowned as she looped the belt about her waist.

"Unhappy with the dress or with the meeting?" he asked.

"The dress is fine."

"What network is it?"

"FBS."

"Barnett Roderick just had a heart attack," he remembered. "I had my secretary send him a get-well letter."

"This is the man taking over for him, Greg Lyall."

Chris waited for Ken to ask more about him, but perhaps because he did not recognize the name, he thought she did not know him either.

172

Only Marian was aware of her affair with Greg, which had long been over before she met Ken. She could have told him, of course—she could tell him anything, she knew, and he would still love her—but there had been no need. Both of them acted on the premise that their lives started fresh and anew and unhindered on the day they met.

Ken was studying her. "You aren't happy that it's FBS."

"Not very. Its news operation isn't very good, and the ratings are abysmal. I'd start with a lot going against me."

"It would be nice to wake up next to you in the morning again and have breakfast together and be able to stay out till a normal hour at night." He hid his own concerns.

She smiled back at his reflection in the mirror. "And not have me fall asleep over dinner. That would be lovely."

She took a last glance at herself. Like many women born beautiful, she was innately confident about her appearance and did not usually fuss much over it. Now, however, nothing seemed quite right. Giving up, she reached down for her handbag and turned around to kiss her husband good-bye.

He flashed a smile that expressed the love and admiration he felt for her. "I'm sure you'll knock this Lyall guy dead."

"I'm sorry he ever called."

Ken lifted her chin to meet his lips. "I think you're worrying needlessly. He's giving you exactly what you always wanted."

"Is he?" she mused. "That sounds like something you find in a fortune cookie: 'Beware of getting your heart's desire.'"

As an agent for many of the highest-paid newscasters and producers in their contract negotiations, Carl Green had been a pivotal figure in the eighties' escalation of salaries for TV newspeople. Network anchors like Tom Brokaw commanded upward of two million dollars a year, and Diane Sawyer and Connie Chung had switched networks for more than a million and a half. A wiry, driven man, proud of the luxuries his success had brought him, he spent nearly as much time trying to relieve his clients' anxieties as he did negotiating for them. Although he had not let on to Chris, unable to develop any leverage on his side of their network negotiations, during recent weeks he had become the one who was anxious.

Carl's sense of an adversary's strength was tuned like a fine instrument. Chris's network needed her drawing power for its morning show, "Starting the Day." Yet, as time passed with no concessions from the president of its News Division, he became increasingly certain that the accounting types who now ran her network believed they could sit tight and make the deal on their terms. He had put out feelers at all the other networks, trying to spur competition for her talents. All had been eager to hire her, but not in the slots she wanted, where their own high-priced newscasters with long-term contracts were already firmly ensconced. The problem was that the heads of her own network knew it. Despite her eagerness to leave "Starting the Day," they were sure Chris would have to re-sign with them and at the salary they dictated.

The phone call from Greg Lyall had been "like seeing a goddamn desert bush burst into flames, a miracle," Carl recounted to his agency colleagues in a conflicted, but vivid simile. "Now, we can get some competition going here. She'd be crazy to go to FBS, as weak as its ratings are, but her network will have to play ball in our court now. Have any of you ever dealt with this guy?" he asked.

None had.

"I was introduced to him once," Carl recalled. "Just a hello. Hardly remember him—I was trying to get Roderick alone to make a pitch." He pondered for a moment. "The way I see it, we've got a real amateur here. Dumb son-in-law who doesn't know dipshit about news or much of anything else, but who's just been put in charge of the candy store. He's a patsy. How does three million a year sound?"

By the time seven o'clock came around, the number glittered in his mind in rainbow hues. He had advised Chris to be late, to keep this Greg Lyall off balance so that he himself could make a hard pitch without her there, but she arrived punctually.

He seated her in the living room and began to outline his strategy for the meeting when the doorbell rang.

"Just let me do the talking," he cautioned Chris. He sensed she was reluctant to go through with this meeting, but didn't know why.

Greg entered to find Chris sitting in the large armchair in front of the mantel. She was wearing a black silk dress. A single strand of pearls dipped a couple of inches below her neckline. Her blond hair was shorter than in 1981. He halted in the archway. Having seen her innumerable times on television since then—and thought about her far more often—he should not have been surprised by anything about her appearance, but he was.

"You look beautiful," he said almost involuntarily.

Chris's mouth tightened in anger. She stood up. "This meeting was a big mistake. I figured you could keep it on a mature, businesslike level, but I should have known better." She turned to Carl. "That's it. Please get me my coat."

"Oh, Jesus," Carl moaned under his breath. For some unknown reason this meeting had spun out of his control and was about to crash before it had begun.

"Chris, honey," he said soothingly, "why don't you just sit down and we'll have drinks and we'll make a little small talk? Get to know each other."

He flashed a warning glance at her. She had to understand how important this meeting was. Even if this guy was Adolf Hitler, they needed some kind of an offer from him to be able to get her own network to up the ante.

Unmollified, Chris resumed her seat. The maid entered with a tray of drinks, and Carl engaged Greg in a conversation about FBS and its prospects.

By the time they went into dinner, Chris had regained control of her temper, but she had not spoken. She had resolved to treat Greg like any other television executive with whom she might deal, but he had immediately tried to vault the business barrier and win her over by resorting to what he must mistakenly have assumed was the attraction she still harbored for him. Devious. Totally lacking in character. His behavior confirmed the ruthlessness he had demonstrated when he left her. She had agreed to hear him out, but there was no way she would work for that bastard.

The small talk continued as they ate. Greg remarked favorably on both the salmon-mousse appetizer and the veal-tournedo main dish. Carl was pleased that an elegant society guy like Greg Lyall was impressed—it was worth every penny the cook was costing him.

"Chris said you offered her the anchor job. Ray Strock is an institution at FBS."

"That's my problem," Greg pointed out.

"You're talking sole anchor here, right? No co-, no partner."

Greg nodded.

Carl relaxed; he had the ball now, no question about it. "Well, Chris is very happy where she is. We're maybe this close to signing a new contract with them." He held up a thumb and forefinger a millimeter apart. "It would take a huge megadeal for her to consider leaving a place where she's so happy."

Greg's gaze swung to Chris. "I told you on the phone that you'd be our star, not only our anchor for the nightly news, but for every important event and crisis, the personification of news at FBS. You'll be our symbol to the nation, the person they think of when they think of FBS."

Carl was astonished at Greg's openness—no jabbing or weaving; the guy's chin was wide open. "I hope you're prepared to pay what a great talent like Chris is worth, what it's going to take to win the bidding with the other networks who are after her."

Greg's eyes were still on Chris. He wanted her to believe his sincerity. "I'm making one offer. It's what the job is worth. No bargaining. Do you want me to spell it out here or wait until I'm alone with Carl?"

He knew Chris was too straightforward and her curiosity too great for her to wait.

"How much?" she asked.

"Chris," Carl interceded, "this is just a get-acquainted meeting."

She nodded at Greg for an answer.

"Two million dollars a year," he said. His intelligence report had been extensive and specific. "That's twice as much as you're making now. I want a ten-year contract."

Chris did not react.

"That's almost insulting," Carl declared. "It's ridiculous. We're not prepared to even start the conversation at less than three and a half million dollars a year. And we've never given more than two years."

"We'll need ten. You know the other networks get it for an anchor. We all want to be sure that our figurehead doesn't run off somewhere else with our audience. It works to your advantage, too. Chris gets security."

Carl tried a different approach. "She may turn out to be so unhappy at FBS that she'll want out after five years. She should have that right."

Greg glanced at Carl. "So you can hold us up for more money in five years? Let's confine our conversation to this particular galaxy. Ten years with a cost-of-living increase based on the CPI after five. The network she's at right now is holding firm at a million, and she hates doing 'Starting the Day.' FBS is the only network prepared to give her the one job she's wanted all her life. She'd take it at the same salary she's getting now, and I'm offering twice that."

"You're insufferable!" Chris suddenly declared, her eyes blazing.

"Now, Chris—" Carl interjected. It was beginning to dawn on him that for his client and Greg Lyall this might not be a get-acquainted meeting after all.

"What part's insufferable?" Greg asked her. "The two million dollars a year or that it's the job you want?"

"That you seem so smugly sure I'll jump at the chance to become FBS's anchor and work for you."

No matter how sincerely Chris might deny her desire for the spotlight and ascribe her motivation to wanting to make a difference, wanting to be heard, Greg knew intimately how powerful, if unacknowledged, was her ambition for fame and prominence. It had already propelled her to immense renown. He was proposing to lift her even higher, to the pinnacle of journalistic stardom.

"Chris, this job has always been your dream, to be the most powerful newscaster at a major network and bring the truth to people. I'm offering it to you."

Her face was a thunderhead. "You son of a bitch! You crawled and kissed ass and betrayed whatever is decent and fine between two people, and now that it has finally paid off for you, here you are trying to buy me, too."

"Let's not make this personal. I'm here because you're a great broadcast journalist, and FBS needs what you can bring it."

"That's really the point, isn't it?" Carl said to her, confused by the byplay, but frantic for her to concentrate on the chance being offered. She ignored him.

"I know you too well, Greg," she declared hotly. "Oh, do I know you! I would want everything spelled out in the contract, especially how much control I'd have to pick stories and the people working with me."

"Within reason you'll have all the control you'll ever want," Greg promised. "Chris, I want to remake FBS's nightly news program from top to bottom. The kind of news broadcast we always hoped we could create but never had the clout to. Now we do."

Chris was still ablaze. "I don't intend to take a job where I'm going to have to knuckle under to some nincompoop psycho of an executive producer."

Greg smiled slightly. "Like Ron Skink? Your network has belittled you and undervalued you. I know how good you are. I want to give you the prominence and the opportunity you deserve."

"She has to be 'managing editor,' " Carl asserted, emboldened by Greg's remarks.

"She has it," Greg agreed. Arrangements at other networks where the anchor could dictate staffing and stories had sometimes been criticized, but Greg sensed the point would make or break the deal. "Chris, I intend to take personal responsibility for rebuilding the program. The only one who can overrule you is me."

"Oh, God!" she retorted. "I don't even want to see your face. You know what the worst part would be? Your becoming head of the network, getting all that power, all those people working for you, dependent on you, will finally justify all the wrongs you've ever done."

Greg halted. His gaze engaged hers. "You might not believe it, but this meeting isn't easy for me either. We both know I'm here because I need you. With you as our anchor, we'll pick up a lot of viewers in a hurry, especially the younger ones sponsors want. Ratings will climb. That was true every place you ever worked, and it will happen for us. But that's just a start. You're the best newscaster I know, and I want the best news program—the best news *organization*—in America. I'm up against it at FBS. We're bringing up the rear in every category there is. But whatever you might think of me, you know that I'll move heaven and earth to change that. And the only sure, long-term way is with quality." His voice softened. "Better than anyone else in the world . . . you know that what I've always wanted most is to run a network as well as I can. To be the best. That's why you should say yes to my offer. That's why you should believe me."

"I detest you, you know."

"You have every right to," he admitted. Yet, his expression was intense with excitement over what he envisioned. "FBS News—the whole damned company—has been sitting on its fat laurels for years now, while the other networks trimmed their staffs and their costs. I intend to get rid of the deadwood—anyone who doesn't measure up—and to raid the other networks for the top correspondents and writers and producers. You know who the top people are at your own shop. We'll get them for you. Chris, I promise to put the best news team in broadcasting behind you."

Chris's gaze lowered to the tablecloth. She deliberated silently for a long while, focused only on her thoughts. Carl wanted to jump into what he understood of the negotiation, but something in her concentration dissuaded him.

When she finally looked up, she said, "I want Manny Ramirez as executive producer."

"Terrific," Greg agreed. "Where is he?"

"Still with FBS," she said caustically. "Buried at your overnight news program."

"You've got him."

"Finally!" she exclaimed as she stood up. "It only took me nine years."

"What's happening?" a confused Carl asked them.

"Congratulations," Greg happily informed him. "You just made a deal. Christine Paskins is coming to FBS."

12

~~~~~~~~~~~~~~~~~~

After many years running the Buenos Aires bureau, Manny Ramirez had been repatriated, only to be exiled to FBS's bleak two-to-six-in-the-morning news program that sputtered along on few viewers and a meager budget. He knew that he and everyone else connected with it were considered expendable in this purge to cut staff. They were the outcasts, those who had not made it onto the secret A-list of favored news producers, writers, and reporters—or even onto the B-list.

Manny considered sending Greg a note when his old boss was named to head the company. But after the passage of so much time, it seemed like brownnosing, and the proud Latino decided not to. He alerted his wife to prepare for the worst and began making phone calls to friends in the industry about a new job. But having been abroad so long, he lacked the good contacts others could count on in a job search.

A few minutes before seven o'clock in the morning, Manny began to straighten up the desk one of the daytime producers would use later in the day.

"In the mood for some breakfast?" a man's voice asked him.

Everyone here knew that he went straight home after the broadcast, returning later only if he had a story to tape that day. He glanced up at the speaker to refuse the invitation. Greg Lyall stood across the desk from him.

"Breakfast sounds good," Manny said, the ends of his mustache curling upward with his smile. "Just what I was hoping for."

By noon, an FBS press statement alerted the rest of the world that Christine Paskins had switched networks and would go on the air as FBS's news anchor in two weeks, as soon as her contract expired with her present network. The News Division president at that network immediately called a press conference to declare that "Starting the Day" 's rating would not suffer because of her absence and that the firing of Ron Skink as producer had been in the works for a long while before Chris left. No one believed him. His voice was faltering, and word was already circulating that his neck was now on the chopping block.

Biff Stanfield had worked late at the nightclub and had slept only three hours before waking to get ready for his appointment. Clean-cut and black, in his midtwenties, he made his living as a comedian, and he hated it. The club, where he had a semipermanent job, was in a bad section of Los Angeles and attracted a violent crowd. What he wanted to do with his life was create and produce television shows.

He had gotten a few writing jobs on sitcoms, but a lot more writers were out there than there were series to employ them. He scrambled from show to show trying to obtain assignments. He was lucky to get one or two a year. It seemed tougher somehow for a black man to get hired as a writer. Producers who had liked the way he read his material told him he ought to do stand-up. That had infuriated Biff. The old prejudices still prevailed. Blacks were entertainers, athletes, monkeys dancing at the end of a leash, not considered smart enough to create the shows.

They were right about his knack for stand-up comedy, he found out. He did it now for the money, but he'd be damned before he'd cater to their stereotypes and demean himself by enjoying it or succeeding at it. He intended to succeed in the white man's world on his own terms. That was why he had substituted Biff Stanfield for his real name, Leroy Washington. The new name was an aggressive slap at white people's preconceptions; producers who would never see a Leroy Washington would take a meeting with the person they thought was a Biff Stanfield.

"That's right, my name is Biff Stanfield," he would explain on stage. "My folks were hoping for a blue-eyed, blond white boy . . . who could slam-dunk."

The audience invariably laughed, and the young man would be off and running. He was funny, but the humor cut with a bitterly hostile edge.

Right now, for the first time in the four years he had been trying, he had a real shot at having a network pay him to write the pilot script for a series idea he had come up with.

Nicky Willard, Biff's agent, had said he loved Biff's series idea and that he had pitched it in vain to every broadcasting and cable network, to every studio. Raoul Clampton, at FBS, had turned down Biff's project twice, so had the people at NBC.

Just recently, in what seemed to be an annual ritual bloodletting, the head of Programming at another network had been fired and replaced with Nicky's close friend, who had loved the series idea over the phone. The two men had set up a meeting with Biff for today. Nicky assured him that selling the project to his friend was a sure thing.

Now Biff was waiting in the network's reception area to meet with this new Programming chief. He had been waiting for nearly an hour. Almost as upsetting was that Nicky had not arrived to join him for the meeting. That wasn't like Nicky. He had always been punctual, always there at Biff's side to support him, a rock. Biff felt warmed by the recollection as he waited for the appointment.

Just then the elevator doors opened. For a moment Biff thought Nicky might be arriving, but two other people emerged. They seemed to be old friends who both had appointments here and had encountered each other by chance in the lobby. Biff recognized one of them: Danny Vickers. Biff had seen his photo in the trade papers, but here was the man in the flesh. Vickers was a legend, a kind of divinity to Biff. A high-school dropout, Danny Vickers had started out with nothing and produced several long-running series that made him a giant in television. The parties he gave at his Bel Air home were legendary, with champagne said to spurt from the fountain in his garden. Just seeing him renewed Biff's own hopes that a man possessing only a belief in his own talent could make it big.

"I've been looking to come up with a good action-adventure show, Arnold," Danny said to the other man. "They're buying reality this year, you know, something like 'Wiseguy.'"

The other man was Arnold Mandel, Biff realized, a film writer and producer. The trades had mentioned that he had been developing a sitcom set in a weirdly off-kilter future with goofy parallels to today's social ills.

"I've shot two pilots for them," Arnold confided to Vickers, "and they still can't make up their minds."

"I heard about your show, Arnold," Danny said. "Too outrageous. Too different. What do you expect?"

Arnold gave a Talmudic shrug. He had overcome his aversion to the rat race of weekly television because this was a project he believed in. But afraid of the controversial subject matter, network programming executives had wavered and done the prudent thing: requested changes and a new pilot. Now they continued to test the new pilot in front of focus groups and to vacillate.

Mandel and Vickers wished each other good luck and gave the receptionist their names. She immediately ushered them through the door behind her.

Even though Nicky had still not arrived, Biff took a cue from Mandel's and Vickers's boldness and stepped up to the receptionist. To his surprise Nicky's name seemed to confuse her, and she phoned inside to the offices.

"He'll see you now," she said.

That was more like it, Biff said to himself. Even without Nicky, he could handle it. Hadn't Nicky said that he pitched his own projects better than anyone? More important, hadn't Nicky told him that this new Programming guy was already crazy about the concept?

Biff straightened up his jacket and strode through the doorway into the inner portals of the network.

The secretary guarding the corner office waved him through.

A curly-haired man was seated at a desk at the far end of the large office reading some papers. He raised his head.

"What do you want?" the man said.

The man was Nicky!

"It's you! You're here!" Biff ran up to him. He was thrilled.

"They fired that no-talent S.O.B. last night and hired me."

"This is great! I can't believe it. We can do my series now."

"What series?"

"You know, *my* series, the one you've been trying to sell. That's why we had this meeting today."

Nicky tried to remember. Then when he did, he shook his head. "Not interested. A piece of shit."

"But you can't . . . That's crazy . . . You loved it!"

"That was selling. This is buying."

Nicky had a meeting scheduled elsewhere in the building. Biff chased after him into the reception area.

"Let me give you a piece of advice, kid," Nicky said, a moment before disappearing. "Don't try to sell something to a network without an agent."

Biff felt faint, unable to breathe. The receptionist directed him to the men's room. He leaned over the sink and began splashing his face with cold water.

Danny Vickers, too, was heading for the men's room. The network's programmers had just canceled the only series he had left on the air. He had been prepared to propose several ideas to juice it up: Give the detective protagonist a sexy female sidekick he'd like to boff, but she plays hard to get; bring in a new guest star every week to play that week's killer; and the old standby, add car chases. One look at the programmers' faces as he entered the room, though, and experience told Danny his show had already been pulled. The meeting was a courtesy because of his past successes for them.

Biff glanced up as Danny entered the men's room and went to the urinal. He looks sicker than I do, Biff thought.

Bad investments and several marriages had reduced Danny's net worth drastically. He had lost the Bel Air house to his last wife and was living at the beach house in Malibu. The latest calamity was the show's cancellation at a time when it was $12 million in the hole.

Because of the stars' salaries, the posh sets, and the chic costumes, the hour series was wildly expensive to shoot: $1.2 million an episode. The network was paying him only $900,000 for it. So he was losing $300,000 on each episode, which he had borrowed from a bank and counted on recouping when the show was syndicated to independent stations after its network run. But the series had just been canceled before he had enough shows to syndicate. With the expenses of his life-style and his bad luck the last few years, the $12-million loss would wipe him out.

Danny had been in trouble before and considered himself a fighter. He would just have to play games with the bank, he determined, and in the meantime, break his ass to come up with a hot new show for next season. He could just about make it to next year. But he needed a blockbuster.

"Excuse me," Biff said.

Danny looked over and froze. A *schvartzer!* he thought fearfully.

"Don't touch me!" Danny screamed. "Mike Tyson is a personal friend!"

Biff extended a hand to shake Danny's. "It's really an honor to meet you, Mr. Vickers. I'm Biff Stanfield. A writer."

"I'm a little occupied right now."

Biff was apologetic. "Oh, gee, I'm sorry. It's just that I overheard you talking about a show like 'Wiseguy,' and I've got it."

"What a lucky break for me!" Danny remarked sarcastically and turned back to the urinal. Now that he knew the *schvartzer* was some half-assed writer, he was no longer concerned about his safety. Writers were like toilet paper. You just pulled more off the roll when you needed them.

With Danny a captive audience, Biff quickly outlined his series idea. Entitled "Under Cover of Darkness," it was about a black undercover TV reporter who broke important stories by using hidden cameras and by assuming a variety of false identities: a maintenance worker, a file clerk, a telephone repairman, a butler—black menials who were virtually invisible in the white world, particularly to the rich, powerful, and corrupt. Although tempered by humor and honesty, the world depicted in the show would be dangerous, often terrifying, and peopled by harsh, unconventional characters; this was the world from which Hollywood was insulated, but which Biff knew only too well. The main character was funny and outspoken, his comments and criticism of the life around him serving as his release from that grim and outrageous reality.

"I hate it," Danny told him.

The last flames of Biff's fervor about the project, about his future in television production, were extinguished in that instant. He had been deluding himself all this time. The guys at the top in this business could see how poor his ideas were and how meager his talent. Biff slunk from the men's room.

At that same moment Arnold Mandel was entering it.

"How did it go?" Arnold asked Danny.

"Canceled," Danny admitted. "Maybe they'll give you half an hour of my slot."

Arnold shook his head. "They still haven't made up their minds. Their option runs till midseason. I've got to start looking somewhere else to sell it."

"Arnold, I just had an idea for a show. What do you think?" Danny recounted Biff's concept for "Under Cover of Darkness."

"Terrific," Arnold said enthusiastically.

"You mean it?"

Arnold nodded. "Unusual hero. Intriguing, gritty milieu. Suspense." Danny rushed for the door. "I've got to see someone."

He ran to the emergency stairway. If he hurried, he could catch the *schvartzer*—what did he say his name was? What a great idea the kid had! Of course the show's hero could never be a *schvartzer*. Make him the sidekick, like in *Lethal Weapon* or the technical guy like on "Mission: Impossible." And they'd be cops. Having reduced the concept to a familiar formula, Danny felt more comfortable with it. The real genius was his own, he decided, in being able to recognize how to make an ordinary idea valuable.

Danny was puffing like an ancient steam locomotive when the elevator doors opened on the ground floor to reveal a forlorn Biff. Danny rushed forward.

"Why did you run away when I told you how much I liked your idea?" Danny managed to get out between great gulps of air.

"You said, 'I hate it.' "

"You didn't hear me right. I said 'great,' not 'hate.' "

The closing elevator doors knocked them into each other. Danny swung an arm around the bewildered young black man as they staggered out.

"Did I ever tell you how close I am to Diahann Carroll?" he asked.

* * *

184

The status and influence of the select few who anchored network news broadcasts were towering, at times almost inseparable from the news they presented. The modern shamans of American culture, they described and made sense of events. Covering catastrophes, they expressed the nation's shock and sympathy. At their best they helped to keep government honest. When the country's most trusted newscaster, Walter Cronkite, attacked administration claims about the success of the Vietnam War on the "CBS Evening News," Lyndon Johnson understood that because he had lost Cronkite, he had lost the support of the American people.

Chris was no stranger to the national spotlight, having been a White House and foreign correspondent, the co-host of a network news-and-talk show, and raised to gossip-column celebrityhood by marriage to a notable political figure. However, her prior experience had not prepared her for the intensity of interest that focused on her now, for having her motives and abilities dissected so critically and prominently, and for the attention she drew in public, like an actor with a hit series or a rock star. Interviewers had always treated her gently, like America's darling. To generate more controversy for their pieces, they now attached barbs to their questions. Would the public accept a woman as full-time anchor? Wasn't her salary exorbitant? Why did she think she could replace Ray Strock, one of the nation's most honored newsmen? Wasn't she being picked for her looks and glamor?

Greg immediately set about restructuring the company. An entire level of vice presidents was eliminated, a level that had evolved with no other function than to supervise lesser vice presidents. Many operations were streamlined and combined. Despite generous severance benefits, the extensive firings and changes throughout FBS increased resentment against Greg. Many people expressed their displeasure anonymously to the press, who settled on Greg as an easy target, characterizing him as "a midget," "a lightweight," and "a figurehead who was in way over his head."

A couple of small changes he made went almost unnoticed: He beefed up the very-late-night news broadcast and added another brief news update to prime time. The few critics who noticed his introduction of a nightly two-minute spot exploring democratic values derided it as a misguided attempt to win a pat on the back from do-gooders, the FCC, and his socialite friends, a further indication that this Lyall was all surface show and little business substance. Few discerned that both that segment and the news update slipped in extra commercials, while spreading the News Division's costs over more airtime.

*   *   *

185

Diane's daytimes were busy. She had cut back on many of her charitable activities, so as to spend more time with her father during his convalescence and to devote the bulk of her energy to the predominant cause in her life: building the children's hospital to be named after him. She had quietly been lobbying hospital directors, believed she had the votes needed to approve building the new facility on an empty lot the hospital owned, and was canvassing wealthy friends who might make major contributions. She hoped to announce the new children's hospital at the annual dinner for the children's wing that was coming up in a few weeks.

For the first time in her marriage, however, she was forced to spend many evenings without Greg. She felt awkward at social events without him—almost widowed. She missed him. She tried to be awake when he arrived home late and was more eager to make love to him.

On Monday morning, a week before she was to begin anchoring its nightly news, Chris walked into the FBS newsroom at ten o'clock, as requested. She knew a few people here. FBS had already hired away from her old network a producer of whom she thought highly. More new hirees would be arriving over the next few weeks, even as many present employees were being laid off or told that their contracts would not be renewed when they expired.

Chris had decided to soft-pedal her entrance as much as possible and had dressed in jeans and a blue sweater. All this week, as the old format anchored by Ray Strock was produced and broadcast, a new vision of the news would be crafted, with a dress rehearsal after the regular broadcast on Friday. The veteran newscaster had been asked to become an elder statesman, doing opinion pieces nightly and during special events. But no one could guarantee that either Strock or the format would work out.

"Hi, I'm Chris Paskins," she said, introducing herself to those closest to the door: a desk assistant and two cameramen.

As if they did not know. The staff was paralyzed by dread of the changes that would continue to decimate their ranks over the coming weeks and months.

FBS's News Division was bloated by any standard, with over thirteen hundred people and a $350 million budget. High in good times, those figures were lethal now. Before the Reagan years, broadcasters kept hands off their news divisions, afraid that the FCC would lift their licenses for failing to use their monopoly over the airwaves in the public interest. Now, however, the political climate had changed, cable and VCRs were luring away a large segment of the networks' audience, and news now had to pay its way.

To cut costs, Greg and Alan Howe, who had recently been named to head the News Division, were reducing the number and size of domestic and foreign news bureaus, which would now rely more on free-lancers and on local reporters if a network correspondent was unable to get to the news scene in time to cover a story.

When Greg announced that he was personally taking on the responsibility for revamping the nightly news broadcast and increasing its audience, Howe was grateful, rather than miffed. He did not know Greg well or whether Greg was competent in that area, but recent years were littered with the bones of news executives who had failed to raise Ray Strock's rating.

Greg, Howe, and Manny Ramirez were already waiting for Chris when she arrived. Greg was carrying a bouquet of white roses. A calculated risk. Would she be touched or angered by his remembering she liked white roses?

"On behalf of all of us, welcome to FBS," he said, handing her the bouquet and hoping the salutation from "all of us" would weight her reaction to the favorable. She smiled.

He continued, "I thought I'd give you an hour to settle into your office before we get together to go over ideas for the new broadcast."

Chris noticed Manny had joined the group gathering around her. She gave him a hug. "It's going to be fun."

"Just like it used to be," Manny replied.

He glanced at Greg to include him in his meaning. Chris did not.

The other people standing around felt awkward and disloyal. Only two days earlier another executive producer had relied on their loyalty. Although most thought now only of survival, a few were delighted at the upheaval, eager for the coming of a new regime.

"It's great to have you here," one of the young women said and extended her hand, introducing herself. Her name was Hedy Anderson. She was a handsome, big-boned young woman who had risen swiftly as a reporter after being hired from a local Chicago station.

"You made a lot of women in this industry very proud when you were named anchor. I look forward to working with you."

"I've seen your work. It's good," Chris said.

"Thanks. Thanks very much."

Others stepped up to make her welcome.

Chris recognized a face at the back of the group staring stonily at her. Ray Strock. The lines plowed by time across his forehead and from nose to chin like parentheses about an angry mouth expressed the antagonism of a man shamed by displacement after a lifetime of esteem and achievement. Chris went up to him.

"It's an honor to be on the same broadcast with you," she said.

187

"We'll see," he answered.

He stared at Chris for a moment, then turned abruptly and walked out of the room.

Stew Graushner finally managed to land a job writing at scale wages for a lurid syndicated tabloid TV-news program called "The Guts of the Story." The program had fenced off for itself the lowest level of what passed for news. It went after the audience eager for cheap thrills and titillated them with the frightening, the lascivious, and the grotesque. Favored subject matter included celebrity love affairs, murder, rape, child molestation, and UFOs. The people on staff were suited for their jobs, Stew decided; they seemed as strange as the subject matter.

A sign one of the producers had placed on his desk summed it up well: "No Story Too Weird, No Gossip Too Raw, No Smut Too Filthy." Stew suspected that the man was not joking. His own brain kept hearing a far-earlier phrase, the words Dante had placed above the Gates of Hell: "Abandon All Hope You Who Enter Here."

Stew approached the weekend like a man gulping air after freeing his leg from a shark. He had written several shows his first week—he no longer called them programs or broadcasts or kept his prose un-emotional. One of the tamest had been about a whorehouse madam murdered by her dwarf maid, who was believed to have escaped under the skirt of one of the prostitutes, the maid's lesbian lover. Next week he was slated to work on "bizarre sexual practices of an IRS coven."

Until the moment he was handed his paycheck for the week, Stew was sure God would figure out a crafty way to stiff him. One of his coworkers gave him a lift to the university bursar's office, where he exchanged the check for an extra two-weeks' grace period to come up with the rest of the tuition. By the time he paid off the bill, next semester would be upon him. The dream of owning a car receded into the mist of the distant future.

Walking back onto the street, he was stopped by a woman he knew casually at the university who had heard about his separations from Patty and teaching. He expected at least polite sympathy, but instead she expressed delight. She was having a party tomorrow night for other singles and badgered him to come. Apparently, eligible men were at a premium. She gave him the address, an apartment in Marina del Rey.

Ordinarily, parties and unattached women, especially in large numbers, dismayed Stew. He had dated sparingly before meeting Patty and married young. It was a "brave new world" out there, from all accounts, one he doubted he was prepared for.

By the next afternoon, though, the urgency of his need for companionship overwhelmed him. He had to start his single life sometime.

Deciding that one more night spent finding faces in the water stains on his walls would make him a prime candidate for insanity, he got dressed and hitchhiked out to Marina del Rey. He would worry about a ride back when the time came.

The apartment was large and crammed, mostly with women. The door was open. People sipping white wine or red spilled out into the hallway. Several near a table in the dining room were eating raw vegetables they had carefully drowned in a runny dip. Haute cuisine did not seem to be the attraction here.

Many of the guests knew each other, Stew observed, doubtless veterans of such get-togethers. He tossed back two white wines before turning around to confront his social life.

"Professor Graushner," a woman's voice called out above the din. For a moment he did not remember that the person referred to once had been he.

"Professor Graushner," the woman repeated.

She had now slipped around a knot of people and stood before him. She was short, in her midthirties, with an appealing face punctuated by a small nose and eyebrows darker than her long hair, which was streaked through with several designer shades of blond. She was smiling. He decided that he liked her smile because the corners of her eyes crinkled and made the smile seem wholehearted. He remembered having liked it sometime in the past, but could not recall the name attached to it.

"I'm Susan Glendon," the woman announced. "I took your creative writing course, oh, years ago."

"Of course," he said, recalling a woman who dressed then in sandals, handwoven skirts, and peasant blouses, a sort of refugee from the previous decade. She now wore cream-colored slacks and a purple silk blouse that appeared too casually chic and well pressed to be inexpensive.

"You made a big difference in my life," she confessed.

"Didn't someone used to pick you up after class on his motorcycle?"

She laughed, the eyes crinkling attractively again. He recalled slim, tan legs revealing themselves as she hiked the handwoven skirt high on her thighs and took her place on the back of the motorcycle.

"My first husband," she told him. "I worked as a secretary to put him through welding school—God, can you believe it, *welding school*—then I found out he was cheating on me. My second husband was better educated and a lot richer, but just as rotten. You said some nice things about my writing. That gave me confidence to try writing for a living."

Stew searched his brain for a recollection of her writing, but the memory of her legs blocked everything else. She seemed genuinely grateful for what he had taught her. He, in turn, felt grateful for the first therapeutic words applied to his battered ego in months.

"But I'm blocked right now," she said glumly. "I've been trying for months to come up with a good idea and can't."

Oh, no! Stew thought. Not another blocked writer! It would be like looking into a mirror after the summer he had spent immobilized before blank typewriter paper. But she was attractive, seemed eager to be with him, and did not consider him an irredeemable failure, as he had begun to think he might be. It occurred to him, with a shock, that perhaps, if the evening went right, he might get to see those legs again, and all the way up this time.

"Are you working on anything?" she asked.

"What?"

"I heard you weren't teaching at the university anymore, so I figured you're probably working on a story or a novel."

To give himself time to think he handed her a white wine and poured another for himself.

"Actually," he said, at a loss for a more original answer to hold her interest and esteem, "I'm working on this idea for a novel about a college professor who takes a job at a sleazy tabloid TV-news show."

Stew began to describe the eccentric people he worked with and the sorts of subject matter the show dealt with. Susan seemed entranced.

"I don't think it's a novel," she finally told him.

"It's not?" His mind's eye could see the skirt dropping abruptly over those legs like a stage curtain, someone else spiriting her away into the night on the back of a motorcycle, and himself vainly trying to hitch a ride to follow her.

"No, I think what it would make is a wonderful sitcom." She was bursting with excitement. "It's terrifically funny, especially the way you tell it. The setting is great. It has endearing characters."

"Endearing. That's what I thought," he remarked in amazement.

"All the craziness of life could be inherent in those newsroom crazies and the people they would meet doing stories. All the deceit and self-delusion. The stories would raise intriguing issues the comedy could play off of. You'd never run out of situations and characters."

Stew noticed that in her enthusiasm the tip of her tongue occasionally flicked lightly across her dry upper lip. He stopped breathing as he waited for the next appearance of that pink intimacy.

"And I love the idea of the college professor," she added. "It was really a stroke of genius putting an innocent with integrity right at the center of all those amoral people who don't care in the slightest about the difference between truth and fiction."

"Well, thanks."

"Look, I don't want to impose on you. It's your idea. But this is the most exciting idea for a sitcom I could imagine. I'd love to work with you on it."

Stew roused himself from meditation on the cunning attraction hidden in the secret cavern behind her lips. She seemed to be asking him to do something with her. He pieced it together out of bits of phrases still floating about his memory. She wanted him to develop this silly idea he had tried to impress her with—for lack of anything better—into something she could try to sell as a TV series. They would start by writing some sort of proposal, she seemed to be saying.

Weeks earlier, staring down the gun barrel of poverty, he had resolved to renounce pie-in-the-sky fantasies and not waste his time trying to write some piece of fiction no publisher would ever buy. He was a talentless wannabe, not a real fiction writer. He must think now only of making a living. He had a daughter to put through college. Shoe leather to save. Bunions to shrink. It was time he grew up.

Selling a sitcom was even more absurd than hoping to sell a book. Thousands of books were published each year; only a handful of new series got on the air. But he was enjoying the unfamiliar sensation of a woman's adulation, and more important, he was pretty sure that if he turned her down outright, the chances of spending the night with her would drop to zilch. That last point was the clincher: He would wait until the morning to tell her that he had changed his mind.

"Sure. I'd be glad to work on it with you. You know, maybe sometime when we both have a few spare hours."

She threw her arms about his neck and kissed him. "This is just the kind of idea I've been looking for. Running into you here was a miracle. I have a feeling you've changed my life again." She smiled her unreserved crinkle-eyed smile at him. "I had a crush on you in class, you know. To be able to work with you . . . Oh, Lord, I'm excited!"

She grabbed his hand and began pulling him toward the front door.

"I haven't even said hello to the hostess," he called out, lifting a last white wine from the serving table.

"Send her a note," Susan called back over her shoulder.

Stew Graushner woke up in an unfamiliar bed in a darkened room. He carefully felt around and established that the other side of the bed was empty. He remembered a very long night, moaning, not much conversation, and a lot of body parts.

He wrapped the top sheet around himself and walked out of the bedroom. Bright sun flooded a room to his right, too brightly for him to see into it. He followed the smell of coffee into a large kitchen on his left that might have come out of *Architectural Digest*, all maroon-and-black

191

lacquer and stainless steel. Susan was preparing breakfast on a stainless steel counter. She beamed at him and bounded over to kiss him.

"Last night was wonderful, wasn't it?"

The memories were becoming clearer. He had never made love to any other woman but Patty and had not done that for half a year. Last night had been terrifying at first. He had felt like a first-time sky diver hanging on to the wing's trailing edge for dear life. He vaguely recalled finally letting go and more or less getting the hang of it before he would have splattered. And how it felt when the chute gloriously opened.

"Last night," he admitted, "was an earthquake."

"Three point two," she said, nodding in confirmation. "The radio said it was centered in the Valley. Breakfast will be ready soon. You might want to shower."

The bathroom was as large and lavish as the kitchen: pink marble with a built-in hot tub and a stall shower. The toilet was housed in a separate enclosure, the bidet in the open beside the sink, which seemed to signify something about modern morals, but he couldn't quite figure out what. One thing he did conclude: Her second husband must have been very rich.

He showered and found the new toothbrush and fresh shaving paraphernalia she had placed beside the sink for him. He thought the razor might be a hint. In a rush of self-improvement, he trimmed his beard down to what looked to him like a triangle of unruly pubic hair, but what he hoped might be mistaken for a raffish Vandyke. By the time he began dressing, he was humming happily to himself.

Susan was placing plates of food on the breakfast table when he returned. Her eyes brightened at the sight of his diminished facial hair.

"I like it. But don't shave it all off." She smiled. "It tickled in several appropriate places."

She took the seat across from him and was about to cut into her melon when she stopped and gazed straight at him in wonder.

"I can't believe I'm actually going to write with Stewart Graushner."

He suddenly remembered the nonsense about the sitcom. He was going to tell her this morning that he couldn't do it. But then his hunger asserted itself. He had lived on Twinkies all week. Death by either tooth decay or a sugar overdose was imminent, he rationalized, if he did not get a healthy meal into his system. The price of the breakfast set before him was letting her rattle on about her ideas for the sitcom. He heard little, however. All his concentration was on the delicious tastes his mouth and stomach were thanking him for.

As he sipped the last of his coffee, though, he reflected that two unknown writers had about as much chance of selling a comedy series

192

to a network as he did of guest-hosting for Johnny Carson. Maybe with alimony paying all her bills, she could afford to fritter away time on projects that would never happen, but he worked hard all week. He needed this day off. What he wanted most right now was to lie in his own lumpy bed and read the Sunday paper.

"The maid will be in later and do the dishes," she said as soon as he set his empty coffee cup on its saucer. "Come on."

The exterior of the house had been unlit when they arrived last night. As Stew followed Susan out the front door, he realized that although the house was small, it was magnificent, all windows and balconies. It sat high above Los Angeles and beside a swimming pool with the look of a mountain spring in a rocky cove.

He had taken no notice of her car last night either. Now he did. A white Maserati convertible. He had never been this close to one, much less ridden in one. As he slid into the enveloping tan leather seat, he decided to postpone the moment of truth awhile longer.

"We have to pick up your car," she remembered. "We left it in Marina del Rey last night."

"It's at a garage being repaired," he lied. The lie came easily to him; he had used it several times at work this week.

"Then we can go right to the studio," she said.

She hit the accelerator and hurtled onto the road that dropped precipitously down from the hills. The G forces slammed Stew up against the headrest. Only a few seconds seemed to pass before she was slowing at a guardhouse stationed like a portcullis in the middle of fortress walls extending many blocks on every side. Over the entrance were the words "Monumental Productions."

Instead of being barred, they were waved straight through. Because it was Sunday, the streets separating the cavernous sound stages were empty. Susan pulled into a parking place, at the end of which was a small sign that read Susan Glendon.

Once more, Stew decided to defer for a time breaking the bad news to her and followed her into a four-story office building.

Her name was also on an office door and beneath it, the words Productions, Inc. As she turned on the lights, a display case to one side of the reception area lit up. Inside were statuettes and plaques.

"What are those?" Stew asked.

"Oh, you know, Emmys and stuff."

"They wouldn't happen to be for writing sitcoms, would they?"

"Some for writing. Some for producing."

"This sitcom you want to write with me. You don't see much trouble in selling it to a studio? Monumental maybe?"

"Monumental and I have a deal. They pay me a million dollars a year for two years. Anything I come up with, they get first crack at. If they like it, we go forward together."

She returned to him and put her arms around his neck. "That's why I'm so grateful to you. I felt guilty just sitting around taking their money, unable to come up with a good idea. You can understand that, can't you?"

He tried to appear as if he did.

She kissed him. "I hope you don't mind that your idea won't be a novel now. But we'd be partners on the series."

"Sometimes a man's got to stand up and be counted," he said with brave irrelevance. "What would my share be for this, you know, for being your partner?"

"You'd get one-half of what I'm entitled to—that is, once the studio gives us the go-ahead on a script. That would probably be after they make a network deal for it. We'll split all the writing and producing fees." She began enumerating the actual dollars for him.

"Stop!" he cried.

He had never been so aroused in his life. He stoppered up the extravagant litany by kissing her mouth and swiftly removing her clothes. He feared delay might waste the orgasm about to overcome him. He tried to focus his thoughts on only his first $12,500 payment and being able to travel by car all the way from his apartment to his job.

They coupled in front of the display case, with the Emmys glinting flirtatiously at him and one tiny bunker of his brain awaiting God's certain double cross.

13

~~~~~~~~~~~~~~~~~~~~~~

E very morning Greg met with Chris and Manny and a small cadre of producers and news writers with kindred vision and taste to craft the new version of "This Is FBS News Tonight." The two men had already done a lot of thinking together, but now Chris was being introduced to it.

Greg was convinced that networks had to differentiate themselves from local newscasts. Despite Ray Strock's assertion of high-minded journalism, FBS had tried for years to raise ratings by presenting the news much the way the worst of the local newscasts did, by arousing viewers' emotions: "If it bleeds, it leads." Imparting information had become secondary.

Greg believed that viewers depended on the network to explain the social, economic, and political conflicts tearing apart the country and world. "We live in confusing times. The Iron Curtain is collapsing. Drugs have become as destructive a force as nuclear weapons. The environment is degenerating. The people want us to analyze the news for them, make sense of it. Local hasn't got the commitment or talent to do that."

The format he had devised was for Chris to go with more hard news items, but most of those reports would be brief. More significant or complex topics would be given lengthier treatment than usual. Correspondents always insisted they needed more time than the usual minute and a half in order for the "why" and not just the "what" of the news to be conveyed. Let's now see what they could do.

For all its aggravations, morning television had honed Chris's skill as an interviewer. The news broadcast would feature live interviews of important newsmakers, usually by satellite. Some interviews she would have to tape earlier that day. A network half hour had only twenty-two minutes of content, with more news to cover than there was time available, but if the interviews could concentrate on essential matters, viewers would feel they were getting the inside story right from the person making news.

Chris liked Greg's plan. But when he contended that the more serious content had to be counterbalanced by clearer and simpler writing and more exciting visuals and graphics, she scornfully understood that it had been devised not out of a commitment to the public good, but solely to attract more viewers. That had always been Greg's primary concern, she knew, and always would be.

She also was not surprised to learn that the present pink-and-blue set that might have come from the lounge of a cruise ship circling Disney World would be scrapped. Designing a new set was invariably a new regime's initial measure to cure a news program's "bad numbers," its low rating. For the present at least, viewers would see the busy newsroom behind her, and the busier the better. Greg was determined to communicate the sense that Chris was at the central point where the world's news first arrived, that viewers would miss something if they chose another network over FBS. When an urgent bulletin came in, the camera would show the head writer at the end of the desk hand the bulletin to Chris. Maybe he would do it for effect, Greg joked, even when there was no bulletin.

On Friday night Ray Strock did his last newscast as anchor. A dress rehearsal of the new version of the program was scheduled to be taped for practice right afterward, with Chris, instead of Ray, as anchor.

With ten seconds left in the broadcast, the director cut from a taped piece back to the anchor desk for Strock's final words, his customary sign-off. But Strock added something more.

"As many of you know, after twenty-four years, this is my last newscast as anchor for FBS." His mouth curled disdainfully. "After me, the dancing girls."

Greg had been watching the broadcast from the glass-walled room where executives customarily gathered to watch the broadcast. He stormed out to confront Strock. The older man was removing his lapel mike and earpiece. He held up his other hand to stop whatever Greg was about to say.

"Forget it," Strock declared. "I've given too much to this business and, I hope, to millions of Americans who've relied on me over the years for me to be shoved aside like dog meat in favor of the latest news starlet. That was my resignation."

He stood up and walked stiffly out the door. His office belongings, it was later discovered, had already been packed and sent home. He had planned his departure carefully.

Manny was the first to speak. "He kept asking me all week if I thought he could come up with something significant in an editorial every night. I think he was afraid he wouldn't be able to. This grand good-bye was easier."

Greg was staring at the ceiling to contain his rage. "What difference does it make why he did it? He hurt us badly." Greg turned to a desk assistant. "Get our PR people on the phone right away and tell them to field the press calls."

Chris was still in the executives' room, staring out at them with shock on her face as if some unrecognized tactlessness on her part had precipitated a suicide. Greg rushed back to her.

"It wasn't your fault," he said as soon as he was in the room.

Her head slowly turned to him. "I used to idolize Ray Strock. We both did. Remember? He was one of the first to stand up and report on civil rights, to express doubts about Vietnam."

"He had also gotten ponderous and self-important. He thought the news wasn't the news until he told America it was. I'm glad he's gone. That gives us back three minutes a night."

Chris turned on him. "How can you be so callous! The man was a giant, and we discarded him."

Greg shook his head. "I offered him an honored elder statesman's role, like Eric Sevareid, John Chancellor. His editorials would have given him a lot more influence to change the country's thinking than most senators have—ask your husband—but he couldn't bear to give up center stage. He thought it was his by divine right."

"And somehow it's mine?"

"Don't start doubting yourself now." Greg remembered the Chris of ten years before who could so easily be stirred to righteous anger. He needed now to incite that in her. "Ray Strock wasn't just saying those things about *you*. He attacked *every* woman. If you don't believe a woman's good enough to do the job, that she's just a dancing girl, then I made a very big mistake."

Chris took a big breath and stood up.

"You really *are* a manipulative bastard!" she snapped.

At that instant, for no reason that seemed logical to him, the memory of his conflicted feelings about her broke over him with the suddenness of a summer squall. Greg remembered why he had fallen in love with her. And why he had chosen to leave her. Worst of all, he thought, was how powerful the memories still were—as if no time had passed—and how pointless. He put them out of his mind.

The anchor desk had already been repositioned to include much of the newsroom activity behind it. Technicians were repositioning lights on the overhead grid. A new script was being put into the teleprompter. A few minutes later an entirely different version of "This Is FBS News Tonight" began to roll.

As he had a decade before, Greg Lyall stood in the back of the control room watching the graphics and music come up on screen and fade into a close-up of Chris, her composure fully restored. Little seemed to have changed. The blond hair still framed a perfect face, a touch older, but more self-possessed. The large eyes still startled and transfixed one, like lasers vibrating out of sapphire. Time seemed only to have made the sincerity she radiated more certain, more dependable. Changes would have to be instituted between now and Monday, no doubt, and continue to be instituted over time. But those would be in the presentation, agenda, approach, coverage, news gathering—not with Chris herself. He realized that the task would be to create a newscast that could approach the plane on which she naturally, effortlessly presented the news.

Instead of a small clique's retreating to a conference room afterward, Greg chose to have the postbroadcast dissection out in the open, with everyone connected with the broadcast sitting informally on chairs and desks. If this news organization was going to become a team, people would have to feel they were all in this together. He looked over at Manny, who was already staring at him.

"What are you thinking?" Greg asked.

"I have a feeling it's the same as you. Why does this world need one more anchor behind a classroom desk like a schoolteacher?"

Greg nodded excitedly at the shared thought. "The news is happening out there, not here in a New York studio." He spun around to Chris. "To the extent we can, not every night, of course, but when we can, what do you think about broadcasting directly from where the news is happening?"

The other networks were doing that from time to time. Greg wanted to do more of it than ever before, much more, to put Chris right in the midst of the big breaking stories.

"Viewers would tune us in because if the action is in Moscow, say, they'd know you'd be there and would be interviewing the top newsmakers. We'd have to spend a lot of money we should be trying to save, but the expense could well be worth it. I think you'd grab a big chunk of new audience."

Chris's eyes were lit with what her mind's eye was envisioning. "I'd love it. But not just to sit in a studio somewhere else. Really out there wherever the news is happening. Really reporting and taping some of the stories, as well as anchoring."

"It will take a lot of planning. And good guesswork."

"And having to work very fast wherever we are," Manny added. "And traveling a lot."

"But you like the idea, too?" Greg asked.

Manny nodded. Greg's eyes swept the room to take in everyone, to include them in his fervor.

"I'll tell you where I think we should go. To Kenya. The developing countries are meeting there next week to consider joint action on a lot of major issues. Our secretary of State will be there and the Treasury, our environmental people, all the Third World presidents and finance ministers—every nation in Africa and a lot from Asia and Latin America. We descend on Kenya and send correspondents to other African countries—not just do South Africa, but all of Africa—and hit it hard. Africa is rich and diverse. There are important stories everywhere. What do you think?"

Chris's eyes were gleaming. "It's terrific. We really start off with a bang."

"Okay," Greg declared to the others. "Africa. By tomorrow afternoon a lot of you have to be on a plane. Manny, see if we can rent one to take everyone and all the equipment. It would stop at one or two cities on the way to Nairobi to let off our people covering other African countries."

Manny had once done a series of stories in Kenya and knew it well. He was already barking directions to his key producers and the unit manager. "See about renting a 707." "Just in case that falls through, block out a hundred seats on regularly scheduled flights to Kenya over the weekend." "Alert our Nairobi bureau chief to find us hotel rooms—preferably at the Norfolk and the Nairobi Safari Club because they're near each other. He'll have to contact the right government minister for permission to shoot inside the conference center and to put a portable anchor booth outside the building." "Start notifying the correspondents and producers and cameramen we want to go." He began listing them and the destinations for each.

Within a couple of minutes each person responsible for an area was on the phone or conferring with staff. Mobilizing and going off like this was second nature to them. That was what news was about. Always being ready to go somewhere.

Greg had been charged up during the planning just moments ago, as he remembered having been a decade before when he himself was producing the news. Now he felt a letdown at the realization that control of the broadcast had left his hands; he was the only person in the newsroom with nothing to do. Even Chris was on the phone with her husband explaining that she would be in Kenya for the week. Greg had devoted so much of himself to conceiving the new program, but his function was now peripheral to the action taking place around him. He became keenly aware of how much he would have to rely on others as CEO. He had confidence in Manny, who had replaced him at KFBS-TV. Now, though, the stakes were infinitely higher. Any failure would be Greg's and absolute.

Since becoming CEO, Greg had been in the eye of the hurricane, the person around whom all the action rotated, making vital decisions in dozens of areas of FBS's business, the object of all attention. After a decade of impotence, the turnaround had been exhilarating. Whenever he had entered the newsroom this week, everyone there, whether openly or surreptitiously, had kept a cautious eye fixed on him. Now, no one noticed him leave.

Chris's favorite restaurant was Symphony Cafe. She and Ken ate there often. The food was wonderful, and they felt at home in the spacious, softly lit interior with its warm woods and high ceiling. But as the car she had called drove her there, she was still too agitated by recent events to relax.

Ray Strock's comment had unnerved her—the need to defend herself against a false impression fostered by a resentful man had been added to the pressure of preparing for a new broadcast. Excited as well by the decision to take the program to Nairobi, she was going over in her mind what she would need to pack tomorrow, the commitments she would have to cancel, the details to inform her secretary to handle in her absence.

Also on her mind, however, was her phone conversation with Ken from the newsroom, when she had called to inform him both that she would be away next week and that she was about to leave for the Symphony Cafe. The conversation had turned contentious for no reason she could grasp. She had broken it off. They would speak further at the restaurant.

The car turned onto Fifty-sixth Street and stopped at the entrance between Broadway and Eighth Avenue. Two couples arriving for a late dinner recognized her as she stepped out of the car. One of the women immediately began to whisper to the others. Chris was sure the woman had caught Ray Strock's broadcast that night.

Ken was already at the table. As she kissed him hello, Chris noted that indeed something was disturbing him. The cause turned out to be her trip to Kenya.

"You have to call it off."

"The decision's already been made. It's out of my hands."

"Damn it, they wanted you badly enough. They can put off your starting as anchor for another week."

Chris waved off the waitress who was approaching for drink orders and faced Ken directly. "There's a problem here that I'm just not getting. Why do you not want me to go to Kenya? You've already told me you'll be away the early part of next week as it is."

"I can't tell you why."

Chris tried not to look exasperated. "It's top-secret government stuff?"

He nodded. Both understood that occasionally matters came up he could not talk about to her. But his trying to prevent her from traveling with her broadcast seemed outlandish.

She pressed him. "Somebody intends to shoot down airliners flying over Africa? Communist guerrillas? Poachers? Give me a hint."

He shook his head.

"I'm supposed to stop an entire broadcast from going to Kenya," Chris said, "and you can't tell me why?"

Ken's normally serene brow clenched as he nodded. "It's very important to me that you not go."

"If you could give me a good reason, maybe I could—"

She waited while he wrestled with the problem. He turned to her.

"You can't repeat to anyone what I'm about to tell you. You never heard it."

She nodded.

Ken glanced about to make sure no one could overhear him before whispering, "The President plans to surprise everyone by flying to the conference on Monday to take part personally in the talks and sign several multilateral treaties. He wants to show his concern for Africa and the Third World. You know what a security risk he faces down there, so the Secret Service has asked the White House to keep the visit secret until he arrives. He'll be taking along several newspeople from the White House reporters' pool and a pool TV crew. They won't know ahead of time where they're going. A few congressional committee heads who've been working with him on some of the matters that will be discussed at the conference have also been asked along."

"Oh," Chris said, comprehending, "and you're one of the senators picked to go."

He nodded. "None of the other TV networks have a clue what's happening. They might not even have a news bureau in Nairobi. They'll have to rely on the pool. But if you're waiting in Nairobi with dozens of FBS people when he arrives, it will look as if I tipped you off and

201

compromised security. The rest of the media will be sure I gave you an edge. The President hates it when his plans leak out beforehand."

Chris was deep in thought.

"What I should do is phone the President personally and let him know what's happening," he said.

"So he can alert the other networks in time for them to get down there. Our foresight in covering this conference will be trashed just because my husband happens to be a senator. Instead of you being compromised, I'll be the one."

"Checkmate," he agreed. "I was afraid this new job of yours was going to create problems for us. But you had your heart set on it."

She laid her hand lovingly on his. "There are husbands and wives who come from entirely different races. This is minor."

"It won't be when that plane lands and you're standing there with a microphone. If I don't go, I'll look even guiltier."

"What if we hadn't told each other any of this?"

"Same thing."

"Then I guess that's the way it will have to be."

Ken was angry. "We're talking about national security here."

"No, we're talking about what claims of national security often turn out to be: embarrassment."

Ken's mouth tightened in frustration. "I can't believe you won't do this for me. You never back off the slightest bit when your career's involved. Being a United States senator—the responsibilities—aren't exactly insignificant. When do you give in for my career?"

"There's no reason either of us should ever have to give in." Ken's question troubled Chris although she did not say so. The Constitution prescribed no resolution for the conflict between the government and the press. She never suspected it might enter her home. As a reporter and a woman, she had always put her faith in the truth. "Neither of us knew about the other's plans when they were made. People will just have to believe us."

Ken hoped she was right, but despite his personal honesty, he was too savvy a politician to believe in the truth.

The week after meeting Susan Glendon was the most hectic and debilitating of Stew Graushner's life.

Each morning she would drop him off at the bus stop. She was very understanding about "his other projects" and the frustrations of getting his car repaired. Then, unknown to her, after the bus left him off, he would walk the mile to the offices of "The Guts of the Story," where he wrote scripts for new shows. Privately, he was also taking mental notes on the oddballs surrounding him: the massive woman tape editor who lifted him overhead in a perfect clean and jerk as a warning she was not be trifled with; the paranoid producer, whose limp turned out to be caused by a rifle strapped to a leg, which everyone discovered when his big toe was accidentally blown away; and the staff's best researcher, who proudly informed the others that her psychoanalyst claimed her sex practices were so bizarre that most had not yet been described in the literature, which she spent the bulk of her time on the job reading.

Or at least those were the television characters his colleagues evolved into as he and Susan collaborated late into the late night on the series. And later, in bed.

Susan bounced out of bed bright and early every morning. Stew crawled.

By the end of the week, their short proposal spelling out the concept for their new show was ready. They set up a meeting on Saturday morning with the head of television for Monumental Productions, Mickey Blinder.

Like many television executives, Mickey had held jobs on both the network side and the supplier side, dealing all the while with the same people, who possessed similarly checkered résumés. Their careers were a series of choose-up games, where the same people were reshuffled: Competitors became colleagues became competitors again; suppliers of programming became buyers and then suppliers again. Rarely were any of these power brokers capable themselves of creating a story that would captivate audiences, the final purpose for their employment. Yet they were the ones who decided what would get bought for production, what would go on the air.

Monumental Productions had hired Mickey Blinder away from a network after his predecessor was hired away from Monumental. The job required him to induce the networks to finance pilots of Monumental's proposed series and then buy the shows for broadcast, while Monumental accumulated them for syndication.

Last year, his first at Monumental, Mickey sold the networks three pilot shows. One was picked for fall presentation. It had not lasted out the year. The only Monumental show still on television was the long-running sitcom "I Love Luba." No one seemed to care that it was a rip-off of "I Love Lucy," as well as "Perfect Strangers." This was its fifth year on television, and it was just about the only popular show FBS still had. Yet, his predecessor and not Mickey had sold that show to FBS.

The rule of thumb was that a TV executive had two seasons to prove himself. This was Mickey's second. Unless he got at least one strong Monumental show on TV, he was through.

After his first year, Mickey convinced his bosses to make long-term deals with proven creators of successful series. Susan had been one of those. He had been waiting months for her to create a new show. Whenever he passed her in the commissary or the parking lot, he would anxiously ask if she had come up with anything. She would shake her head sadly and keep walking. Each headshake drilled a separate ulcer in his stomach, he was sure.

Now, to hear that she had a project she wanted to meet with him about, he told her, was like hearing the Mormon Tabernacle Choir sing "Happy Birthday" just for him.

Mickey's career had been built on being liked. Suddenly realizing that he did not know Susan's religion and might have offended her, Mickey rushed to assure her that he "deeply respected the Mormon religion— all religions, in fact, regardless of color or creed." He himself was not a Mormon, he added. He had been careful to divorce each of his wives before marrying the next.

Mickey's office was the largest Stew had ever seen. He could picture jetliners being serviced at one end. Mickey was middle-aged, chunky, balding, energetic, tan, and smoked a cigar. He looked to Stew like every other entertainment-industry executive of that indeterminate middle age. He was dressed in tennis shorts and a warm-up jacket. A case containing several tennis rackets leaned against a wall. He had a doubles match scheduled later that day with several other TV executives, among them an ABC guy with whom he was hoping to make a deal for a show about a loudmouthed working-class wife who was really a robot.

The air conditioner was on high, but Mickey kept wiping sweat from his forehead and neck. He seemed to Stew a very worried man. Particularly after Susan "pitched" him, as she called it, their new series, "Lowdown."

Mickey's eyes rolled wildly. "You really mean to tell me that you expect a network to buy a show about how bad those syndicated news shows are they put on TV?"

Susan reminded him, "Mary Tyler Moore worked in a third-rate TV newsroom."

"Mary Tyler Moore was a saint," Mickey pronounced reverentially. "Those ratings, those reruns . . ."

" 'Murphy Brown' takes place in a newsroom and attacks news shows," Susan said, hoping he would draw comfort from another show with the same background that was presently on network. "But the important thing is that the newsroom in 'Lowdown' is a funny place full of funny people."

"Weirdos."

Mickey had no idea whether the public would like the show or even whether the idea was a good one. He knew only that the show was too unusual for him to be able to sell to network programmers, who thought exactly as he did. They wanted the security of concepts and characters that had proven successful in the past. His eyes were pleading.

"Give me a family. I can sell that. Make the mother a smartass. Great. I can sell that. Even a family with an alien for a smartass. A snap. But these degenerates . . ."

Susan could not shake Mickey's negativism. His only hope to make a deal for a pilot script, he said, was FBS. "Marian Marcus is just crazy enough to go for it, but she'll never convince Raoul Clampton."

"Try," Susan urged him. "Let's you and I take a meeting with Marian as soon as we can. I love this show."

Slogging back from Monumental's office building to where the producers were housed, Stew tried not to look at the cars parked in the lots. Even a rusted Yugo would break his heart.

Diane invited Barnett for dinner on Saturday night, the night after Ray Strock's tumultuous sign-off. Barnett was now well enough to leave the house for short outings. When Greg returned from a workout at his health club, for which he had had little time in recent weeks, his wife and father-in-law were chatting in the living room.

Greg commented that Barnett looked a lot stronger.

Barnett's eyes were cold. "I saw the news broadcast last night. Ray Strock's humiliation was disastrous. Utter clumsiness. FBS News has been left looking like a cheap traveling circus."

"You're *sounding* a lot stronger, too. Ray Strock had agreed to do regular editorials on the broadcast instead of anchoring. There was no reason to suspect he would knife us in the back. Our feeling is he was afraid he might not have the depth or imagination to give a significant opinion every night." Greg matched Barnett's stare with his own. "Or perhaps his ego couldn't relinquish the spotlight. A lot of older men get like that."

"I hired Ray Strock because he was the finest newscaster of his generation."

The statement contained its own answer, and Greg held his tongue. He perceived that Barnett was trying to make this a fight over turf. Barnett would avoid taking his stand over the corporate reorganization—cost-cutting was necessary and he was glad to have someone take the heat for firing people. Barnett cared passionately, however, about everything that was broadcast. That was how he and his network had built their reputations. That was what his friends would comment about to him at parties.

No program ever went on the air without his personal approval. When he abdicated after his heart attack, he understood intellectually that the decisions that used to be his would now be Greg's, but viscerally he never acknowledged it, and like the old lion on the plains whose wounds were starting to heal, he had circled back to test the interloper once more. He had chosen the Ray Strock demotion as the battlefield because the media uproar made Greg weakest there.

Greg chose to reply with logic and not emotion. "Ray Strock's low rating was costing us about fifty million dollars a year in lost revenue. I think Christine Paskins can help us make that up. That's what I was hired to do."

Barnett was not ready to break off the fight. His glance flicked toward his daughter.

"When Diane told me you intended to replace Ray Strock," he went on, "I held my tongue. I was sure you'd convinced an established anchor to come over from another network to replace him. But when she told me a few days later it was going to be one of those . . . those interchangeable women reporters you can't tell from one another, I was sure she had to be mistaken."

Greg's gaze pierced Diane's as he asked Barnett, "When did Diane tell you that?"

"The morning after you hired the woman."

"You mean before it was announced."

"Of course. What good would it have done to tell me when it was too late for me to stop you from making a mistake."

Greg looked back at Barnett. "But you didn't *try* to stop me. Why?"

"I figured all the eggs had already been broken," Barnett replied, but with noticeably less firmness than before.

Greg suspected no call had been made because the old man feared that his own decision in the matter might not be correct, that his instincts had become fallible. The company's decline and then his heart attack had undermined his self-confidence; he had learned he was mortal and had become afraid he could be wrong. He had raised the matter now solely to demonstrate that while ill health had forced him from the corporate fray, he was still supreme in the family.

Greg felt a cold, lonely wind curl about him. Right after the dinner with Chris and Carl Green, he had excitedly informed Diane what had happened, to share his delight in the strategic coup that would commence his reign as CEO. He impressed upon her that the information was absolutely confidential. Never before had she had to choose between the two men in her life—one or the other had always yielded at the last moment. Worried that Greg's maneuver might be a mistake, at her first opportunity the very next morning, she had confided it to her father—and he wanted Greg to know that.

While Greg was deceiving himself that his new corporate authority would create a more equitable balance with Diane—and build the closer relationship he desired and Barnett had demanded—Diane had deserted Greg for her father's side.

After Barnett left their apartment, she tried to defend her action by arguing that she could not know Greg meant her to keep the information from her father. Barnett was, after all, still FBS's chairman. Greg said only that the decision as to who should be informed was his to make, not hers.

He still felt obligated to Diane for the advantages she had brought him and the duties he had pledged to her. The only change was that the invisible line separating him from her, that he had hoped to eradicate, had turned fluorescent. He could never trust her.

Two days later Mickey and the creators of "Lowdown" were at FBS's Programming Department to meet with Marian Marcus. She was enthusiastic about the series, so enthusiastic, in fact, that despite her habitual caution about sticking out her neck, she went so far as to march Mickey, Susan, and Stew out of her own office and into an impromptu meeting in Raoul Clampton's.

Beneath the pleasant, boyish face and casual, open shirts affected by many in the entertainment industry, Raoul Clampton was a frightened man. His new prime-time lineup, as the ones before it, had sunk lower than the previous year's. He had no idea what the public would go for and what it would not. He had seen too many can't-miss new ideas fall from the sky like shot birds—and too many promising executives—so he cautiously hewed to the tried and true. If it worked before, he believed, there must have been a good reason for that, and with some new little twist, it would work again. Raoul found "Lowdown" too original to feel comfortable with.

Marian argued that Susan Glendon was a proven quantity, that this show was just different and wacky enough to attract an audience. Raoul said he would read the proposal, but did not really like the concept and was pretty sure that the reading would not change his mind.

As Susan was leaving, he asked her whether she had any ideas for a show about a family. How about an alien?

Raoul asked Mickey to stay behind. If Susan hoped that the latter would use the opportunity to argue for their show, she would have been mistaken. Raoul wanted to discuss "I Love Luba."

Its rating had been weakening, he said, but he would consider renewing the show for another year. Mickey comprehended immediately that the problem was not the show's rating, which was the best of any show on FBS, but that Raoul was angling for something else. Raoul's position at FBS was doubtless shaky now that a new CEO had been named. Mickey suspected the programming executive might want to use the leverage of renewal to make a personal arrangement with Monumental that would come into effect if the ax fell on him, as it had on hundreds at FBS. He needed an insurance policy, a little side deal that could never be revealed.

With Mickey as desperate to get and keep shows on TV in order to save his hide as Raoul was for a parachute to save his, the two men quickly made a deal. Raoul would renew "I Love Luba" for a year and give a firm commitment for a new series starring Annette Valletta, the actress who played Luba, for the year after. Mickey would guarantee that if Raoul was fired at FBS, a production deal at Monumental awaited him, with a quarter-of-a-million-dollar salary, offices, and a chunk of any profits that resulted from TV shows he developed.

Annette Valletta's five-year contract would expire at the end of this TV season, and Mickey had to convince her to sign for another year of "Luba" and to commit to the new series after that. He thought he might dangle some TV movies in front of her, and of course an increase in salary for doing the last year of "Luba." FBS was presently paying Monumental a licensing fee of five hundred thousand dollars to broadcast each half-hour episode twice. With Raoul now in his pocket, Mickey decided, he might as well ask to increase that licensing fee. Some of it would pay Annette's larger salary, but most would reduce the deficit Monumental was racking up because each episode cost nearly six hundred thousand dollars to produce.

Eager to win points with Mickey and Monumental, Raoul approved another hundred thousand dollars an episode. The increased payments would start, not next year, but immediately—and be paid retroactively for shows already shot this year. Finding no resistance, Mickey pushed further.

"One more thing, Raoul," Mickey said, "if I *can* convince Annette to come back for another year, I think Monumental deserves a guaranteed thirteen-week commitment next year for a new series."

"Hey, come on, Mickey, that would guarantee you two new shows: one next year and the new series for Annette the year after. The initials here are FBS, not HUD."

"If you're no longer here by then," Mickey offered, "that first one is yours to produce."

"You've got a deal."

Both men understood that the new series could not be something so loony and sure to fail as "Lowdown." Mickey pulled a new proposal from his briefcase.

*　　*　　*

Marian sat glumly in her office. She had phone calls to return, material to read, but she was too upset by the meeting just ended in Raoul's office to rouse herself. If FBS was to have any chance to build ratings, Marian believed, it would be by putting on new and innovative programming that offered viewers something different. "Lowdown" was just that, and Susan Glendon had a real feel for that sort of material. Her last series, on a different network, had been funny, but short-lived. Marian was convinced it had been badly placed in the schedule and its proper audience not given enough time to find it.

Raoul entered her office. He carried two proposals. He dropped the first on her desk, for "Lowdown."

"Don't ever do that to me again," he warned, "surprising me like that."

He could be brutal with subordinates, and Marian had taken a risk, she knew. Oddly, though, he sounded in a good mood.

"Did you read the proposal?" she pressed him.

"Piece of shit," he grumbled. "Mickey thinks it's shit, too, but he couldn't say that in front of what's her name." Raoul handed Marian another proposal. "After you guys left, he pitched me a project he really liked. I think the concept has great possibilities." Raoul's voice softened with emotion. "It touched me a lot more deeply than I was ready for."

"What's the concept?" she asked.

"This really warmhearted woman alien runs a crowded day-care center and can communicate with infants. It's called 'We're Out of Space.' Catchy title. You know how big that film *Look Who's Talking* was at the box office. This is a switch on that. Let me know what you think."

As soon as the door closed behind him, Marian angrily threw the proposal for "Lowdown" into her wastebasket and dutifully picked up the one for "We're Out of Space." Even without reading it, Marian knew what she would think.

14

~~~~~~~~~~~~~~~~

Air Force One landed at the Nairobi airport to be greeted by a Kenyan honor guard, an American Secret Service contingent, and an array of FBS cameras. Chris awaited the President in front of his limousine.

Chris was banking on the relationship she had developed with the Bushes in Washington to gain her an impromptu interview. She smiled as the couple strode toward her beside the squat figure of Daniel arap Moi, the Kenyan chief executive, who was there to meet the plane. Glimpsing the plea in Chris's eyes and realizing that this was her inaugural broadcast, the First Lady placed her hand on her husband's arm, halting the men.

Chris had prepared a first question she hoped both men would want to stop and answer, about the drastic threat that poaching posed to the continent's wildlife. The opportunity to show his concern for animals was too propitious for the American president to decline. She quickly followed with a question about African drought relief and then about economic matters.

Whenever the American president seemed about to end the interview, Chris directed a question at the Kenyan president, and Mr. Bush had to display courtesy and wait out the answer. She saved her most telling question for last, asking Mr. Moi how his country, which received substantial American aid, could claim to be democratic yet permit only one-party rule, allow no political opposition, and fail to investigate rumors of corruption by high government leaders. Furious, he curtly replied that the country could not tolerate the divisiveness a multiparty system would cause and then stomped away. The pungent exchange would add fireworks to her lead story. The reporters in the pool were still trying to get off the plane.

Mrs. Bush delayed her husband a moment longer. "Oh, Chris, your husband flew down with us."

The President had seemed pleased by Chris's impertinent final question, possibly planning to ask his Kenyan counterpart something similar in private, but now his expression grew cross.

"My husband is on the plane?" Chris quickly asked in feigned astonishment before Mr. Bush could speak.

The First Lady winked at the younger woman. "What a lovely coincidence! Good luck on your broadcast. It's about time a woman regularly anchored the news."

" 'This Is FBS News Tonight,' " the announcer's voice smoothly intoned, "with Christine Paskins, reporting from Nairobi, Kenya."

New animated graphics dissolved into a medium shot of Chris standing in the outdoor courtyard of the spotlit Kenyatta International Conference Centre. Behind her loomed two dark-brown structures: a twenty-seven-story, cylindrical office tower and an enclosed amphitheater designed in the shape of a traditional hut. Out of camera range police ringed the site for security. It was three in the morning Kenyan time.

After a dozen years of experience, Chris told herself, it should have been like any other moment in front of the camera, like anchoring in Los Angeles or Wichita. But for just an instant, she felt her throat constricting and a teariness coming over her. Although she was too professional to allow her feelings to show, deep inside she wore a smile a yard wide. She was the anchor, the cutting edge, and as much as she hated the word, the "star" of FBS's network news. This was the moment for which she had worked and hoped all her life.

"Good evening. I'm Christine Paskins, speaking to you from Nairobi, Kenya. President and Mrs. Bush made a surprise visit here today for an important conference with African leaders."

The tape segment rolled that showed the plane landing and the couple descending to the tarmac and walking to their car with Moi. Her interview ran two minutes. "This Is FBS News Tonight" with Christine Paskins was off and running.

Public curiosity, piqued by the broadcast's publicity, promotion, and advertising, had produced an enormous audience, topping the other networks' news offerings in the ratings regatta. Chris's being on the spot for the President's unexpected trip and getting the interview made FBS look like a leader in news gathering, rather than the follower it had been for so long. The pool coverage seemed paltry by comparison. Satellite technology allowed Chris to serve as anchor with the apparent ease she would have in New York, as she reported on and introduced several domestic stories. But viewers primarily saw features about Africa, often against exotic backgrounds.

As soon as the program ended, Greg was on the open phone line to the mobile control room parked outside the conference center. Manny had the call routed onto the intercom system. Everyone within earshot heard Greg's congratulations to the staff on a superb job, a great start. Manny was laughing as he had the call routed back into his receiver to report that people were exchanging high fives and the director was dancing on his chair. The two men would compare notes later about changes for tomorrow night, but first Greg wanted to speak alone to Chris.

She was removing her microphone as the phone rang beside her at the anchor desk. Greg's voice greeted her.

"You were terrific," he declared. "A smash opening night."

"It was really okay? I was afraid I was going to lose it at the start. A couple of times maybe I rushed and didn't get across well enough."

"You were terrific." He paused. "I apologize."

"What for?" she asked, surprised.

A long silence ensued. For a moment Chris thought the line had gone dead. Then she heard Greg's voice again.

"For a lot of things," he said quietly.

That was not something she wanted to hear. She had made up her mind to work with him, but she had resolved long ago never to forgive him. He had once said to her that some things can never be forgiven. Time had taught her that he was right: Some things never can be.

An instant later the humor was back in his voice. "One thing I apologize for is not pushing harder ten years ago for you to anchor on KFBS."

"Thanks," she said, but she always distrusted praise. "Now tell me what was wrong with the broadcast."

"Not much," he said honestly. "A little too much local pageantry maybe. I'd like to see the graphics improved and put more of the tape footage for the short pieces you report into a box next to you on the screen, so we still see you. Make the viewer feel you were there."

"But if I wasn't there—" she started to protest.

"We'll discuss all that when you get back to New York. It couldn't have been better."

Returning to her hotel, Chris was shouting silently inside herself with such exultation she was sure her colleagues crowded with her into the rented bus could hear and would gag her.

212

"This Is FBS News Tonight" with Christine Paskins, she kept repeating. Anchor Christine Paskins.

Ken was asleep when she entered their bedroom at the Norfolk. He came awake when she slipped naked into bed and kissed him.

"How did it go?" he mumbled.

"Okay," she whispered. "It was okay."

His eyes started to close again. She rolled on top of him and kissed him again.

"Don't you dare go back to sleep," she said.

Newspaper reports of Chris's premiere were uniformly favorable, but many raised questions about why FBS was able to anticipate the presidential trip and the other networks were not. FBS's Public Relations Department tried to forestall criticism by issuing a statement that the decision to be at the conference had been made for good journalistic reasons and before the President's plans were known. Senator Chandler's office issued a similar statement. Enraged at being scooped, the other networks besieged the White House press office with complaints. It was too late. Chris Paskins and FBS News had been launched.

Because the President remained in Nairobi, rather than the broadcast's rating dropping after viewers' natural curiosity to watch the first show had been satisfied, enough others tuned in the second night for FBS's temporary ratings lead to hold. Chris's interview that night with the secretary of State produced a big piece of news: The South African government would soon be releasing long-jailed officials of the outlawed African National Congress. On Thursday, President Bush would meet in Zambia with ANC leaders during a trip there, in hopes of initiating a dialogue between the two sides. Chris announced that she and FBS would be covering that trip and would continue on with the President to his meeting Friday in Cairo with Egypt's President Mubarak.

FBS had been lucky. Greg did not underestimate the amount of hard work and stamina still needed to lift the broadcast's popularity and quality, but its news organization had loudly, unmistakably, announced to the world that it was on the way back. Many executives with FBS affiliates, heartened by the speed with which he had delivered a more competitive news program, had already phoned him with compliments. Some had even enhanced their local news programs with clips from the African tape.

Greg did not expect to maintain the news broadcast's current ratings. By next week—probably even by the end of this week, as other networks flew in their anchors and more reporters—viewers would tend to return to their customary news favorites. But enough would have sampled the program to be aware of it and to peg Chris's rating substantially higher than Ray Strock's. Advertisers would have to pay more for scatter spots, bringing in more revenue, and even his strongest doubters would have to take him seriously now.

Although FBS remained the doormat of commercial television, Greg had the breathing space he had hoped for.

"That's Sally Foster!" a woman called out.

Sally smiled and lifted her chin and breasts higher as she walked past those waiting on line for a table at Los Angeles's Spago restaurant; such recognition was occurring less and less frequently. She was a couple of minutes late and knew that her punctual best friend, Annette, despite pressing demands, would already have arrived from the set of "I Love Luba." Annette Valletta did not wait on lines for a table.

Annette's life ran as precisely and unfailingly as a clock. But why shouldn't it? Life was so easy for Annette, Sally knew. "Luba" was bringing her several million dollars a year in salary, and she would eventually earn many millions more from residuals and syndication. Offers for movies and other TV work poured in. She lived in a large home in Holmby Hills with a pool and tennis court and gardens. The best restaurant tables were always available for Annette. The world indeed loved Luba and Annette.

Sally tried not to think of the disorder and failure that had nearly destroyed her own life. Self-pity, she had learned to her sorrow, only got you into deeper trouble. Since leaving the drug rehabilitation clinic, she had adopted the resilient Scarlett O'Hara's positive philosophy for her own: "Tomorrow is another day."

Annette had saved her life by taking her there. Annette was a major star, but Annette had never abandoned her. In a town where friendships die in tandem with declining Nielsen ratings and film grosses, how do you repay that sort of steadfast loyalty? Sally would be grateful to her friend until the day she died.

Sally had been out of the clinic for two years now. Drugs had harmed her in many ways—she was broke, for one—but she had not lost her looks. Although she might not be recognized so quickly now, heads still turned when she passed. And she was still taking acting classes and working out every day. At a time in her life when she should be luxuriating in success, she was still hustling for a break and living with a creep like Danny Vickers. Among many other flaws, he was a liar and secretly given to dressing in women's clothes in their bedroom. He made her skin crawl, but he represented her best chance for a comeback.

Annette's face lit up when she spotted Sally approaching, in the way that delighted millions every Wednesday night. Her blue eyes and mouth were pretty, but oversized, so her smile was bigger and her eyes livelier against the red of her hair when that smile took command of her face. Sally half-expected to hear Luba's endearing Russian accent call out to her, "Ha-llooo, Selly."

Annette was talking with a chunky, balding man who had come over to her window table. Behind them Los Angeles's lights sprouted prodigiously, like flowers in an infinite black lawn. She introduced him as Mickey Blinder, head of TV for Monumental.

He recognized Sally, said some nice things about her, and asked what she was working on. Sally's only prospect was the series concept Danny was trying to sell to the networks, but she answered in a way that made her sound in demand, yet still available for something Mickey might have for her. He stood aside to allow Sally to take her seat.

"You think about it, honey," he said to Annette. "It's a sweet deal. One more year for that kind of money. Think how much more your share of the residuals and profits will be worth with another year of episodes in the can."

Annette replied with hard-eyed practicality. "If FBS wants me for another year, they ought to be willing to guarantee me twenty-two episodes of a new series the year after."

"Monumental would love to do another series with you, you know that—" he began smoothly, pleased that he had anticipated her request.

She interrupted him. "Not Monumental, Mickey. Me. My own production company. Directly with FBS. I own the new show."

Mickey felt sweat wetting the back of his shirt collar. "You don't want all those headaches, the hiring, the accounting, the—"

"My own company. All the profits. A firm commitment for twenty-two episodes of any show I decide to do. And I want to pick a new executive producer for 'Luba.' "

"I'm sure your agents would tell you that—"

"Good-night, Mickey."

Mickey uttered effusive good-byes and returned to his own table. The two women leaned forward to exchange delayed kisses.

Annette explained that Mickey Blinder was trying to induce her to sign for another year of "Luba" after this one. Sally would have given an awful lot for *any* employment, and here was her friend declining to continue with a show that could easily run three or four more years.

Annette shrugged. "The way FBS treats me, I'd just as soon quit now and take my chances on coming up with a new series for another network."

Sally had heard the usual complaints over the years about inconsiderate treatment by network executives, but those were excuses for refusing to sign on again, not reasons.

"What's really bothering you?" Sally asked.

"Johnny," Annette confessed in a whisper to keep others from overhearing. "He hasn't been able to get any of his projects off the ground. My success and his failure is driving him crazy. He might just up and leave."

"And so you figured if he became 'Luba' 's new executive producer . . ."

Annette nodded. ". . . and he could also develop and produce the new series for our company, it might save my marriage. You know the way Johnny is."

Sally nodded. She knew very well how Johnny was. Italian. They had once been lovers, and afterward she had introduced him to Annette, who was also Italian and had melted. Many women considered Sally an excellent resource for dates. The list of her lovers was a long one.

Annette turned the conversation to Sally. She wanted to know how things were going with Danny Vickers. Embarrassed by the coldness of her feelings for him, Sally replied only that the TV series he had developed for her had still not been sold to the networks. More concerned about her friend's personal life, Annette expressed the hope that the couple's living together indicated a serious relationship forming for her friend. Sally practiced her acting by sounding enthusiastic about Danny.

December was the most incredible month for news since the end of the Second World War. Bush and Gorbachev met aboard ships off the Malta coast. Soon after, the Berlin Wall was breached, and thousands of East Germans surged into the West to taste freedom and buy the foodstuffs and electronic gadgetry they had long been denied. Chris and the news staff hopscotched across Eastern Europe as Communist dictatorships toppled like dominoes.

"The real Domino Theory turned out to be based not on conquest by warfare," she told her audience, "but by an idea, the idea of democracy."

She also joked that with visiting East Berliners rushing to spend the West German government's cash in West Berlin stores and the Eastern Bloc peoples' hungering for consumer goods, this might be called the Shoppers' Revolution. Her comment was widely quoted.

Each night after the broadcast, whether in person or by telephone, Greg oversaw a strategy session to improve the presentation. Chris was troubled by the number of his changes that dealt with the look of the production, not the substance of the news. They made sense, but at bottom they were purely cosmetic. This was a historic time. What difference did the angle of the camera's placement on her or the graphics' colors make?

She fell into the habit of discussing her feelings about the changes with Gerry Torborg, whose thoughtfulness seemed accentuated by his habit of pushing his half-glasses onto his forehead when not reading. He had been a news producer at the network for twenty years and before that, at several midwestern stations. Some criticized his slowness in preparing stories, but she found his journalistic integrity a strong buttress to her own arguments against Greg's sometimes overbearing certainty about the need for such changes. In her mind Gerry became her moral umpire overseeing television news's often mindless rat race to meet deadlines and raise ratings, a kind of St. Christopher's medal to remind her of her values. She made sure that he survived the staff cuts, and she steered stories his way that required thoughtful discernment about controversial issues.

Chris and Hedy Anderson had become friendly during the Africa trip. One night while the Senate was in session and Ken in Washington, the two women dropped into a local delicatessen for a late supper. Chris liked the other reporter's lack of pretension and earthy candor; they had a lot in common.

Hedy brought up how impressed everyone on the staff had been to discover that Greg Lyall, the new CEO, was so committed to the news. Chris immediately set the other woman straight.

"It's not integrity. He has no integrity. For him it's a business strategy, its numbers. Greg thinks more people will watch if they believe they're getting more from FBS. You know, a marketing bonus deal, like getting extra steak knives in that TV ad. If he thought the audience'd buy dirty limericks set to music, he'd push us to take singing lessons."

That weekend Chris flew down to Washington to join Ken at a White House dinner. Foreign dignitaries and luminaries from a multitude of fields had been invited. Several well-known musicians entertained. Chris was able to contrive a private moment to thank the President and First Lady for their graciousness in submitting to the interviews in Nairobi and Cairo.

During cocktails she found herself conversing with a Latin American businessman. Something about his face was familiar, but his name was not. A lifetime's experience had taught her to listen to the premonition that jangled like a small bell deep inside her subconscious. She had an idea who he might be.

Chris made several phone calls the next morning and had a researcher at the Washington bureau do some checking. Her mistrust and the sound of that internal bell continued to amplify.

At two-fifteen that afternoon, a phone call reached Chris with some of the answers she had been seeking. George Bush had never satisfactorily brushed away the suspicions about illegal dealings with the contras when he was vice president. Now, it turned out that one of the men named during the Iran-contra hearings, who had disappeared after being indicted for his part in the illegal transfer of funds, may have been an honored guest at that White House dinner. The phone call also raised one very large question.

She took her apprehensions and the facts she had unearthed so far to Manny, and then, with the News Division's president on vacation, both immediately went upstairs to see Greg. They waited in his outer office for a prior meeting to end.

Greg was meeting with Ev Carver and Bill Jorgenson. The three men agreed that the first prescription for the company's recovery, the cost-cutting, was going well. But programming was the heart of any network and the company's most critical area. Greg was planning a trip to Los Angeles to meet with Raoul Clampton and to spend time becoming reacquainted with the Hollywood creative community that FBS needed to attract if it was to gain access to better shows. Ev, to whom Clampton reported, would join him.

Chris and Manny replaced the two executives in Greg's office. She surveyed the immense space as she took a seat. The wall behind her contained a line of color photos, portraits of major performers on the network. Hers was the first. Ignoring the compliment, she began to recount the matter they had come to discuss, her eyes pugnaciously fixed on Greg's.

When she concluded, Greg asked, "Did this fellow you met at the White House admit he was the man named in the hearings?"

"I haven't confronted him and don't intend to until we have all the evidence and are about to go on the air."

Greg agreed. Not wanting to lose the exclusive, only at the last moment would they offer the man an opportunity to answer the charges—when enough time remained to insert his statements into the piece but not enough for the story to leak out.

Greg fell into the devil's advocate role he had once automatically assumed with her in such discussions. "How can you be sure it's the same man?"

"Except for a mustache, he resembles photos of him for one thing."

"He could be a look-alike. And Lopez is a common Hispanic name."

Manny had made the same comments and nodded.

Chris rejoined, "My contact has arranged a meeting for tonight with a source he says has documents that will prove the two men are one and the same."

Chris paused, anticipating the problem her next words would cause. "He wants twenty-five thousand dollars for the documents."

"Oh," Greg said, with a sound like air rushing from a punctured tire.

The question of whether to buy incriminating testimony was touchy for news organizations. The decision had to be made at the highest managerial level. Most responsible daily newspapers took the position that they would not buy information, that the act undermined their credibility. Broadcasters, however, had done it in the past. Nixon's chief of staff, H. R. Haldeman, was well paid for a Mike Wallace interview. Book publishers paid people for "insider" books as a matter of course. Those opposed to buying information expressed the fear that if an auction market existed, informers would tend to hold back information they now gave freely.

"Forget about the morality for a minute," Manny remarked. "On price alone I told her the deal is crazy."

"I'll go there with you," Greg decided. "We'll play it by ear."

15

~~~~~~~~~~~~~~~~

After that night's broadcast ended, the three FBS people were
driven down together to Park Bistro, a restaurant on lower
Park Avenue, and given a large table in the rear. They
ordered dinner and waited for the informers to arrive.

Manny returned from the rest room just as the waiter was placing
their appetizers on the table. Greg was seized by a startling reminis-
cence: Nine years before in Los Angeles he and Chris, then secretly
living together, were dining at a small restaurant when Manny entered
with a date.

Greg glanced over at Chris. Her delicately delineated profile was
pointed at Manny, who was speaking. Greg thought he detected a flush
on her cheek, but his angle to her made him unsure. Did she remember,
too, or were his own thoughts imposing themselves on his perception of
her? He longed to see her face. Had a blush overcome her? Turn, he
pleaded silently. Turn and glance at me and let me know that you share
my nostalgia.

"Butter?" he asked her.

Only her eyes shifted to take him in for an instant. "No, thank you."

His gaze slowly traced the edge of her profile, commencing at her
careless blond locks: A long crescent of brow ended at the notch where
the impeccable straightness of her nose began; her soft top lip curled
upward, mirroring a lower companion that dipped down in the suggestion of a pout; her chin was a soft prow that suggested her determination; her long, sloping neck elevated her head as elegantly as a Carrara
pedestal. She was beautiful in a way that seemed limitless to him, that
needed no mental allowance for the slightest defect.

She turned at that precise moment. He smiled at her, his pulse
racing.

"Then you do agree," she said, her expression intense.

He was disheartened to observe no residue of a blush on her skin. He could not tell what she had been thinking, just as he could never be quite sure all those years ago.

"Do you agree with me?" she repeated.

"I wasn't listening," he admitted.

Chris's expression turned guarded and stern at his inattention. "If the material proves without a doubt that the man I met last night at the White House is the man who's under a federal indictment, then we have to buy it. Look at it this way: If this Lopez is doing something illegal and the President's implicated, we would be morally remiss in *not* paying for it and broadcasting, right?"

Greg nodded. "Everything's for sale in one way or another. The trick is to try to retain our principles."

Ordinarily, Greg's professing virtue would trigger scorn from her, but she was too intent on winning her argument. "So it's not the principle of payment," she concluded with a tinge of triumph in her voice as she turned back to Manny, "but *what is being paid for* that's crucial."

Manny rushed to differ. "Buying this proof troubles me. The President just might not have recognized this guy last night. What if our money goes to finance some South American terrorist group? How would we look?"

Greg weighed the contentions. "The President knew Lopez fairly well. He would certainly recognize the guy when he was introduced to someone called Lopez-Melendez, with or without a mustache. And because of the hearings, he would know the guy was a fugitive. If so, he shouldn't have posed for pictures with him. That seems pretty major to me."

Chris smiled at Greg and impulsively gripped his hand, a kind of recognition between teammates. Greg's pulse pounded in his ears. Her hand snapped back as if singed. Greg assumed she had glimpsed desire in his eyes.

I'm acting ridiculously, he told himself. He straightened up in the booth and plunged his fork into his nearest *moule.*

Two swarthy men of medium height entered and peered reticently around. Spotting Chris in the rear booth, they shambled toward her. The spokesman for the pair was the man with whom she had spoken on the phone, a minor official with the Venezuelan consulate. His companion was a clerk at a Maryland bank. Both men spoke overly correct English with heavy Hispanic accents.

The second man apologized for having to ask for payment. "I fear the people who own the bank where I work. If they determine I was the one who gave you these"—he held up a manila envelope—"I will need the money to run."

Lopez owned an interest in the bank, a fact that had never come out during the Iran-contra hearings. The speaker placed on the table photocopied corporate bank records, dated prior to the hearings. For purposes of registering with various regulatory commissions, Lopez had changed his name to Lopez-Melendez (which added his mother's last name to his father's in Hispanic style). Photographs were attached to several documents. The speaker had thought it wrong at the time that Lopez, a fugitive, was involved with the bank and was sure the FBI or a regulatory commission would track him down. But none did. He himself was too frightened to speak out until his friend said Christine Paskins had been making inquiries about the man.

"We want the documents," Greg admitted after he and his colleagues had examined them, "but I don't think you really want to cheapen what you're doing by putting a price on it. You have my word that we'll keep your identity secret. If a problem arises with your bosses and you fear for your safety, the money will be there for you, as well as legal help no matter how much that costs."

The speaker turned to Manny, whom he recognized as a fellow Latino. *"Quién es este hombre?"*

"El jefe de FBS," Manny answered.

The man thought for a minute and then nodded his agreement at Greg. Chris's hands darted out at the documents now sitting in the middle of the table.

After several seconds, perceiving that the transaction had been completed, the South Americans pushed back their chairs and hurried from the restaurant.

"I admire your refusing to pay," Manny said to Greg.

"He was just trying to save the money," Chris remarked cynically, and turned to Greg for confirmation.

Greg pulled a check from his inside jacket pocket. Already made out to cash, it lacked only an amount and Greg's signature to be bankable.

Like a second cellophane gel slipped over the first, Chris's skeptical glance back at Manny was colored by the satisfaction of having detected Greg's materialism. The waiter arrived at that moment with the main courses.

The three were silent for several minutes, enmeshed in their own thoughts. Chris was the first to speak up.

"What if this story is bigger than an innocent mistake in the White House invitation list?"

"Let's hope so," Greg replied, and smiled wryly at her.

Chris returned the conspiratorial grin. She had hungered for this excitement during her exile to the morning show, this rush that came as if her foot had suddenly slammed pedal to metal. They had shared kicks like this once. With Manny, too. The three grinned broadly at one another.

For several days the news was filled with the story Chris had broken. The White House contended at first that the President had no idea who the man at the dinner really was, but then changed that story to say that the invitation had been part of an elaborate sting operation to convince Colombian drug lords that he was protecting the man, so they could rely on the man's banking empire to move their funds out of the United States. American and Colombian authorities would then capture the drug lords and seize their funds.

Most Americans who thought about it were outraged that Chris Paskins's disclosure had ruined a chance to capture drug kingpins. Why had she run the story anyway? Wasn't she just trying to smear the President, to look like a crusader at his and our country's expense? The drug cartel could have been crippled, isn't that what the President said? And the irresponsible journalists at FBS had ruined any chance of that. Where was their patriotism, their concern for America?

Few stopped to consider the flimsiness of the White House's story or that the plan might not have worked or that a federal fugitive was being shielded without the approval of the court that had indicted him. The President looked like a hero. He had been trying to do something to free the nation from drugs. A television network had thwarted him. Goddamn reporters!

Ken Chandler was furious at her. A guest at the White House, Chris had violated the President's hospitality and breached the confidentiality of a private evening. Didn't she think enough of Ken's position at least to inform him beforehand what she intended to do? She was destroying his relationship with the President, his party, and every voter who respected this country.

Several angry FBS directors and affiliate executives blasted Greg over the phone. The angriest phone call was from Barnett Roderick, who had himself just received a personal phone call from the President. The nation's chief executive had expressed his extreme dismay at FBS's actions. The two men had been close friends for many years and had once discussed the possibility of an ambassadorship for Roderick if the network owner ever retired. Because such antagonistic reporting could foreclose that possibility if Barnett ever decided he wanted it, he was doubly furious that FBS News had acted "so unpatriotically."

Barnett ordered Greg to fire Chris and the executive producer for acting "irresponsibly." Greg replied that he himself had authorized the story after the White House refused to explain why the story should not run.

"Damn it!" Barnett growled. "You really let your new power go to your head. Who the hell do you think you are to insist that the President give you an answer?"

"That's *supposed* to be the press's job."

"You've got a short memory. When Nixon and Agnew went after the TV newspeople, we were terrified that our stations might lose their licenses. We tiptoed for months."

"Not that short. I remember what happened to Nixon and Agnew. They had good reason to fear the truth from the press."

The answer angered Barnett more. "Your job is to make money, not headlines. Offending the government and your viewers is not smart business."

"Greg Lyall and I will be flying out for programming meetings," Ev said to Raoul over the phone.

Ev sat propped against his headboard, fully dressed, phone receiver to his ear, stockinged feet extended before him. Night now in New York, office hours still prevailed on the West Coast, where it was three hours earlier. Raoul Clampton was still in his office.

"You have the dates we'll be out there," Ev continued, "and know that we want a full-scale rundown on problems in the current schedule and on what you have in the hopper for pilot shows."

"What's Lyall thinking?" Raoul asked.

Ev could sense the Programming vice president's apprehension. The man's fear was the reason Ev trusted him. Raoul was really asking, "Am I safe?" and "What kinds of programs does he want?"

"I imagine he's thinking the same thing I'm thinking. If you don't give us higher-rated shows next fall, we take you out and shoot you."

Raoul was always nervous dealing with Ev Carver and knew he never quite sounded in control of matters. Carver's ruthlessness even underlay his jokes.

"It's tough when you're not the number one network," Raoul complained. "Suppliers don't bring the best projects to us because we don't have hit shows we can schedule before theirs to deliver a big audience."

"I heard that bullshit last year, Raoul. This year we want ratings."

"A lot of great concepts here," Raoul said quickly. "We're testing every last detail. We're pretty hopeful."

"You sound more anxious than hopeful."

Ev's doorbell rang.

"Come in!" he called out. "The front door's open."

A moment later Hedy Anderson entered Ev's bedroom. He patted the bed. She sat down beside him. Ev returned to his phone call.

"I had to get the door," he said into the phone. "Lyall and I want you to set up a big party when we're there: spectacular, the best caterer, whatever it takes. Invite the stars and creative people behind our present shows."

"Could you get Chris Paskins out here for it? The community here is impressed that we hired her. They think it demonstrates we're committed to doing what it takes to rebuild."

"Newspeople always impress them. They think of them as intellectuals. Maybe I can convince Lyall to send the whole broadcast there. Do some sort of arc on California and the West. That way all our top correspondents could be at the party . . ."

Hedy was waiting to learn whether she would be asked.

". . . like Hedy Anderson," he said into the phone, and winked at her. Ev slid the tab of his fly zipper down and gestured for her to play with his cock. Hedy hid her grimace from him as she pulled the long, flaccid hose free and began to manipulate it.

Ev turned his attention back to the phone conversation. "But the point of this shindig, the whole reason we're putting on this show, is because we want you to invite the top creative people in Hollywood— producers, writers, stars, you know who I mean. We want to convince them that FBS is a great place for their shows, to sell them on bringing their new shows to FBS."

"Do you think Lyall would like me to have women there?"

"If you mean whores you claim are starlets, no. This is pure business."

"Ev," Raoul brought up, "we might have some trouble getting Annette Valletta there. Mickey Blinder says she's being difficult about doing 'Luba' after this year. You got my memo. Is Lyall concerned about it?"

"He will be when he finds out. Resolve it before we get out there."

"She's asking a lot."

Ev was growing exasperated. "Who the hell else do we have in the top fifteen?"

Ev's penis had hardened. He motioned for Hedy to suck him off. She suppressed the ripple of nausea in her stomach. The bastard had not even said hello to her.

During a visit to FBS's Chicago station, Ev had plucked Hedy from near obscurity as one of its street reporters. She had given him a wild night and two weeks later, was in New York with a network contract. But she knew that standing up to him could end her career just as fast as he had boosted it.

Dutifully, she lowered her head and enclosed him with her mouth. She hoped to bring him off quickly, before he began thrusting into her and she choked on the excessive length.

"Right, Annette's important to us," Raoul agreed. He always felt he had to placate Ev Carver when dealing with him, never more so than now. "If Monumental does get us another year of 'Luba,' we'll have to guarantee they get a new series on next year's schedule and that the year after Annette gets a new one of her own on."

Ev asked incredulously, "We have to do them a favor for keeping their goddamn show on the air?"

"If my memory is right," Raoul said quickly, "isn't your birthday coming up? Mickey Blinder wants to be even more generous with you this year. He's thinking you might like one of those big Mercedes. He could leave it for you at your hotel."

Ev grabbed Hedy's hair to stop her oscillation.

"Are you crazy?" he shouted into the phone. "I tell you I'm coming out there with the CEO who's been firing guys right and left and you want to know if some supplier can slip me a new car when I arrive? You've got to have shit for brains. I might not like Lyall, but at least I'm smart enough not to expose my ass to his gunsight."

"Look, I didn't mean it like that, Ev. It's just a gift."

Ev wanted to end the conversation. "You know the dates we'll be out there. Make the arrangements."

Hanging up, he released Hedy's hair and clasped his hands behind his neck. He liked the way Hedy gave head and chuckled at the aptness of her name. She kind of dragged her bottom teeth lightly along the underside. There was a lot to be said for Hedy. Big and good-looking. Presentable in company. Good reporter, too. Kept her eyes and ears open for information he could use, like that stuff about how Greg Lyall was at the center of the White House story. She knew her place. She owed him a lot and was smart enough not to step out of line.

Hedy glanced up at him. He smiled at her and patted her cheek. He thought he'd give her a little help and began thrusting deeply into her.

"Was I wrong to go with the story?" Chris asked, voicing her private apprehension to Gerry Torborg. "Maybe I didn't have enough facts yet. Or maybe it was wrong even to run a story that might embarrass the President unless I out-and-out caught him with his hand in the cookie jar."

The middle-aged news producer thought about this before answering. "You had enough facts to raise the issues you did. And they were good issues, and necessary."

"Then why am I getting attacked like this?"

"The government and the press are natural enemies. Each keeps the other honest. The government's always sure their secret maneuvers are for the best, or they want to cover up their fiascos and are furious to have them discovered and questioned. We're sure they can become tyrants or can endanger us in some other way unless we expose them. Natural enemies. It can be painful until the dust settles and the truth vindicates you."

Chris bit her lip. "Or maybe it never does."

Gerry slowly nodded.

In this case Chris had to wait only until the third day, when FBS's South American correspondents beamed up unedited footage proving that Lopez's banking interests down there were scanty—not by any stretch of the imagination the empire the White House had suggested—and what was most critical, that bank-fraud charges were outstanding against him in Venezuela.

"Yes!" Chris cried out as she heard the revelation on the videotape.

Her eyes ablaze with the zest for battle flaring within her at that moment, she turned to Greg. "I think we both want to be very sure we handle this right, Greg. Would you help me edit this material and write my remarks?"

He was as exhilarated as she. After years spent pursuing his career with caution and restraint, he burst with enthusiasm, burned with ardor, exulted in achievement.

"I'd have been looking over your shoulder every minute anyway."

"Just like the old days."

The White House quickly backtracked to distance itself from Lopez-Melendez, admitting that its eagerness to fight drugs may have allowed itself to be conned a bit. The new disclosures, everyone agreed, went a long way toward reestablishing FBS's credibility and enhancing Chris's reputation as a reporter.

Greg noticed that some of the sharpness of her attitude toward him seemed to have been sanded down by their working so closely together during the crisis. She no longer always appeared poised to bite off his head, and could deal unemotionally with him. She might not like him—she probably never would, he was sure—but at least he had won back a bit of her respect.

He wished with all his heart that he could deal as impassively with her. Proximity stoked embers within him he had told himself had long since died out. His flesh burned as hotly now as when they first met. The same fire, that hunger to possess her, consumed his groin. His emotions were contending what his reason had always denied: that he still desired her. By choosing opportunism over integrity, over love, he had gained the advantages he had sought. He was head of the network, one of the most powerful men in television. But his life away from work was loveless and superficial. He felt now as if he had just awakened from a decade of sleepwalking.

With so much else on his mind, he did not need those disturbing thoughts shouting for attention in his brain.

Once or twice Chris had noticed him staring at her. She had smiled self-consciously, but had appeared annoyed. He would have to watch himself more carefully.

One other thing he would have to watch out for: Someone in the newsroom was obviously leaking reports to newspapers. Several had named Greg as having personally directed "the attack against the President." FBS's directors would surely love that.

"Surprise!"

The guests bunched from wall to foyer wall grinned at Greg, who had just returned from work and let himself into the apartment.

Diane rushed into his arms. She was laughing at his confusion.

"You won't remember in a million years what this anniversary is."

He shook his head.

She kissed him. "You and I met exactly nine years ago tonight." She kissed him again, laughing. "You do remember that?"

"At the Beverly Hills Hotel. You thought I was your chauffeur."

"How times have changed," one of the men called out.

"I was in love with you by the end of that night," Diane reminded him. "I've never asked how you felt."

"It took me a little longer."

"At least you can lie a little for the sake of our guests and my romantic soul."

"I was always a little retarded," Greg joked.

"There wasn't somebody else, was there Greg?" Diane's friend Libby teased.

Diane wrapped her arm around his waist as she guided him toward the guests. He draped an arm on her shoulder.

"I know nine isn't a round number, but I wanted to give you a party," she said. "Were you really surprised?"

He nodded.

"Pleased?"

He nodded again.

She laughed once more. "You look like a bomb fell on you."

"I feel that way. Giving this party is really a lovely idea. Thank you."

Diane leaned her head onto his shoulder for an instant, then turned to face him, both hands about his waist. In years past much of her free time had been spent with him. She had looked forward to it.

"I know I've been very busy lately," she admitted. "And so have you. But I wanted you to know that you've been a wonderful husband and make me very happy."

She waited for him to say something similar. He bent down and kissed her.

"Happy anniversary."

They made love several times that night. That had not happened in many years. All the while Greg thought of Chris. Even when he was exhausted and on the edge of sleep, he still felt unsatisfied. He also felt like a heel.

The next morning he told his secretary to have a huge floral bouquet sent to Chris. Not white roses. The card should read "For courage under fire" and should be signed "A still-admiring Greg Lyall." He assured himself the sentiment was as proper as any network CEO would have sent his anchor after such an ordeal.

At lunchtime he stopped off at Harry Winston and sent Diane diamond earrings to commemorate the anniversary. The note was warm and loving.

16

〜〜〜〜〜〜〜〜〜

C hris was worn out. The duel with the White House had taken a lot out of her, the tension more wearing than the investigation. She was grateful for Friday's arrival.

Ken was in Washington, and she flew down there to join him for a dinner party with administration insiders and wealthy contributors. He and her hosts knew when she accepted the invitation that her job would keep her from arriving on time, but earlier that day she had gotten a strong impression from him on the phone that he and they would rather she not attend. Because she was so exhausted in mind and spirit, she almost acquiesced, but then she decided that staying apart would solve nothing in what promised to become an ongoing cause of conflict with Ken and might even indicate cowardice to her hosts.

She caught the eight-o'clock Trump shuttle at LaGuardia. She had hoped to sleep, but too much was still on her mind.

Now that the confrontation with the White House had ended, she tried to weigh what the fight had gained her and what she had lost. Her journalistic reputation had been enhanced, but the gate had doubtless closed on the easy access granted her in Africa by the President and First Lady, who would now be openly hostile. Did they believe the invitation had somehow bought her complicity? Did they really expect her to ignore their harboring a fugitive? The prospect of coming upon a story like that was what had lured her into journalism.

One result of coming under pressure so quickly in her new post was learning she could rely on many of the news team to do their jobs well. Hedy, for one, had dug up a strong story outlining Lopez's political connections to Bush loyalists. Chris's greatest surprise during the uncertain days just past was Greg. He had stood his ground beside her when the safer course for the network would have been to order silence. Why? She had brooded over that since the first meeting in his

230

office with Manny, and she still couldn't find a satisfactory answer. Ten years before he had sold her down the river for personal advantage, but now when his safer course as head of the network was to kill the story, he had refused. What was different now? The circumstances? The times? The most improbable reason she could come up with was that Greg might have changed.

She had convinced herself after he left her that Greg Lyall was an easy man to decipher, one of the legion of the immorally ambitious, a shark who kept mindlessly swimming and feeding his growth from birth until death. But more than simple self-interest had motivated him, something smacking of principle—or she assumed, that he had hoped might pass for principle. But she could not be certain of his selfishness. She remembered instances at KFBS when he fought to maintain the integrity of the news. Chris did not like feeling respect for Greg. It complicated her cynicism about his motives.

The plane landed gently along the carpet of lights and taxied to the Trump terminal. Chris turned her thoughts to the dinner party and her husband. As a reporter she was used to being considered the enemy by politicians: If they couldn't manipulate you, they feared you. She refused to think of her husband that way. But with him, too, the situation had become more complicated.

Chris had arranged for a limousine to drive her to the Georgetown town house where the party was being held. The guests were already seated at the long dinner table when she arrived. Ken rose and stepped forward to meet her. She noted his hearty campaign smile, which meant that appearances here were uppermost in his mind. She kissed him lightly and greeted the others with a general salutation meant to cover them all.

What struck her as she took her seat beside Ken was how silent had become a room that the moment before she entered had been an aviary of sound. Chris decided that if she did not break the ice, the evening would be unbearable for everyone. As usual she chose to do it head-on, like an Arctic freighter.

"Sorry I'm late, but George and Barbara couldn't bear for me to leave."

Laughter cracked the strain. The dinner party started up again.

Chris sneaked a glance at Ken. He was laughing, with a kind of pride in his expression.

That's the way it is, Ken, she told him in her thoughts. It isn't going to change. What you saw on TV was what you got.

Stew Graushner's pride since learning how unenthusiastically the networks had received "Lowdown" could be measured with an eye-

231

dropper. He was gaining the impression that Mickey Blinder had just about run out of places to sell the project. Stew was living with Susan now, using what would have been rent money to pay down the loan he took out for his daughter's tuition. Susan bought the food, as well as "little gifts" of clothing for him that now comprised a complete wardrobe. He drove a car she had rented for him while his own was "being repaired." Just about his only remaining independence derived from his hateful job at "The Guts of the Story," which Susan did not know about. He feared that if he gave it up, he would lose "those wonderfully off-center ideas about characters" and "that wild dialogue" that Susan believed were being born directly out of his imagination. But what would he have to offer Susan when the project's last turn-down was announced? Why would she want to stay with him then?

"I love the fact that you can let me do things for you and not feel you've somehow lost your manhood," she said, pausing to touch his cheek. "About last night . . . I hope you're not still troubled by it. That happens to every man once in a while. Sometimes even as often as it's been happening to you."

She took a deep breath and smiled brightly. "It doesn't bother *me* a bit. Really. I just jog an extra two miles the next morning."

Her thighs, he recalled, were now rippling with muscles.

Greg stood in the back of the control room as the news broadcast wound down. Its rebuilding was going well. Other programming areas now needed his energies more, but few offered so apparent an opportunity for quick repair. One disaster that he might just have to live with for the time being was sports programming.

FBS had not won the bidding for a major sports package in years and was gradually running out of viable sports programs. He cringed at the knowledge that until the succession of senior golf tournaments kicked in early next year, Saturday afternoon's highlight was a contrivance called "Celebrity Darts."

NBC had captured the '92 Summer Olympics, CBS's top-dollar bid had won the '92 and '94 Winter games, NCAA basketball, and four years of major-league baseball playoffs and World Series games. CBS had argued that the late-season baseball championships, for example, were an excellent promotional platform for its new fall shows and so were worth more than just the advertising revenue they could earn. Contending that the prices were far too high, Barnett had dropped out of the auctions; he was interested in the bottom line, he said, not hype. The head of FBS's Sports Programming Department jumped at the chance to evacuate a sinking ship when the severance package was offered.

Because any package he bought would not be on the air for at least a year, maybe two, Greg decided he would just have to go with a weak sports-magazine show filled with second-rate sports and raid the other networks for a new sports programmer. Meanwhile, he would have to fight preemptions from the affiliates for movies and local sports and hoard his funds for use where it would do the most good: developing the best prime-time series, movies, and miniseries to refloat the good ship FBS. With so much sports on TV now, he hoped that market was overloaded.

"I think the format's pretty much there," he remarked to Manny as Chris signed off at the end of "This Is FBS News Tonight."

Manny had been making a list of items he wanted to fix. They had to be small ones, Greg thought. The program had a distinctive character now that approached what they had been trying for.

Greg went out into the newsroom to tell that to Chris.

"You sound a little sad," she noted after he had told her.

Walking back to her office with her, Greg realized that he was. After years of careful paper-shuffling, once more he had burned with zeal and experienced real satisfaction. But his work here was more or less done.

Chris offered encouragement. "You've got a whole network out there waiting for you to lead it."

"This was a lot easier than that will be. I don't have many tricks left up my sleeve to dazzle them with . . . like a Chris Paskins I could throw at the news ratings."

She decided that the moment was right to ask him something that had been on her mind for days. "Why did you give me the go-ahead to do the White House story in the first place? It would have been a lot safer not to."

"I figured you needed to break a big, controversial story," he answered. "Viewers had to think of you as more than just a pretty face on the dial. Your image needed stature. Going up against the President was chancy, but perfect."

"So, it was for ratings again, not truth or the people's right to know or any ideal like that."

"Idealism is a luxury I can't afford right now."

Instead of being scornful, she was intrigued. "Why are you admitting it to me? You could easily lie to make me think better of you."

They were just outside her office now.

"I lied to you once and I've never stopped regretting it. I never want to do it again."

His gaze was relentless. Chris glanced away and ducked into her office. She was frightened of the feelings breaking shackles within her.

*　　*　　*

233

Raoul Clampton was jiggling his foot. That was not a good sign, Marian knew. It meant he was scared and might act erratically.

She and the other programming executives were seated around the conference table. Raoul had spent the morning with his scheduling people, frantically shuffling plaques around on the magnetic board to devise lineups that would improve FBS's prime-time ratings against its competitors. From his development people this afternoon he wanted to know their best prospects for pilot shows, which they would then present personally to Greg Lyall and Ev Carver at the upcoming meetings. Marian understood that meant Raoul wanted to spread the blame.

Earlier in the day one of the lawyers in Business Affairs had sent her a note to ask if she knew anything about a new financial arrangement for "Luba." Clampton had just sent him a memo directing him to increase the license fee in Monumental's contract for "I Love Luba" by a hundred thousand dollars per episode—retroactively to the start of the fall season. FBS seemed to have gotten nothing in return. That was an outright grant to Monumental for the year of $2.2 million, a lot of money for a company tightening its belt. Clampton's memo also asked the lawyer to add a clause that gave Monumental a blind thirteen-week commitment for a new sitcom next year.

She had copies of both Raoul's and the lawyer's memos and wanted to check later with Clampton about them. She could not conceive of his having given away a slot in next year's schedule sight unseen without even mentioning it to her.

Barry Collins, in charge of developing dramatic series, was extolling what Marian judged to be very predictable choices he had tried to make even safer by casting stars as leads. The stars, though, seemed lackluster and ill suited to their roles. Stars don't guarantee TV hits, she had always believed; TV makes its own stars. As Collins neared the end of his presentation, she admonished herself not to scream out loud if he lauded another cop show or some variation.

"Oh, there's one more we ought to be very excited about," he added. "It's called 'Squad Five.' It's about a group of five cops, all with special talents, who take on the toughest police assignments in the city. It's a gritty combination of 'Mission: Impossible' and 'Hill Street Blues.' The head honcho of the squad was a Green Beret in Nam whose wife was killed by drug dealers out to teach him a lesson. He volunteered to form the squad in order to find them and bring them to justice. One member of the squad's a rock singer in his spare time. A second's an ex-tennis star. One's this really gorgeous chick who's a karate champ, but used to be a hooker, so she knows the underworld. Realism, that's what we're after here. A great feature is that if one of the actor's Q-ratings drops, we can kill him off on the show and add one who's more popular."

"I love it, Barry," Raoul praised him, his voice registering more pep than it had since the meeting began.

"Great, Barry."

"Very creative."

"Good going, fella," two others simultaneously chimed in.

Marian had been made uneasy by Raoul's comment that she and her colleagues would have to claim the choices they were presenting to the top brass were their own; she would be held accountable for shows she despised.

As Raoul called on her for her presentation, Marian made a crucial decision. She slipped the pages before her into a folder and pulled out new ones. She began to speak.

"I've given a lot of thought to our comedy lineup. I'm convinced that because we're last in the ratings, we have to be daring, experiment, try for something new to get attention from viewers: new formats. So . . . these are the comedy proposals we ought to back."

Marian began to list those she believed in and wanted to present to Lyall and Carver. She had eliminated ones Clampton truly hated, but every choice she now proposed he had clearly vetoed.

In very short order he angrily cut her off.

"I think I have a pretty good idea of the comedy series concepts I want to go with. I'll present them myself."

He then called on the woman in charge of long-form drama-movies-made-for-TV and miniseries to brief the group.

When the meeting ended, Raoul asked Marian to follow him to his office, where he closed the door just long enough to fire her. She started to argue—not for herself, but for the shows he should be supporting.

"That's now my worry," he told her curtly. "You're nothing anymore. Be out of here in twenty minutes."

Marian was gone in ten, her personal belongings in a cardboard carton that filled her arms. Sentimentally, she had thrown into it a pile of discarded comedy proposals she liked. Out of the corner of her eye, she spied her former second-in-command—now her successor—coming down the hall with her own carton in her arms. Marian did not slow down to offer her best wishes.

She placed her belongings in the backseat of her car. Her only stop on the way home was Baskin-Robbins, where she bought a quart of Rocky Road and a quart of Jamocha Almond Fudge. Then she drove straight to her house.

"Fuck Raoul Clampton!" she screamed at the top of her lungs as she braked to a stop before her garage. Several birds atop her bushes flew off in fear.

"Fuck cop shows!" she shouted, and ripped the tops off the ice-cream containers.

"Fuck cookie-cutter sitcoms!"

She attacked the ice cream.

"Fuck my hips!"

Her gaze swung up to pierce firmament visible above the open sunroof. "And as long as I've got You're attention, fuck television and all the assholes in it!"

While she scooped large dollops of first one and then the other ice-cream flavor into her mouth, tears rolled down her cheeks.

Greg and Ev arrived at FBS's Los Angeles headquarters early in the morning after a late flight and some sleep at a hotel.

Ev was just here for show, Greg suspected, awaiting the palace revolution after next year's season went down the tubes and took Greg with it. Ev was already making clear to one and all that Greg had taken over responsibility for fashioning the new lineup.

As he walked down the corridor, Greg was struck by how many people were employed in the Programming Department. Some were seeking and overseeing the projects that would result in next season's new shows, one or two were experts in placing shows on the schedule to best attract viewers away from rival networks, and many oversaw current shows: evaluating new story lines, requesting script and cast changes, and frequently fighting with producers.

Although Greg had heard good things about Raoul Clampton from others, his own impression had always been of a nervous man, always moving, a weathervane responding to the corporate mood.

The first order of business was evaluating the current schedule. Greg did not want to take the time right now to examine the few dayparts that were holding their own against the competition. Saturday morning was decent: a mix of cartoon and live children's shows with adequate ratings. Late night was acceptable, too, a hot young comedian whose talk show was building against Johnny Carson and the rest of the competition. Greg was interested in the other dayparts.

"Let's start with morning and work through to prime time," Greg requested. In other words, he thought, let's examine the heart-attack victim's failing heart last.

At FBS the network's morning program was the Entertainment Division's responsibility, as at ABC, rather than the News Division's, as at NBC and CBS. The idea was that viewers seeking lighter fare—less news, more chatter and features—might choose FBS in the morning.

Raoul seemed to be content with the program, until Greg told him to start looking for new hosts and a new producer to inject some vitality into two very boring hours.

"Absolutely right," Raoul agreed. "My people have been considering Ron Skink to produce it."

Greg's glare prompted instant retreat by the programming chief, who quickly added, "But I told them that was a terrible idea."

Next came daytime. FBS was holding its own better there than during any other daypart. A couple of good soap operas and a network-owned talk show led into late afternoon—known as early fringe—and then to prime access. Except for the half hour of network news, the latter periods were reserved to the local stations, which fought their own regional rating wars with syndicated talk shows such as "Oprah" and "Donahue" and "Geraldo" and game shows such as "Wheel of Fortune" and "Jeopardy."

The three-hour block from eight to eleven P.M. was prime time, attracting the greatest number of viewers and the greatest number of dollars. Only on Friday night was FBS competitive, when "Luba" drew a large early audience and helped pull along the shows that followed.

Raoul nervously explained the series arrangements he had made with Annette Valletta and Monumental to obtain a renewal for "Luba."

Greg stopped him. "I understand why you gave Annette a series commitment for doing another year of 'Luba.' Any new show we put on the air with her after that will have as good a chance of making it as anything else we could put on. But why the commitment to Monumental?"

"Without Monumental," Raoul replied, "we couldn't have gotten Annette to renew."

"That seems odd if she's willing to do her next series without them," Greg said, and turned to Ev.

Ev nodded in agreement. Raoul Clampton would have to sink or swim on his own. If he sank, Ev did not want to be the man seen trying to toss him a life preserver.

Raoul tried to embroider his explanation. "They would have canceled 'Luba' on us."

Greg cut off the discussion. "You've already given them the deal in writing, so we're wasting our time raising objections. From now on no new deals get made without my approval."

Raoul stepped up to the magnetic scheduling board to present the changes he proposed to make in the current prime-time lineup. It was divided into wide vertical columns for each night, within which were narrower columns representing each network's fare on that night. Across the top were the days of the week. Down the sides were the evening hours from eight to eleven. Rectangular plaques listing an FBS show could be moved around the board into different time periods and compared to the competition at that time. Greg noted there were no plaques for standby series. The network retained an option to broadcast through the spring those series not chosen for the fall.

"We have some pilots for midseason standing by," Raoul stated, "but we have no respect for them. We have to go with these."

In order to conserve cash, Ev had vetoed the practice of putting any of those potential replacement series into production ahead of time. Given Raoul's evaluation of them, Greg decided, that was probably just as well. Raoul and his schedulers were limited to moving around the existing shows into slots where they might draw more viewers.

Greg said nothing until they were through, but he was troubled by several moves. The proposed Saturday-night changes, for one, did not make sense.

"Why do you want to put 'Hot Time,' which should be attracting a heavy teenage and early-twenties audience, into nine o'clock Saturday night?"

"The idea is to counterprogram against 'Golden Girls,'" Raoul explained. "We're sinking fast where we are now."

"Saturday night's audience is primarily older people and young kids. That's the audience 'Golden Girls' was designed for. 'Hot Time''s audience is young adults, and they're out of the house on Saturday night. Who's going to watch it?"

Raoul looked to Ev for support. The latter said nothing. Raoul then looked to his subordinate in charge of scheduling. That man was carrying out an urgent inspection of the table's grain.

"Well, none of these suggestions are final," Raoul asserted. "We wanted this meeting to get your ideas."

Greg stepped up to the scheduling board. He was not an experienced scheduler, but he had a pretty good idea of the basic ideas involved. Overall, you tried to present shows that would draw the largest possible general audience. Comedies played as a block, but you tried not to schedule a comedy, for example, if a rival had a strong comedy on at that time. You "counterprogrammed" by putting on a different program type against it, say a melodrama. If a rival's show primarily attracted males, you might put one on that primarily drew females; if it attracted the young, you might go for an older audience. Adult audiences from eighteen to forty-nine years of age were the most desirable to advertisers, who would pay more for that demographic. You hoped to start out the evening with a strong family show and then attract a compatible audience from one show to the next, so as to maintain what was known as "audience flow."

Greg moved several of the red rectangles on which were written the names of current FBS shows.

He turned to the others in the room. "I think this might give us a better shot at second place in those time periods. What do you think?"

Raoul suggested reversing two shows that Greg had moved, and Ev found a better night for "Hot Time." That was the best they could do with what they had, it was agreed. The changes would go into effect in several weeks; time was needed to gain the advertisers' approval (they had the right to cancel), to notify the affiliates, to change the listings in *TV Guide* and newspapers, and for the network to run promotional spots alerting viewers to the new days and times.

"One last thing," Greg remembered. "I got a chance to see 'Hot Time' the other night. The show only came alive for me when that guy was on screen who owns the nightclub and tries to be cool and attract women and is always striking out."

"Rick?" Raoul remembered.

"Right. He's trying so hard to be Humphrey Bogart and always falling on his face. We can all identify with a guy like that."

"But he's only a peripheral character."

"I think we ought to make him more central, to put more scenes in the bar. He's human, and more important, he's funny and makes everyone else funnier." Successful television series were built on characters an audience liked to spend time with week after week.

"Do it!" Raoul ordered the young man in charge of current comedy series. On the odd chance that the change worked, Raoul wanted to be recalled as having been behind it all the way. In the second year of "Happy Days," a similar prominence was given to a tough greaser type who was a secondary character. The Fonz's ascent became the stuff of programming legend.

The meeting then shifted to the subject of the shows under development as concepts, outlines, and scripts for the coming television year. Twenty-five to thirty-five of those would be made into pilot shows. A few of the latter might be chosen to go on in midseason. Most, though, could not be readied until September.

From the corner of his eye, Raoul watched Greg as each of his programming executives described their prospective new shows in detail and the talent associated with them. He had been hoping for enthusiasm or at the very least, agreement on the choices. Greg listened through the rest of the morning and much of the afternoon and said nothing.

When the presentation was finally finished, Raoul suggested three possible replacement shows that might be ready to go on the air by February.

"Is that all there is out there?"

"These are the best that producers are bringing us. Sometimes we suggest an idea to producers to develop for us. These are top producers, people with heavy track records."

Although he did not allow it to show on his face, Greg was deeply depressed. The concepts behind a couple of the TV movies and one of the miniseries had been interesting, but a network's strength resided in its continuing series, for which audiences tuned in week after week. Not a single series in development had excited him.

FBS needed hits, one or two shows that would break through and really catch the nation's fancy, such as "Cosby" did and "Roseanne" and during an earlier time, "All in the Family" and "Happy Days." Those were rare, but if you found one, you could build an entire night's lineup around it and wipe out the competition. You could even spin off new shows from its characters. His feeling was that a show had to be distinctive to catch on like that, something new, something that developed a little chemistry with viewers. But Raoul and the others had spent months searching out new projects, which they had narrowed down after the most exhaustive testing. They were sure nothing like that was out there. Or at least nothing with that potential was being offered to FBS.

"A couple of our standby series could start shooting quickly," Raoul offered. "Monumental has already got scripts coming in on a show I think we ought to use for their commitment and just move it up to midseason of *this* year. It's called 'We're Out of Space.' "

Raoul was pleased to be able to demonstrate a valid reason for the commitment he had given Mickey Blinder. He outlined the concept of the show.

"Set up a meeting for tomorrow morning at his office," Greg said. "He's a big supplier. I ought to meet him and at least talk about it." He closed the thick presentation folder and slipping it under his arm, he stood up to leave. "But I have to admit the concept doesn't really excite me."

Greg had an office in the building, but he headed for the KFBS-TV newsroom, where "This Is FBS News Tonight" was broadcasting. Key members of the network's news staff had flown west to do the program for three days from Los Angeles, ostensibly to kick off the first in a series about the country's major geographical regions. But the scheduling had been moved up a couple of weeks so the network's top correspondents could add to the glamor of the party being hurriedly organized for the third night.

Greg arrived to find the network news being broadcast and transmitted to the East Coast, where it was three hours later. He found an empty chair on the far side of the room, where he soon fell into thought. A hand tapped him on the shoulder.

"KFBS News has the room now—or don't you remember?"

Greg looked up. Chris was sitting on the corner of the desk in front of him. He glanced at the clock. The network broadcast had ended five minutes earlier.

"It feels strange to be back here," she admitted. "Even stranger because you're here, too."

"It's as if no time has passed. We're the same two people. And yet everything has changed."

"We're both married for one thing."

He nodded. He could not tell whether she intended her remark as a reminder to him. She could not tell whether his expression hinted at ruefulness or simply acknowledgement.

"We've gotten a lot of what we wanted in life," she declared with a firm sense of satisfaction.

"Not always the way we had hoped for, but I guess overall that's true."

"Greg, I was going to call you. I have a favor to ask. I want you to meet with a friend of mine. She used to work here—first for me in news while she was finishing college and then in the Entertainment Division until she was fired a few days ago."

"Look, I'm sorry she was let go, but things are tight around here. I'm not going to go back and second-guess her boss."

"She's not looking to get her job back. I don't think she'd ever work for him again. It's just that she's troubled by some things that happened in the department and thinks you ought to be aware of them."

"I don't trust unsolicited altruism. People always have a hidden motive; usually it's revenge."

"In this case I think it might be apprehension. Now that she's out, she's afraid that the head of the department may try to blame things on her that were his doing."

"A very paranoid lady, your friend."

"She doesn't think so."

Greg was confused. "He might blame what *kinds* of things?"

"She said something about Monumental Productions being given an extra hundred thousand dollars a show and a firm commitment to do a new series next year."

Chris observed sudden attention straighten Greg up in the chair.

"What department did your friend work in?" Greg asked.

"Programming."

"Doing what?"

"She was in charge of new comedy series, but she's done a little bit of everything there. She'd like to talk to you."

"I think I'd like very much to talk with her."

"We're getting together for dinner in a little while. Maybe you could join us for a drink."

Chris told herself that she was pleased for Marian's sake that he could make it.

Mickey Blinder had canceled his morning appointments to meet with Greg. Raoul Clampton arrived at Mickey's office a few minutes early to brief him on the conversation he and Greg had had yesterday.

When Greg showed up, he was accompanied by an unexpected companion, Marian Marcus.

"You might not know this, Greg," Raoul quickly asserted, "but I fired this woman last week."

"I rehired her," Greg said.

Mickey extended his hand, a wide smile on his face. "Glad to meet you at last, Greg. Heard a lot about you. I'm Mickey Blinder."

"I made a wild guess and figured since this was your office and you're sitting behind the desk, you might be. I'd like to know more about the deal you made with Raoul here for a hundred thousand dollars more an episode—retroactively—and a blind thirteen-week commitment for next year."

"If you're suggesting something wasn't aboveboard, Greg," Mickey rejoined, "then I feel a little insulted here."

"Let's start with the extra hundred thousand a show. What did we get for it?" Greg took a seat and gestured to Marian to take the chair beside him.

"Well," Mickey replied, "Annette was really against doing another year of 'Luba.' We had to sweeten her salary."

"I spoke to her agent this morning. She's getting twenty thousand more a show. But next year, not this year. I still want to know why you're getting a hundred thousand a show—even for shows you've already shot."

"You have to understand," Mickey answered. "We couldn't afford to keep doing the series with the losses we were taking."

"The show's a gold mine. Our financial people tell me every episode you shoot is worth two to three million dollars to you in syndication."

Raoul crossed his legs and sat back with what appeared to be composure, but his foot was jiggling wildly. "I guess you could say it was an option to make sure we got Monumental's *next* series, Greg.

242

That's why they agreed to give it to us. We aren't exactly the first choice when producers are peddling their new product."

"Some suppliers have five, six, seven hours a week on network," Greg replied quietly. "Monumental has half an hour. Ours. Nobody's been breaking down the doors to make deals with Monumental."

"Well," Raoul said with a chuckle, "we sure wouldn't have had a prayer of getting 'We're Out of Space.' "

"Now that also seems odd to me. Your memo authorizing that commitment never mentioned any project. No writer or producer or star was tied to the commitment. Monumental had carte blanche to put on anything they wanted. A couple of days after that you had the contract amended to commit us to thirteen weeks of that space thing." Greg glanced at Marian. "Sound funny to you, too?"

Raoul jumped in before she could answer. "She'd love to smear me."

"Not like your good friend Mickey here," Greg said, smiling benignly. "He wants only the best for you. It says so right here in this memo. Remember it, Mickey?"

Greg handed over a photocopy of a secret memo Mickey had written. The round-faced production executive turned ashen. "Oh, Jesus!" Mickey started to hand the memo to Raoul.

"I have a lot of copies," Greg assured him, and handed one to Raoul.

Last night had been an eye-opener for Greg in many ways. The tall, somewhat ungainly young woman with frizzy hair and clever brown eyes whom he and Chris had met for drinks showed him two memos. Clampton's authorized the questionable arrangement for "Luba" and thirteen weeks of any Monumental half-hour sitcom. But she also had with her a copy of another memo, a secret memo on Monumental stationery that a friend at Monumental had slipped to her out of its confidential files.

In it Mickey Blinder described the deal he had just made with Clampton, including his promise to hire Clampton if he left the network or was fired. Out-and-out bribery. That memo could put both men behind bars.

"You're fired, Raoul," Greg announced, "and as of this moment FBS's deal with Monumental is canceled. That's just the beginning."

Mickey's brain, always so good at tap dancing him out of trouble, was failing to operate.

"Could I have five minutes to talk to Raoul?" he asked.

"Take ten," Greg offered magnanimously, and strolled with Marian into an adjoining office.

Over dinner last night Greg had admitted to Marian and Chris how disheartened the Programming Department's new projects had made him. Marian explained that all the new and interesting ideas she had seen had been rejected in favor of clones or recombined versions of already popular shows that possessed no singular or compelling concept or execution—whether of writing, casting, or direction—nothing that could grab the audience. All the networks had played it safe this year, she pointed out, which had resulted in only one new fall series' thus far producing even middling success, and that one was built on an unusual concept: It was about a sixteen-year-old doctor.

Marian had then outlined to Greg a few projects Raoul had rejected that had excited her. Greg had grown as excited as she. They thought remarkably alike. She was as convinced as he that the only way to come up with the breakthrough shows that would take off like a skyrocket and shower ratings fireworks over an entire night was to be innovative, even daring, in ways an audience could relate to. And only breakthrough shows could dramatically reverse FBS's slide.

The cocktail hour had stretched into dinner, but still the discussion continued. Greg and Chris had gone back with Marian to her house and sat on the floor till very late, talking and reading proposals she had kept while they sipped beer from the bottle and dipped into a huge bowl of microwave popcorn. Without anything's being said, it was understood that Marian had been rehired. And also without anything's being said, that the near-decade-long state of hostility between Chris and Greg had ended.

He had driven her back to the hotel where both of them were staying. Although in some ways being together seemed natural, both had felt the tension humming silently between them. And electricity coursing through their bones.

She had gotten off the elevator on the fifth floor. He had wanted to follow her. She had halted for an instant, searching in her handbag for her key. Or was she waiting for him? he wondered. But he had let the doors close between them, had stayed on until the sixth floor, and had gone to his suite.

He had then phoned Diane, as he did every night when he was away. She had missed him and had a dozen stories about her day to entertain him with. But despite the virtue in which he had steeped himself, he had not slept well.

"I had to take so much crap with a smile from Clampton over the years!" Marian exclaimed as soon as she and Greg were alone in the small office adjoining Blinder's. "Revenge really is sweet."

Greg laughed. "If anybody knows how it feels to turn the tables, I do."

"When you showed them Blinder's secret memo," she joked, "I thought I'd have to apply CPR to restart their hearts." She grew reflective. "You don't want to put them in jail, do you?"

"I don't know. Is there anything we want from Blinder? We have him now where we want him."

"You'd do business with him?" Marian's ethical sense was affronted by the thought of making a deal with someone who had acted so dishonestly.

"A lawsuit gets us a lot of legal costs and dubious publicity, especially when we want to look like good guys to the creative community out here. But the *threat* of a lawsuit. That can be very useful."

"I guess I'm not used to acting so cynically."

"You pick it up fast when your back is to the wall. So, any ideas?" She shook her head.

The walls were lined with shelves containing scripts and treatments and proposals. Out of habit she skimmed the titles on the spines. But it was a proposal in a pile on a chair that caught her eye. She grabbed for it.

"On second thought!" she said excitedly.

Written brightly on the cover was its title: "Lowdown."

A few minutes later, the door opened. Mickey's shirt was soaked in sweat, and he was wiping his forehead with a handkerchief.

"We'd like to know if it's possible to make some kind of a deal with you," he said.

"You know, gentlemen," Greg replied as he walked back into the room and resumed his seat, "I have a feeling that a deal may just be possible."

17

~~~~~~~~~~~~~~~~~

Mickey could not believe his good fortune. Even when your back is to the wall and the firing squad is taking aim, you've got to keep fighting because you just never know. He would have given Lyall the world to get off the hook, but instead, after canceling the giveaways to Clampton, the guy actually bought a pilot from him. Unfortunately, it was that idiot project "Lowdown."

"I've just made a fabulous deal for you," Mickey phrased it when he summoned Susan Glendon and her partner to his office to meet with the "new big guys" from FBS. "You go right to pilot. No waiting for FBS's script approval. Am I out there fighting for you, or what?"

As soon as Susan walked in and saw Marian Marcus and not Raoul Clampton, she understood immediately why FBS's interest in "Lowdown" had been kindled. The women immediately began to discuss possible casting.

Greg was astounded to see, entering just behind Susan, his old newsroom boss and mentor Stew Graushner, looking totally dumbstruck. He was the "S. Graushner" named on the proposal's cover as co-writer and co-producer. Greg was delighted. He had not seen or heard anything about him since the latter left KFBS.

Greg joked, "Afraid that creditors might find you if you used your full name?"

Stew's coughing fit covered the awkward moment quite nicely.

As soon as Marian and Greg departed, Mickey informed the writer-producer team that the deal with FBS had one little wrinkle he had forgotten to mention amid all the excitement. Raoul Clampton was now executive producer of the series. FBS had insisted on it, Mickey tried to claim.

Susan did not believe a word and correctly guessed that, for some undisclosable reason, a spot had to be found quickly for Raoul, obviously now persona non grata at FBS. Susan declared she would refuse to do the series if Clampton's name was on the screen or if his salary was in their budget or if he came within a hundred yards of the set or the production office or if he even dared to speak to her.

"Hey, I've got no problem with any of that," Mickey assured her. "Which sound stage do you want to shoot in?"

"E," she said, and departed with Stew.

Mickey quickly ordered his secretary to inform Raoul Clampton of the arrangement and rushed upstairs. He had one last personal task to attend to. He used his key to slip into the locked file room where the studio's secret memos were kept and yanked every copy of his incriminating memo.

At about that same time the new executive producer of "Lowdown"— at least that was what it would say on Raoul's weekly paychecks—was observed climbing the catwalk ladder up to a cubicle just beneath the roof of sound stage A, at the other end of the Monumental lot from where that show's pilot would be shot. Within days the strange, silent figure would become known to the lot's wisecracking regulars as the Phantom of the Upper A.

An ebullient Susan, on the walk back to her own offices, was beginning to discuss ideas for the pilot script when it finally struck Stew that lady luck had suddenly, improbably kissed him square on the lips.

He interrupted her. "Excuse me, but how much do I have coming to me at this very moment?"

She calculated quickly. "We share equally in whatever I get for writing and executive producing the pilot and of course, for creating it. . . . We get half now. . . . Your share is about twenty thousand dollars—"

"Twenty thousand!" he breathed.

"—and another twenty thousand when we finish the pilot."

"Another twenty thousand!"

"If the network picks up the show, you get closer to forty-five thousand for every episode after that. That's twenty-two episodes. Just under a million dollars a year."

"A million dollars!"

"And of course, half my share of the profits in syndication. That's the big money."

"The big money!"

"Are you all right?"

"I have to use a bathroom. I'll be right back."

He must have to go badly, Susan thought, watching him sprint back to the administration building.

Stew knew that Monumental's checks were issued there.

247

*   *   *

Marian drove her car behind Greg's from the Monumental lot to FBS. She had no idea what sort of job he had in mind for her. She guessed she would be a kind of assistant to Greg, advising him on new shows, looking at the pilots when they came in. She needed an office somewhere.

"Where do I go?" she asked when they were inside the lobby.

Greg had weighed his options for Programming during the drive back. He could try to hire a top programmer from one of the other networks, but those types were not likely to jump right away. They were already locked into lucrative arrangements and at the least, would wait to be paid their year-end bonuses before risking preliminary conversations. They would take weeks more to negotiate a deal and then, in the end, might use it to win an escalated deal where they were. He did not have that kind of time to dawdle away. Even if he did, as likely as not they might turn out to be like Clampton. Not dishonest, but so cautious that they no longer had a fresh opinion or the courage to act on it.

His ready alternative was Marian. She had wide programming experience. Not at the top, but she had certainly dealt with many of the town's leading television creators and judged their work. She also had the advantage of knowing the projects that had already come into FBS.

But Greg was aware that she had never had the ultimate responsibility for picking and shaping the shows to go on the air. He had no idea how she would react under fire, whether that mousy front hid an iron will that would emerge when given command or one that would break under the strain. He would be placing the company's fortunes in untested hands, risking its future fortunes on her untried taste and skill.

Yet, if he was going to fail, Greg finally concluded, he would rather do it taking his best shot—his *own* shot. Marian's instincts matched his own—and she was willing to trust those instincts.

"Programming," he answered her. "You're in charge."

"In charge of what?"

He laughed. "The department. Programming. All the scheduling, new series development, whatever it takes."

"You're kidding." She could see he was not, but she was stunned.

"Keep whoever you think is good. Fire the others and hire people whose judgement you trust. And do it fast. Do we need all the people who supervise current shows?"

"Not all of them. Some just spend their time trying to prove they're smarter than the producers. My money's on the producers. Who do I report to?"

"Nominally, Ev Carver because he oversees Programming and the

Entertainment Division as part of his Broadcast Group. Treat him as if he's your boss. But that's just for form's sake. He'll stay out of your way because he knows I want programming in my hands. And that suits him fine because the odds say I'm going to fail. He wants to be ready and waiting to take over when I do."

"Everybody says he's a killer."

"That's only his better nature. Watch your back."

"In this town that's the side we wear our bulletproof vests on."

"Good. I'll be on the phone with you every day talking things over and out here as much as I need to be."

"People here have to know you're solidly behind me."

"I'll make that clear on Wednesday night at the gala. Incidentally, you'll have to take that over now. You'll probably want people there who Clampton ignored. Invite them. And do it personally. We want to convince the creative community that we're serious about giving them a lot more leeway to try their wings and a lot fewer handcuffs."

"Anything else?"

"A couple of things. We have few replacement series ready we can raise ratings with, so try to develop some good one-shot products we can use during sweeps months—movies, miniseries, specials. Also, the FCC lets us produce more prime-time shows than we do. We've been too timid. If a producer does a show based on our own idea or if he'd have to go to a studio for financing, maybe we should step in and finance it ourselves. That could be big profits if a show takes off."

Marian looked around the lobby for a moment. "It's all a little scary."

"It's a *lot* scary. But just try to keep in mind all the things you said to me last night. Don't lose sight of them. Trust yourself."

"Thanks," she said, and started to shuffle toward the elevator.

Greg stopped her. "If you want people to treat you as if you're in charge, you'd better look as if you're in charge."

For an instant Marian did not understand, but then she noticed Greg's tall, erect bearing. Her own back stiffened upright. Her shoulders pulled back. She smiled at him and strode decisively into the waiting elevator.

All morning people cradling cardboard cartons in their arms streamed from the building.

Greg and Marian spent lunch, cocktail hour, an early dinner, and a late supper that night pitching FBS to key creative people in series television.

Greg liked the way Marian handled herself. Several times producers tried to sell her mediocre shows that other networks had rightly rejected. She declared that the advantage of bringing a show to FBS was not that the network was desperate enough to take anything, but that it had nothing to lose by keeping hands off a show they cared a great deal about doing; they'd get a lot of creative freedom.

Ossie Krieger, for one, derided the pitch. FBS had already destroyed one of his series with its interference, he told them, and he wasn't about to risk another. With a series presently on the air, he did not need FBS and had, in fact, vowed never to go back.

"Does that mean you've got a new series you're thinking of doing?" Marian immediately asked.

"NBC is looking at it."

"What's it about?" she asked.

Marian had always been straight with him, Ossie reflected, one of the few in programming at FBS who had. He'd try it out on her.

"I think it's a funny idea," he began, and disclosed the premise. It was set in a shabby girls' boarding school always on the brink of insolvency. The headmaster, who also owned the school, was a sly but not very capable con man who was always involved in a new scheme: sometimes to earn the funds to keep the doors open and sometimes to become wildly, exorbitantly rich. Although a few innocents had come to the school to learn, many of the girls were as cunning and wayward as he and invariably had their own scams going on, sometimes to sneak boys in, sometimes to sneak themselves out, sometimes to fleece the headmaster out of what he had just connived to gain. The series and the school were both called "Miss Grimsby's Academy for Young Ladies." When it was absolutely unavoidable that she appear, the headmaster dressed up as, of course, the nonexistent Miss Grimsby.

Greg and Marian shared a glance. Greg spoke up.

"We'll give you a hard-and-fast commitment right now to do it as a two-hour movie. That will serve as the pilot. If we like the way that turns out, you'll get a full year's commitment to do it as a half-hour sitcom. FBS will produce it in-house and put up every bit of the financing. You'll get the same profit share you would from a studio."

Ossie was taken aback. "But first you'll want to see the script, right, and make just one or two 'little' suggestions."

"Probably," Marian offered. "But I won't have the right to veto a thing. You can take my suggestions or ignore them. I trust you to be reasonable. As long as nothing's patently offensive, you can shoot your script. The only approval I really want is on casting for the continuing characters. That's it."

"I'd want the show put into a nine or nine-thirty time slot. This won't be a kids' show."

"We wouldn't want it to be," Greg assured him, then pointed out, "NBC is riding high in the ratings. They might not have *any* slots open up for your show."

"Parents might complain that we're corrupting their school-aged children."

"This is entertainment, not a Sunday-school lesson. People know the difference. Or should." Greg extended a hand. "Same terms you'd get at NBC. Do we have a deal?"

"This is crazy," Ossie observed with a laugh.

Marian smiled. "We told you this wasn't the old way of doing business here."

Ossie shook Greg's hand.

His lawyer and agent met with FBS's Business Affairs people at ten o'clock the next morning. The deal memo was agreed upon by lunchtime.

On Tuesday *Daily Variety* headlined the story that Raoul Clampton had "ankled" FBS for Monumental, and Marian Marcus was now in. That was already yesterday's news as their reporter, a jaded veteran at recognizing and stepping around Hollywood hype, tried to elicit some new angle from Greg in the minutes before guests would enter the ballroom for the start of FBS's party. The press had been invited to make sure that word of the network's new attitude went out to those not there tonight.

A smirk forming on his mouth, the reporter asked, "You mean no more sitcoms and action-adventure series? Only superbly creative and significant dramas?"

Greg answered frankly. "TV is built on the old standbys. People want them. They have since they told stories around a fire in the cave. I just hope we can do them better, add a little something new and interesting to the plot or a character that catches the audience. Look, we need those ratings, but you don't get them with the same old stuff. If viewers were as dumb as a lot of programmers believe, the networks wouldn't be losing viewers and getting in a new bunch of shows and programmers every year."

The night's theme, which underlay the presentation, was "We're on our way." Chris's appearance provoked loud applause. She and Hedy and several other correspondents spoke briefly after the showing of a montage of taped highlights from recent news broadcasts. Then stars from several FBS current series and a miniseries being completed came on stage to say a few words.

Annette Valletta as Luba got the audience laughing with her innocent-seeming, Russian-accented comments. She ended with a couple of sly questions planned in order to confront with light-hearted humor what had to be on everyone's mind. "How did you happen to get such a good job, Mr. Lyall? Maybe you knew somebody?"

"You've got to start somewhere," he answered her. "The top is as good a place as any."

He got a good laugh. She flounced off. And Greg grew serious. Viewers had sampled all of the network's uninspired new shows this season, found little of interest, and gone back to old favorites, mostly on other networks. FBS wanted to enter next season with more daring, more original choices in the lineup. He claimed that FBS was prepared to go further than the other networks to give suppliers firm deals and creative freedom. He ended with a glowing introduction of Marian that emphasized his full support.

For the first time in her life, Marian had not let her physical appearance be dictated by her anxious psyche, but by experts. Makeup, hair, and clothing stylists had been called in and given carte blanche.

The Marian Marcus who walked briskly across the stage to the podium was a tall, eye-catching figure in a flamboyant red dress and a frosted-blond hairdo that whipped vividly about her head. Her large features would never allow her to be pretty, but she would never again be plain. The speech she read recounted more or less what Greg's had, but she added to her and FBS's credibility by announcing her first deal, a two-hour movie pilot with the superstar writer-producer Ossie Krieger. The excited murmur and then applause as she ended the presentation indicated the new respect that deal had just given the network.

Then she and Greg and her staff began to work the room. This was a buffet. No fixed seating. They wanted to be able to move freely. To cultivate top producers. To stroke top stars. And just as eagerly, the room worked them.

Danny Vickers had been invited and brought Sally Foster. As soon as Sally fell into conversation with Annette and her husband, Danny slipped away to assault Marian with his bag of projects. To his consternation Marian knew them all and politely declined them all, the one with Sally Foster for the third time. Its premise was trite and the writers mediocre.

Danny suddenly remembered. "I've got this great young black writer working on this fabulous action-suspense series for me. It's about a white cop—he's the main honcho—and a black cop. They disguise themselves to solve a different big case every week. It's *Lethal Weapon*. It's *48 Hours*. It's . . ." He could not come up with another movie model that he hoped would excite her. "The working title is 'Daye and Knight.' "

Marian thought the project worth looking at further. The title, though, would have to go.

"How about 'Knight and Daye'?" Danny tried brightly.

Marian shook her head. "Let's meet with the writer next week. My secretary will set it up."

When Danny returned to Sally, a big smile lit his face. He whispered to her that he had just gotten "some real good interest" on her new series project from Marian, but that it would take time.

A high-level FBS West Coast sales executive, a bushy-haired, jowly man in his fifties, descended on Marian.

"What kind of a car?"

"What?" she asked.

"What kind of car did they give you?"

"I don't know. Dark blue."

"You don't know?"

She shook her head. The car came with the job. She now left her own at home.

He couldn't believe such a deceitful reply. "What number?"

She was equally confused. He grew exasperated.

"What number parking place did they give you?"

Again, she shook her head. Yesterday, she had found her name on a parking spot close to the office building's front entrance and had simply parked there.

"Number five!" the man barked. "That's what number you have! Number five! And the first four spots are reserved for East Coasters who are never here." He counted them off in order on his fingers. "Roderick, Lyall, Carver, and Jorgenson. I've been a senior vice president eight years. Eight years! And all that time I've never gotten lower than number six. Some snot-nosed kid gets made a senior vice president, and just like that, ten minutes later, she's number five. Who the fuck do you know?"

He stomped away.

Ev Carver had also been pondering the significance of Marian's promotion. He had acted quickly to contain the damage at Monumental. Mickey Blinder had phoned him in desperation when Greg and Marian went into the adjoining room. Ev told Blinder to come up with something valuable to offer FBS in a settlement, on whatever terms Greg offered. Blinder was then to hire Clampton in order to insure that the story not get out.

That solution also disposed of Ev's little personal problem: the gifts Mickey had given him from time to time. Ev had always made sure never to give Blinder anything in return—no deals, nothing. Just goodwill. Friendly gestures. Monumental treated a little more tenderly than the others. But appearances could have hurt him. In fact Ev had been enraged to learn that Clampton had carved himself a deal with Monumental.

253

Ev glanced over at the tall young woman Greg had selected to replace Clampton. Everything he had learned about Marian Marcus indicated that she was a guppy swimming in a tank of piranhas and was certain to get eaten alive in the programming job. The slick operators out here would set her head spinning and sell her crap shows. Because she was Greg Lyall's personal choice for the job, the two would both go down in flames.

Why the hell had Lyall picked her? Was he sleeping with her? The woman had a kind of flair, but she was certainly on the homely side and Lyall had a lot to lose if he was caught dipping his wick away from home. You could never tell, though, about a guy's compulsions or his taste. What if Greg *was* sleeping with her? Ev conjectured. If he himself could somehow find out, Jesus, but wouldn't that give him great ammunition to shoot down Barnett Roderick's son-in-law.

Hedy had already left for New Orleans on a red-eye to cover a story there in the morning, so Ev sought out other company for later in the evening. Toward the end of the party, he managed to find a moment when Sally Foster was alone. He was conversing with her near the dessert and coffee table when he noticed Greg, a few feet away, walk up to Chris. Ev remembered that he used to think the two had something cooking.

"Seems like old times," Ev quipped to them.

Laughing at what he hoped was their embarrassment, Ev drew Sally away to chat in a more private area. Danny quickly moved across the room to intercept them.

"What it really seems like," Greg commented to Chris, "is a bad case of déjà vu. Danny Vickers's party, remember? Ev was also with Sally and making lecherous comments."

She nodded. "It must be the smog out here that has that erotic affect on people."

Greg's gaze locked on hers. "Does it have that affect on you?"

She did not answer right away. She was staring into Greg's eyes, evaluating him. She tried to concentrate on the scars he had left along her heart and ignore the voices singing in her flesh. Her compulsion for honesty won out—and her anger at recognizing a truth about herself she had tried hard to deny.

"Unfortunately, where you're concerned, my body seems to have a mind of its own."

"Mine, too," he answered softly.

A man's voice sounded behind them. "You two again?"

They turned, expecting once more to find Ev. Arnold Mandel was smiling at them.

"I know, I know," he said. "You're just close friends."

254

Greg emitted an abashed little laugh. "How are you, Arnold? It's been a long while."

"It looks to me like only a couple of minutes ago. I don't see either of you for ten years, and when I do, you're still together and still look like you can't wait to get your clothes off and jump on each other. But you're always just good friends. Everybody should be so lucky to have such friends."

Greg wanted to get on to another subject quickly. "Marian says you have a pilot show that's getting the runaround at one of the other networks. Can we see it?"

"It's not FBS's kind of show. Your shop is always too worried about its reputation."

"We're trying to do the things again that got us that reputation."

"Greg, my show is controversial, and I believe in it too much to pull my punches and soften it."

"Try us out, Arnold. Just let us look at it. I'll be here till Friday."

"All right, but you know my ground rules up front." Arnold eyed Chris and Greg once more. "Now you two can go back to being just good friends."

When the party ended and Greg had concluded his last conversation, he looked around for Chris. She was gone.

He had been afraid that revealing how desperately he wanted her would offend her and shatter her gradually renewing respect for him. Instead, she, who had every reason to hate him, had confessed tonight to that same carnal attraction. But she had termed the attraction "unfortunate," and wisely demonstrating the self-restraint he himself might not have been able to, had left.

That was better, he thought. They were both married, she doubtless a lot more happily than he. She would hardly be willing to jeopardize her husband's love and trust for a night's fleeting satisfaction. Greg would be risking a lot more than his wife's trust. His job could be at stake. Moreover, Greg had given his word to Barnett that he would work at his marriage, and he had.

Greg was grateful that Chris had clung to more enduring priorities and had made the right decision for both of them by leaving.

Greg refused a studio head's invitation to go somewhere for drinks and more talk and went upstairs to his room.

Ev Carver and several others who happened to have found themselves in conversation together went across the lobby to the hotel's cocktail lounge. Invited by Ev, Marian was among them, the only woman in the group. His interest in her was twofold: Although she did not have a great face, she looked as if she might be a lot of woman in bed; and seducing her might win him an ally.

After being deftly fended off for several minutes, however, he decided to take off for the Polo Lounge with an old buddy from the KFBS days who was now a producer. Ev recalled that he had usually gotten lucky at the Polo Lounge.

With a whisk of Greg Lyall's hand, Marian had become a very powerful woman in Hollywood. The men still at the table were trying their best to develop a cordial relationship with her. An amorous one could be even more useful. Marian basked in their regard. She had never been an object of men's attention before. Months could pass without so much as a phone call from a potential date. She had not made love to a man in over two years, and even that one had been a mistake on her part, not much of a man and less of a lover; he had hardly aroused her.

Yet, here were a well-known director and a studio executive broadly hinting at asking her out later in the week. She tactfully discouraged them. Marian understood that her newfound allure derived not from her new hairdo and dress, but from her power to finance and schedule their projects. She was not about to allow herself to be compromised.

After a second drink, the get-together broke up. As they were all filing out, Marian hung back to converse with the youngest in the group, a producer's assistant given his invitation to the party by a boss who could not make it tonight. The young USC film-school graduate had been so dazzled by the crowd into which he had somehow wandered that he had not said a word at the table. He could barely believe that a television titan like Marian Marcus, the woman in charge of FBS's programming, had dropped back to speak to him.

She took his phone number and told him to keep next weekend free. "Maybe I'll make dinner for us at my house. We'll play it by ear."

Before rushing off, she prudently cautioned him that a young man seeking to make his career in television would be wise not to mention this to anyone.

Greg could not sleep. He was obsessed by thoughts of Chris. He ached for her.

Finally, near midnight, he threw on some clothing and took the elevator down one flight. She had the corner suite, he knew, directly under his.

Even as he knocked on her door, he told himself how insane this was, how ridiculous he would look to her, how her anger at his advances would damage their working relationship forever.

"Yes?" her voice called from behind the door a moment later.

"It's Greg. I have to see you."

"I thought it would be you."

She drew back the door to admit him. She was naked.

"Don't talk. Not a word," she whispered.

They kissed with an urgency repudiated and dammed up to overflowing for ten years. No one else had ever aroused her so or ever could.

Tonight felt new, yet resonant with memory, and thus, infinite. They inhaled all the remembered smells and touched all the sweet, remembered places: her small, lifted breasts and the perfumed skin between; the furrowed muscles guarding his ribs; her flat abdomen rising into transparent blondness at the delta between her thighs; the smooth, musky baby skin behind his testicles; the silky little pillows that her vagina swelled into when she was ready and eager for his entrance; his hardness that seemed as if it could reach no deeper or get no harder, yet somehow did inside her.

Inside her.

In that initial instant of inward and outward embrace, each of them felt complete—a conjunction, as always, glorious and perfect.

And when they came—each time during that long night that they came—they were blinded by fulfillment.

Guilt did not lead the two other faces into the room until dawn, with the sun.

18

~~~~~~~~~~~~~~~

"I guess once every ten years my body is entitled to a night like that," Chris said, pushing herself into sitting upright against the headboard.

After a moment Greg did the same, gazing straight ahead as she did. Both wished to avoid the hazard of looking at the other and a binding sense of complicity about what they had done. It was morning, and now that their passion had been slaked, time for reason to prevail.

"It was a mistake," he agreed.

"We got carried away."

"Anyone could slip . . ."

"Being together away from home like this . . ." she added.

"In a city where we used to live together."

"That doesn't mean we don't love our spouses."

"Or that there has to be a second time."

She turned sharply toward him. "There *won't* be a second time."

He nodded. "There *can't* be. We'd be risking too much."

"We'd be hurting people we love."

"And who love us."

"I won't go sneaking around behind Ken's back," she said firmly.

"And if it didn't work out before between us, who's to say it would now."

"It worked out fine," she reminded him. "You just saw a chance to better your prospects through another woman and grabbed it."

"The reasons I left ran a little deeper than that," he replied testily.

"See"—she smiled—"we're starting to argue already."

"Last night was wonderful, but never again."

"Absolutely." She got out of bed to walk across the room to the bathroom. "Just like it never happened."

"We're mature enough to exert self-control and simply treat each other like old friends."

"In a purely professional way."

"And go back to the people who really love us and need us."

"Back to our real lives."

"It would probably be better, though, to stay away from each other for a while," he suggested. "You know, in a few weeks we'll be able to deal with each other a little more dispassionately."

"That would make it a lot easier for both of us."

They glanced once more at each other's eyes, to confirm their agreement.

As Chris hoped, when she emerged from the bathroom, Greg had left. She packed, dressed, and was on the nine-o'clock plane back to New York with those on the news staff who had not returned the night before.

While the end credits ran, Arnold Mandel observed the faces of the other five people in the room and tried to gauge their responses to the pilot they had just seen for his series "What's the World Coming To?" Greg was thoughtful. Marian was unreadable, as was the fellow from Research. Her two smiling subordinates in comedy development surreptitiously glanced over at her to gain some clue to her reaction. On the whole they had all laughed a lot in the right places, and Arnold considered that good. But they were network people. Now they would second-guess themselves.

"Well, you weren't kidding about its being controversial, Arnold," Greg began. "It's outrageous. But it's also funny as hell."

Marian liked that Greg had definite opinions and did not hide them behind platitudes. He was prepared to take the heat for his mistakes and expected nothing less of her. She believed, as he did, that the network could not afford fainthearted hesitation at this critical time; better to try something that failed than to do nothing and continue to deteriorate. After years of concealing her opinions, to voice them and act on them was liberating.

"I laughed my sides off," Marian admitted, "but almost felt guilty about it, like when someone is telling shocking racist jokes."

The young woman Marian had recently elevated to her old job agreed. "While you're squirming at the comparison to present-day reality, you're laughing in spite of it."

"That's the reason I set it in the future and made the situations so ridiculous on the surface," Arnold pointed out. "It makes the humor at the comparison to today more acceptable."

259

Greg looked over at the West Coast vice president in charge of testing audience reaction to shows. "Will we draw viewers or turn them off?"

The man locked and unlocked his fingers as he spoke. His face was grim. "My honest opinion is that I think this is probably the most offensive show I've ever seen. Many of these futuristic characters are so odd and have no redeeming qualities for the audience to identify with and like. The jokes might be about this future society, but they're transparently relatable to today. That's the point. I counted at least half a dozen special-interest groups that were attacked and would protest: blacks, Jews, homosexuals, the poor—"

"Italians," added one of the executives, chuckling at the recollection.

"So you think it's too risky to put on?" Greg asked him.

"We'll practically need bodyguards when we leave the building."

Arnold was ready to put his videocassette back into his briefcase and depart. "Do you all feel that way?"

"I'd like to test it to see whether viewers are too offended to watch," Greg replied.

"Your biggest problem might be sponsors," Marian reminded him. "They'll steer clear of this show like it has the plague. We'll practically be running a full complement of public-service announcements."

Greg added with some chagrin, "For the same groups the show is offending. It kind of balances out. But the show is too good and too funny to give up on without thinking it through."

Arnold was annoyed. "Look, that's the same reaction I got at the other shop. Testing is always easier than making a decision. All right, I'll give you thirty days."

"Is thirty days enough?" Greg asked the researcher.

The man nodded. "We can show it to small focus groups and have them talk about it and analyze their reactions for you within, say, two weeks."

Greg silently polled one after another of those in the room for their opinions about whether they liked the show enough to move to the testing stage. Marian nodded adamantly. Perhaps following her lead, perhaps out of true conviction, her two subordinates nodded as well.

"Okay," Greg agreed, turning to Arnold. "We have thirty days. If testing shows the reaction to the pilot's positive, not negative, that it doesn't actively turn viewers away, we'll give you a commitment."

Arnold took out his appointment book. He would not abide delay. "Thirty days," he had granted, and that was all he was prepared to wait. "All right, make it Monday a month from now. That gives you an extra day or two over the last weekend. I'll be at your office in New York for your answer at nine o'clock in the morning that Monday."

*   *   *

With scant days remaining until the annual dinner for the children's wing, Diane won approval from the hospital board to build a full children's hospital. But on the Friday of the dinner, as Greg was flying back from California, all her meticulously organized plans began to fall apart. When she called up the Waldorf for a final conversation with the banquet manager, she learned that he was out sick and that his substitute knew nothing about the extensive details the two had agreed on. Then in quick succession, three celebrities on her guest list, all with excellent reasons, canceled. The last and most damaging to her was the governor, who was to speak at the dinner. His office called to say that he had just caught the chicken pox from a grandchild and both were now quarantined in the nursery.

Diane immediately phoned Sen. Ken Chandler, who owed her and her father a good deal for their past financial support. He was facing a tough reelection fight this year and would need their help more than ever. Would he and his wife come to the dinner tonight and replace the governor? A few minutes later he called back to assure her that the two of them would be honored to attend.

Diane would have been furious if his wife, an FBS employee, had refused the invitation. Still, she found herself exhaling an enormous sigh of relief. A speaker and a second celebrity replaced with one couple.

Greg had just arrived at his New York office when she phoned to ask whether he could arrange for one or two FBS stars to attend the dinner tonight.

"Only the soap operas are shot in New York," he informed her.

"I guess on short notice that's the best we'll be able to do. But only one soap-opera person. More would look tacky, as if we couldn't do better. Oh, by the way, Senator Chandler and his wife will be replacing the governor. She'll be arriving as soon as her news broadcast is over. What's her name? Christine something?"

"Paskins," Greg said, carefully straining all the color from his tone.

"She's been in the magazines a lot. Pretty woman. She'll add some sparkle."

Diane was concerned that Greg's crammed schedule might interfere with the dinner's careful timing. "Please, Greg, I know you're busy, but I really need you there right from the start."

"I promise."

"And you won't forget that soap-opera person. With an escort, if they wish."

"And the soap-opera person."

"Oh, one more thing," Diane remembered. "The Chandlers are at our table. I'm sure she'll feel more comfortable beside someone she knows. I've put her next to you."

*   *   *

Greg was troubled by the prospect of seeing his wife for the first time after his trip. With Chris often intruding into his thoughts these last two days, he feared to make some little mistake that might alert her.

He arrived at the foyer outside the Waldorf's Grand Ballroom a few minutes before seven. Diane was bent over some papers, in discussion with another woman. Because of Diane, this event had become a must obligation for the various coteries of old and new society. She was making a last-minute check of the table assignments and placements to make sure they had been allocated as diplomatically as possible.

Don't appear anxious, Greg told himself as he approached her. The affair with Chris is over and done with, prudently and mutually ended. Think of it as something in the distant past, like the earlier romance; Diane had never suspected that. His only concern must be the present.

Diane glanced up. Her face exploded into a smile. She threw her arms around him and kissed him exuberantly.

"I hope you'll forgive me, Annie," she said to the other woman, her arms still around Greg's waist, "but I haven't seen this handsome man in nearly a week."

Greg nodded a greeting at the other woman.

"How's it going?" he asked Diane. He flailed about in his mind for something else to say after that, but a single fleshy word threatened to pop onto his tongue: "adultery." Despite his recent mental preparation, he could not forget that two nights earlier he had made joyous love to another woman.

"It's been a horror," Diane replied, "but hopefully all the problems are behind us. I'd have one thing less to worry about if you'd stand by the elevators and wait for Senator Chandler. He should be here in a few minutes. His wife will miss cocktails, but a limousine will bring her over as soon as she's through with the broadcast."

Although Greg had obviously seen Senator Chandler on television many times, he had never met him. Used to politicians who create attractive media images that hide their characters, Greg had all sorts of preconceptions about what the man was actually like: several years older than Chris, so perhaps a bit paternal; a professional handshaker without much substance; when not cut down to five-second sound bites, long-winded and pompous. Greg did not expect to like him—he did not *want* to like him and certainly did not want to chance the guilt feelings that liking him might impose.

The man who stepped off the elevator turned out to be both likable and not pompous in the least. They fell into a conversation about America's recent invasion of Panama and then about several media issues currently before the Senate. The man was not a sprightly conversationalist, Greg decided, a bit bland, a bit studied, but there was no mistaking how well-meaning he was.

Ken brought up another matter. "I just want you to know that I think you've handled my wife quite well."

"What?" Greg was startled.

"Oh, that's right," Ken recalled, "she once mentioned that you two have done this sort of thing before."

"I'm afraid I don't—"

"The news program, it's very good. You use her talents well. She was concerned that the style might be too show business-y, but it hasn't been, not at all. We're both very pleased."

"Yes, we've worked together before," Greg tried to say matter-of-factly. "I was her executive producer in Los Angeles."

"What a wonderful coincidence!" Ken commented enthusiastically. "You know, she had some misgivings about FBS at first. I guess I have you to thank for her being so satisfied lately. How did it go in L.A.?"

"Her being there helped a lot. Important TV people were at the party. They were all very impressed that Chris had come over to FBS."

Ken's forehead wrinkled. "I know she can take care of herself and I'm probably being overly protective, but these long, hectic trips take a lot out of her. She seemed exhausted when she got back."

"Could I get you another drink?" Greg asked.

Greg had spent a lifetime disguising his feelings, but nonetheless had felt uneasy and suspected he looked flushed meeting Chris's husband. Too little time had transpired since that night he and Chris had made love. He was sure that if she had stepped off the elevator with her husband, her reaction would have looked even guiltier than his; Chris possessed great self-discipline, but she was also very straightforward.

Once his watch indicated that the second feed had been broadcast, he anxiously began to calculate the minutes before she would arrive: the time she would need to get downstairs to FBS's lobby, to travel east to the Waldorf, and then to come upstairs from the Lexington Avenue entrance.

Greg was actually grateful when he spotted Barnett and could bring Ken over to him. This was Barnett's first public appearance after his illness, and he had undertaken it only because of Diane's announcement. Ken deftly shifted the conversation from the old man's improving health to his own upcoming reelection effort and began soliciting their support.

*   *   *

263

Chris arrived just as the others were walking to their table near the steps leading up the ballroom's stage. Greg saw worship in Ken's eyes as he kissed her and began the introductions. She did indeed look tired, he thought.

Greg anticipated fireworks exploding from his father-in-law upon being introduced to the anchor who had succeeded Ray Strock, but the recuperating Chairman had obviously been keeping an eye on the Nielsens.

"I've truly enjoyed your contribution to the news," he told her.

She was flattered by the compliment from a pioneer champion of television journalism. She was introduced to the other two couples who would be at their table: the male pediatric cardiologist and the female ghetto educator who would be receiving awards tonight, and their spouses.

"You know Greg Lyall, of course," Ken then went on, "and this is his wife, Diane, our hostess."

Greg had been watching Chris's eyes. She did not glance directly at him when his name was spoken, but turned to Diane. Surely Diane would find Chris's nervousness suspicious.

"How pleased we are to be here," Chris said.

"You and your husband were very kind to agree to attend on such short notice," Diane replied.

"I was delighted for such a good cause."

Chris was smiling and seemed at ease. Greg could only surmise that she had erased the short-lived resurrection of their love affair from her memory as efficiently as they had agreed to do before parting in Los Angeles. Where he was concerned, she seemed sensibly determined to conduct herself with arm's-length civility.

Diane placed her father on one side of her chair and Ken Chandler on the other. To enhance the dinner conversation, she customarily seated spouses apart.

"Mrs. Chandler," she said with a stubbornly formal, old-fashioned usage that would not be dropped until the second time they met, "please sit over there, beside my husband."

In that instant Greg observed a flash of panic on Chris's face so fleeting that, if he had not known her well, it might have passed unnoticed. As he held out her chair, she finally glanced into his eyes. Again, he saw panic and understood. The prospect of their being so close had set off the same stampede of passion within him. The barbed-wire willpower that had been fencing in good sense snapped before it, railings of self-interest were leaped, efforts at self-control were pounded beneath its hooves like long grass.

"Thank you," she murmured as she let him slip the chair under her.

Her eyes implored him not to do or say anything that might arouse her further.

He sat down. Inadvertently, his thigh slid along the satin that clothed hers. She shivered. The spasm passed though his own body—an earth tremor liquefying the substance it rumbled through.

She gazed down at her plate and spent an inordinately long time unwrapping the fan shape of her napkin. She dared not look at Greg beside her or Ken across from her.

It seemed to Greg that minutes passed while he and she sat immobile, unconscious of the world outside their skins. Finally, anxious that someone would notice their silence, he turned to her.

"Did you have a good flight back from Los Angeles?"

The face that lifted to his was in agony, whipped by despair and by desire.

"What did you say?" she muttered.

He did not reply and finally had to look away. He watched the waiters progress toward the tables with the appetizers.

Soon, the lights dimmed, and a man's sonorous voice issued out of the public-address system to welcome the guests to the tenth annual dinner for the children's wing.

First a film was shown describing the work of the children's wing. Then the hospital's chief administrator came on stage, a tall man going to gray, with gold-rimmed glasses and a poised manner at the microphone. He made the surprise announcement that construction would soon start to expand the wing into a new, full-service children's hospital that would treat children regardless of race, religion, or ability to pay and would be a center for research into childhood illnesses.

"The hospital will come into existence mainly as a result of the dedication of one person. You all know her as a tireless fund-raiser. But I also know her as a tireless worker among sick children and a grateful staff. She and her family have most generously donated twenty million dollars to enable us to begin the work of building the new children's hospital." He paused for the applause. "In their honor the directors of the hospital have voted to name the hospital after a very great benefactor of the hospital and children everywhere, her father, Barnett Roderick."

The spotlight picked Barnett out. Slowly he stood up and tipped his head slightly to acknowledge the applause. That so many there knew of his recent illness magnified the response. As he sat down, he impulsively leaned over and kissed his daughter on the cheek, publicly acknowledging his love and his thanks.

"Ladies and gentlemen," the administrator concluded, "I am honored to introduce to you our chairperson for this dinner and the president of and the moving force behind the new Barnett Roderick Children's Hospital, Diane Lyall."

Applause rolled forward like the tattoo of a thousand drums as everyone stood to honor Diane. She rose up into the spotlight, which glittered from her sapphire parure, the beading on her blue gown, and the highlights in her chestnut hair. Her smile gleamed as brightly. Tonight was her triumph, the culmination of so much that was important in her life. The hospital was about to be launched. She had honored her father as grandly as she had always dreamed of doing.

She climbed the steps to the stage. Looking out onto the dark, roaring sea of people at her feet who meant so much to her, Diane felt loved. Although she would never display the vanity of admitting it, she wished the applause could go on forever.

Diane spoke about the new hospital and the additional contributions already donated.

"The rest of you aren't off the hook," she joked. "I'll be calling on each one of you for a contribution. And I'll keep after you until I get it. So make it easy on yourselves by giving more than you can afford right away."

As the guests laughed, three small children moved out onto the stage, one on crutches. Diane took the microphone in hand and dropped onto her haunches beside them. She introduced each and elicited briefly their stories of successful treatment at the children's wing with a sweetness and gentleness that communicated her love for them.

"She's magnificent!" Chris whispered to Greg.

"Sometimes she really can be," he agreed.

He glanced at Barnett. Pride and love glowed on his father-in-law's face. Greg envied him so devoted a child.

At the end of the evening, as everyone around the table was standing up, preparing to leave, Greg was able to turn his back on the others and speak privately to Chris.

"We have to see each other alone," he whispered.

"I don't know when we could."

"Do you and Ken have any plans for the weekend?"

She shook her head.

Diane appeared at Greg's side to say good-night to Chris and thank her for coming.

Greg turned to his wife. "I thought it might be fun to have Chris and Ken join us in Connecticut this weekend."

"You usually hate when I invite people." She smiled at Chris. "He says he can't really relax if he has to be a host. He must feel very comfortable with you and your husband."

Diane supposed Greg wanted to strengthen FBS's relationship with

266

its valuable anchorwoman and her influential husband, who she had learned sat on the Senate committee that oversaw the FCC. She herself relished the opportunity to lobby the senator for federal funding for the children's hospital.

"Please come up with us," she said. "It would be fun."

"Ken," Greg called out, "we've invited you and Chris to our country house for the weekend. We'll fly up in a helicopter first thing in the morning."

Ken nodded to Chris to indicate his willingness. A weekend such as this could solidify an important source of support for him.

Chris's attention shifted back to Greg. "Are you really sure about this?"

Her voice conveyed her doubts about going—and her inability to resist.

"I can't think of anyone I'd rather spend the weekend with." Greg's voice was low and assured.

"I don't understand what you're doing in an area like this," Sally said.

Danny had pulled over to double-park for a moment and check the map. He had never been in Watts before. All the faces were black. He was having trouble finding the address he was seeking, but was afraid to put down the window and ask directions.

"There's this old black guy who's really sick. He used to do gardening for me before my ex-wife got the Bel Air house. I want to stop in and cheer him up. You know, give him a couple of bucks for bills."

"That's really a nice thing to do, Danny." Sally was genuinely moved by the unexpected kind streak in Danny.

"Down deep I'm all fucking heart."

"Two blocks farther on you make a right," Sally said tightly.

"How do you know?"

"When I was on dope, if I couldn't contact my seller, I'd come down here and buy it on a street corner."

"Jesus, down here?"

"I can find my way around Watts blindfolded in the middle of the night. . . . Sometimes I did."

Danny located the low-rise apartment house built among single-family dwellings and parked. He waited a moment for some men to walk by and then dashed into the building.

In the vestibule, he rang up and was admitted into the interior of the building. Biff Stanfield was waiting at the door to the second-floor apartment when Danny climbed the flight of stairs. But so was Biff's girlfriend, Lily, a lawyer with a firm representing people in the music industry.

267

Danny thought she was some kind of put-on, at first. Black women lawyers were only something they invented for TV because it looked as if you weren't prejudiced if you put one into a show. He himself had done it twice.

But she sure sounded like a lawyer.

"Biff doesn't show you the proposal," she insisted, "until we get a piece of paper that says he and you are partners."

"So, now you don't trust me," Danny railed at Biff. "I spend a lifetime building a reputation in this business, a name that means integrity, but suddenly the old values don't count for anything. I tell you, it's an insult to ask me for a piece of paper. I'd rather rip out my heart than give you a piece of paper. Because that's what I'd be doing. Without a good name, a man is nothing."

"Lily?" Biff asked.

She folded her arms. "No contract, no proposal. And there's another thing. Why couldn't Biff meet in your office?"

"An office is cold, unfriendly. Partners meet in a home."

Lily had a different explanation. "I figure you didn't want anybody there to be able to testify that Biff had meetings with you on the project."

"I can't believe this." Danny turned wounded eyes on Biff. "This is the thanks I get for convincing the head of programming at a major network to meet with me on this project Tuesday?"

"A meeting on this?" asked Biff eagerly. "Who with?"

Danny avoided giving Marian's name. "A giant in our industry, that's who. A powerhouse. A legend. Someone with whom I'm very close."

Biff was elated. "And this network powerhouse wants to meet us on Tuesday to talk about 'Daye and Knight'?"

"*Me*. This person likes the idea and wants to meet with *me* on Tuesday to see the full proposal. This person hates writers. This person would kill the whole project if I show up with a writer. Incidentally, this person also hates the title. It's got a new one: 'Danger, Stranger.' "

" 'Danger, Stranger'?"

"How about 'The Danger Guys'?"

"That's worse than the other one."

"The important thing is the proposal. We've got to go over it."

Biff turned to Lily. "We could let him look at it."

She relented only slightly. "While you two are going over the proposal, I'll draw up a quick letter agreement to acknowledge that you're partners."

Danny smiled. "Makes a lot of sense."

He read the proposal closely and wanted a number of changes made.

Some, Biff admitted, enhanced the show. Many were designed to enhance the presentation. Danny rarely read all the way through a script, but proposals were the heart of the sale. And short. Danny had a showman's flair for selling that he wanted reflected in the proposal.

"How long will it take you to redo it?" Danny asked.

"A couple of days at least."

"I'll come back Monday night, about the same time, to pick it up."

"Just sign this before you leave," Lily said, and handed him the short agreement she had drawn up.

He folded it and thrust it into his inside jacket pocket. "I'll have my lawyer look at it."

"All it says is you two are full partners as producers and Biff is also the writer."

"Hey, I don't send box tops in without having my lawyer read them first."

Lily exchanged a glance with Biff before she spoke again. "Just bring the signed contract back with you on Monday night. No contract, no proposal."

"No problem." Danny smiled accommodatingly.

In the vestibule behind the front doors, he encountered a tall black prostitute who had stopped to check her mailbox. She wore spike heels, and her long legs were clothed in black stockings held up by a white garter belt over lace-trimmed white panties, an outfit intended to draw customers on the street. Danny stopped for a second look.

"Those are fabulous panties," he exclaimed. "Really gorgeous."

She winked. "For fifty bucks we can go back up to my place, and I'll take 'em off so you can get a better look."

"I'm in a hurry. I'll give you hundred for them right here."

The woman burst out laughing.

"What's so fucking funny?" Danny asserted defensively.

"We've got a lot in common."

She quickly stripped off the panties. A large penis popped into view.

"How about we go back to my apartment," the transvestite asked seductively, "blow a little stuff, try on some dresses, get it on?"

A guy! A fucking black queen was propositioning him. He was revolted. But he had been having trouble getting coke lately. A guy needed a little something to help him relax after a hard day, but Sally watched him like a hawk. She would not allow the stuff in the house and would probably leave him if she knew he was still using it.

"You got some stuff on you?" Danny inquired.

The black formed his lips into a kiss. "That ain't all I got, sugar."

"Just the coke. How much you got?"

The transvestite pouted, disappointed at being refused. He drew a second pair of panties from his handbag and slipped them on, carefully tucking his penis back between his legs. The little white guy was kind of cute, he mused, except for that awful toupee. The gold watch and ring look as if they weighed a ton, so he must be loaded. It would have been great to try on clothes together and make a night's earnings without having to get over to Sunset and hustle. But what the hell? Two hundred was a great start on the night. He drew a clear envelope from a hidden pocket in his bolero vest.

"That'll be another hundred."

Danny nodded. He pulled out his cash and peeled off two bills. The black man gaped at the roll of cash, all hundreds.

"You sure I ain't got nothing else I could sell you? I got gorgeous bras, honey, and a camisole to die for."

Danny stuffed the lace panties and the envelope into his jacket pocket and rushed from the building.

"This is insane," Chris said worriedly to Greg. "I'm scared stiff."

She glanced to her left, where their spouses stood anxiously watching them.

"It will be easy," Greg said soothingly. "Trust me."

He leaned close to her and turned on the ignition. "You know how to drive a stick shift. That's all it is. Just be very gentle with the gas pedal."

They were sitting in the red Lamborghini on the long, winding driveway leading out of the estate. Chris lowered her foot onto the gas pedal and raised the clutch. The wedge-shaped vehicle shot forward. Her eyes widened in synchronization with her smile as the car raced past spider-armed winter trees. She turned the steering wheel slightly at the exit. The car whipped into a ninety-degree turn and rocketed down the country road.

A short time later, seeing that they were approaching a stoplight and a junction, she slowed the car to a halt.

"My God, that was incredible!" she exclaimed.

"The exhilaration of acceleration."

"What a feeling! This car! When did you get it?"

"A while ago. It was a gift from Diane."

"For your birthday."

"No, just a gift."

"Oh."

Chris stared straight ahead. The light turned green, but she did not start moving.

"I didn't really believe that people lived like you two do. It makes

'Life-styles of the Rich and Famous' look like a homeless shelter. You know, when we landed in the helicopter, I thought we were coming down at a prep school or a college because the buildings were so huge. When all those people came running—gardeners, maintenance men—I thought they were angry we'd landed on their property. I couldn't believe they were all your servants."

"You figured we were flying to a little country hideaway the Lyalls just sneak off to."

"Until now, until this"—she gestured at the car enveloping them—"I never really understood what it was you had left me for."

"For God's sake, Chris, just promise me one thing. Promise me you won't forgive me."

"I sound like I'm about to, don't I?"

He nodded.

"I never realized that I wasn't just competing against another woman," she told him sadly. "But a whole other dimension of living. I feel like a peasant trudging manure into the palace. It's almost too splendid for me to comprehend." She reflected for a moment. "And worst of all, I like your wife, Greg. I had pictured some bony, useless creature whose days are taken up shopping for the dresses she'll wear at night."

"A lot of it is."

"But that's only the smallest part of her. She's interesting and can be funny and she's—"

"Are you trying to convince me my wife is worthwhile?"

"When you left me, I think I convinced *myself* that you were a bastard who sold himself cheap to a . . . what? I guess to a woman who couldn't get a man any other way."

"And now you don't think I did."

Very slowly, as if the moving parts of long-unused machinery were cracking apart rust that had fused them together, she began to move her head from side to side. "No, not anymore, I don't."

"Listen to me. I sold myself as surely as if I were up for auction. I had a choice. To grab for all of this. Or to stick with love. It was as cold and logical a decision as I've ever made. I did it because I was sure in the end it would make me happier."

"God, I can see why."

"But when I was with you in Los Angeles, everything inside me that isn't cold and logical finally rebelled and showed me I had lived a lie for ten years. I was happier in that bed with you than I've been for all thirty-six hundred nights with Diane combined. You and I were kidding ourselves to think a little self-control could stop all the feelings that came pouring out of us the other night. When you're near me, those feelings, they overwhelm me. All my emotions are hungry for you. And yours are for me, I know they are."

Chris's head slowly sank onto her chest, her honesty struggling with her values.

"Yes," she finally said in a small, plaintive voice.

She raised her head and sought Greg's eyes. "I don't want to feel this way. My husband loves me. And I love him—I really do. He's kind and principled and he cares about me and worries about me. He gave me back happiness."

"That I took away."

"I owe him so much. I don't *want* all the turmoil that boils up in me when I look at you and makes me forget that. I hate myself for it. Do you understand?"

He nodded. "Diane trusts me. She needs me. And she's given me so much. Everything I hoped for when I married her."

He paused to consider. "This job I finally have, I'll lose it—and everything else that I gave up a decade of my life for—if the slightest whisper of infidelity reaches her or my father-in-law. You could lose your job, too. They'd have to pay you, but they could keep you off the air for the whole ten years of your contract. That would be like death for us."

Chris's gaze swung back to the road. "I was foolish to agree to come up here this weekend."

"It was my fault for inviting you."

"We have to end it, right? As hard as it is, it can't go on."

He nodded. "It's over."

After several seconds he reminded her, "We'd better get back. Ken will want a chance to get behind the wheel."

Chris made a U-turn and slowly drove back to where her husband and Diane were patiently awaiting them.

"I want us to leave," Chris told Ken that afternoon after they returned from the tennis court roofed by a bubble for the winter.

Ken and Greg had hit the ball awhile. Greg was a far better player so a match made no sense. Chris and Diane had chatted on the sidelines, which to Chris seemed hypocritical and made even less sense.

"But I thought we were all having a wonderful time," replied Ken.

Chris was sitting at the dressing table. He leaned over and kissed her cheek reassuringly.

"You're just a little intimidated."

"I am," she agreed, guilt churning other emotions. "I'm out of place here."

"They're probably just as impressed with us. We aren't unimportant people."

She perceived in his voice his pride at having risen to a prominence that could attract the friendship of people who lived like this.

"We can't be rude," he added. "We agreed to spend the weekend. They'd be offended if we suddenly picked up and left."

Chris was silent.

"You know that's true," he pressed her.

Chris nodded with resignation. She would stick it out. This was the penance for her transgression in Los Angeles.

At breakfast Diane invited her guests to attend church with her.

"Chris doesn't go in much for organized religion," Ken apologized for his wife. "But I'd like that very much."

"Ken's the virtuous one in our family, I'm afraid," Chris affirmed. Her father had raised her as a practicing skeptic.

"Well, you can stay here and keep Greg company," Diane replied brightly. "I usually have to swear he'll witness a miracle to convince him to go."

A maid was holding the platter of silver-dollar pancakes before Ken.

"Take more," Diane advised. "They're very good."

Diane was only a sporadic churchgoer herself. Greg assumed she was attending today because her guest, New York's junior senator, would impress her friends at the service even without his wife.

"I'll be fine alone," Greg said, shifting to Chris. "You don't have to stay on my account."

She pondered for what seemed a long while before she shook her head. "I'll keep you company."

Greg and Chris stood at the picture window waving good-bye to the limousine as it pulled out of the driveway. He stepped back into a corner of the room and drew her to him.

"Any luck so far in convincing yourself that it's over?"

"No. You?"

"I didn't sleep much last night."

"I thought I was the only one. I wanted you so badly."

"I want you now." He cradled her face in both his hands and kissed her deeply. "The wonderful thing about my wife's minister is how long-winded he can be. Let's go down to the boathouse. We can be alone there."

"Greg, we ought to be sensible. Think of the consequences."

"There don't have to be any if we're careful."

"There are always consequences."

273

"Now that I have you again, I don't want to lose you."

"And you don't want to lose what you have. You can't have everything. It never works like that. Let's stop now, before it's too late to turn back."

"I've sacrificed all my life, always given up one thing to get another. I won't do it anymore."

Chris pulled away, but her hands still gripped Greg around the waist. "And you expect us to hide and try to live a lie forever?"

"Only till the end of the year, when my contract becomes ironclad at the network. I thought about it all night. Once I put the network into profits, Barnett won't be able to do a thing to me. I'll be in full control and can protect you, too."

"And if it doesn't become profitable?"

"Then we'll still have each other. But that won't happen. I'll turn the network around if I have to do it with my bare hands. We just have to hide what we feel for each other until the end of the year."

She emitted a sharp sigh. "We always end up hiding, don't we? That eats me up. But you could promise me nothing and my body wouldn't care. It just wants you."

"I love you, Chris. I always will."

Her hands moved compulsively down his flanks. "Love right now seems almost beside the point."

19

~~~~~~~~~~~~~~~~~~~~~~~~~~~

Danny would have arrived earlier, but he got lost again in Watts trying to find the address. When at last he did turn into the right block, the only parking place was near the corner. Danny recognized one of the blacks standing against the building, the transvestite he had dealt with last time he was here. The other men were dressed normally.

"Hey, it's my main man, the stud," the queen greeted him. "Looking to get some blow?"

He found the double entendre funny and began chuckling. None of the others did. One of them asked, "He a buyer?"

"Got a roll could choke a whore." The queen found that even funnier.

The other man became interested. "You like some stuff?"

"How much you got?"

The speaker's eyes narrowed greedily. "Whatever you can afford."

"You ain't got more than—" the queen started to say to his companion, but was cut off by a sharp elbow.

"Got some great stuff."

"How much can a couple of thousand buy me?" Danny asked.

"You're in luck. We're having a bargain sale today."

"Let me see it," Danny said.

"Not out here. You want to get us all busted?" He motioned toward an alley separating this corner building from the next.

Biff returned to the window after getting himself a cup of coffee from the kitchen. Danny was still not in sight, but he noticed a new car parked near the corner that was out of character with the neighborhood and had to be Danny's, a Rolls convertible. When no one rang up after a few minutes, Biff became worried.

"Something's wrong," he told Lily. "I'm going to go down and look around."

"Not alone, you're not," she asserted.

No one was around the Rolls, and they began to widen their search.

At first they did not pay attention to the mound in the shadows at the end of the alley between the two houses. But as they turned away, Biff decided the form was too long to be a garbage bag. He moved forward to investigate.

"Oh, Jesus, it's him! He's dead!"

A pool of blood had formed under Danny's head.

"You're sure?"

"I don't want to touch him and find out."

Lily bent down and placed her hand against the side of Danny's neck. She could feel no pulse. He was already growing cold.

"He's dead all right," she confirmed.

"Look at his hand."

In Danny's fist was a package of white powder. Lily felt in Danny's pockets. They were empty.

Biff was bitter. "I'm waiting upstairs for my big break and this son of a bitch gets suckered for his roll trying to buy coke."

"We'd better phone the police," she suggested.

"And be tied up for a month answering questions? All I know is that Vickers had an appointment at a network tomorrow to sell my show, and I'll be damned if I'll miss that shot."

"But you don't know which network or who with?"

"Maybe he has an appointment book on him."

"Nothing. I already went through his pockets."

"The car?"

After a quick check to make sure no one was watching, they rushed out of the alley. The Rolls was locked, but nothing lay on its seats.

They hurried back to the apartment. Biff phoned Danny's office, silently praying for someone to answer.

"Vickers Productions," sounded the young secretary's voice.

"You're still there."

She recognized Biff's voice. They had spoken several times. "I was just waiting for Mr. Vickers. He worked at home all day and was just coming in for a little while. He wanted to dictate some letters."

"He and I have a meeting tomorrow at a TV network. Do you happen to know which one?"

"No, he took his appointment book home to Malibu this weekend."

"Well, maybe it's in the files. He and I were working on a series idea together."

"If it's a new series, those files are at his home, too. That's what he was working on this weekend." The professional tone crumbled a bit. "Actually I'm getting a little worried. Mr. Vickers should have been here already. You don't suppose something is wrong, do you?"

"No," Biff exploded. "What makes you think I know something?"

"I just asked what you thought."

"I'm looking for him myself. Remember, I said that, that I'm looking for him, too."

Biff regained control of himself. The young woman gave him Danny's Malibu address and phone number. He hung up.

"I'm going out to Malibu."

"I'm going with you," Lily declared.

"I don't want you in any deeper than you are now," he said.

"The way your luck's running, you may need a lawyer before the night's over."

Chris stumbled twice over words in the first feed, which was not like her. No updates had come in, but she would have to redo those segments to get them right for later viewers.

She had so much on her mind, so much roiling her mind. The two hours making love to Greg yesterday had been rapturous, but the rest of the day had been disorienting. She had expected to feel mortified in front of Ken and Diane, but she had not. She had felt euphoric and grandiose, as if nothing could ever again harm her. Life was rich and full and gratifying. Bountiful love cascaded over her from every direction. Last night, back in their own apartment, she had even made love to Ken and enjoyed it enormously. For a while she had thought of Greg as she made love, but then had thought of no one, only how good her body felt and how remarkably Greg had reawakened it.

This morning, however, the troubling thoughts had again assailed her. She had tried to compartmentalize her mind, but she was all of one piece, she knew, for better or worse. All day she sagged with guilt and worry and shame.

After the second feed, she met with Manny and Alan Howe to go over for the final time the list of those to be fired in the second round of cuts. Greg had held off completing the reorganization of the News Division until the new team could evaluate people's capabilities. Now, as managing editor she had to participate in the wrenching consequence of taking on that role: deciding which nightly newspeople working at headquarters and in news bureaus around the country and the world were to be laid off when the next round of "outplacements," as they were euphemistically termed, were eventually announced.

One more news producer had to be cut. Manny insisted that it be Gerry Torborg. Chris argued vehemently that she and the broadcast needed him.

"He takes twice as long to get out a piece as anyone else," Manny maintained, "and agonizes over every cut as if he were supervising the Crucifixion. The other night a late story had to be inserted into the lineup. I told him he had to cut his own piece by thirty seconds, and he just about refused to do it. I finally ordered one of the tape editors to do it without him. We haven't got the budget for that kind of producing anymore."

"You don't like the fact that he stands up to you. He's not one of *your* people. But that's just why he's important. He has an integrity that we sometimes lose track of."

"I know you're close to him . . ." Manny began.

"Damn it, he's given twenty loyal years to this company. He's got a sick wife and two daughters in college."

"We pleaded with Greg and the Budget people to let us keep *this* many on our staff." Manny thrust the list at her. "Who would you fire instead?"

Chris took a long while to peruse the list. Finally, she handed it back to him. "They're all good."

"And they're all turning out twice as much work as Torborg."

"Then are we agreed it has to be Torborg?" Alan asked, directing the question at Chris. He would not make the decision without her approval. Because an anchor drew ratings and, thus, income to the network, Chris was far too powerful to risk crossing.

Reluctantly, she nodded. "When the time comes, I think I have to be the one to tell him."

By then Chris was in no mood to return home for a dinner that required her to heat up the main course the housekeeper had prepared during the day and to cook vegetables and maybe something else. Instead, she phoned Ken, and they met at the Symphony Cafe. Early diners would have left for the theater and concerts by now. The restaurant would be relaxed and full of celebrities, so she and Ken would receive fewer stares.

He was already seated and waiting for her when she arrived. She could tell he had something he wanted to talk about.

"Ken, could we put off bringing up any major new matters tonight?" she asked. "It's been a hellish day."

She ordered a glass of wine and was sure she would want another soon.

Ken's animation did not subside. "This is something good, Chris. I think you'll be happy to discuss it."

"Ken, honestly, if you knew what I've just gone through—"

278

"Trust me on this." He took her hands in his. "Chris, I think it's time we had a child."

After a long beat, she replied, "For a politician, your timing can sometimes be abominable."

"I was sure you'd love the idea. You've always told me you wanted a big family. We've been married two years. It's time."

Chris pulled her hands free and began to straighten the dinner utensils before her. "Ken, I've just taken on a massive responsibility as anchor, and the jury's still out on my performance and will be for a long time. When Brokaw, Jennings, and Rather are racing to the latest catastrophe, I'll be a balloon. Viewers will be less worried about the victims than about me toppling over in a hurricane or the ground giving way under my weight."

Ken was deeply disappointed. "That isn't going to change if we wait, Chris."

"No, but at least I'll be more of a fixture on the air and can take off a month without destroying our ratings." She eyed him suddenly. "It just occurred to me. At least for your own purposes, your timing may be right on the nose. You didn't happen to choose this particular time for me to get pregnant because you have a tough reelection fight coming up and a pregnant wife would look good?"

"Believe me, Chris, that had nothing to do with it."

"That upstate Democrat who might run against you has a big family, doesn't he?"

"Five children. But I swear to you that didn't enter into my thinking at all."

"God, you sound so sincere. You always sound so sincere. Is it only the men *I* know who can sound sincere when they're being totally devious?"

Ken was genuinely hurt. "Chris, you know how much I want children."

"I know you do. I'm sorry. I've just got a lot on my mind. Right now having children is out of the question."

Ken shrugged. "I understand."

Oh, no, she told herself, please don't. I couldn't bear it right now if you really did understand.

Sally Foster was reading a magazine by a small light in the living room that overlooked the darkened beach. Suddenly, between the periodic whoosh of waves, she heard a scraping noise in the far bedroom. For a moment she thought Danny might have forgotten his key, but then realized he knew she was home and would have rung the bell.

She quickly turned off the lamp and went to the desk drawer for his pistol. He had fumed, "Goddamn *schvartzers* are everywhere!" when showing her where he kept it. She had been appalled by his racism, but remembered the pistol. A Southern girl, she had grown up with rifles and shotguns and had learned to handle a pistol when making her cop show.

She checked the barrel in the dim light to make sure it was loaded and then knelt down behind the desk. She could hear someone entering the front bedroom through the window, then some whispering, and then a second person.

"I thought you were bringing the flashlight," she could hear one of them say.

"Well, we're just going to have to turn on a light," a woman's voice whispered back.

"Let's do it in the living room."

Sally heard them enter and stumble around a bit searching for a light switch. The lights went on.

She jumped up. "Don't either of you move."

"Oh, Jesus!" Biff cried out. "Don't shoot!"

Neither appeared armed.

"I'm calling the police." Sally always thought Danny was paranoid-crazy on the subject of blacks breaking in, but was he ever right!

"Don't do that," Biff implored her. "We're not thieves."

"Sure," Sally scoffed, "you're building inspectors working overtime."

"No, I'm a writer. I'm working on a project with Danny Vickers."

"Who's she," Sally inquired sarcastically, "your agent?"

"No, my lawyer."

Sally's eyes snapped open with incredulity. "That's it! I'm calling the police. When Danny finds out, he'll raise such a ruckus, you two will never get out of prison."

Lily's expression became sympathetic. "Are you his wife?"

"Thank God, no. I've been living with him and having my doubts about that."

"Well, I think I've got bad news for you. Danny's dead."

Lily recounted what had occurred that evening.

Sally's face was drawn. "I was pretty disgusted with him, but I didn't want him dead."

"I'm really sorry for you," Biff commiserated.

"He was a cockroach."

"Well, still, he must have had some redeeming qualities," Biff continued.

Sally thought that over.

"No," she concluded.

"None?"

"He was a degenerate. Even his taste in lingerie was tacky. But he was putting together a new series for me."

"Still, you must be very upset by the news." Biff took a step forward to comfort her.

"Make one more move and I'll blow you away like face powder!" Sally warned. "You two figured now that he was dead, there'd be no one home to stop you from looting the place." Sally had barely a cent to her name, but hoped that before Danny's death was discovered, she could stash away a few valuables to tide her over for a while.

"I remember that face-powder line from some show," Biff recalled. "Wait, you're Sally Foster, right? That was from your show."

She nodded with some pleasure at his recognition.

"Sally," he said, trying to put as much reassurance into his voice as he could, "all we want is a look at his appointment book for tomorrow."

"His what?"

Lily thought she might sound more convincing. "Biff and Danny were producing a show Biff created. Danny had a meeting at some network tomorrow that was interested in it."

"More bullshit! He's got an appointment to sell *my* series tomorrow."

The three shared a sudden, worried realization.

"Where's his appointment book?" they exclaimed at once.

They rushed to the desk. It was locked.

Sally grasped an empty vase on the desk. "He keeps the key in here. He doesn't know I know that."

She turned the vase over. A small key tumbled out.

The appointment book was locked in a top side drawer. Under eleven o'clock Tuesday was written: "Marian Marcus, FBS, Day and Night."

Sally was furious. "He must have been planning an orgy with her. The guy was the lowest—"

"No, 'Daye and Knight' was the working title of my show. He just didn't spell it right."

"He was dyslexic. He couldn't spell to save his life."

"Spelling wouldn't have helped."

"That bastard!" Sally cursed, irate at what the appointment book had revealed. "He swore to me that the meeting tomorrow was to sell *my* show."

Biff remembered. "His secretary said he had his files home."

Sally unlocked the bottom desk drawer. The project files were laid in alphabetically. She pulled out the file for her show and the one for Biff's. The most recent correspondence in hers comprised formal rejection letters from networks. Two were from FBS.

"I'll kill him!" Sally screamed, waving the gun. "That lying bastard, I'll kill him!"

Biff and Lily dove at the other file. Inside was Danny's handwritten note that Marian Marcus liked the idea and had asked to meet with him and the writer.

"With the *writer?*" Biff roared. "I'll kill the lying bastard myself!"

It was left to Lily to remind them. "You're both a little late."

"I'm going to that meeting myself," Biff announced.

"You won't get past her secretary," Sally pointed out, "even if you do manage to get into the building. Marian Marcus won't see you without Danny there. You have no package. Danny was a top producer. They would have relied on him to put up the deficit financing. Now, if you were bringing them a package, say some stars . . . What's your show about?"

Biff explained that it was an hour-long action-suspense series about white-and-black buddy cops who used disguises to break big cases.

"Why does one of them have to be a black guy? A woman would give you the same contrast. Me, for instance."

"Oh, no. That was the whole point of creating the show. It was originally supposed to be about the black, but Danny convinced me you needed a white hero to sell a drama show."

"It won't sell without a package. If I can get Chad Laidlaw to play the white guy, would you be interested? You'd have to make the other part a woman, and I'd play it."

"Laidlaw would be perfect, but he's already got a series."

"It's getting pulled in midseason. He's worried out of his mind because the pilot shows at the other networks are already cast and set to shoot. Chad's up to his eyeballs in mortgage payments and alimony to ex-wives. He's also being blackmailed by the mother of some kid he knocked up who'll spill the beans if he falls into arrears. The only network it's not too late to make a deal at is FBS."

Lily was not about to see this opportunity slip by. "Biff, you can become the messiah for African-Americans with your *next* series. Let's not lose this one. What do you want, Sally?"

"I'll want a quarter ownership and so will Chad, I'm sure. We'll bring in an experienced producer who the network will approve, and he'll get a piece. The last quarter's yours. You know, plus our salaries."

"Okay," Biff finally declared. "Is there a typewriter anywhere, or better, a computer and a printer? I have to redo this proposal before eleven tomorrow morning."

Sally pushed a button. A computer rose up out of a cabinet to one side. "Am I a great partner or what?"

Biff pulled the desk chair over.

"We need a title," he remarked. "Nobody really liked 'Daye and Knight.' "

" 'Adam and Eve'?" Sally offered.

Biff nodded and began typing. Sally phoned Chad Laidlaw, who loved the concept. The package still needed a production company or studio to guarantee any deficit if the series went over budget, but that would be no problem. Lily began to write up a short letter agreement that would bind them all. She halted and looked up.

"You know, we really ought to do something about Danny."

"You just told me Danny's dead," Sally replied.

"His body's just lying in that alley."

"Oh. Maybe somebody found him already."

"Not where he is," Biff pointed out. "He might not be found for days."

Sally was practical. "Look, you can't call from here. The police could trace it. You have to use a pay phone near the body." Sally knew about such things. One show she had done trapped a killer who used the wrong phone. "Don't give your name or anything."

Lily shivered. "It's not *altogether* impossible that by the time we get back there tonight someone would already have found him and called the police."

The three nodded, relieved by that thought and by their own decency at not having forgotten the deceased completely.

By noon the next day Marian had given the "Adam and Eve" package the go-ahead. Biff would write the pilot script. He would have to work fast. She liked the contrast between grim situations and flippant humor. There could be a light comic side to the couple's relationship and to the characters they took on with disguises. She astonished Biff by remarking that she had seen both a sitcom episode he wrote and him perform as a comedian. She thought he had the sort of humor to pull it off.

At the time the newly formed "Adam and Eve" production team was jumping up and down outside the FBS Building, an assistant medical examiner was sliding Danny Vickers's unidentified body out of a refrigerated locker. The crushed skull was immediately obvious, but he would still go through the entire autopsy to be sure that was the cause of death.

Because the Rolls was stolen before the body was found, two days would pass before Danny was identified, and then only because Sally called the police to say he was missing.

The newspapers played up the story and the fact that he was found with cocaine in his possession. Although the police made determined noises to the press, they privately doubted they would ever locate his killer. They were right.

Danny's death proved a benefit to his ex-wife, whose young son inherited Danny's estate, despite most people's being sure that her fitness trainer was really the father.

It benefited Sally, who got to stay in the Malibu house rent free after she threatened to contest the estate's distribution. She intended to spend the next month or so there consulting on Biff's script and trying to find the combination to Danny's safe, while living off discreet sales of his artwork.

Television critics believed that Danny's death benefited America's viewers most of all.

Greg temporarily held off announcing the planned News Division terminations while he pondered expanding its activities to solve the problem of low ratings being generated by an expensive, lumbering drama on Tuesday nights at ten. Some of those newspeople would be needed if he counterprogrammed in that hour with a much less costly news-magazine series that the News Division would produce itself; he would save six hundred thousand dollars a week in a time slot he was certain to lose anyway. If enough viewers displayed interest, the hour might even be profitable.

Every network was trying to come up with viable prime-time news hours for the same reason. The trick was to figure out a new format. The news documentary "48 Hours" filmed an ongoing story. Sam Donaldson and Diane Sawyer did a mix of news reports, live interviews, and conversation no one was yet comfortable with. Connie Chung had tried a couple of concepts on Saturday night. NBC's News Division was perpetually flailing around to come up with a format that could hold an audience.

Greg also had to keep in mind that viewers were being flooded with syndicated tabloid-news shows on local stations, often during a prime-access half hour before the networks took over for the night. The crudest of those was a popular show he had recently seen called "The Guts of the Story," which produced stories remarkably like those Stew Graushner and his partner's series satirized.

"There's a reason those Barbara Walters interview shows are so popular," Greg reasoned aloud. "People like knowing personal stuff about famous people. Let's have Chris do three interviews with important people every week."

"On top of the nightly news, that's a good way to kill her," Matt Blanchard pointed out. Greg and Alan Howe had selected the young senior producer to oversee the program and gave him his choice among several field producers and writers for his staff.

"All right," Greg agreed, "she'll just be the host, and we can film a

284

little background about each person along with some file footage and spend a lot of time having the person talk very personally into the camera. If it's someone important—say, the inside story of Japan's new emperor, if we could get him, or Sandra Day O'Connor—Chris would do the interview. You know, their personal feelings, some light gossip they might not have revealed before. Otherwise the producer or a correspondent will ask questions from off-camera to get them talking. We cut the questions out of the soundtrack and just have the person's intimate talk to the viewer."

"How about calling it 'Intimate Portraits' or 'Confidential Story'?" was Howe's suggestion. A florid complexion made him appear embarrassed by it.

"The last one's punchier. Somebody already has 'Inside Story.' Maybe we'll come up with something better. I want to be on the air in a month."

Blanchard stood up. "That doesn't give me much time."

"If we can cover breaking news in minutes," Howe declared, rising to leave as well, "a month's practically a vacation."

Greg did not know whether the last remark had been made to demonstrate a can-do attitude, but it pleased him nonetheless.

Greg and Chris had not spoken in several days and had not been alone since the weekend at the country house. She looked up with a start when Greg stepped into the open doorway of her office.

"I was just thinking about you," she said.

He closed the door and went around the desk to kiss her. She savored it.

"It's always as good as I hope it will be," she whispered. "Okay, what's up? Couldn't get wonderful me out of your mind?"

Greg explained the new prime-time news hour to her. Her contract allowed for such a series and occasional specials. FBS had to capitalize on her popularity if a news-magazine program was to succeed.

"It's going to be serious, though," she wanted him to assure her. "I wouldn't want to be doing, you know, 'Inside Jessica Hahn.' "

"We'll have some lighter pieces, but the idea is to focus on people who have real significance to all our lives, do a little minidocumentary about each, which would include a long segment in which they tell us about themselves."

"Sounds terrific."

She asked Greg a few more questions about the proposed program and then fell silent. They were both thinking the same thing. Chris voiced it first.

"When do you and I get time alone? Where? How? I can't walk into a lobby without being recognized."

"I'll rent an apartment in someone else's name. With a private entrance. Maybe in a brownstone. We won't be able to get much time together, but at least it will be something."

Chris began to laugh. "You're the best person at secrecy I know. You reminded me of a place. A friend is thinking of giving up her apartment."

She became pensive. She was thinking of Ken. "It won't be that easy for me this time, Greg."

"For either of us. Just keep in mind, we only have to hold on until the end of the year."

"The end of the year," she repeated.

"And then we can live happily ever after and have lots of kids."

"Sounds wonderful. We'll just have to wait a couple of years for the first one . . . you know, until the program's established. Ken has a hard time with that, but you and I have the same priorities."

He bent forward and kissed her again. "I made a terrible mistake when I left you. I chose opportunism over love. How often does a man get a second chance to correct his life?"

Chris met with Matt Blanchard to convince him to hire Gerry Torborg for the planned newsmagazine program. She could pull rank and demand it, but sensed determination in the young man to stand his ground now and demonstrate that he was boss, regardless of her power.

"Gerry's a fine producer," she argued, "a fine man."

"I like Gerry personally. But we don't have time for his kind of contemplation over every little thing. We're going to be going at a pace that will wear out someone half his age. If he slows up the process so that we don't get something on the air, it's my ass. I can't take that chance."

There was an additional reason, she sensed: Blanchard wanted to be surrounded by his own people and not have in his midst someone known to be an ally of hers. But his argument about the need for a quicker, less meditative producer was unassailable. Gerry could never work at the required pace. She nodded and stood up. Tomorrow the terminations would be announced, and she could not prevent Gerry Torborg from being among them.

Chris did not sleep much that night and came in early to be sure to catch Gerry as soon as he arrived. She brought him to her office and, as gently as she could, told him he was being let go. She had expected dismay and then worry. She had not expected that his understandable anger at the company would be directed toward her.

286

"I thought you, of all people," he said, "would have the principles not to knuckle under to the news-as-entertainment thinking."

"It wasn't like that. I fought for you, but it was impossible."

"This isn't the Saturday morning cartoons or 'Wide World of Entertainment.' This is the news, the information that's essential for us to provide to a free people. I'm being fired because I took that duty seriously."

"You have every right to be upset. But choices had to be made. The budget was just too high."

Gerry Torborg gazed at her with the full dignity for which she had always admired him and then he rose and went to the door. He had one last thought to express before he left.

"Nobody ever said the budget was too high before we had an anchor who made two million dollars."

Stew Graushner parked his Jaguar in the office building's basement garage. He ran into the men's room and hurriedly changed from the plaid vicuña jacket and the silk slacks his private tailor had just run up to an old K Mart ensemble he had worn before Susan Glendon scattered magic dust on his life. The new clothing was then hidden in the Jaguar's trunk. A cab awaited him on the sidewalk, which let him off a block away from "The Guts of the Story" 's ramshackle offices. He walked inconspicuously the rest of the way.

To determine whether he could risk giving up the job that was providing what Susan believed to be his inspired imagination, he had once called in sick and stayed home to work with her. All that day he was devoid of ideas. He returned to "Guts" the very next day. The excuse he gave Susan for disappearing was that he could write only at night and must go off into the mountains each day to pursue deep intellectual thought. He told her he was pondering a paper to be entitled "The Semiotics of the Semaphore, Five, and Six."

Susan was awed. She revised her own work schedule to write with him after he returned at the end of the day (once more back in his elegant clothing after having secreted K Mart's finest). She marveled at the new plots and details he managed to come up with each night about their series's characters. She was humbly grateful for the chance to work with him.

Susan was troubled on the personal level, however. No longer was impotence the problem. Now, after their writing was done for the night, she seemed unable to interest him enough to keep him awake. She feared that a man of such towering imagination and intellect would soon grow tired of their conventional lovemaking and thus, of her.

Each day, while he was gone, she labored to devise new scenarios and techniques to maintain his sexual interest. She bought weirdly lascivious outfits and prowled the most disreputable sex shops for kinky implements and for books with scurrilous plots she might adapt for their bedroom. They seemed, in fact, to catch his attention. But she knew if she was to retain it, she would have to invent ever lewder and more unconventional pleasures. She was falling apart, but dared not let on for fear of losing him.

Stew thought he finally and truly understood what hell must be like. He had finally seen his dreams realized: He was on the brink of success as a writer, he was making a lot of money, and the most incredibly sexy woman plied him with erotic delights. But success had turned out to be a curse. He could barely keep his eyes open. He dared not confess his fatigue resulted from holding down a job at "Guts" because that would undermine the cause of her respect for him. So, after working at two jobs, in order to prove his infatuation he had to make love in everything from a Saran Wrap toga (he was Zeus) to, on this particular night, a rubber Santa Claus outfit (she was Vixen). On his shoulder he hefted a bag full of the most bizarre toys.

She ignored his pleas that Christmas was long past. Attached by the reins he held, she galloped around the house crying out, "To the top of the rooftops!"

Finally, getting into the spirit of the game, he cracked a velvet whip over her naked rump and demanded to know whether she had been "naughty or nice."

She stopped so abruptly when he reined her in that her antlers nearly poked out his eye. Yet, he still retained the presence of mind to declare with more pain than lustiness, "I can't wait to slide up your chimney, babycakes."

"Oh, Santa," she cooed, "I just love your North Pole."

He snorted brazenly. A cloud of talcum powder whitening his beard flew up into his nose and sent him into a fusillade of sneezes. By the time he had recovered, his North Pole was pointing solidly south.

Greg listened through the oral presentation given by the three impressive gentlemen from Research. He had already read their voluminous written analysis. All of the groups on whom they had carefully tested Arnold Mandel's pilot show for "What's the World Coming To?" had had the same reaction: They were scandalized.

"I told you they would be," maintained the West Coast researcher of new shows.

His boss, the head of the Research Department, was even more pessimistic about the series's potential. "It might even pull down shows that come *before* it."

Greg thought for a while. "Something bothers me. Very few people said they found it funny."

"If you'll notice, one of the subjects mentioned that it was amusing 'if you like that sort of thing.' "

"Has Jimmy Minh seen this?"

The Research v.p. was startled. "No, of course not. This isn't his area. He just tabulates our ratings."

The man had no idea that Greg Lyall knew Jimmy Minh. Actually, he had no idea that anyone knew Jimmy Minh, who had been entombed in the same office and position for over a decade.

"Ask him to come up here," Greg ordered.

"He'd probably be embarrassed . . ."

Greg picked up his receiver and punched in the number from memory—Jimmy had counseled him many times over the years. The vice president turned white.

A few minutes later, the wiry Vietnamese ambled into the room. His shirtsleeves were rolled up, and his shirttail had climbed out of his pants. A shock of black hair dipped down in front of his large eyeglasses.

Greg explained their problem. Jimmy perused the report for a few minutes. Then pushing his glasses higher on the bridge of his nose, he looked up.

"Greg, you say this show is really outrageous?"

"Pulls no punches. I thought it was wildly funny, but these people didn't seem to agree."

"They wouldn't have with so many others in the room. They would say what they thought would sound respectable. You have to test that sort of show where they'll really watch it: in the privacy of their own homes. That's where they'll be honest."

"Can we do that?"

"Sure, we can get a cable company to play it in a sample area next week and then we phone up the viewers on a random basis for their opinion."

"Handle it, Jimmy. I need an answer no later than two weeks from last Monday."

Jimmy's boss tried to assert, "If we had known you were looking for that sort of answer . . ." His voice faded away under Greg's glare.

It was inconceivable to the vice president that the chief executive officer would consult directly with his subordinate and not leave that to him. But shocking form or not, the conclusion was inescapable that despite having always conducted his corporate life with exemplary political caution, he had suddenly and without the slightest warning come face-to-face with his personal apocalypse. Over Jimmy Minh, of all things. He wondered if it was too late to take advantage of the severance package offered a few months back.

The party was a dazzler, one of the kind she only used to read about. But Marian Marcus received dozens of invitations a month now. Tall and erect, chicly gowned, she was an impressive and glamorous woman, but most important, she was a *power* in Hollywood, feted and flattered everywhere.

Her escort this night was an intriguingly muscular young assistant director she had come upon while viewing a rehearsal for a dramatic pilot. She ignored him most of the evening. After they returned home would be time enough to turn her attention to him. Parties such as this were for business. She conversed with several studio heads about buying a group of their latest theatrical films for showing next season. Most of the films were committed first to cable, which had laid out preproduction cash. But if she could obtain a package of films that had not yet played on cable or had perhaps played only sparingly, and then added to those some movies FBS had itself financed, two attractive hours every week would be accounted for.

As she and her escort left the party, one of the young people parking cars came up to take her ticket. Her heart nearly stopped. Before her was the face enshrined in the deepest vault of her memory.

"Excuse me," she asked, pulling back the parking stub, "aren't you Derek Peters?"

The well-remembered smile shyly lit his face. "Yes . . . yes, I am. Do we know each other?"

Derek Peters, she thought, you are still the most beautiful creature on this entire earth.

"No reason why you should remember, I guess," she said aloud. "We used to go to UCLA together."

He looked a little puzzled. "I usually have a good memory for faces."

"I'm Marian Marcus."

Most of the young people who parked cars at such events were actors trying to make ends meet. She asked if he was.

"Not a very lucky one," he admitted. "A couple of shots on 'Tour of Duty,' a walk-on or two, some little theater. I always end up getting beaten out for the part. What do you do, Marian?"

"I'm head of Programming for FBS."

Once more his smile formed, but astonished now and eager and gleaming. "I think I remember you now, Marian. At UCLA."

290

"We have a lot of catching up to do," she assured him. "Are you doing anything later tonight?"

"No. I'll be through at one."

"Well, I'll just drive my friend here home and come by for you then." She turned to her escort. "Derek and I practically grew up together. I know you won't mind."

His muscles seemed to sag a bit under the tuxedo, but after all, this was Marian Marcus he was talking to. He told her he didn't mind a bit.

Marian tried to catch as much sleep as she could on the red-eye to New York for the Monday-morning meeting. Derek had driven her to the airport. A week had passed, and they had seen each other every night. Only with the greatest effort had she torn herself away from him now for the two days the trip would require.

She had just enough time for a shower at her suite at the Plaza and to freshen her makeup before quickly slipping on one of her new dresses. She rushed over to the FBS Building for the meeting with Greg and Arnold Mandel. Afterward she and Greg would review the list of shows going to pilot.

At Greg's office she was introduced to a Vietnamese named Jimmy Minh, whom she learned had just been promoted to head of Research.

Jimmy revealed that Arnold Mandel's show, "What's the World Coming To?" had tested much better with a home audience, as he had predicted it might. "It had some high negatives, but those who liked it, really liked it."

The response had been particularly good among the eighteen- to thirty-four-year-olds, the most desirable audience segment. Although that was encouraging, Jimmy warned that many people were offended or thought they should be. Arnold would have to tiptoe along a fine creative line.

Ev Carver reported that the ad agencies had shied away from the show, preferring to wait until it had proved itself. When pressed for an on-the-record opinion, he advocated not picking it up for that reason and because it would almost certainly arouse the affiliates' animosity.

"Even so," Greg disagreed, "with all the series we want to replace, what the hell do we have to lose? At least the show tries to say important things. Let's face it, we don't have anything else."

Marian agreed. "I say we go with it in a late slot—maybe Wednesday at ten-thirty—when we can't be accused of corrupting children. Do a lot of publicity about how controversial it is, try to calm the affiliates' fears while building a cult audience, and then wait in the bunker for the results."

Jimmy liked that idea. "We can do an audience-flow survey to see how many viewers come back to the show over time and how many quit."

Arnold, who had feared the show would never get on the air, now argued that Greg was in too much of a hurry. No scripts were yet ready. He wanted to premiere the show in the fall.

"This show will get lost in the fall," Greg maintained. "If it's to have any chance at all to find an audience, it has to go on now, when people aren't confronted by dozens of new choices."

Arnold reflected for a moment. "I like what you've done with 'Hot Time.' The producers tell me the changes came from you guys. I'll gamble you're right here, too."

He would just have to drive everybody hard—himself most of all—to get enough scripts. He'd probably be writing next week's while shooting this week's.

"Please understand," Greg concluded, "I want you to be careful, but don't pull your punches. If this show is to have any chance at all, it'll be because you shock people into laughing at things like bigotry and official stupidity. The controversy should get the show noticed. Once you get chicken, we have no chance at all."

"It's nice that you think we have *some* chance."

"Arnold," Marian finally answered him, "huge hordes of smart, hip, young viewers will have to get hooked on the show for it to have a chance. Unfortunately, a lot of television producers have gotten very rich underestimating the taste of the American public."

"Derek's really wonderful. He really *is* wonderful. Not fantasy now. We've spent every night together since we met."

Marian was aglow. She and Chris sat across the dinner table set up by room service in Marian's suite at the Plaza.

"Can you believe that after all these years he's come back into my life?"

Chris grinned. In the oddest way, Marian thought, but she was so full of happiness about her news that she rushed on.

"His career really hasn't gone well. He lives from hand to mouth. He drives two hours into L.A. every day because he rents a room in some little farming town for practically nothing. If his car should break down, he probably hasn't got the money to buy a replacement part."

"But I'll bet you've simplified that long drive for him, by letting him stay overnight at your place."

A peal of laughter rang from Marian's throat. "All right, I did tell him that it was dangerous for him to drive back so late at night and why shouldn't he just stay over."

"And now you're getting used to it."

292

Marian nodded. "I've never been so happy. All my adult life I've come home to an empty place and forced myself to make dinner and . . . Well, you know. But he's there when I come home now. And usually he hasn't had an audition, so he's made dinner for us and can't wait to see me. And I can't wait to see him. We rip each other's clothes off while the pasta is boiling over. Crazy?"

"That's the way it should be."

"You went a long time with no one in *your* life," Marian remembered. "Those nights when Ken comes back from Washington must be like a vacation for you guys."

Marian noticed the shadow pass behind Chris's eyes. With anyone else Chris might have tried to hide it.

"Uh-oh," Marian sighed, "something's rotten in paradise. You're unhappy."

A soft smile slowly suffused Chris's expression. "On the contrary, I'm the happiest I've been in a very long time. It's just that the cause isn't Ken."

"Then I really do mean that 'uh, oh.' I *was* wondering why you didn't have me to dinner at your apartment. Who is he?"

Chris pondered awhile. "You're the only person in the world I would tell this to. I've known him a long time."

Marian emitted a deep sigh. "I was afraid of that. Greg Lyall already has you wrapped around his little finger again."

"It isn't like that. It's just that the same old feeling comes over both of us when we're together. As if Ken and Greg's wife and all the time in between never happened."

Marian eyed her friend sternly. "But they did happen, Chris. They happened, and you were devastated. He saw a chance to get ahead and all he thought about was himself."

"I know," she replied softly. "But I think I understand now why he did it."

"Oh, Jesus!"

"Look, I don't forgive it, but I understand it."

"And what about Ken and the Crown Princess Roderick?"

Pain was apparent now in Chris's expression. "For the present nothing." She explained how everything depended on Greg's plans for FBS working out by the end of the year.

"Thanks for the extra pressure," Marian responded with wry sarcasm. "Now both of us are chained to whether he can pull it off."

"Don't you think he can?"

Marian thought for a moment. "I think he's smart and charming and a guy who really means well when he can afford to. He changed my life. But for you, more than your career's at stake."

Marian broke the silence with another thought. "In the meanwhile what happens? Do you think you're the type who can live with one man while having an affair with another?"

Chris shrugged; she did not know. So many questions confronted her.

"I didn't choose this. I wouldn't have chosen this for anything. I just can't help myself."

Marian hugged her friend. "They get into your bones early, and no one else seems right."

" 'The fabulous, flawless Derek Peters!' " Chris recalled with a laugh. That was what the two of them jokingly used to call him.

Marian remembered another epithet they used to use. " 'And that bastard Greg Lyall!' "

20

~~~~~~~~~~~~~~~~~~~~

"That new show about the future is detestable!" Barnett proclaimed in disgust to his son-in-law.

Greg assumed he was referring to Arnold Mandel's series, "What's the World Coming To?"

"The same old product won't sell anymore," Greg answered. "Look at the real hits so far this year—"America's Funniest Home Videos," "The Simpsons," "Twin Peaks." They're all recent midseason replacements and all distinctive. Our show is honest, funny, and may just be daring enough to make it."

The two men sat in the large salon at the rear of the country house, looking out on a lawn that sloped down to the lake. With late April had come greenery and flowers in the garden and along walking paths. Diane sat at a desk to one side half-listening while attending to her own matters.

"If I had any idea you intended to put that hate material on the air . . ." Barnett let the sentence hang. "Don't you consider anything sacred?"

Greg knew Barnett to be a thoroughly amoral man, except where family was concerned. At times, Greg suspected, even an immoral man. His ethical grievance about "What's the World Coming To?" had to be a ploy to gain a different objective. Greg's rejoinder was pragmatic, not theological.

"All the press it's getting, that controversy, is helping to find an audience in a very bad time slot. That half-hour slot is doing better than it's done in years. People seem to be finding the show, younger people who could be renting movies or watching shows on cable." Greg displayed a teasing smile. "For the May sweeps we're moving it to an earlier hour. We think it will do even better when there's a full-size audience out there."

Greg outlined FBS's plans for the sweeps that would set rates for the ad agencies' upfront buying in June, at which some $4 billion would come in to the networks. FBS would try to overcome its lack of strong series with specials, miniseries, made-for-television movies, and a couple of the stronger movies from next season's package. The other networks would be scheduling special programming as well, but this year they had also held back episodes or shot extra episodes of many of their strong series. Everyone had moved programming around like dominoes to devise the strongest possible lineup against the others. The revamped morning show would travel to Australia and New Zealand for two weeks. Greg admitted to the hope that FBS would increase its ratings with all this sweeps footwork, but the key determinant for how it would do next year was the series pilots that would soon be chosen for the fall schedule from those now being produced.

"I'm feeling like my old self again," Barnett declared, taking a different tack. "The doctor says he wouldn't be surprised to see me putting in a full day's work soon. I've been thinking I might sit in next week when you're watching the pilots. Keep my eye on some of those hotheaded decisions."

So, that's it, Greg recognized. Your health is improving, the crisis is over, and you're bored. You want to get back in the game again. Sorry, old man. It's my bat and ball now. Greg noticed out of the corner of his eye that Diane's head was raised like a hunting dog's, watching, listening.

"We can't play it safe anymore. Are you sure you want to share the blame if next fall's lineup is a bust?" Greg inquired of the Chairman. "Ev Carver doesn't. He's already slid away from the table. Come the fall he wants to be able to blame everything on me."

Barnett bristled. "I've never been afraid of responsibility." But then he added, "Your contract puts those decisions into your hands. I wouldn't want to be accused of going back on my word."

Greg observed to himself that Barnett had never been stopped by that in the past, but said aloud, "I appreciate the confidence."

Diane's head lowered again to her own work.

Greg leaned forward toward Barnett. "Short term we have to raise ratings with a better lineup. But with the broadcast networks all just fighting for a bigger piece of the same total audience, unless we make long-term structural changes in the way we do business, I think over the long haul we're just rearranging deck chairs on the *Titanic*."

Greg needed Barnett's aid to win board approval for the new directions he had begun contemplating when he was in charge of future development. Barnett had ignored them then.

Station ownership was the most lucrative part of the television business. Why should a network pay a prosperous station to carry shows the station needed as much as the network? Moreover, if IBM and General Motors were worldwide businesses, why not American TV broadcasting companies? Although the FCC still forbade them from syndicating shows domestically—they and the other networks were fighting the studios and independent producers over that—FBS should be trying to syndicate abroad and to co-produce shows with foreign broadcasters or buy into them.

"We should also do more in cable," Greg said. "We're not allowed to own cable systems. But we should certainly be buying into or starting up the networks that go on the cable systems. That's our business, delivering programs to viewers."

"Over the air," Barnett reminded him. "Not on cable."

"ABC's share of ESPN is worth over a billion dollars now. GE sees that owning NBC isn't enough; it's jumping into cable joint ventures and even to beaming direct to home satellite dishes with Rupert Murdoch, who controls Fox. We have a News Division, why don't we have an all-news cable service? If we'd invested ten years ago, a lot of those viewers we lost to cable would be watching our cable networks now, not Ted Turner's."

Barnett was frowning. "Now isn't the time to throw money away."

"If we have to borrow to go where television is headed in the future, then we have to borrow. But more to the point, right now we, CBS, NBC, ABC—we're the biggest draws on cable. But we have only a single income stream: advertising. The cable networks, like CNN, have two income streams: advertising *and* what the cable systems pay them out of each subscriber's fee to the system. How many people would buy cable if they couldn't get the broadcast networks on it?"

"The law requires they pay a small amount for the copyright on shows when they transmit our local stations. You want it raised?"

"No." Greg was adamant. "I want the law abolished completely so the cable companies would need our permission to broadcast our local affiliates *with our programming* on their systems. And they would have to pay *us*."

"You're missing the point, Greg. If cable cut us off, our viewer base would be smaller. We would have to charge less for commercials."

Greg diplomatically refrained from mentioning that Barnett was the one missing the point. Once a visionary, in recent years Barnett had allowed his thinking to become habitual.

"Barnett, without being able to put on the over-the-air stations the cable companies would be in deep trouble. They'd start losing masses of viewers."

297

Barnett suddenly glimpsed the possibilities Greg saw. "They'd have to give in to us, just to stay in business."

Greg nodded. "The heads of some of the other networks and I are beginning to make noises about it. Look at a company like Time Warner. They own a studio that produces TV products they're allowed to syndicate. They own cable systems and networks. We can't do any of that. It's wrong. All kinds of proposals are percolating in Congress to reform cable TV. We might not get the proposal through them this year, but we have to start lobbying for it now."

"Ken Chandler heads that Senate committee, doesn't he?" Barnett remembered.

Greg nodded. Inducing Ken Chandler to aid him was a troubling prospect.

Diane suddenly spoke up. "I'm inviting Ken and Chris to a small dinner party. I want to follow up on the children's hospital. You can approach him on your matter."

"Let's keep business and friendship separate," Greg replied. "Make a separate lunch date with him or go to his office. I'll do the same."

"Nonsense. Dinner at our apartment would be perfect. The man was thrilled when we invited him here. He's a poor boy who can't quite believe he's rubbing shoulders with people like us."

After a decade of marriage to you, Greg thought, I'm finally included. Too small a victory come too late.

Diane picked up the phone and called the Chandlers' home. Ken answered, and they agreed on the date.

"It doesn't work. I'm telling you it doesn't work."

Biff Stanfield was nearly insane with worry. He had watched the rehearsal just before the initial take of the first scene between Sally and Chad and had nearly thrown up. The woman character he had created so carefully now seemed as contrived as a Saturday-morning cartoon, Chad's as stiff as an ironing board.

"It'll be fine," the man in the safari jacket answered.

John Rosenthal was a red-bearded producer-director who had cut his teeth at MTM and directed fifty straight episodes of "Gang Way," a runaway hit, and probably another hundred shows over the years. The high fees he now received and the residual checks that came in each month had made him a rich man. He was heavily in demand during pilot season because of his touch with comedy. This year, though, the project he and his wife, Marti, an experienced producer, had personally developed had fallen through at the last minute, and Marian Marcus had talked them into joining the team for "Adam and Eve." They would own 25 percent on top of hefty salaries. John had taken a liking to the script and to this kid who had written and created the show. More important, he had reasoned that if Marian Marcus was that interested in the project, it might just get onto the schedule.

"You keep telling me not to worry," Biff was agonizing, "but *you* sure as hell aren't worrying and *somebody* sure as hell better!"

John smiled. He walked over to Sally and Chad. "Take it a little faster this time. And move a little closer."

"That's it?" Biff moaned when the smaller man returned to his chair. "If the world was collapsing right in front of Steven Spielberg's eyes, would he just say, 'Move closer'?"

"Marti!" John called over to the pretty, round-faced woman in discussion with Marian Marcus near the side of the studio. "You've worked with Spielberg. Would he have told them to move closer?"

She noted the hint of a smile as he spoke, and she shook her head. "Farther apart."

John turned back to Biff. "I guess you have your choice."

Unnerved, Biff rushed away.

"Let's shoot it this time," John directed the cast and crew.

From his new perch atop a ladder in the back of the studio, Biff watched as the words "Take two!" and then the clap sticks sounded. Sally leaned closer to Chad. This time their repartee ricocheted back and forth. Biff was amazed. It sounded exactly as it had in his head when he wrote it. Better. Maybe this show really had a chance.

From now on, he decided, he would descend from this ladder only when John absolutely needed him. That would doubtless be, he was sure, during the very next scene.

Marian and her staff had spent the week racing around Los Angeles theaters and sound stages, worrying through last-minute changes with the producers and writers. At times, Marian suspected, her people were as much of a hindrance as a help, but she wanted to be sure no unpleasant surprises would turn up on the videocassettes of the finished shows. Every project seemed disastrous now, the memorized lines slow, dull, and trite, the interaction between the actors labored. But she knew that something magical could occur as soon as the cameras began to roll, as it had the other day on the set of "Adam and Eve." No matter how high the expectations, though, until the shows were edited, the sound mixed, the music added, and the images finally pranced across the little screen, no one could foretell whether the magic would result in enchantment or doom. And then only after millions of viewers had been exposed to the spell.

Marian had managed to look personally at rehearsals or shooting for over a dozen FBS pilot shows.

299

"Tinsel Town," a musical which centered on young actors, writers, and directors trying to make it in Hollywood, hadn't yet jelled. The cast seemed to lack vitality, the direction urgency. Her hopes for the pilot were dropping fast. A show called "Castaways" seemed more promising; unlike on "Gilligan's Island," these shipwreck survivors constantly struggle for dominance and survival and sometimes, to assert their humanity, as they create a society with many of the problems of our own.

In a couple of weeks, Ossie Krieger would begin shooting the two-hour "Miss Grimsby" movie-pilot. A half-hour slot was being held open for it as a fall series because everyone was so sure it would play well.

"Bottom Gun," about a bumbling Air Force pilot who somehow always manages to come out on top, had already shot its aerial footage, which looked good, and would soon go inside for interiors.

Marian had special affection for "Lowdown" and thought its often shocking humor and outrageous characters might just have a chance; the writing and the cast and crew generated a crazy chemistry that might carry over onto the screen.

What else? Marian tried to remember as she drove back from Universal City. The hour was late, and she had just watched a run-through of the Benny Blakely sitcom. Early tomorrow morning, she would be on the set of "The Neighborhood," an hour-long dramatic series she had bought from Monumental in addition to "Lowdown." God, who knew anymore?

She did not look forward to going home tonight. Derek would not be there. He had finally won a small part in a TV film and would be shooting on location in San Francisco. They had been separated only once, when she went to New York for a meeting. It worried her that he would be away, with other women all around him. At the one or two parties they had attended together, women had buzzed around him as if he were a honeypot. Beautiful women. Because *he* was beautiful. So she did not like to go out much with Derek anymore. But he would be alone in San Francisco, on a shoot with a lot of young actresses. One might make him forget the plain, graceless woman awaiting him in L.A.

Marian did not want to delude herself that Derek could love her for herself. All that was holding him here, she was convinced, was the penury that his unlucky career so far had imposed and his hope that she might change that luck for him.

One casting director had told him, "No man as pretty as you is going to be believable to the average shnook sitting at home with his six-pack. He'll probably think you're gay."

Derek was a dreamer, a little at loose ends in the practical world. He depended so heavily on the few, practical people in his life. His agent. Her.

Marian wondered, as she had so many times before, whether she should use her influence to help his career. She believed that people such as Raoul Clampton were corrupt in more significant ways than simply taking money; they were adrift without values, unable to judge accurately the projects presented to them because they had substituted apprehension and self-interest for judgement. She feared that insisting someone give Derek a role would weaken the integrity on which she prided herself, the integrity that she considered essential for succeeding at her job. Would owing the producer a favor tempt her to order episodes of the show instead of passing on the pilot? Would Derek's having a part sway her? Would he hate her if she canceled?

Once more Marian came to the same conclusion: Helping Derek get work would undermine her only true qualification for her job, her integrity.

To her surprise the lights were on in the house. Derek was in the kitchen.

"What happened?" she asked. "You were supposed to be in San Francisco."

"I was about to leave for the airport when my agent called. They were running badly over schedule and cut my scene. They'll just add a couple of lines and stretch some scenes in the editing."

Derek had tried for a tone of carefree acceptance, but the hurt stabbed too deep. Marian could hear the misery. The long eyelashes were downcast, the lush mouth drawn tight. She put her arms around him.

"Don't worry, baby," she whispered soothingly. "Mama loves you. Mama will always love you. Someday it will happen for you. I know it will. You're going to be a star. Mama believes in you. Mama loves you."

Derek put his own arms around her and laid his head against hers. "It kills me that I have to take from you and rely on you all the time. At least I can get a job waiting on tables during the day. Bring something in."

Marian kissed him. "You have to keep taking acting classes and being available for auditions. Don't ever think you have to do a thing for me to love you. Whatever Mama has is yours. Just be here. That's all I ask. Just be here."

Chris exploded. "This is not the script I approved!"

All the changes she had made yesterday in the script for tonight's "Confidentially Speaking" should have been typed into the new draft by now. Yet here she was on the set to shoot her on-camera material and to record an audio track to be added to the edited picture, and many were absent. Little incidents such as this had been happening continuously.

Matt Blanchard, the executive producer, tried to divert her. "I promise you the script works."

"I don't want your promises. I'm looking for competence. If you're so sure it works your way, *you* read it on the air."

Chris turned on her heel and marched out of the studio.

"Anchors!" Matt spat like a curse, embarrassed in front of the staff waiting for shooting to begin. He had hoped she would forget several of her requested revisions, which he liked better his way.

Matt turned to Hedy Anderson. Although the concept had been retained of having the interview subjects speak directly into the camera, as if confiding to the viewer, Hedy and one or two other prominent correspondents, along with Chris, now appeared on camera at the start of their segments to do short background bios on the person they had interviewed. Hedy had a piece on this week's program and was slated to chat on camera with Chris before and after. She was closer than anyone else to Chris.

"See what you can do," Matt asked. He was glad to shove the task of dealing with Chris's tantrum onto someone else.

Although not egotistical, Chris possessed a strong ego that had powered her hunt for fame and recognition and had made her a creature she claimed to despise in news, a star. Every time that red light went on atop the camera, she was the one who put herself on the line. That risk separated her from all the others working on the program, no matter how important their contributions.

Heavily overworked, she had been made edgy by a succession of sometimes small, sometimes larger problems the young newsmagazine program had encountered. Matt Blanchard seemed to be fighting her instead of cooperating. The program's early ratings were lower than the program's it had replaced, bringing into question her ability to draw a prime-time audience. In the last few days several TV columnists had suggested that the few interviews she actually did herself were simply window dressing for the format, like her introduction of other correspondents' reports; that she wasn't really working as a journalist on the program. Because she did have so little time to devote to reporting for "Confidentially Speaking," the vein of truth in the comments rankled.

"Matt sent you again," Chris observed as soon as Hedy entered Chris's office.

"He hasn't got much of a bedside manner." Hedy took a seat beside Chris on her small sofa. "You look tired."

"I've had exactly one full weekend off in the last two months," Chris replied tensely. That had been the weekend at the Lyalls' estate. "I've been out of the country six times and in other parts of the country fifteen times since I came here as news anchor. The Berlin wall opens up, an earthquake hits somewhere, and it's a race to see which network's anchor will get there first—not to mention people from every foreign network. And it never stops. We keep trying to find new places to take the broadcast. Look, that's the format we settled on, so I can't complain. But Matt ought to understand that the time I give to *his* program is valuable. I can't waste it on his games."

"Being the boss is still new to him."

"You've got to be exhausted, too."

Hedy shook her head. "After working at local, the time I get here to do a story's a luxury."

The women exchanged a smile recalling the daily marathon as street reporters.

"Are you going to be able to get away this weekend?" Hedy asked.

"I'm leaving for Moscow on Sunday." Chris grinned conspiratorially. "An interview with Gorbachev and his wife. In their home. You know, before they come here in June for the summit."

"My God! That's incredible!"

"I got lucky. We're trying to keep it a secret so the other networks don't muscle in. We'll use the entire hour next week." That would be her answer to charges that she was not truly acting as a reporter on "Confidentially Speaking."

"Matt has to be thrilled. He's crazy to be provoking you."

Chris sought Hedy's gaze, to reveal something else. "I'll probably do a story or two from there for the nightly news, but it'll look too awkward for me to anchor that broadcast from there. I've asked that you sub for me until I get back."

Hedy was stunned. "I'm . . . I'm . . . Thank you."

"No need to thank me, you're good. I've also told Greg he should consider you to anchor the weekend news on a regular basis."

"He won't think it's just too many women?"

Chris laughed lightly. "Do you mean, 'Is Greg a male chauvinist?' "

"Something like that."

Chris considered for a moment. "His only concern will be whether viewers take to you. He's like a circus juggler keeping track of the things that can turn on or turn off viewers."

"You two know each other so well. You seem to have a shorthand when you discuss things."

"We worked together for a year in L.A. and you know, since he hired me to come over here to anchor the news."

"God, it's got to be so great to be respected like that . . . someone

303

who knows your work and hires you because he respects you as a professional."

"Not really. Someone had to respect *your* work to pull you out of local and bring you to network."

"But I mean someone who doesn't want his pound of flesh for it, whom you won't owe your soul to."

Hedy's eyes dropped, and her head turned away. Chris suddenly suspected that Hedy had given up the little ground-floor brownstone apartment in Greenwich Village and sublet it to Chris—swearing her to secrecy—in order to move somewhere she could not be found. Compassion welled up in Chris for her friend. She bent forward and kissed Hedy's cheek. "What matters is that you've made good on that opportunity to prove yourself."

"Well, thanks again for mentioning me to Greg," Hedy said, chagrined by how emotional she had allowed herself to become. "I really admire him. He's a terrific guy." She chuckled. "You know, the kind of attractive man they always say about, 'It's too bad he's married.' "

Hedy was surprised to glimpse what she thought might have been a flash of sorrow in Chris's eyes.

"Oh," Hedy said in realization, "he's the one."

Reluctantly Chris nodded. She felt she had to explain.

"We both thought it was over years ago. It wasn't." Her eyes implored secrecy. "Please, Hedy."

"Not a word to anyone. I promise."

Impulsively, Hedy hugged her friend, sensing the enormous and ambivalent sorrow inhabiting her.

Finally, Chris stood up. "Do you think our young executive producer has had enough time to put my changes onto the teleprompter?"

"I think he understands that from now on he'd damned well better."

Hedy put her arm around Chris's shoulders as they walked toward the door. "I'll just tell him you were hell on wheels in here."

The afternoon light squeezed through the closed curtains and upturned blinds to suffuse the little ground-floor brownstone bedroom with gauzy illumination. Chris lay naked across Greg's chest. Apart for weeks, they had made love almost frantically.

She lifted her head to look at him. "This was the only thing I could think about all last night and this morning."

"You probably said the same thing to Gorbachev to get that interview."

"It would have been too crowded there in bed. Me, Gorby, Raisa, the interpreter."

"The language of love needs no interpreter," said Greg with feigned dreaminess.

"One of the great lies of the Western World. Men and women speak a totally different language. If it weren't for biology . . ."

"You'd be, what? A lesbian?"

"No," Chris answered with a seriousness that surprised them both. "Happily married."

"I don't believe you really are. I've watched you and Ken together. Civility isn't love."

"No, but it's steady, peaceful. Before you came back into my life I didn't question or hate myself."

"Aren't you happy now? With me?"

"Yes. But tonight, at your dinner party, I'll feel like a total shit. 'Nice to see you again, Diane. I do so enjoy having your husband inside me.' And 'Ken, you know Greg, don't you? Would you believe that not three hours ago he was fucking my brains out?' "

"That reminds me, there's some legislation I want to talk to him about."

Chris frowned. "Doesn't it strike you as just the littlest bit, say, low and exploitive—even a touch despicable—that you're lobbying the same man whose wife you're sleeping with?"

"Would you rather I stopped sleeping with you?"

"Damn, these are the times when I really don't like you."

"Of course it troubles me. But doing business with him won't change the fact that I love you or want to be with you."

Chris took a while to reply. "I wish you hadn't invited us tonight."

"Not guilty, judge, to that particular idea."

"I'll watch Diane looking happy beside you and feel rotten for her sake and worse for my own."

Greg had no reply and decided to strike out in a different direction. "I hate to add to that rotten feeling, but . . . The Gorbachev interview was great and drew great ratings for "Confidentially Speaking." But those don't come along every week. We've got to do more celebrity interviews, lighter stuff, to keep pulling the numbers."

"Oh, no, I can tell what's coming. 'The first interview direct from Warren Beatty's bedroom' and 'Roseanne, is it really true you tried to commit suicide by swallowing an entire freight car of Nestlé Crunch?' "

"Would probably draw a forty share."

Chris glanced down. "Greg, is there some evil fairy godmother who waves her wand and turns everything good to garbage?"

He kissed her. "Not this."

Her lips hung on his.

"You and me," he said softly, "is the only thing that keeps me sane."

305

Ken was a step behind Chris walking into their bedroom after the dinner party. Her slim body that always moved with an easy economy walked more stiffly along the hall with each step. Her head glinting gold specks in the dim light gradually tipped downward.

He thought he had been in good form tonight. Told a couple of good stories and hit it off well with several excellent prospects for campaign contributions. He was pleased that each of the Lyalls sought him out privately to raise matters on which they hoped to gain support. He knew Chris did not like these parties much, but she was usually a good sport about extending herself. Tonight, however, she had hardly spoken, had barely kept up her end of the conversations.

Taking her elbow an instant after she stopped to turn on the bedroom lights, he moved in front of her.

"Chris, something's bothering you." Instantly he knew he had made a mistake bringing it up, but the words could not be retrieved. "What is it? Is there something that isn't right between us?"

Her head felt like a slow-motion explosion, bursting outward from the mix of volatile substances his questions ignited. For weeks she had tried to live the double life of wife to one man, lover to another, and had been tortured every moment.

"I want a divorce," she said.

"Oh, Lord!"

"You once said that if it wasn't right, I could end it, I could leave."

"Just like that!"

"I thought it could work. It hasn't."

"For two years it worked. You were happy. I know you were happy."

"Maybe I was fooling myself. I don't know. But things have changed for me, and I have to get out. Pretending to be happily married is a lie I can't live anymore."

"Is there someone else?"

"It's just over, Ken."

She hoped she had not hesitated in answering. But even if Greg were no longer a factor in her life, she would have ended her marriage now. Once passion fled elsewhere, it could never return; you could never put an omelet back in the shell. Only respect for Ken was left—and pity.

"I want a divorce," she repeated.

Ken exploded. "Without a thought for what I'm facing? You picked a great time. The toughest election of my life coming up this fall, and you just consider yourself. Do you think voters will stick with me if they see my wife didn't?"

"Oh, God, I forgot all about your campaign."

"Honoring your obligations probably isn't at the top of your shopping

306

list right now, but getting reelected happens to be damned important to me. If you ever loved me at all, if you have any regard left for me—"

"You know I do."

"Then you'll keep this whole thing just between us until after the election."

All Chris wanted was for the complications to end, but they were entangling her more and more. She could not extricate herself without hurting Ken.

She nodded. "I won't leave you until after the election. I'll move into the guest room." This was the first time either of them had called it that; with its desk and book-lined wall, it had always been known as the library.

"And you'll campaign for me."

"Yes. I still believe in you."

"I thought I might have to commission a last-minute poll to see whether your support had switched on that, too."

"Please, Ken, don't make it worse."

"I want it to be worse. I want it to be tough as hell for you. One minute you love me, the next you don't. I don't understand it. Maybe it's the pressure of the new job. Well, I don't fall in and out of love that easily. I love you and I think down deep you still love me."

As Chris lay under the covers on the convertible sofa, for the first time since Greg left her a decade earlier, she cried herself to sleep. Even when Greg brought her happiness, he still brought her sorrow as well.

21

～～～～～～～～～

Mickey Blinder was in his bedroom packing for the flight to New York. During these next three days in May, FBS would choose its fall schedule, the last of the networks to do so. Out of the thirty-two pilots it had financed, maybe eight or nine would make it onto the schedule—and more at midseason. FBS had to make the most changes to lift its ratings. A few additional shows would get the nod to shoot perhaps six episodes as standby replacements for later in the year. The rest of the pilots, in which so much time, money, and hope had been invested, would be tossed onto the scrap heap. All of Mickey's pilots for the other networks had struck out. His last hope was FBS.

Each time a network convened in New York to choose among the pilots, he and the other studio and production-company heads and the shows' producers flew east. They filled the hotels and hung out at the same bars surrounding the network's headquarters where the triage was taking place; they wanted to protect against a show's being dropped from consideration solely because no one connected with it was available to answer a question.

"Does the show have legs?" one network executive might ask, meaning, Is the concept capable of generating a new plot every week? Each producer would have a batch of twenty or more plot outlines with him just in case.

"Is the country really ready for that kind of show? Our testing wasn't sure." The studio producing the pilot would have its own research ready to counteract a show's potential negative aspects.

But most of all, Mickey and the producers of his two shows and all those other producers and studio executives were flying to New York because it was easier to wait for the word there than three thousand miles away with the hundreds of others—actors, writers, directors, associate and co-producers, production-company executives—whose future depended on the network's decision.

The phone rang. A producer friend wanted to let Mickey know that he had run into one of FBS's programming executives at the L.A. airport.

"He mentioned that 'The Neighborhood' had tested great."

"Really, he said that?" Mickey was buoyed by the news.

"He even said a couple of people there thought it was the best thing of its type since 'Hill Street Blues.' "

"Hey, that's great. Thanks. I appreciate it. Anything about my other show? 'Lowdown'?"

"No."

"But thanks, that's really something. Keep me posted if you hear any more."

Mickey hung up, his spirits temporarily lifted by the phone call. Earlier he had heard a rumor that Barnett Roderick told someone he was worried that putting on another controversial show on FBS like "What's the World Coming To?" might prompt a viewer campaign for sponsor boycotts or even a congressional hearing. Arnold Mandel's show was starting to pull good numbers, but you could never be sure what finally decided a network one way or another.

Mickey's wife came in with the extra shirts she had asked the maid to iron for him. She looked as anxious as he did.

"Hey, not to worry," he told her. "The law of averages is on our side."

That did not seem to reassure her. He locked his suitcase and carried it out to the car. He felt like a dying man on a pilgrimage to Lourdes in search of the miracle to save him.

The captain's voice interrupted the quiet murmur in first class. "On our left side you can see the city of Denver. We should be reaching New York in . . ."

Marian's and her top lieutenants' hand luggage were stuffed with video-cassettes of the pilot episodes they were bringing to New York, and she was pleased with them. She had asked for some reediting on a couple to speed up the pacing, and that had been done. "Tinsel Town," though, never quite worked. She still loved the idea, but wanted to rethink it. The show needed a few more interesting characters and cleverer lyrics. If it came together, the show might be reshot for next spring.

There were some shows nothing could save. Benny Blakely's, for one. She had brought the cassette, but would not recommend it. The rest seemed strong, she felt, several of them maybe even with the kind of breakout potential FBS needed so desperately. What was the old saying about bringing the pilots east, though? Everything turns to shit over Denver.

Her mood plummeted. She even flashed a glance out the window to make sure the plane was still level.

Derek had dropped her off at the airport and would be back home by now, she assumed, getting the bedroom ready for repainting. She had moved her clothes out of one closet, so Derek could have it for his clothing. She had asked him to surprise her with a new wall color he would be happy to live with. He might even be applying it by now. Marian had purposely not hired a painter so Derek would have something purposeful to do for the next couple of days. He claimed to have an audition coming up for a little theater thing, but she suspected he had said it solely to maintain his pride. He seemed to have given up hope. If only he could be happy with things just the way they were.

After UCLA, Derek had knocked around the country awhile. A role in an amateur theater production in St. Louis, where he was working as a construction laborer, so excited him that he returned to Los Angeles to pursue an acting career. That was three years ago and he had little to show for all that time, ascribing his failure to bad luck, bad timing, his type not being in demand—a dozen different excuses. Until he met Marian, he had lived from day to day, working as a waiter or a carpenter or a salesclerk long enough to pay the rent and keep going, sure that his big break was about to come.

Anxious not to be considered a fortune hunter, he told none of his friends about their relationship and kept it from his agent. Living with Marian forced him to confront what he now felt was his irresponsibility in not having built a future for himself. Guilt about always taking from her and giving nothing back weighed increasingly heavy on him, he told her. She was such a success, and he such a failure. He said he had fallen in love with her because of her intelligence, her strength, her verve, her warmth and humor, and her love for him; that he felt inadequate and sometimes even awestruck in her presence.

Marian did not believe a word. She knew infallibly in her heart that what had attracted him to her was the influence she wielded and how much that could help his career.

"The Terminator's deep in thought," a friendly voice said, cutting off Marian's brooding.

Marian looked up. John Rosenthal was standing in the aisle. He, Marti, and Biff had finished editing and sound mixing on the "Adam and Eve" pilot early that morning. Ten days earlier Marian had seen a rough cut of thirteen minutes and had liked what she saw. The finished show would be tested today at Preview House, where each audience

310

member's reaction to every moment would be carefully correlated with that person's answers on a questionnaire asking such specifics as age, income, and background. A hundred fifty would be chosen as the sample to represent the correct cross section of the viewing public.

"I was just talking to Fred," John began. Fred, seated just behind Marian, was in charge of Dramatic Series for FBS. "He says you might be worried that Chad Laidlaw won't come across strongly enough opposite Sally Foster. This probably sounds self-serving, but I think they both hold their own. I think you'll like the chemistry between them."

"My real worry is that he'll end up in jail and not be able to do the show if we decide to go with it."

"Oh, you mean that incident with the teenaged girl."

She nodded.

"He swears the girl and the mother have signed papers that clear him of everything."

"Can you get them to me?"

"Right."

John went back to his seat and the in-flight telephone. If his having wangled a seat on this flight did nothing else but allay her fears about Chad, it had paid off. He phoned Chad's lawyer and told him to fax the papers to Marian in New York.

He placed two other calls as well: to Sally and Biff, to assure them that Marian did not seem to be holding the lateness in delivering the show against them.

By the third day the network executives involved in the selection process had been narrowed down to Greg, Marian, Ev Carver and his v.p. of Sales, Jimmy Minh for Research, and several of Marian's senior people in programming. But the true decision-making rested now with Marian and ultimately, with Greg.

Those present had been moving the magnetic rectangles, the "cards," around on the scheduling board for hours, trying to set the lineup for Wednesday night. The white cards represented new shows. One would go up on the board only to be pulled down a few minutes later when a different possibility occurred to someone. Occasionally, a red card representing a current show would come down only to be reborn a few minutes later. Because FBS was later than the others in establishing its fall lineup, it knew what the competition would be and did not have to rely on the intelligence gleaned by spies close to the enemy camps, such as agents and ad-agency people.

"There's no sense in going with 'Bottom Gun' unless we have an eight-o'clock slot," one of the programmers pointed out. "We need the kids and their parents because no adult with an IQ above room temperature will watch this one alone."

Everyone agreed that "Bottom Gun" was wrong for Wednesday, either at eight or eight-thirty. They moved it to Monday. Benny Blakely was somehow resurrected for eight o'clock Wednesday. He lasted twenty-three minutes on the board before someone remembered that Ossie Krieger's show, "Miss Grimsby's School for Young Ladies," would almost certainly make the schedule. To no one's dismay, Blakely came down. But no one was satisfied when "Miss Grimsby" went up because the show would have no strong lead-in to establish it. Then someone recalled that they had just about promised Ossie he would get the coveted Friday-night spot at nine o'clock, right after "Luba," one of the few sheltered time periods in the schedule. It was shifted over.

"Adam and Eve" was up and down several times. "Castaways" beat it out for Thursday at ten o'clock. The only other night on the schedule that seemed to provide a compatible audience flow pitted it against another network's drama that attracted the same demographics and was still too strong to unseat. But a shifting schedule might still open a slot for it.

"Lowdown" was a show everyone liked. But would Mr. and Mrs. John Q. Viewer? The humor and characters were unconventional and thoroughly adult; it had to go on no earlier than nine, when the percentage of children watching TV dropped and young couples, having put their tots to bed, were finally free to sit down in front of the set. Woodruff, the Sales v.p., asked Jimmy whether the actor playing the professor had tested well. He had.

Pushing for the show, Marian said, "I think it will build once viewers become familiar enough with the characters to like them. They're quirky, but very strong. This show's got the younger demographics we're going for." The concept behind all the new programming was appealing to the eighteen-to-forty-nine-year-old group for which advertisers would pay more and which was, fortunately, more willing to sample new shows.

She read aloud synopses of several additional plots Glendon and Graushner had supplied. Susan had wisely written them up to evoke laughter, foreseeing just such a moment. She got her laughs.

Greg said, "I see it as a real breakout possibility, if it does catch on. We ought to open it in a way that gives it a running start. But how do we protect it on the regular schedule?"

"Put it after 'Luba' and 'Miss Grimsby,' " Marian suggested.

Greg again turned back to Jimmy. "Do they attract the same audiences? 'Luba' doesn't seem as sophisticated."

Jimmy shook his head. "Different demographics. How's Tuesday at nine-thirty. 'Coach' is vulnerable—its audience share drops six points after 'Roseanne.' Viewers might switch channels."

Greg vetoed the idea. "Why counterprogram with our best shows just to get second place? We should be sheltering the promising shows and then building them into blockbusters."

"Monday?" Ev Carver suggested.

"An all-white night?" Marian pointed out incredulously, referring to the color of the magnetic cards used for new shows. Wouldn't Ev Carver just love to see us gamble on a night that had all new shows? she thought. Much too risky. "I've been thinking of making Monday our movie night and maybe moving 'A Funny Marriage' to an early slot on Wednesday. I don't think we should risk changing 'What's the World Coming To?' from Wednesday at nine. It's catching on there."

Greg agreed. Arnold Mandel's show had been gathering steam and controversy in equal measure in that time slot. Sponsors had even started to knock on the door. The employees at FBS were holding their collective breath. Jimmy Minh had put himself on the line by predicting it would make the top ten by fall.

Greg stood up and went to the board. He picked up the rectangle labeled "Lowdown" and placed it into the Wednesday nine-thirty slot, right below "What's the World Coming To?".

Greg stared at both cards. "It's too late for caution. We all wish we had a hammock for it."

Everyone knew that the ideal place to introduce a new series was between two already popular shows, the new one in the middle sagging initially in the ratings, supported by high viewership front and back. "M*A*S*H" was almost canceled its first year, but zoomed to fourth in its second year after it was moved between "All In The Family" and "The Mary Tyler Moore Show."

"But since this whole damned exercise is a crapshoot," Greg continued, "we might as well gamble on having two shows in a row come up big the same night. If they do, we dominate and knock 'em all off."

With no one willing to refute his reasoning, the group then began to construct the rest of a viable Wednesday night around those two shows.

In the end, everyone knew, some worthwhile shows would not make it onto the schedule because the correct slot was unavailable—they would not provide effective counterprogramming against strong shows already drawing the same audience or the audience flow was wrong. A show on which no one was high might sneak on simply because it was the only one that fit the criteria.

*　　*　　*

Late that night, after next year's schedule was finally set, Greg made the obligatory phone calls to the program suppliers: first to those whose shows had been canceled for next year and then to those whose new series had failed to make it onto the schedule and finally, to the lucky ones whose pilots had won them a place in the lineup or were at least put on hold for possible introduction at midseason. Marian sat with him to make sure no one was forgotten, especially no one whose shows were not picked up. The worst rudeness would be to forget someone waiting anxiously by the phone for word, who would have to find out the bad news late and secondhand. These were talented people. They would be back. A little graciousness now would be remembered when they had a new project.

Sally had programmed her telephone to switch any phone calls over to Annette's house. John Rosenthal had promised to call her as soon as he knew. Sally sat all afternoon with Annette and Johnny around their pool, and then they had dinner. None of the telephone calls had been for her.

"You're going crazy staring at the phone and you're making me crazy," Annette finally declared. She pulled Sally to her feet. "We are going for a walk. To the end of the block and back."

Sally resisted, but Annette insisted a ten-minute walk would clear everyone's head.

When they returned, the maid handed Sally a message. John Rosenthal had phoned from New York. He was leaving for the airport, but she should call Marti, who would explain what had happened.

"I knew we shouldn't have left," Sally wailed. She tried to decipher the cryptic message. "We didn't make it. I know we didn't. He would have said yes or something like that if we made it."

Annette, always practical, refused to conjecture. She picked up the receiver and punched in Marti's number, written on the phone message. She handed Sally the receiver as soon as she heard a ring.

"Marti? It's Sally. What happened?"

Annette watched for jubilation or grief. Sally's expression did not change. She hung up.

"We're being put on hold as a possible midseason replacement. They like the show, but say it's too low-concept to go on with everything else—it'll get lost. They say it needs to build and will have a better shot after the dust settles. They didn't order any episodes, though."

"Ladies and gentlemen," the deep announcer voice cut through the chatter. "The chief executive officer of the Federal Broadcasting System, Mr. Gregory Lyall."

314

The Hilton meeting room was filled with several constituencies: members of FBS's affiliate board flown in to screen the new shows and be briefed—they were station executives elected to represent the affiliates' interests with the network; ad-agency people and some of their clients ringed many of the tables; and of course the television press was there. The purpose of the breakfast was to announce FBS's fall schedule. The next step would be for the rest of the affiliates and then the advertising people to view the new shows, in preparation for the upfront commercial-time sales. Greg was here to begin the process of marketing the goods.

He acknowledged the applause. The FBS logo on the large screen behind him dissolved into a photo of Annette Valletta as Luba.

"This is going to be a great year for FBS," Greg declared exuberantly, "the year FBS begins to come back big. We've already started with 'What's the World Coming To?' And you've seen the improvement in 'Hot Time.' Well, we've got some terrific new shows, the strongest group of new shows in our history. This fall the rest of the FBS schedule will blast off. Luba is going to have some great company this year."

Greg began to describe the new schedule night by night, show by show, while clips from each pilot were displayed on the large screen behind him.

Mickey Blinder sat forlornly in the back of the room. He had stayed in New York an extra two days on business and would be returning to L.A. later today. "The Neighborhood" had bitten the dust—not even put on standby. He stared at the clip from "Lowdown." The only pilot from Monumental to make it onto any of the fall schedules. Who would have thought it? he reflected. Of all the great projects he had had this year, who would have thought it? What the hell was this business turning into?

Two nights ago, he had phoned Monumental's CEO in California. With all the false enthusiasm he could muster, he tried to make the single commitment from FBS sound like a victory. "They're crazy over this show. They say this could be another 'Cosby,' another 'Cheers.' "

But the truth, he was sure, was all too evident. Two years of pilots plus millions in producer advances had all gone to get one lousy half-hour show on the air. One. A show that had as much chance of lasting out the season as a World War Two training film on the proper cleaning of a latrine.

"So that's it, ladies and gentlemen," Greg concluded, "that's the first stage of the rocket that will carry FBS to the top of the ratings in the nineties. We want you and your clients along with us on that ride to the top. Thank you."

The applause was loud and sounded sincere. But Greg knew he was only the last in a succession of network heads from whom the advertising people had heard a version of that speech within the last month. And the one they were all sure was most likely to fail.

Book Four

PRIME TIME

JULY 1990

22

~~~~~~~~~~~~~~~

Much of the half-hour news broadcast emanated from Berlin late that Friday night in July, Chris's image and words beamed up to a satellite from Unter den Linden, the Brandenburg Gate behind her. She was in a rush to leave Berlin after her sign-off. A private plane was standing by to whisk her from Tegel Airport to Geneva, where she would be driven to a small Swiss town for a long weekend of vacation. Greg, negotiating links with foreign television broadcasters, would be arriving there from Paris at about the same time. So as to gain viewers while the other news anchors were vacationing, she was taking her summer vacation in small snatches. It was also a way of spending some of it with Greg.

She had interviewed a small group of American soldiers stationed in West Germany who were soon to leave for the States. One of them had waited around for the broadcast to end and then diffidently stepped up to walk beside her as she was departing.

"Ms. Paskins, ma'am. Could I speak to you alone for a second?"

"I'm in a bit of a hurry, soldier," she said.

"I think it's important, ma'am."

"You'll have to ride to the airport with me. The driver can take you wherever you like afterward."

The soldier climbed into the limousine's rear seat beside her. As the car headed north out of the city, she raised the barrier isolating their conversation from the driver and waited for what the soldier had to say.

He spoke slowly, halting between sentences as if testing them first to determine whether they contained good sense. "Ma'am, I'm Technical Sergeant Benjamin Craig. My background is nuclear missiles. You know, they're being deactivated and dismantled here under the disarmament agreements with the Russians. My younger brother and me, we're both crazy about rockets. That's why we enlisted."

319

"Go on," Chris said, waiting for the point.

"My brother's missile unit in Germany was disbanded, and he was sent home, too. But the very day he arrived, new orders were cut assigning him and two of his buddies to a brand-new unit. He wrote that day to tell me about it. They were sending him to a town in Maine. Well, I've asked a lot of the brass around here about that town, but none of them ever heard of a military base near there. What's even stranger, the letters I get are all postmarked Washington, D.C."

"And you're concerned for some reason?"

"Ms. Paskins, why should three expert rocket jockeys be sent to the middle of the woods when the military needs all of us now to dismantle these babies?"

Chris turned that question over in her mind all the way to the little Swiss inn overlooking the snow-fed lake in the Alps. A message awaited her there from Greg: Diane had surprised him in Paris; he could not get away.

Chris drove right back to the Geneva airport in the same taxicab. If Greg had met her, she might have forgotten the soldier's questions, but she had nothing ahead of her for the weekend. Ken would be campaigning in New York City. She had agreed to appear with him at a few key rallies, but she was wary about compromising her journalist's objectivity by active campaigning.

When her plane arrived at JFK, she took the helicopter to LaGuardia and the shuttle to Washington. She had slept over the Atlantic and immediately began to hunt down her Defense Department contacts.

"Whatever your plans were for the weekend," Diane remarked to Greg when she arrived in Paris, "we can do together."

"I didn't have anything much planned."

"Well, what I'd like to do then is make quick stops in the morning at a few designers, maybe pick up some winter outfits, and then we can spend the rest of the weekend together."

They lunched at Taillevent on Saturday before a helicopter flew them to the Loire Valley. It hopscotched from one great château to another: massive Chambord, topped by turrets, spires, and chimneys and surrounded by endless woods in which Francis I loved to hunt; Azay-le-Rideau, a jewel of a Renaissance edifice set amid trees at the edge of a river; and Chenonceaux, where Henry II's mistress planned an extension bridging the river, but was evicted by his widow, who completed the bridge as a great gallery over the water.

"What are you thinking?" Diane asked as they walked out through the gardens at Chenonceaux. A car and driver awaited them in the parking lot to take them to their hotel.

320

"That all the big shots who swaggered around these cold, drafty places are as dead as their servants and peasants." Greg grinned at the irony. "The lowliest family with a television set today has access to more news in half an hour, more entertainment in a night, than kings may have had in a year. Technology has democratized the world. It's made kings of commoners."

"It only appears that way. That's what keeps the commoners from revolting against the kings." Diane pondered a moment. "You're the exception. You were more determined to go from commoner to king than anyone I ever knew."

"Sometimes I wonder if all the anguish and frenzy is worth it. For what? A castle in an age when the average guy has a decent house anyway? A limo when the average guy can drive himself wherever he's going?"

Diane thrust her arm through his as they walked. "You're kidding yourself, Greg. You can't bear to be ordinary. You want to be special, on top, controlling others and not being controlled."

"In other words it's still better to be king."

"I can't see that I'd ever have to fight another woman for possession of the château," she said laughingly. "You're definitely not the type to have a mistress."

"I'm not?"

She shook her head. "You aren't the self-indulgent type. You always try to do the right thing. I'm much more likely to have a lover than you."

"Do you?"

She laughed again. "You're jealous. I haven't been able to make you jealous in years."

She threw her arms around his neck, halting their progress along the gravel. "I love you much too much. We argue at times, but I've never wanted another man. You make me happy."

She kissed him quickly. A family was approaching: the husband holding a tot's hand, the pregnant wife carrying an infant. The site became too public for Diane. She took Greg's arm and continued the walk to their car.

"You know what made me feel odd in the château? That Henry the Second's mistress was named Diane. I kept thinking she should have been the wife."

"And the king should be named Gregory?" Greg tried out the sound: "Gregory the Second. Sounds more like a pope than a king."

"Definitely not you. Popes are supposed to have at least a nodding acquaintance with God."

And not just his competition, Greg finished to himself.

*   *   *

321

Despite the lateness of the booking, a business colleague was able to arrange accommodations for them at Château d'Artigny, a spacious country mansion converted to a luxury hotel. In the dining room Greg ran into a good-humored Los Angeles lawyer specializing in the music business whom he knew, who was there with his wife. Although the evening was far pleasanter than he had anticipated, too often Greg's thoughts strayed to a small inn in Switzerland and Chris. Early that morning he had tried phoning her there and was told she had received his message, but had chosen not to check in.

A hazy wine-lit glow had descended on the couples when they bid good-night after dinner and made their way up and down stairs and corridors to their quarters.

Greg made love to Diane because he missed not being able to make love to Chris, because today, tonight, Diane had been tender and compliant and had not tried to be both king and queen, and because they had both drunk too much to be on guard.

"I traveled all that way just to see you." Chris was steaming. "You could have told her you had a business meeting in Switzerland and would be back on Monday."

She was speaking on the phone to Greg from New York. He was still in Paris and would be going on to London. Diane had already left him to catch the Concorde home.

"Think it through," Greg said. "She'd have wanted to come along."

"I suppose, but that was going to be our weekend. We get so little time together. You made love to her, right?"

"Yes."

"Damn."

"What about Thursday night?" he asked. "I'll be back by then."

"I can't. I agreed to speak at a benefit. Ken has a fund-raiser Friday night. I've got to be there."

"I know. He invited Diane and me."

"That bothers me, Greg."

"I got out of it. Besides, whatever we could legally contribute to his campaign, we already have."

"Saturday morning?"

"We're giving a brunch at the country house for a group of our bankers." He thought he heard a painful sigh through the receiver.

"And so, Diane gets another weekend."

"If it's any consolation, I'm not happy about it either."

"And you'll make love to her."

"I doubt it."

"Now, *that's* some consolation. Anyway, Hannah Rafael and I are flying to Maine this weekend."

"A story?" Hannah was a senior producer for FBS's nightly news.

"Don't know yet. I have to talk to you about it though."

"Big stuff?" he asked.

"Could be. I'll try to get myself on your calendar for Thursday."

"Seems like a long time from now. I miss you."

"Love is really shitty sometimes," Chris said.

Applause broke out the moment Stew and Susan were spotted entering sound stage E. They had spent most of the night polishing the script for the episode to be shot this week and were about to distribute revised copies to the actors and crew.

"Congratulations," the set designer called out. He was supervising construction of the additional sets required this week.

"Congratulations on what?" Stew asked with calculated ingenuousness.

"The *People* magazine story. It was great."

"Oh, that," Stew said nonchalantly.

Susan laughed. "Don't let him fool you. He's thinking of having it bronzed."

The article and the photos had been the opening salvo in the publicity campaign that would run through the first months of the fall season to attract viewers to "Lowdown." The piece described the series and how Stew and Susan had met at a party years after she was in his class and how they had fallen in love while creating what the magazine called "the fall's hot new show for FBS."

Recent months had seen a lot of changes in Stew. He was well rested because he had given up the job at "The Guts of the Story" after discovering in the bedroom that if he and Susan played the parts of characters from their new series, his imagination could whip up the most delicious plots and dialogue—while keeping Susan happy and satisfied.

His appearance had changed, too. His mustache and beard were now gone and his straggly hair transformed into a helmet of permed curls. He was considering an eyelift to enhance his now more youthful image. His shoes now cost twice as much as his monthly rent once had. His wardrobe now occupied a good part of Susan's second bedroom. The Jaguar had been traded in for a BMW and the BMW for a Mercedes. That just meant bigger car payments. The money was flowing in, so what did it matter? Life was really good, he had finally begun to believe. He possessed everything he could possibly want.

The stage manager gestured toward the rear of the sound stage. "She said she has some business with you," he told Stew.

Stew peered into the darkness at the figure walking purposefully toward him. Large sunglasses hid her face. She removed them as she stepped into the light.

"Patty!" he exclaimed. He had not seen his wife since the day they separated.

"I just stopped by to serve you with some papers," she said pleasantly. "You must be Susan," she acknowledged, and extended a hand.

Greg introduced them. Patty's law firm did some business with Monumental. She had come by after a meeting.

"What papers?"

"Divorce."

"I thought we *were* divorced. I signed something when we split up."

"That was just a temporary separation agreement."

Susan stepped courteously away. This matter was between Stew and his wife.

"Well," he wondered aloud, "isn't the other part automatic?"

"Not quite. There's the matter of community property."

Stew was aghast. "All you wanted was the house and tuition for Wendy. I'm paying that. Ahead of time," he added proudly.

"But that was before."

"Before what?"

She drew *People* magazine from her briefcase. "Before you were doing well enough for it to matter. If what they say about the television series is true, we should be worth several million dollars at least."

"We?" he bellowed.

"Stew, dear," she said amiably, "we're still husband and wife. And of course, it was also before I discovered you were having an affair behind my back with your friend there."

"This is crazy."

"You can't deny you deserted me and left me without a cent."

"Deserted you without a cent? You kicked me out when I had nothing."

"Isn't that really a matter for the court to decide?" she asked sweetly.

"Court?" He was beside himself.

"The divorce laws are intended to protect wives from being taken advantage of."

"You can't be serious."

"I'm sure when you hire a lawyer, he'll explain it all to you," she intoned soothingly.

324

Stew hung his head, as if stretching his neck for an ax's fall.

"As long as I'm here," she added, "why don't you show me around our set? I'm really very proud of you, dear. And I'm sure when you read the divorce complaint, you'll be very proud of me."

"You owe this story to me, Greg," Chris asserted. She was sitting in his office with Alan Howe and Manny Ramirez. "You wanted lighter interviews from me on 'Confidentially Speaking.' I gave you pure helium and didn't make a peep. I've run my tail to hell and back for the news broadcast. Well, I want this. It could be a big story. That's why we didn't want to go any further without your approval."

"We'd be taking on the secretary of Defense," Greg pointed out, "and for all we know, the President."

"The President may not even know what's happening up there," Chris said. "But something sure is."

"That's still supposition."

"At a time when the U.S. and the Soviets have committed to dismantle nuclear-missile bases, our army may be adding to our ICBM arsenal by secretly building one in the woods in Maine."

Greg rejoined. "*May* be. You have a lot more digging to do. All you have are the names of a missile technician posted there and some source in Defense who won't say anything on camera."

"So far the story makes sense: The secretary is a superhawk; he's condemned the disarmament pacts right from the beginning. Just last week he warned that it may be a Soviet trick that will leave us defenseless if they attack."

"Alan?" Greg inquired.

"This is a big news story," the News Division president shot back. "That's the business we're in."

No doubts there, Greg noted. Manny was nodding his concurrence.

Chris spoke again. "Greg, I don't understand why you're suddenly so worried to take on the government. You never were before."

"Because right now we're seeking the administration's cooperation for legislation we need, for one thing. And for another, our focus should be on a fall season that will make or break us."

"What does that have to do with anything? This is a news story."

He grew irritated. "It has everything to do with whether this network survives."

"And whether you survive!" Her voice softened. "I'm sorry. But this story is important, Greg. You know it is. If the secretary really has gone off on this secret agenda, he could be endangering a world peace that's closer than it's been at any time in history."

No one spoke after that. Greg stared out the window in thought.

Chris had elevated the issue far above questions of his best interests or the network's. She was challenging his principles.

He turned back to the room, exhaling. "Okay, we have to pursue it." He pointed a finger at her. "But you better make sure every fact is nailed down twice."

"You'll see the piece first," she promised gravely. A twinkle returned to her eye. "We're even now. You remember that Swiss assignment I wanted."

She stood up. "Please wish Diane a nice weekend for me, will you?"

Ossie Krieger and two of Marian's people were waiting for her in a screening room at FBS's Los Angeles office building when she arrived from a breakfast meeting. He was there to show them the just-completed two-hour film that would serve as the first episode of "Miss Grimsby's School for Young Ladies."

Marian had already committed to financing a full season of half-hour scripts for a series. If she gave approval now, Ossie would start production on the first immediately. FBS was putting up all the financing.

"Overall I love it," Marian assured him when the lights came up. "But I have some reservations. One of them is that nude scene. The movie and the series will both go on at nine, right after 'Luba,' which skews young. You wanted that slot. We gave it to you. There will be a lot of kids in that audience with their parents. It's okay to have sexy innuendo that goes over the kids' heads, but visible T and A is out."

"All right," he replied grudgingly. "What else?"

Marian turned to the other two programmers. "What did you think of the leads?"

"Except for the actor playing the hip guy from town, they were fine," the young woman in charge of comedy development answered. "I hated him."

A major catalyst for much of the action was a guileful young male character from the nearby town who often sneaked into the all-girl boarding school to pursue money-making scams with some of the young women, while romancing them as well. Halfway through the film, he moved into a room in the attic and had to contrive elaborate ruses to keep from getting caught. Occasionally, disguised as a student, he would bump into the headmaster, dressed up to impersonate the nonexistent Miss Grimsby.

The other programmer agreed. "The part calls for someone who can be a glib, scheming charmer and a ladies' man without seeming like a rat. We have to like him. With the right actor, the character could take off with viewers. But the guy you've got is boring. Everything slows to a crawl when he's on."

"My feeling, too," Marian confirmed. "You've got to recast the part."

"That would mean reshooting about forty minutes of this movie," Ossie warned.

"We'll pay for the reshooting. Tack the extra days onto the schedule before you start shooting the series."

Ossie agreed to begin the search for a replacement immediately. Marian and the others mentioned several actors he should look at. She made clear that FBS would not approve the series until he found one FBS approved.

He stood up. "Back to the glamor of big-time TV."

Marian wanted to keep the pressure on Ossie. The truth was that her flexibility to substitute another series in his time slot was not so great as she let on. Several shows in the lineup were having production problems. "I Love Luba" had not even commenced shooting yet for the new season, which was scheduled to commence next month. Although her salary had been raised and her husband named executive producer, Annette Valletta had suddenly made new demands and had refused to start shooting until she got her way, obviously believing she had FBS over a barrel.

In addition to her problems at work, Marian was increasingly preoccupied by worry over her personal life. The long stretch with no work and no prospects had persuaded Derek—made him "see the truth," as he put it—that he lacked the talent to succeed as an actor. Marian had suspected as much from the first. He was now considering leaving the West Coast for good, not because he wanted to get away from her—he didn't want to do that, he assured her—but because he couldn't bear to be that close to the center of the profession.

She had left the house early, before Derek was awake, so she phoned him as soon as she had a free moment. She learned that he was packing to leave California. Marian was distraught.

"But I love you. I can't live without you."

"I love you, too, but I'm at the end of my rope. You'll be better off without me . . . and with a guy you can respect."

"Promise me you won't leave until we can talk it over. Promise me that. When I get home tonight, we'll discuss it." She refused to let him off the phone until she had his promise. She immediately ran down to Elaine Kanter's office.

An old friend who worked under her, Elaine was in charge of casting. Marian told her to get to work immediately to find parts among the network's projects for Derek Peters. Preferably nothing that took some talent and that he might mess up. They didn't have to be too big. The important thing was to do it immediately and have producers call his agent right away, today, to set up auditions. And, oh, yes, she shouldn't mention Marian's name. Seeing the strain on her boss's face, Elaine asked no questions.

Marian returned home to find Derek ecstatic at the miraculous turnabout in his fortunes. He had an audition the next day for a small part in a miniseries; his agent had told him the producer happened to have his photo and résumé on file and thought he'd be right for it. Derek was the only one up for the part, so the chances were he'd get it.

"There's a possibility of some other things, too, she told me. It's incredible. Just when things seemed hopeless . . ."

"I'm really thrilled for you," Marian told him.

"It's not much, but it's a start."

"I'm sure your luck has changed."

She hugged him tightly for a long while.

Sally and Annette sat on the brick terrace overlooking the latter's swimming pool. Annette was stretched out on a chaise. It was a bright, cloudless day. An umbrella shielded both women from the sun. Sally had been admitting to her friend how badly the tension was getting to her as she waited to learn whether FBS would order episodes of her show, "Adam and Eve." The network would not make the decision until after the fall lineup premiered and it had some notion of which shows were doing well and which were not.

"In my heart, I know we won't get a commitment," Sally confessed. "What will happen to me if we don't?"

"You can't be sure. I liked the show. It's probably just a matter of their wanting the right time period to open up."

Annette shifted on the chaise overlooking the pool and reached for her iced tea. The glass slipped through her hand and shattered on the bricks.

Sally jumped. Annette did not move.

"Would you do me a favor and get the maid to clean it up?" Annette asked.

"Are you all right?"

"Just a little accident."

Annette dabbed on some of her new perfume. Sally noticed something.

"Your hand is shaking."

Annette dropped it to her side. Her other hand flew up to cover her face. She was crying.

"What is it?"

Annette continued to cry for several minutes. Sally, now on the chaise beside her, tried to comfort her, but did not know what was wrong. The maid had heard the crash and was sweeping up the glass.

When Annette regained control, Sally started to ask again what the matter was, but Annette gestured for her to keep quiet until the maid went back inside.

"All the maids trade gossip," Annette said when the woman was gone. "I sometimes think the *National Enquirer* has them on retainer."

"What's wrong?"

Annette stared upward into the cloudless sky. The house was high in the hills, above the smog. Annette took a long time to decide whether to answer. She had not told anyone except Johnny, but she and Sally had shared so much over the years. Needing her friend's support, she relented.

"The doctors think I have some kind of nerve disease. They're not sure what it is. I'm losing control of my muscles."

Sally embraced her friend. "You poor baby."

"They're doing all kinds of tests, but it's been getting worse. This morning I had trouble walking."

"Oh, God! I've been chattering on so self-absorbed. You couldn't even work right now if you wanted to."

Annette nodded. "We always tape the show with three cameras, in front of an audience. There's no way." She paused to catch herself from losing control of her emotions again.

"There must be something they can do."

"Tests and more tests. My own feeling is it's one of those irreversible diseases where you end up a vegetable. They're afraid to tell me the bad news before they're absolutely sure. You know, malpractice."

"Then all those demands you made on Monumental and FBS—"

"I needed more time for the doctors to figure out a medicine to give me so I could do the show." Her eyes beseeched her friend. "That's why you can't tell anyone about this."

"Of course not."

"If I couldn't do the show"—Annette's voice caught—"I'd know that I was dying. I'd *want* to die."

"Don't say that. You have everything."

"I feel I'm watching myself fade away. But I keep telling myself, as long as the show is still there waiting for me, I've got a chance. . . . I've never missed a show, so I won't miss this one. I can lick this thing."

"You bet you can," Sally declared, hugging her again. Annette's stamina was legendary. "Why didn't you tell me? I'll be with you every moment, just like you were for me."

* * *

The two-engined Cessna located the old logging company airstrip and descended into the narrow rectangle shaved out of Maine's north woods. It taxied to the now-vacant dispatcher's shack. Chris, her producer, and a cameraman stepped onto the hard-packed dirt. Parked by the shack was a station wagon and driver sent out for their use from the Bangor affiliate. This was the height of the state's summer tourist season, but this town was too far north to attract many tourists and the coast too forbidding. Obtaining three rooms in the town's largest hotel on a weekend had not been a problem. The news team planned to claim they had come to do a story on rural economies, so as to be able to inquire about new construction in the area without arousing suspicion.

The station wagon traveled a number of miles to the coast road and then turned onto it in the direction of the town. On one side the land plunged straight down to the rocky seacoast.

"This whole thing might just be a wild-goose chase," Chris warned her companions. She had preempted their weekend and was apologizing ahead of time.

"Stop!" the cameraman shouted.

He grabbed for his videocamera, shoved in a cassette, and pointed it out the window. A dark speck had risen up out of the sea at the horizon and was gradually growing into the shape of a large military helicopter flying low over the water. Nearing the cliff that defended the land from the sea, it shot upward until it was about a hundred feet above the road along the rim.

The cameraman followed the helicopter in his optic as it crossed the road in front of the car and became lost to sight behind the treetops on the road's inland side. He did not remove his finger from the button until he had tipped the camera down to take in the road sign announcing that the town was five miles away.

"And then again," he said, "it might not turn out to be a wild-goose chase after all."

At the hotel's front desk, the manager eyed Chris as she signed her name on a register card.

"I thought it was you," he said delightedly. "The missus and me watch you on the news all the time. Enjoy you, too."

"Thanks. We're here to do a story on how rural economies in various parts of the country are faring."

"Well, this town could use a little publicity."

"That military base they're building outside of town must have helped some. You know, buying lumber, concrete, fencing, hiring construction workers to put up the barracks and so forth."

"A little, but they do most of that work themselves. Keep to themselves, too, so it doesn't help the restaurants and bars much."

"What kind of base is it?"

"They say it's a weather station."

"You sound like you're not sure."

"Lot of secrecy for a weather station." He eyed her shrewdly. "If you're aiming to find out more about that base, I'd have to say that you fellas have got a lot of hard digging ahead of you."

"The hotel manager was sure right," Chris said dejectedly. "Everybody in town knows a military base is out there in the woods. We even got a couple of merchants to say on tape that strangers bought supplies from them. But none was ever in uniform."

Sitting across from her at his office desk, Greg was caught up in Chris's intensity as she conveyed her thoughts. That intensity was integral to her sincerity on the air and to what made her so magnetic. In their little apartment he would have swept her up in his arms and covered her with kisses.

"Thinking of giving up?" Greg teased, allowing his smile to reveal itself. The obstacles, he knew, would only sharpen her determination.

"We know where the access road to the base is, but you can't see a thing, not even a clearing, from the air. We tried. All the supplying isn't by helicopter. Townspeople say supply trucks enter all the time. Manny has arranged for a local ENG crew in a disguised van to spend some time cruising back and forth in front of the turnoff onto the access road."

Very concerned that the ENG—electric news gathering or videotaping—crew not be discovered trying to get shots of trucks and military vehicles entering and leaving, Chris had insisted that they switch vehicles often and that her producer go out with the crew to supervise.

"You don't need me to tell you pictures of trucks and jeeps aren't enough," Greg said.

Instead of discouragement shadowing her eyes, they were filled with excitement. "Remember that soldier I met in Berlin who originally told me that his younger brother was at the base? He's back in the States now and going up there on Saturday to see him. They both have the weekend off."

"Will the one at the base talk on camera?"

"The older brother thinks if I disguise his face and voice he might."

"Sounds promising. I wish I could go with you. A weekend in Maine together would have been nice."

"I could be back by Sunday," she said hopefully, "if you can get away."

"Sunday morning," he confirmed.

"Ten o'clock?"

He nodded. "I'll call you in Maine on Saturday, just to be sure."

She broke into a smile. "I can't believe I'm actually going to steal some of your weekend away from Diane."

"I keep telling you: You think too much about her."

"I try not to. If I do while we're together, I feel guilty. If it's when we're apart, I get jealous and lonely."

"You have no reason to be jealous. I love you."

"No reason?" Chris objected. "Diane's happy as a clam because she doesn't know about us. You have both of us, like some Turkish pasha, so it's heaven for you. I'm the one who gets the short end of the stick. Literally."

"This isn't like you."

She nodded. "I hope not. I don't like myself much when I feel and talk like this. The situation is beginning to wear me down."

"I'm sorry, Chris, but we're too close to the new season for me to let it get to me right now. Too much is at stake."

"And I've got my work, too, I know," she said standing up. "But we haven't made love in weeks. When that happens, I get anxious and begin doubting you and me and why we're putting ourselves through all this."

"Sunday."

"Sunday." Once again her gaze grew intense. "But if you dare tell me you made love to your wife between now and then, I swear to God I'll cut your heart out."

Sally accompanied Annette to the hospital for the tests and kept the vigil with Johnny in the waiting room. The doctor met with them all after Annette was dressed to report that the tests he had been so sure would diagnose her illness had been inconclusive.

"Medicine doesn't really know everything, although we sometimes try to sound like it does," he temporized. He wanted to bring in a colleague for another test that might pin it down. He was going to try to schedule it for next week.

Annette was morose on the ride back to her house. "I'm wasting away to death," she said, "and there's nothing anyone can do."

"Hey, don't talk like that," Johnny told her. "You're going to be fine."

Annette did not reply and said nothing more during the rest of the ride. Johnny put her to bed as soon as they arrived home.

Sally sat on the terrace, waiting for Johnny. A good-looking, large-shouldered man, with abundant black hair and a ready smile, he was glum when he appeared, the optimism he had exhibited for Annette now absent.

"She's asleep. Those tests knocked her out. I had to carry her from the bathroom to her bed."

"She tries so hard not to give up hope . . ." Sally let the sentence drift away incomplete.

"But she's fooling herself. Is that what you were going to say?"

"It's very sad. The doctors can't seem to do anything for her. She's the only one who really believes she's ever going to be able to work again."

Sally let her words hang in the air while she again meditated on a thought that had insinuated itself into her mind, almost against her will.

"What will happen to 'Luba'?" she finally asked. "Production is already behind schedule."

"Without Annette how can there be a 'Luba'?"

"That really seems a shame. It's such a successful show. And this year was really your big break. You were totally in charge. Important salary. A chance to make a name for yourself in television."

"You're telling me."

"I guess you'll have your hands full here at home, taking care of Annette as she becomes an invalid. By her side night and day."

Johnny's mouth showed the glimmer of a grimace for an instant; he was not the nursing type. Sally moved her chair closer to his. Her hand fell lightly across his knee.

"It really doesn't have to be that way," she said. "If FBS knew the truth about Annette's condition, they wouldn't want 'Luba' to end. Monumental wouldn't want it to end. There's a lot of money at stake here. They'd probably be very grateful to someone who could save the show for them."

Johnny shifted to face Sally more directly, her hand slipping down and onto his thigh. She left it there.

"You have something in mind," he said.

"I wouldn't want to hurt Annette for the world, you understand. I'd cut off my arm before I'd act against her. She's my dearest friend. But she's too distraught to think properly now, to think about what's best here. We have to do that for her."

"I'm listening."

"Johnny, have you ever heard Annette and me when we're joking around together with Russian accents? Even she says how well I do her."

"You don't expect to go in and make people believe you're Annette?"

"No, of course not. There's only one Annette. You know how much I admire her, Johnny."

"Hey, there's no one like Annette," he repeated.

333

He shifted more toward Sally, until he faced her directly and the backs of her fingers lay atop his fly.

"Johnny, do you remember when Valerie Harper was locked out of her show and they brought in Sandy Duncan? As a sister or an aunt."

"Sure, there was a big lawsuit."

"But the important thing is that the show is still on the air. With Sandy Duncan."

"You already have a show."

"A backup," she replied contemptuously. "FBS might never go forward with it. But they *need* 'Luba.' "

Johnny stared at Sally, assessing the idea. "If Annette were well, it would be a different thing."

"Absolutely, but the poor dear's getting worse and worse."

"You, me—her best friend, her husband—it's up to us to think things out for her when her thinking's not quite, you know, sensible."

Sally stroked gently up and down the bulge lengthening between his legs. "To keep straight what's best for everyone at a time like this."

"Exactly."

"We wouldn't want to shatter that wonderful will of hers to beat this thing by telling her what we have in mind."

"Let's see how it works out first."

"Annette will be asleep for a couple of hours. Why don't we try to see Mickey Blinder right away?"

Johnny nodded, already thinking out possible deal terms.

"Tell him this is urgent," she added, and gave a little tug to hold his interest for later.

Ev Carver had become anxious in recent months. Instead of discrediting himself as CEO, Greg Lyall seemed to be doing well at the job Ev believed an act of gross nepotism had snatched away from him. Greg was making friends among the company's directors and even possibly laying the groundwork for the beginnings of a turnaround in the fall.

As crazy as it seemed to Ev, that weird show "What's the World Coming To?" had become hot during the summer, when the established shows were just sliding by mostly with reruns and bored viewers were more willing to spin the dial in search of something diverting. The change of focus on "Hot Time" had improved the ratings, and it was now a solid second in its time slot. Ad buys in the upfront selling were higher than the year before; the media buyers liked some of the oddball shows the new programmers were coming up with. Even the sports division had won a few packages of regional college football and basketball games.

Because of their rivalry, Ev anticipated Greg would be likely to terminate him as soon as his protected year ended. He would have to act immediately if he was to have any chance at all of unseating Greg and taking over the network.

The first opportunity came from an unexpected quarter: Barnett Roderick phoned him. He was in from the country for a few days and thought they might have lunch. "Just to get a feel for how things are going around the company," the old man said. Interesting, Ev thought. Why hadn't he asked his son-in-law?

As he entered Barnett's fabled apartment for the first time in his life, Ev found himself greeted at the door personally by the previously imperious chairman, as if they were the oldest and closest of friends.

Within minutes, Ev surmised that he had been asked to this private lunch because Barnett had been growing restless. The man seemed to be back to full health, but bound by the terms of Greg's contract, unable to reassume control of the company. Surreptitiously, he was seeking an ally atop the company's operations who would provide the kind of inside information that rarely reached the board of directors, the kind he could never extract from Greg Lyall because it would put the latter in a bad light. Barnett could capitalize on such information to make his own return to power possible. Yet, Ev sensed ambivalence in the old man. He probably did not want to oust his son-in-law, but he certainly wanted to regain the power he had relinquished.

But if he did return and Greg still remained in place, then Ev would be pushed even farther from the top than he was now. On the other hand, if Ev could come up with explosive information, perhaps Greg could be blasted away. Ev's first thought was fiscal misappropriation. A possibility here because Greg's wife had the money in the family, not Greg.

As soon as he was back at his office, Ev entrusted a loyal subordinate in Finance with the task of going through Greg's expenses and all the deals he had approved since taking over. But Ev had no confidence that something negative would turn up, and time was running out. Ev could not afford to wait.

Late the second afternoon, through the intercession of a powerful friend on Wall Street, Ev found the two of them in the midtown headquarters of Basil Markham, a billionaire who had constructed a worldwide communications empire in print and television. The largest gap in the empire that included newspapers, book publishers, broadcast companies, satellites, and cable facilities in a dozen countries, the jewel he was rumored to be seeking, was a television network in the United States. Markham was in the city for a single day before returning to a vacation home on the Riviera. He had given the visitors precisely one-half hour of his time.

335

Ev's friend presented a hostile-takeover plan under which Markham would bid publicly for all the FBS stock. He would retain eighty percent of it. Ev would run the company and end up with the other twenty. The investment banker assured Markham that his firm could obtain the necessary financing for him.

Markham had studied FBS's financial statements and had been watching the company for many months. He was interested, but he was a patient man who had learned that eventually the right moment to pounce would present itself. He told the two men to count him in, but only if the price of FBS stock fell sufficiently. At the present price, the company was still too expensive. With stock market conditions unstable right now and a fall season about to start that might depress FBS's prospects further, he preferred to watch and lie in wait until something, anything, sent the stock lower.

The meeting restored Ev's spirits. He now had a real shot at taking over FBS. Dusk was graying the light as he stepped out onto the street; dinnertime was approaching. He had made no plans for the evening and was in the mood for company. He thought about whom he might call up. He had not seen Hedy in a few weeks, what with both of them traveling and his having other plans. But there was no better companion for a good time than Hedy.

He phoned the newsroom from the street. One of the desk assistants confirmed that she was still there. He decided to surprise her.

Hedy was alone in her tiny office when Ev arrived.

"Hello, Ev," she said indifferently.

"Is that all the greeting I get after all the time we haven't been able to see each other?"

"What do you want, Ev?"

"I want to take you to dinner. I've missed you, Hedy."

"It's Friday night. People usually call beforehand to make plans for Friday night."

He stepped to the side of her desk. "I've been really busy."

"I have plans for the evening, Ev."

"Break them."

"That isn't possible," she answered carefully. She feared his temper.

"Hey, this is for me, Hedy. You're my girl."

"It's over between us, Ev."

"I don't brush off that easily!" he hissed with sudden vehemence, his jaws tightly clenched. "You were nobody when I found you in Chicago. I made you. I can break you, too."

"I'm grateful for your help, but I don't intend to spend the rest of my life paying you back. I've built a reputation on my own now."

He grabbed her wrist, twisting her to her feet. "Who are you fucking?

You've got to be getting it somewhere—I know you. Who's the guy?"

"It's over, Ev. Leave it at that."

He released her wrist, smiling again, trying another approach. "Hedy, you've done great. But with Chris Paskins ahead of you, you'll never get the big job. I know you want her job. I can help."

"It's over, Ev."

She slipped past him and out the open door before he could stop her. Goddamn cunt! Goddamn ingrate cunt! He had made her, and she was welshing. No woman ever walked out on him. He was the one who decided when it was over. Whoever she was fucking, he would find the son of a bitch, and if he was in television, he'd destroy him. She'd crawl back begging.

Chris sat all morning in their connecting hotel rooms with her crew and Technical Sergeant Benjamin Craig, the soldier she had met in Berlin. Often he would go to the window to look out on the jumble of streets squeezed between pine-covered bluffs that comprised this Maine town. Near noon, with everyone growing increasingly anxious that something had gone wrong, Ben Craig received a phone call from his brother. The latter's replacement had taken ill, and his pass had been canceled. He would try to get there tomorrow.

Chris repressed her disappointment and invited everyone out for a lobster lunch. Thousands of dollars and many hours had been expended over the last two weeks. She still had no story, only suspicion. For all she knew this soldier had no brother and had turned a large weather station into a large hoax.

That afternoon, when Greg phoned her, she told him they would have to postpone tomorrow morning's tryst. Down deep she wanted to hear him tell her that he was immediately dropping all his plans and flying up to be with her. That was ridiculous for her to expect, she knew, and of course, he didn't. She felt spurned and resentful the rest of the day.

23

~~~~~~~~~~~~~~~

It's the most up-to-date missile base I've ever seen, but as I understand things, according to our treaties with the Russians, it's illegal."

A man's black silhouette was centered on the television screen. His electronically altered voice was describing the base he was recruited to work at: how it was constructed and operated in utmost secrecy in contravention of treaty terms. Despite the disguising measures, the man's distress at violating orders by revealing the truth came across.

"That just doesn't sit right with me," he said. "Everybody wants peace so badly, I just don't think our country should be trying to sneak one over that breaks the agreement. We hear more bases like this one will be going up other places."

The tape ended. Chris and the field producer, Hannah Rafael, turned to Greg, Alan Howe, and Manny Ramirez, who had all crowded into the editing room. The Maine material had included shots of the military helicopter swooping over the cliff road and military trucks entering the access route to the alleged base. A road-construction project had been set up there to block off the road from unwanted vehicles. Chris explained that, once, the ENG crew had raced past the barriers, as if failing to understand that they were not permitted to enter. A car quickly caught up with them and forced them to turn around and leave. In the distance they could see what appeared to be the guarded entrance to the base, but were unable to get a shot of it.

"The interview sounds pretty strong," Greg concluded.

"An eyewitness," Alan Howe agreed. "I wish we could get pictures inside the base itself."

Chris reminded him. "We flew over it and saw nothing. You heard the sergeant: It all looks like forest from above because everything is either built below ground or camouflaged on top to evade detection." The man had described silo covers with bushes planted on them that swung away just before firing.

"I guess we go with what we have," Greg declared, looking to the others for their opinions.

Howe suggested the company's general counsel review the material to be sure they were on firm legal footing in broadcasting it. Chris then spoke up again.

"There's one more thing I'm trying to get hold of to put the last nail into the coffin. I hear there's a top-secret document from the Defense secretary himself that authorizes these bases. I've got my Pentagon sources trying to find it."

"How long do you want to hold off broadcasting the story?" Manny asked. One mustache end was turned up quizzically, the other aggressively down.

"Till the end of the week."

"A lot can happen between now and then," Greg observed, more presciently than he could foresee. "The more we have, the better we can stand up against the firestorm. It's sure to hit."

A rueful smile swung out from Chris's face like a sign on a broken hinge. "Ray Strock, come back. All is forgiven."

Ossie Krieger's enthusiasm was once more at a high, Marian noted as he bounded into her office accompanied by a couple of slim young men on his production team. The men around him, she discerned, were getting younger and wearing heavier makeup the older Ossie became. She could expect adolescent drag queens in another few years.

"We've narrowed it down to two actors," he said. "The second one on the tape is the one we want to go with. Marian, let me tell you, we saw dozens of actors to find someone who could handle the part—and we'd already seen dozens before this. We're really cutting it close with the schedule. We have to work out this guy's contract and start shooting by Monday or else there's no way we can meet the air dates."

Marian slid the videocassette into her VCR and took the seat beside Ossie on her sofa.

The first candidate was a former child actor named Miller. His test wouldn't win any Emmies, but he could carry off the role in a solid way. She was startled when the second actor's face appeared on the screen.

"His name's Derek Peters," Ossie told her. "We're really high on this guy."

For the first few seconds, Marian heard nothing Derek said. Then, gradually, the pounding pulse in her ears diminished, and she could observe his performance. And it was all she had hoped for when she had insisted the part be recast. Derek was comically sly and seductive and charming. His extraordinary beauty fit the role precisely.

"You can't believe how lucky we were to find him," Ossie gushed. "Your casting woman told us to look at the guy, but he stumbled all over the reading. The worst cold reader I ever saw—he must be dyslexic or something. I'm surprised he ever got a part in anything. But we were testing everyone on camera, so we had him memorize a short scene and do it on tape. He knocked us for a loop. This guy just comes alive in front of a camera. He's so gorgeous, it's tough to believe there's all that talent inside." Ossie suddenly remembered that he needed Marian's approval. "It's up to you, though."

Marian was frightened. No longer was she worried about criticism for his getting the part—he was too good for that to be a consideration— but that he might become a star.

She stood up. "Leave the tape with me. I want to think about it some more. Call me in the morning."

Ossie and the others began to file out. "Remember, though," he stopped to remind her, "we've got to have an answer."

Marian nodded. As soon as they were gone, she rewound the tape and watched Derek's performance again. She ran the tape several times. She watched it until tears were running down her face.

Derek did not tell Marian about the impromptu screen test he had done for Ossie Krieger, certain he would be disappointed once more. Once or twice before he had told her he was up for a part and had come home disappointed and feeling like a bragging fool. Gripped by the fear of yet another failure, he decided that only if he won the part would he divulge the good news.

That night neither raised the matter. They hardly spoke. Derek could not sit still. He looked at a magazine for a minute or two, then turned on the TV, then turned it off and went out to the driveway to wash the cars. Marian watched him and brooded.

When they were in bed, she drew him to her breast. He kissed her nipple, sending the familiar thrill throughout her body.

"Do you love me?" she asked as she had a dozen times before.

"More than I've ever loved anyone," he said softly, glancing up into her eyes. "I can't believe how happy I've been with you."

"And if you were a star?"

He laughed happily, thinking of the part his agent said he had a real shot at getting. "I would love you more. I wouldn't be ashamed to love you."

Marian kissed him and held him against her and thought about what he had said and how much she loved him and how empty her life would be without him.

Greg was already inside the brownstone apartment when Chris arrived by cab. She let herself in with a key, as he had. He had just laid out on the small dining room table the sushi dinner he had bought them. The television set was on in the bedroom.

"How was the broadcast?" she asked after an ardent embrace.

"Fine. No complaints."

"Enough foreplay, let's make love."

She flew into his arms and began kissing his ear.

Later, they sat down, unclothed, to the dinner, aware that sexual hunger would blossom again as soon as the last piece of *uni* or yellowtail disappeared. Her feet were up, resting companionably on his lap.

"Anything new on that rocket base?" Greg inquired.

"The older brother called me from Washington. The younger one who's at the base tells him there's been a lot of commotion lately. Someone found out a TV crew was nosing around. Everybody's being questioned. He's worried we won't keep his identity concealed. I told him he can assure his brother there's no way he could be recognized."

"Maybe you'd better go with it tomorrow night."

Chris pondered for a moment. "I'd still like to hold off just a little longer to see if we can come up with that memo. A Pentagon contact swears it exists. Once we break the story, it will be buried deeper than those silos."

"But no later than the end of the week. It sounds like we can't risk delaying over the weekend."

"Manny feels the same way."

"Friday night then, at the latest."

She smiled. "Truth now, Greg. All the important things you do as CEO, all the big decisions, isn't news still the most fun you have?"

He bent down and kissed her ankle.

"It doesn't even come close."

Freeway traffic was brutal, and although she was late for an appointment, Marian went first to the office of the young woman in charge of comedy development, where she played the audition tape. Taking no chances, Marian declared that she thought Derek Peters much the better of the two actors. Her subordinate instantly agreed. Marian ordered her to phone Ossie Krieger with FBS's approval and then send her a memo documenting her choice.

Mickey Blinder, Sally Foster, and Johnny Mannetti were waiting in

341

Marian's office when she arrived. They wore grave expressions, Mickey's almost desperate.

Johnny averred that first and foremost, he himself had come there because of his duty to FBS as the new executive producer of "I Love Luba." Mickey Blinder was quick to claim a similar commitment to duty. Marian's initial impression was that they were really here as intermediaries to settle the issues Annette Valletta contended were preventing her from commencing production.

"Annette's sick," Mickey blurted out. "It turns out that was her real problem all along. The chances are good she can't do 'Luba.' "

Marian felt suddenly dizzy and nauseated, as if her chair had plummeted straight through the floor. "Luba" was the network's only hit show, the linchpin on which an entire night's scheduling strategy had been based.

"What's wrong with her?" Marian asked.

Mickey deferred to Johnny, who explained the medical problems as far as they were known. "You've got to understand," he concluded, "Annette doesn't know we're here. She'd go crazy if she knew."

Sally finally spoke up, conveying a command that indicated she was providing her group's leadership. "Annette won't accept the fact that she's desperately ill. She keeps hoping the doctors will find a magic pill to cure her. They don't even know what she's got. We were worried that if we waited any longer to come here, FBS might lose her show. We didn't think that was fair to you."

Marian was somewhat confused. "But Annette, you say, can't do the show."

"Someday she might," Johnny interjected loyally, "but for now, no."

"Annette's absence doesn't have to mean the end of the show." Sally winked at Marian and smiled. "You see, dollink, ve hev a plen. Meet Natasha. I em Luba's old friend, just arrived from Soviet Union. I em vat you Yenkees call a bumshell. I hev come to dis country to expluhd."

The three visitors watched Marian's face as she digested the idea and assessed its viability.

"Tell me how you see the character playing," she asked.

Sally sketched the revamped concept for the show and the initial episode. Natasha would arrive unannounced in the U.S. just after Luba has left to visit her folks back in Moscow. Luba's bandleader husband is frantically trying to find a live-in housekeeper to take care of their kids while he is at work. Natasha volunteers, falsely claiming expertise with children. Comedy would arise out of her unfamiliarity with American ways and her decidedly undomestic nature in a household inhabited by Luba's very American husband and kids. Another comedy source would be her attraction to the husband, whom she is forever trying to seduce.

Marian turned to Johnny. "Could you still meet the schedule?"

"We have three writing teams. The first one can have a script by Monday while the others are working on the next two."

Necessity and the shortness of time offered Marian little choice. "All right, I buy the idea. We'll finance thirteen scripts and commit to your shooting the first six episodes. We'll want to be on top of everything you do. If ratings hold up, we'll order the rest of the season." Marian focused on Sally. "I'll have Business Affairs contact your agent as soon as our meeting's over."

"I assume there won't be any problem letting me out of my commitment for 'Adam and Eve'?" Sally wanted to confirm.

"The basic premise was a good one, but it never quite jelled." Marian had a more pressing concern. "Who's going to tell Annette? Ten minutes after we make a deal, she's going to read about it in the trades."

No one seemed willing to risk her ire.

"She's your wife, Johnny," Sally pointed out.

"She's your best friend," he replied.

"It's your show," Sally stated to Mickey with the force of an accusation. He could not think of a reply.

"That gets everyone off the hook," Sally insisted. "We could say you and Monumental forced Johnny to produce the show under your contract with him. And that FBS forced me under my contract for 'Adam and Eve' to go into 'Luba.' I finally agreed to do it rather than let some actress come in who would fight to keep the part if Annette got better."

"If she gets better," Marian declared sharply, "she's in and you're out. The name of this show is not 'I Love Natasha.'"

Sally nodded. The important thing was that she was back on top again, a TV star once more, in a series that could now happily run for years. At midseason she could always raise again the question of that bothersome title.

Half an hour later, when the meeting ended and the visitors stood to leave, Sally raised a hand to halt them. "I think it would be appropriate if we all said a little prayer for Annette."

Each head piously bent forward. The phone rang. Marian rushed for it. Enough sanctimony had been shoveled at her this morning to last a lifetime. She waited until the others filed out to take the call.

"Mr. Peters is on the phone," her secretary announced. "He says he has to talk to you right away. He sounds very excited."

Marian took Derek's call and listened with deep ambivalence to the happiness spilling excitedly out of him. The days were numbered until Derek—famous, wealthy, and achingly beautiful—left her for another woman.

When he became CEO, Greg took on jobs usually held by several people. Now he had withdrawn, for the most part, from supervising the nightly news, but he was still putting in fourteen-hour and longer days running the Entertainment Division and the network while overseeing the parent company. Next year he might feel confident enough to move someone up to ease his load, but right now he had to be in direct contact with everyone whose work could affect FBS's profitability in the coming year.

As time had grown shorter until the new fall season premiered and he became more comfortable wielding power, he had grown increasingly short-tempered, even domineering. What he said that morning to Ted Woodruff, the head of the Sales Department, flew around the company at Mach 5 speed.

They were in one of the FBS Building's small TV studios with several other key people and linked by a television hookup to Marian and several others at a TV studio on the Coast. Greg began by summarizing what most of them already knew. To get a jump on the other networks, FBS's fall lineup would premiere in early September, a few weeks from now.

"We're taking two weeks to roll the shows out right, with enough promotion and advertising and the best exposure. Some we may show twice over a couple of days, like we hear NBC is planning to do. Some we'll premiere in showcase slots and then move to different permanent time slots after the public has had a taste of them. We think this is going to be a great season for FBS."

Despite the confidence Greg invariably displayed to instill confidence in those around him, he felt under siege. Everything in his life was riding on how the audience would respond to the new shows: his job, the salary, bonus, and stock options that would give him financial security, his future with Chris. On his shoulders, he knew, he also carried the hopes of so many others at FBS, from those he had elevated, such as Marian, down to mail-room clerks who might be laid off if FBS was forced to cut back again. The ripples of success or failure would spread far beyond employees and wash over actors, producers, directors, writers, camera operators, set decorators, hairdressers, and others; it would also affect the finances of thousands of stockholders who owned shares in the company. The price of the stock, a particularly sensitive meter of the company's success, was never far from his thoughts. His bankers had told him that the company was a prime candidate for a takeover if the stock dipped.

Paul Bell, FBS's head of Advertising and Promotion, spoke next. A frenetic young man of thirty, he and Greg had spent long hours devising the network's plans to market the new fall lineup to the public.

"You all know our promotional campaign is built around the phrase 'star time, good time,'" Bell began. "The idea is that FBS is bringing great stars and good times into your home. The subliminal pitch is: No matter how miserable your life might be, there's always one place where you'll be made happy and feel loved by these glorious people you admire. Kind of like legal drugs. The theme connects well with the younger, better-educated, more urban demographic we're aiming for with our sophisticated sitcoms and the character-oriented and lighter action-adventure dramas we're going with."

He showed them the on-air promos and sketched out the rest of the advertising and promotion, including the coupon game with a national fast-food chain that required players to watch the new series. "It won't bring good ratings to bad shows, but it should increase early viewer sampling."

Then Greg took the floor again. "The affiliates like us to start the campaign months ahead, but I've always thought it was a waste. Viewers get bored with the campaign long before the new lineup is there for them to watch. This year we talked the affiliate board into holding off the campaign until very near premiere date."

That was when Ted Woodruff spoke up. The head of Sales was a longtime protégé of Ev Carver, who was sitting beside him. "I'm getting some flack on that from the ad agencies. They say we won't be making enough of an impact by going that late. They've got a lot of ad money riding on our new lineup."

Greg seethed. Woodruff had been dragging his feet on every new sales idea for months. He had argued with Greg several times, usually contending that Greg would be making a mistake to ignore his greater experience. But this was the first time he had done so in front of others. Greg suspected Ev had put him up to it.

Greg answered forcefully. "I think we all understand that the advertisers have a big stake in the success of our fall season. But we've got a bigger stake. This timing will give us the biggest bang for our promotional buck."

"Wouldn't ad agencies be the best judge of that? We've always done it that way, and they've never objected before. I think maybe—"

Greg thrust his finger hard at the Sales v.p., interrupting him. "Let me make this clear to you, Woodruff—to all of you—so there's no

345

mistaking it. I'm the boss. Either do what I say or get out of the way!"

Woodruff turned white. His voice stumbled into apology. Greg was already addressing the others.

"Once something's decided, I expect complete commitment. Either this ship makes it through this storm because I steered it well or we all go down with it together."

The long, black limousine swung onto Eleventh Avenue and stopped at the corner of Forty-ninth Street. Ev Carver emerged from the rear of the limousine and strode into the aging Munson Diner.

Two laborers were hunched over coffee at the counter on the left, discussing the previous night's Mets game. A black couple sipped coffee desultorily at a booth on the right. In the rear sat a bald-headed man with gnarled browridges cantilevered above wary eyes. He was an ex-military-intelligence officer whose firm was sometimes hired by FBS's Security people to check into the background of prospective employees. Ev had hired him personally for a private job, but had told him to bill FBS in the usual way.

Ev dropped into the chair across from him. "Who's the bitch fucking, Hank?"

"It's all on the film."

"You got her with someone!"

"I'll tell you this, she sure isn't a nun."

"That cunt! I'll stomp her into little pieces."

A Security passkey allowed the investigator access to Hedy's locked office. He had quickly made wax impressions of the keys in her handbag. One of the keys let him into her apartment in the brownstone, where he placed a tiny camera high up in a closet, the view for its high-speed film provided by a tiny hole drilled through the wall above the molding, its silent shutter activated once every ten seconds while there was movement in the bedroom.

"I have the best of the prints," he told Ev, and slid a manila envelope across the table. He had made two sets of each photo. The negatives were back in his darkroom.

Ev bent up the metal clasp and opened the envelope. Enlargements revealed a naked man and woman making love in various positions on the bed.

"That isn't her!" Ev exclaimed. "Hedy's a brunette."

"You said it was the TV reporter. I recognized her right away. That's her."

Ev looked more closely at her face. And then at the man's. Ev was stunned. No mistaking those two: Chris Paskins was going at it with Greg Lyall in Hedy's apartment.

"Holy shit!" he joyfully exclaimed. "Holy mother of shit!"

This was the most lethal ammunition Ev could imagine having against Greg. Barnett Roderick's son-in-law fucking away with America's sweetheart of the news. Faced with the scandal these photos would spark, Greg would be forced to resign in Ev's favor.

"Sorry I couldn't get you what you wanted," the other man apologized.

"This'll do fine." Ev stood up, slipping the photos back into the envelope. "Add a thousand dollars to your bill, Hank. A bonus. You did just fine."

Ev was already out the door before the bald-headed man recalled the audiocassette residing in his pocket. Microphones concealed in several places in the apartment had broadcast whatever was said to a hidden tape recorder. He thought about running after Ev Carver to give him the cassette and then decided to listen to it first. If anything turned up on it, the guy might be willing to jump the bonus.

He asked the waitress for another coffee, slipped the cassette into the little recorder, and sat back to listen. After a while it came to him that this woman reporter and that bastard she was screwing in the photos were trying to destroy America's nuclear capability.

Greg was seated on the sofa reading a report as Ev entered his office unannounced. Closing the door, Ev pulled the photos from the manila envelope and dropped them onto the coffee table.

Greg felt as if they were a concrete block dropped onto his chest; he was unable to breathe. "How did you get these?"

"A little birdie flew up to me with them." Ev's voice was gleeful. "You're a dead man, Lyall. Dead as dirt. I want your resignation or my next stop is Barnett Roderick's apartment."

"Why didn't you just give them to him? Why bring them to me?"

"Too much turmoil the other way, and it doesn't guarantee that I take over. What I want is for you to make sure with the old man that I replace you. You obviously have him eating out of your hand. Tell him anything: that you can't take the pressure, that you realize you're not good enough and the company needs Carver. Anything. Just make sure I replace you. When I do, you get the second set of prints and the negatives. Clean, neat, and no one gets hurt."

Greg was staggered. These photos would destroy his career and Chris's and her husband's probably. Diane would be devastated. Ev Carver could not be bought off; all the man had ever wanted was to run FBS. If Greg refused to resign, Ev would have no scruples about releasing the photos to the press.

"What you're asking will take a few days to work out," Greg stated.

"I understand. Just see that it's done."

Ev had an extra card up his sleeve. If for some unforeseeable reason Greg did not resign in his favor, publishing the photos would doubtless weaken FBS so badly, on screen and off—certainly Chris Paskins's ratings—that the stock would plummet and Basil Markham could swoop in and swiftly swallow the company. In that eventuality also, Ev would be named CEO.

He started to leave and then stopped for a final observation. "You almost pulled it off, Lyall. You built yourself the perfect deal, and then like a dumb asshole, you went and tripped over your own cock."

His laughter was cut off by the slam of the door behind him.

Greg had bought some time to ponder the matter, but right now he saw no alternative to going to Barnett and tendering his resignation in favor of Ev Carver. Too many people would be hurt otherwise. Everything he had ever wanted and worked for had just slipped through his fingers and into Ev's.

He considered telling Chris what had happened and then decided against it. No need to worry her. Once he resigned and got back the photos, her reputation would be safe.

This was the maid's night off. Chris was making herself spaghetti, heating up the tomato sauce in the microwave oven while the pasta boiled on the stove. It was past ten o'clock. Late-breaking news had required three separate feeds tonight, two for the East Coast, one for the West.

The apartment was empty except for her. Ken spent most of his time either in Washington or campaigning upstate now. This coming weekend she had promised to be present while he gave several important speeches. She certainly *did* support him—he was a fine senator, she believed, and a fine man—and still married to him, she had a wife's obligation to appear. But she was a noted newscaster. Appearing with him automatically enhanced his credibility with voters. She feared that it lessened hers and had declared that she would accompany him to key speeches and rallies, as any wife would, but she would not speak on his behalf nor appear in any of his commercials.

The timer rang. She drained the pasta and ladled hot tomato sauce onto it.

Grated cheese, she remembered, and put the container on the table as well.

She finally sat down to eat, rolled several spaghetti strands around a fork, and heard a key in the door.

Ken stepped into the dining room. Usually immaculate, his hair was mussed and his necktie askew.

348

"I didn't expect you home," she remarked. "Do you want some pasta? I made too much."

"No, I came home to talk to you."

"What about?" She would not sit through another plea from him to reconcile. She started rolling a second forkful of spaghetti.

"I just had a private meeting with Phil Grant."

Chris put down her fork. Phillip Grant was the secretary of Defense.

"He says," Ken continued, "that you intend to run a story that will jeopardize America's reputation all around the world and probably destroy the good relations we have now with the Soviets."

"He's worried because he's been found out. Ken, he's breaking our missile treaties by secretly building a new nuclear-missile base. Maybe even more than one."

Ken dropped heavily into the chair opposite her. "He swore to me that wasn't true, that you're about to slander him and really make us look bad around the world. The Soviets will have a field day dragging us over the coals."

"And you believed him."

"He and I go back twenty years. You know how close we are. He wouldn't lie to me, Chris. He says you're being taken in by somebody."

"We have evidence, Ken. Testimony."

"By someone you're sure you can trust? Or a liar with his own ax to grind?"

"By someone I think I can trust."

"But you're not sure."

"I'm sure enough. There's one last piece of evidence I'm trying to get, Grant's secret memo ordering the base to be built."

"There is no base. He would have had to inform the Armed Services Committee if he was building a base, and I sit on it."

"He's a dangerous man."

"Then you won't kill the story."

"Those bases endanger us all."

"Oh, God! I was hoping not to have to do this."

He looked down at his hands as if they held a weapon. They slowly clenched into fists. When he looked up at her, his face was twisted by his inner pain.

"He told me that you're having an affair with Greg Lyall. He has photos showing the two of you making love in Hedy Anderson's apartment. He'll leak them to the press unless you drop the story."

The revelation struck Chris like a mortar shell. She was dazed by it and devastated.

"You say he has photos," she repeated.

"I saw them!" Ken cried out in anguish. "He got them over a

goddamn fax machine. Who the hell knows who else there saw them?"

Chris buried her face in her hands. The love affair that had been a miracle revived had been made to appear squalid and lewd.

"How could you do this to me?" Ken cried out. "People fall out of love, I understand that. But to sleep around behind my back, to let Lyall act like my friend while you were making love to him. . . ."

When she raised her head, tears filled her eyes. "It wasn't done to hurt you or anyone."

"You'll drop that story now. I don't care if the Defense Department is building a weapon that would destroy the world. You owe it to me and to Lyall's wife not to drag us through the mud. If those pictures get out, my political career is ruined."

Chris ran from the room. She needed a phone. She had to get hold of Greg. In the bedroom she looked up his home number and phoned.

"Mr. Lyall, please," she told the maid who answered, and gave her name.

A moment later Greg came on.

"We have to meet right away," she told him. "There are photos of us."

"In my office. In twenty minutes."

24

〰〰〰〰〰〰

Greg arrived at his office a few minutes before Chris. Brooding about the photos had strengthened his decision to resign and thereby save her, Ken, and Diane from the anguish of public ridicule. He would separate from Diane and try to start over again in a new job. He and Chris would divulge their relationship only after enough time passed for blame not to descend on her for causing the separation.

However, Chris's phone call had thrown his thinking into confusion. Who had told her about the photos? Ev, for sure. The guy was evil enough to gain a perverted pleasure out of displaying the photos to her and observing her humiliation.

Greg stood up as Chris entered his office. The emotions she had held back finally broke through. She rushed into his arms.

He guided her to the sofa. Gradually, she regained her composure enough to relate her conversation with Ken and his meeting with the secretary of Defense.

"The secretary of Defense?" Greg was astounded. Why would Ev give the photos to the secretary of Defense?

"He told Ken that the missile-base story isn't true, that I interviewed people who lied to me."

"Do you believe that?"

"I'm not sure anymore."

"You were sure yesterday, when we all reviewed the material. You were confident we had one of the biggest stories of the decade. Nothing about the story has changed."

"Maybe I was pushing my evidence too hard. That interview could have been a setup by those brothers."

"There were other things on the tape," Greg reminded her, "supply trucks entering a lonely access road, a guarded entrance you saw in an area that should only have been forest, the military helicopter."

351

"That still doesn't signify that the base is for nuclear missiles."

A perplexed expression suddenly invaded Greg's features. "Something's wrong. Grant is trying too hard to stop us. If there's no base there, why doesn't he just let the story come out and let us be embarrassed by the truth. Instead he's trying to blackmail a major television network. That's the big artillery, Chris. Why would he do that if the story isn't true?"

"Even if it is, let's leave it to someone else to discover."

"And if they don't?"

"I'll leak it to one of the other networks."

"Then we'll be safe until he makes some other 'request' of us."

She glanced at Greg sharply. "He said he'd give back the photos."

"Why should he? How will we be sure we have all the copies? Do you really believe that a man who may have broken an international treaty, who lied to Congress about what he's doing, and maybe even to the President, can be trusted?"

"I suppose not," she replied in a subdued voice.

He took her hands in his. "When Ev Carver showed me the photos today, my first inclination was like yours, to do whatever was necessary to save everyone's reputation."

"We have to, Greg. If those photos come out, your career is finished, so's mine, and so's Ken's. That's what bothers me most: Ken's only mistake was to love me. That could ruin him now. How can I do that to him?"

"I wish it were that easy to make this whole thing disappear. At least running the story will end the blackmail."

"My God! What's going to happen to my life, my career? Those photos will put us on every shabby news program and in every cheap supermarket newspaper. We'll be a dirty joke."

"I've always admired your integrity, Chris. I haven't always admired my own. But there's just enough journalist left in my soul for me to understand that what we're being asked to do is wrong. And for this country, very dangerous. Do you want that on your conscience?"

She pulled her hands back. "Just about all the load is piled on my conscience that it can take."

"The stakes may have gotten too big to kill the story, even if Grant sticks to his bargain."

"Greg, this isn't about ratings here . . . or about winning some damned time slot. Grandstanding now could be fatal. And not just to you and me. To some innocent people who trusted us and we betrayed."

"All we know is that somebody who could be controlling his own nuclear arsenal wants to kill the truth we're supposed to defend. That could end up really being fatal—and to a lot more people."

"You sound so smugly self-righteous."

"I don't mean to. It's just that I've always made compromises with what was right. Now an issue has come along that's just too big for me to do that." He sat back, decided. "We broadcast the story."

"No matter whom it hurts?"

"We really have no alternative."

She deliberated on their options, her gaze set on the darkness beyond one of the floor-to-ceiling windows. All their escape routes were closed off and their course of action virtually unavoidable after one concluded that yielding to the blackmail would not stop it. Ironically, this was just the sort of gigantic government cover-up she and every reporter dreamed of exposing, that won Pulitzers and Peabodies and Emmys and Columbia-DuPonts. How easy crusading seemed when nothing was at stake.

"Do you love me, Greg?" she asked, not shifting her eyes to look at him. "Will you love me no matter how this turns out?"

"Yes."

"All right," she finally said, turning back to him, understanding that bravery sometimes consisted of having no other choice. "I agree. We lead with the story tomorrow night. God help us."

Before meeting with Chris, a grief akin to that over death had weighed on Greg. The cause, he had comprehended, was the imminent liquidation of all the hopes that had sustained him since boyhood. Afterward, though, he felt light and nimble, uncertain whether that was because he had acted virtuously or because he had nothing left to lose. He began planning actions to meet the new circumstances facing him.

Chris did not return home, but slept in her office. Early the next morning, a Friday, she began to write the piece. When Manny arrived, she looked up only long enough to ask him for a "drop line" for the Defense secretary.

"Secretary of Defense Phillip Grant . . ." she began.

"How about," he suggested, " 'considered the administration's most vehement hawk.' "

"Thanks," she answered, and typed it in.

When the tape editor she wanted for the story came in, she joined him in an editing room to begin cutting the piece.

At ten o'clock the customary conference call among Manny, Chris, all the bureau chiefs around the country, and the senior editors in New

York began the daily process of choosing the night's rundown of news stories. Manny asked whether any of the bureau chiefs had heard rumors about a nuclear-missile base being secretly constructed in his or her region. None had.

Chris worked the phones for an hour, futilely trying to unearth some additional evidence to bolster her story. She broke away to screen a taped piece she and Manny suspected might run too long on judicial measures being taken against unlawful antiabortion demonstrations. They decided that a late-breaking story about new civil unrest in the Soviet Union should be inserted and ordered the abortion piece to be trimmed back by forty-five seconds. Deleted from it was a sequence showing demonstrators being hauled away for blocking the entrance to a Manhattan abortion clinic.

Chris returned to her computer screen to polish the narration for her missile-base piece, knowing she would probably have to make do with what she had. All the while, though, an upsetting thought intruded on her concentration.

In the early afternoon, Hedy Anderson arrived to find a note that Chris wanted to see her, and she walked over to the anchorwoman's office. As soon as the door closed to give them privacy, Chris turned on her.

"I knew you were ambitious, Hedy, and had done things to get ahead you weren't particularly proud of. But I believed you were my friend, that you wouldn't deliberately hurt me to get ahead."

"Of course I wouldn't. What are you talking about?"

"The photos, of course. Of Greg and me in what used to be your bed. Ev Carver is blackmailing us with them."

"Oh, no!"

"Don't act as if you didn't know about them. You had to know."

Hedy sank down onto the arm of a chair. The situation was too far gone to keep her private shames concealed. "Ev was trying to get something on *me,* not on *you.* Sleeping with him was what got me to New York. He became furious when I refused to see him anymore. He thought I still lived there."

"I can't buy that. That lock is pickproof. Somebody had to have your key to plant a camera. They sure didn't have mine. I always keep that key hidden. So does Greg."

"I swear I knew nothing about it."

"I've been thinking back. A few times there were embarrassing leaks from the newsroom we couldn't trace. You were always there, but no one suspected you."

Hedy reddened. She had been feeding Ev bits of information back then, but that had stopped. How could one explain gradations of guilt, that time had changed her behavior? "I swear to you I didn't know he had a camera hidden in the apartment. I don't even know how he got in."

"Someone once told me that when women tasted a little bit of opportunity, they'd become as unprincipled as men in trying to get ahead. Congratulations, your double-crossing paid off. This network may soon be looking around for a new anchor. Thanks partly to me, you're right up there in line for the job."

Chris opened the door. The conversation and the friendship were at an end.

Late that afternoon, Greg flew to the country house by helicopter, joining Diane and Barnett there.

Diane wanted to begin dinner at seven, but Greg insisted on watching the news.

"This is important," he solemnly told the others as the news program's logo appeared on the television screen.

Chris's piece led. She laid out her case for the missile base's existence carefully, claiming no more than she could prove. Rather than relying totally on comments by experts—the so-called "rent-a-bites," "usual suspects," "talking heads"—after the tape ended, Chris herself explained the possible implications.

"If a nuclear-missile base has indeed been built there, that would violate the terms of our disarmament treaties with the Soviets. At a time of lessening tensions between East and West, the base's existence would raise troubling questions: Who authorized it? Was it the secretary of Defense acting alone or did he act with the President's knowledge? Or did someone farther down the chain of command create and implement the plan without the knowledge of either man? Why has Congress not been informed about it? And most important, what is its purpose?"

As Chris turned to another camera to introduce the next story, Barnett punched the remote-control unit to mute the sound. His face was tightened into ultimate condemnation, like the magistrate of a last, apocalyptic judgement.

"Those are scandalous charges. Flimsy and unnecessary. Pure gossip. A total misuse of our news service. That woman made the Defense secretary—a patriot and a friend—sound like some sort of melodrama villain. The administration has every right to be furious and to retaliate."

"We had enough to go on."

"So, you knew about it!" Barnett thundered. "Did you at least check with Grant?"

This is it, thought Greg, this is the moment when my life starts to crumble. "He already knew we had the story. He denied it. We mentioned that he had."

"He denied it, and you still went ahead."

"He wanted to kill the story so badly that he resorted to blackmail." Greg looked at Diane now. "He has photographs of me he said he'd release to the press if the story was broadcast."

"What kinds of photographs?" Diane asked, her back stiffening, preparing herself.

"Of me in bed with another woman."

Profound pain seized Diane's face. Barnett started to speak, but Diane raised her hand to silence him.

"Who is the woman?"

"Christine Paskins."

Diane's gaze swung to the television screen and Chris's likeness that filled it.

"Does Ken know?" she asked after a moment.

"They're going to separate after the election."

"*Does he know?*" she cried out.

"Yes. The secretary showed him the pictures."

"Well, at least I'm not the only fool."

"They'll probably be published tomorrow."

A sob caught in Diane's throat. "You really turned out to be so common. So predictably common."

Barnett rose from his chair to loom over Greg like a column of charcoal-gray smoke topped by fumes of gray hair and censorious eyes and brows.

"What you have done is dishonorable and unconscionable. It's inexcusable. You broke your marriage vows to Diane and your word to me. You're the lowest sort of creature—a social climber with no moral character. You have forfeited all rights to my favor, all rights whatsoever. You should be crawling on your knees right now begging for forgiveness from my daughter and me."

Greg's attention all along had been on Diane. "You know our marriage has been over for a long time."

Barnett's outrage commanded the moment. "You understand that if you leave her, you'll leave with nothing. In any event I am ordering you to submit your resignation from FBS."

"I've thought about that," Greg said reflectively. "I took the job to try to turn the company around and accomplish something worthwhile. We have a chance of doing that. My contract guarantees I stay until year's end, with an option for another five years if the company projects profits at that point. I don't intend to resign."

Barnett's face was now crimson with fury. "You got that job only because I gave it to you. And I can take it away just as easily. A scandal involving the company's CEO and its most important newscaster will provide ample cause for the board to overturn your contract and fire you. I'll see to that."

"So you can take over again."

"Yes, damn it. Take over and bring some morality back to the company."

Greg knew Barnett as someone who claimed whatever principles and assumed whatever pose suited his momentary purpose. "Last November, when I took over, you were only interested in better ratings and stopping the losses. Times change. The company's doing better now. So are you. That's fortunate because you'll need all your strength. I intend to fight you till my last breath to keep the job."

"I'll see you in hell first!"

Standing to leave, Greg placed himself in front of Diane, speaking only to her. "Perhaps the marriage might have worked if Chris and I hadn't fallen in love again, but I doubt it. I think it was bound to end. You and I gave it a lot of years, and very little changed. So much I'd hoped for and looked for in you—that we'd looked for in each other—never materialized. We never had a family."

"You never understood how frightened I get."

"Probably. We gradually became two dissatisfied people separated by all the ways we disappoint each other."

That's what marriage really is, he thought sadly, the slow destruction of the fantasies about the other person we originally got married for. Nothing ever grew in their place.

He paused. This was probably the last time he would have a chance to speak to her directly and not through lawyers. After all these years there must be something else he wanted to say.

But all he could think of was, "I'm sorry, Diane. I'm sorry I disappointed you. I'm sorry that the marriage ended so publicly, with so much embarrassment."

He waited for her to summon her own last words, but she simply glared up at him, her mouth tight. He started to walk from the room.

"Don't go!" she cried out.

For an instant, irrationally, Greg's years of acquired self-sufficiency fell away. The specter of loneliness loomed up before him as fearfully as when he was an abandoned child in an emptying house. But Diane was already swiftly receding into an irretrievable past. I have Chris, he told himself, and I have my talent for this business.

Greg asked the butler to drive him to the railroad station, where he waited an hour for the next train back to New York.

For several days the envelope containing the divorce papers his wife had served on him stood propped up, unopened, on the desk in Susan's study. Occasionally, Stew Graushner would stand before it, like a man praying before a fearsome representation of the Almighty. He knew what they said—she had told him: that she wanted half of everything he possessed and would ever possess from now until the end of time. He pictured her standing in hip boots in the center of his income stream holding a large net to catch his fattest assets swimming by while he, downstream, starved to death.

Finally, like a wild animal sniffing around a baited trap, Stew approached the envelope. He nudged it and jumped back when it fell over, before summoning the courage to approach again and open it. He set the divorce complaint in the middle of the desk and stared at it from too far away to read it, paralyzed by its official-looking appearance. Several minutes passed before Susan, who had been reading a news-paper, intervened.

"You need a lawyer."

She picked up the telephone and as she pushed the touch-tone buttons, continued, "Actually, you need *my* lawyer. He's known as a real bomber—you know, the kind who bombs the other side with motions and papers till they're dizzy and on their knees. He practically bludgeoned my second husband and left him penniless and whimpering, drove him into a sanitarium in fact. Yes, you definitely need Hal Diamond."

Stew brightened. "Hal Diamond. I like the name. It's got a sharp, hard sound."

"Whenever I think of Hal, a nickname I gave him always comes to mind. Hello," Susan said into the receiver as someone answered. "Hal Diamond, please."

"You mentioned a nickname," Stew reminded her as she waited.

"Oh, right. I call him the Wrath of God."

"The Wrath of God," Stew repeated, a huge smile bursting onto his face as he savored the characterization. That was just the sort of defender he needed: a bomber. A starship. The Federation. The Wrath of God.

God's Wrath, it turned out, required a twenty-five-thousand-dollar retainer. As soon as the check cleared, Stew drove to the bank in his new Mercedes and withdrew his last fifteen thousand dollars in cash, which he intended to hide someplace that Patty could never get at.

Early the next day, a wire service distributed cropped photos of Chris and Greg's lovemaking to every major newspaper, newsmagazine, and television station in the United States and overseas. The accompanying story and the flood of others that quickly followed seemed to justify the invasion of the couple's privacy on the theory that viewers had a right to scrutinize the personal behavior of journalists, on whose trustworthiness they relied for their news; that once members of the press began to snoop into the sexual errancies of presidential aspirant Gary Hart or the alcoholism of Kitty Dukakis (who was not even running for political office), their own private morality became fair game.

Few news organs ignored the story—the cast of characters was too juicy: a beautiful, prominent anchorwoman, her senator husband, the head of a network, his heiress wife. The true motive for spotlighting the story was, of course, that the public was interested in gossip about sex and celebrities. A story combining both was irresistible. This was better than "Dallas" or a pop novel, better even than the Trumps, because this scandal came complete with photographs. One of the networks managed to track down Rob Lowe for his comments.

An army of reporters camped out around the entrances to Chris's apartment house the next day. She and Greg could not meet and had to make do with several long phone conversations, which made them feel like prisoners.

Until then, Chris had been America's darling. All through the weekend a hurricane of denunciation descended on her. Every news program or newspaper she turned to splashed her face and often her scarcely cropped torso onto screen or paper. She had instantly become notorious. What had been her private life was now the subject of prurient dissection. With remorse now, she recalled how thoughtlessly she herself had handled such material when it concerned celebrities she did not know. She tried to read a book, but could not concentrate. Like an arsonist returning to watch firefighters battle her blaze, a perverse compulsion drove her back to the stories that were ruining her life.

Guided by the Sunday *Times* real estate section, Greg rented a furnished apartment on Park Avenue and moved himself and his belongings in that very day, before Diane was due to return from the country. Chris thought about joining him, but a call downstairs on the housephone confirmed that photographers were still staked out there, their cars and even a motorcycle at the ready.

Seeking to limit the damage to his reputation, Ken issued a statement to the press on Sunday night—to make the Monday-morning

newspapers—that expressed his shock at learning of his wife's misbe-
havior, but that he still loved her and hoped they could repair their lives
together.

Next morning, Chris called her own press conference in the FBS
newsroom. Always honest before, she was no less so now. She stated
that her husband had long known that she wanted to leave him, but at
his request, so that he and the voters would not be diverted from the
significant issues of his campaign, she had agreed not to announce their
separation until after the November election. She loved Greg Lyall, not
Ken. She was sorry for all the grief that had caused.

She also wondered aloud how the wire service had obtained surreptitiously shot photos that so clearly violated her and Greg's privacy. A
reporter attending the press conference for that wire service had been
given a printed statement to hand out in case the question came up. It
consisted basically of a single line: "In accordance with our Constitutional press freedoms, we never reveal our sources."

FBS's camera crew squirmed in embarrassment through the press
conference and shrugged apologetically afterward. Chris tried to put
them at their ease by joking that at least she would be more attractively
lighted here than in the now notorious photos.

She was sure company directors would want her suspended. Greg
had vowed to fight against it. At least that would give her some time.
But she had no idea yet how she would deal with the issue tonight on the
air. Millions of additional viewers would tune in to see her tonight, she
knew. A very rugged way to raise ratings.

Greg was not used to spending his free time alone and did not like it.
He and Diane were usually out four or five times a week. On other
nights he watched TV to catch the rival networks' offerings, but Diane
was usually there with him. On weekends, even in the country, they
had parties or dinners to attend.

After determining on Sunday that Chris could not join him, Greg
began to go stir-crazy. Phoning friends of his and Diane's for company
was out of the question. Finally, he ran out for dinner to Leo's On
Madison Avenue, a popular neighborhood restaurant, hoping to
encounter someone he knew, then realized word that he was
"prowling" the East Side scene would invariably make its way into the
gossip columns. He grabbed a sandwich in a delicatessen and caught a
movie.

He was in his office early Monday morning, grateful to be able to
throw himself into work. At nine, he began contacting FBS directors by
phone. Barnett had spent the weekend calling them, and Greg, the only

FBS employee on the board, found himself in a race for their allegiance. Nearly all were prominent businesspeople and all but one of them men. Some to whom Greg spoke were outraged or embarrassed by the scandal, especially the older ones who were close to Barnett. Others were willing to extend some sympathy. Most wanted Chris suspended, but found it difficult to vent their feelings fully because Greg was the other person in the photographs. Greg insisted she had the right to defend herself. He did not know how long he could hold back the pressure.

He also tried to prepare the directors for possible repercussions from the Pentagon story. The worst thing in their eyes, he knew, was adverse surprises. What he stressed to each were the company's positive improvements over the year and the need to present a united front right now. He managed to obtain one approval from them that lifted his mood after a weekend of turmoil and distress.

He found himself whistling as he traversed the long corridor from his own office suite and sauntered into Ev Carver's without waiting to be announced. As usual, the curtains were drawn closed, the lighting gloomy. Ev was just ending a phone call.

"I've got some very good news," Greg told him.

"What is it?"

Greg smiled broadly. "You're fired."

Ev snorted. "Good try, Lyall. I figure by this time tomorrow I'll be occupying your office."

"I'll still be here tomorrow. You won't." And one less challenger will be fighting for my job in November, Greg thought. "We located the bill for the private detective. It turns out the directors don't like underhanded employees who try to smear FBS's reputation for their own ambition. Barnett Roderick hates them most of all. Bad mistake."

"You're lying."

"Even your friend Dickenson had to abstain on that one. Try him."

"I sure will."

"But do it from a pay phone on the street. You no longer work here."

Ev evaluated Greg's words and facial expression, and then, convinced, he rose to leave.

"I always figured I'd beat you out in the end, Lyall, because you were hampered by a drawback I never had to worry about."

"What's that?"

"You like to fool yourself into believing you're a moral man. Take it from me, pretensions of a conscience just get in the way."

"We've always provided each other's biggest mistakes, Ev. Mine was taking my eyes off you long enough to make love to a woman I'm in love with. Yours was not firing me years ago in L.A. when you had the chance."

Ev's eyelids hooded slightly and his mouth curved into a slyly reptilian smile.

"I still intend to."

"Take the whore off the air!" one demonstrator screamed into the video cameras.

"Bring God back into our homes," yelled another.

A demonstration had formed outside the FBS Building, with people impassionedly shouting and waving signs condemning both Christine Paskins and abortion.

As soon as all the television crews were present, a small man in his forties named Jonathan Dearey stepped up to the bouquet of microphones. He had organized the demonstration, as well as a recent series of antiabortion rallies in Manhattan, where he had come about a year earlier to gain more publicity for his evangelism. His hair was almost all gone, which accentuated the nondescript roundness of his face and head, like a roseate egg with dark, bright eyes. Behind him stood his small band of followers: five men who looked like bodybuilders and wore yellow T-shirts with the words "Warrior of God" on them.

"God has punished the godless," Jonathan Dearey began in an unexpectedly sonorous voice, "as Jesus said would happen when He spoke through me in prophecy at the site of an abortion slaughterhouse last week. The sinner he punished was Christine Paskins. She kept from her television audience that day the story of the injustice visited on us by the New York City Police Department, who threw our people, doing God's work, into jail."

His fervency vibrating in every word and gesture, Jonathan accused members of the "liberal, leftist press" of banning him from the air in order to keep the nation from learning what he claimed was the truth: that multitudes were joining the Christian fight for morality and against baby murder. He contended that Christine Paskins used her position as a news anchor to promulgate evil and immorality. He demanded that FBS fire her and her "whoremaster boss, Gregory Lyall." He called upon viewers to boycott the network, upon the FCC to force the network off the air, and upon investors to band together to wrest FBS from the hands of "Satan and his minions" and put it into the hands of God-fearing Christians.

As his words came to a ringing end, the strains of "Onward Christian Soldiers" rose on cue from the throats of his followers. At that moment Jonathan Dearey felt his entire body was incandescent with God's power. He was a solitary beacon in the world's black wickedness, God's chosen messenger on earth, his prophet, his Jeremiah come to foretell of doom and destruction if the human race failed to change its sinful ways. But he was also a modern man who understood the power of the media to multiply his audience by a factor of millions and to validate his message by deeming it important enough to broadcast to the nation. By tying this demonstration to the fortunate happenstance of Christine Paskins's scandal, he would get news coverage at last. The news media would be forced to report his call for a boycott and FCC sanctions because Chris Paskins and Greg Lyall were news, and he was right on their tails.

Late that day, Phillip Grant, the secretary of Defense, appeared in the press briefing room of the Pentagon. An athletic man with a military bearing and firmly forthright features, he had been wounded while serving in Korea. He still walked with a slight limp, which Pentagon reporters insisted became more pronounced during military ceremonies. After law school he had gone into politics.

"I have an announcement to make," Grant said into the last of the chatter. Then he began to read. "As many of you know, Christine Paskins and FBS News recently broadcast a report that accused me and this government of building a nuclear-missile base in Maine in contravention of our treaties with the Soviets. That is a lie. There is no such base. We take our treaty obligations very seriously and consider peace our primary goal.

"After consultation with legal counsel, I wish to announce that the Defense Department and myself will be serving papers as soon as they are drawn on the Federal Broadcasting System and Christine Paskins to commence an action against them for defamation and libel. I will personally be asking five hundred million dollars in actual and punitive damages. Ms. Paskins was warned beforehand that her story was untrue. Yet, in an act of gross malice and negligence, she deliberately and knowingly broadcast it with reckless disregard that it was false." Knowledgeable reporters in the briefing room understood that lawyers had inserted that last sentence. The Supreme Court required such elements to override the usual presumption that a public figure can freely be written or spoken about by the press without fear of reprisal.

"We contend that Ms. Paskins manufactured the evidence on which she based her charges against myself and this department. In fact, the soldier she interviewed was AWOL at the time. We believe she induced him to lie on camera so that she could fabricate her malicious story."

363

Grant held up a piece of paper. "I also have a message from the President. The President states: 'I have no personal knowledge of any secret missile base, have not approved any such base, and am certain that the secretary of Defense is completely innocent of FBS's charges.'" Grant stepped away from the rostrum. "No questions."

He turned on his good leg and strode out of the room.

FBS's Pentagon correspondent had been called back from vacation when the missile-base investigation commenced. As he and his colleagues walked up to the front of the room to obtain copies of the statement, one spoke to him.

"Five hundred million! Grant really wants to break you guys."

FBS's reporter was shocked by the figure himself. The amount was one of those government-agency figures so vast as to be incomprehensible. If awarded, it might well bankrupt the already shaky network. Applied to Chris Paskins alone, it was ludicrous.

A simple denial from the secretary would have merited perhaps a sentence or two in a larger story. By initiating a lawsuit for half a billion dollars, he had turned his denial into front-page news.

Chris used the last two minutes of the news broadcast that night to defend journalism and her journalistic honesty. She regretted, she said, the recent revelations about her private life, but they should have remained private and should not be taken as a slur on her honesty as a reporter. She and FBS would not be cowed by the administration's threats. She did not intend to relinquish this anchor chair, no matter how vicious the attacks on her character became. She stood by the truth. She had always believed in the fair-mindedness of the American people and relied on it now.

A moment after Chris retired to her office, she heard a knock on the door.

"Is Miss August in there?" a man's voice called out.

Chris laughed, recognizing Greg.

"Isn't this the Playboy channel?" he said as he entered and extended a single white rose toward her.

She accepted it and kissed him. "Can we go somewhere?"

"My new apartment. It's got an underground garage we can use to avoid reporters."

Chris began to gather up her belongings to leave. "My father called me today."

"Was he shocked?"

"He didn't say, and I certainly didn't ask." Her expression turned

364

shy. "He just wanted me to know he thought I was a chip off the old journalistic block. Something like that."

"Good for him."

"My mother got on the phone, too. She told me that even with all the notoriety, it wasn't too late for me to find a nice boy, start a family, and get into teaching."

25

~~~~~~~~~~~~~~~~

The phone calls from FBS's directors began to reach Greg at home that night. By the next morning he was in conversation continually with one or another of them. Their dismay over the photos had been heightened and given focus by the Defense secretary's charges and half-a-billion-dollar damage claim. This was a quantifiable threat. Sentiment was overwhelming for Chris to be fired, or at least suspended.

Greg argued that notoriety and government indignation had occasionally assailed other network news figures and eventually passed without their ratings suffering unduly. Constitutional issues were involved here: freedom of the press, right to a fair trial, innocence until guilt was proven. Considered pragmatically, replacing a popular anchor temporarily under a cloud would bring accusations of cowardice, and as viewers switched to better-known anchors on other networks, a sharp fall-off in ratings, perhaps as low as they were during Ray Strock's last days. Did the directors want to risk that—or Chris's lawsuit if she turned out to be right about the Defense Department?

One of the older directors replied bluntly, "Hey, none of this gets around the fact that you two were caught in bed together. To a lot of people Christine Paskins is now a wild smut queen who got her job because she was sleeping with you. To be honest, the whole network looks like some kind of orgy den. I understand that she's got a strong contract we can't ignore, but we've got to clear out the stench in people's nostrils somehow."

Another director said, "She deceived her husband, who's an important man in the government. Maybe she lied about the Defense Department, too."

The next regular board meeting was scheduled for mid-November, well after the new lineup premiered and halfway through the sweeps period that would determine the following quarter's advertising prices. By then the present controversy should have simmered down and the company's prospects for the coming year would pretty much be known. If the ratings proved to be lackluster, Greg was out anyway, but if he could point to one or two big shows, a gathering strength in the schedule, an assurance of profitability, then more directors would rally to his side, and he would be in a better position to battle both for himself and for Chris.

Barnett chose that day to return full-time to his office at FBS. He, too, was manning the phone, provoking the directors to take action against Chris. In the old man's eyes, Chris was no longer the woman who had raised the news broadcast's ratings to respectability, but the hussy who had stolen his daughter's husband. He wanted her eliminated, and the Defense secretary's charges provided a more defensible means than leaked photos. Chris also provided the weakened flank from which he could launch an attack on Greg.

Hoping to dissipate this particular issue before the directors' resistance stiffened into a call for a premature board meeting that might end in his dismissal, Greg arranged to meet with Barnett in the latter's office.

Greg walked to the opposite corner of the floor from his own office, remembering his awe the first time he was ushered into the presence of the communications titan—and of everything that day set into motion. As he expected, Barnett kept him waiting.

"If you're here to beg me for a favor," the Chairman announced insolently when Greg was finally admitted, "you came to the wrong place."

Unlike a decade earlier, Greg seated himself unbidden across the desk from Barnett and got down to the point of the meeting.

"Pushing Chris permanently off the air will kill the news's ratings."

Barnett's eyebrows lifted into an angry V. "More than those pornographic photographs did? Just as important, I will not allow a woman to speak for us who might have libeled the government of the United States."

"Without giving her a chance to defend herself?"

The reply throbbed with hatred. "I owe her nothing!"

"The media critics, the columnists, they'll all blast you, saying you either caved into the lowest sort of crowd outcry or you fired her for personal reasons."

"I've been criticized before."

"If her reporting about that missile base is accurate, viewers will side with her, too. So will any judge who examines her contract. How will we look then?"

"So you want your mistress to stay on the air. That's not a surprise. We didn't need a meeting to establish that."

"And you want her off. Also no surprise."

Greg took a deep breath. He saw a way to compromise that would brake both sides before they collided, although not one that was ideal from his perspective. Ratings might dip more than if she stayed on the air—and Chris would be irate. "All of her efforts right now should be devoted to proving she's innocent of the secretary's charges. Maybe she won't buy this, but I think it fair we limit her on-air reporting to this nuclear-missile-base controversy. Take her off 'Confidentially Speaking,' too. If she's exonerated, she goes back on both."

"Not much chance of that happening—" Barnett interrupted to observe. The secretary had given Barnett his solemn assurance that Chris's charges were false and that he had been smeared.

"Just hope she is. FBS's credibility won't count for much with viewers if she's guilty."

"I want that other woman to take her place. The large one."

"Hedy?"

"That's the one. She's been doing a good job on weekends. If we substitute with a man, women will scream we're discriminating."

Barnett's reasoning was persuasive, Greg conceded, but that particular switch would make his selling job to Chris even harder.

"I'll get back to you," he said.

Greg's tact did little to prevent Chris from becoming first furious and then demoralized.

"Roderick was watching out for *his* interests," she railed. "You were watching out for *yours*. As usual mine got lost in the shuffle."

"That isn't fair. They were looking to take you off the air completely."

Chris crossed her arms. "I want my agent here."

Greg felt as if she had slapped him. Jaw clenched, he told his secretary to call Carl Green for him.

An hour later the meeting in Greg's office reconvened, with Chris still glaring at him.

Greg began by once more describing in detail the course the dispute had taken, so as to demonstrate that the compromise with Barnett was the best he could extract.

Carl looked at Greg with soulful eyes. "Greg, I know you've got Chris's best interests at heart. After all you kids have gone through, if you don't, who does?" Although the photos had stunned Carl, he was adroit at adjusting to new conditions.

"But?"

"But not being on the air is living death for Chris."

"She'll still be reporting on the missile-base problem. And when that's resolved, she goes back into the anchor chair."

"*If. If. If. If* not when. *If* she can get the truth out of those Defense motherfuckers."

"If she can't, the directors then have the legal right to suspend her anyway."

"A little *rachmones* here, Greg, a little heart."

Chris leaped to her feet to confront Greg herself. "This is déjà vu: you telling me you did your best to defend me and me screaming that you sold me down the river. I'm surprised you didn't tell the directors I'd do a series on the 'Great Toilets of Fifth Avenue.' "

"Inside joke," Greg muttered to Carl with a grimace, then directed himself to Chris. "Let's not forget that this nation is still reeling over those photos. Not a very dignified pose for a respected news anchor."

"I notice nothing was said about *you* resigning."

"Do you think that would make it easier here for you?"

"No," she admitted reluctantly.

"Then this is the best solution for the time being."

"Damn!" She jumped to her feet. "I always get too loopy over you to see the thorns that end up scratching me later on."

"Your *crown* of thorns?" Greg asked sarcastically. Chris had a tendency to see herself as a martyr fighting alone against injustice. "Admit that the directors have some cause here—like a half-a-billion-dollar liability and the reputation of their news organization."

"Then they ought to back it," she retorted sharply.

Greg put his hands on her shoulders. "This will just be temporary— until you're cleared. You'll get that in writing."

Slowly, the necessity for her yielding to the compromise sank in. "I guess this is as good as we have any right to expect under the circumstances."

Carl stood up to leave. He did not voice his thought, which was that they gave better odds in Las Vegas than he would hazard on her return, and you still came home broke.

"Oh, by the way," he asked, "who's going to sub for Chris till she's back?"

Greg hedged. "That's still up in the air."

"Just as long as it's not Hedy Anderson," Chris declared.

Chris instantly detected the slight sag of Greg's shoulders.

"You son of a bitch." Before all this happened, she could have demanded that Hedy be fired or sent into oblivion, and it would have happened. No longer.

Carl, however, did not object. Hedy was a client.

* * *

Annette Valletta was nearly immobile now, barely able to move to the bathroom or balcony. Some days she had only enough energy to sit up in bed, sponge herself with the help of the maid, and put on a little makeup and perfume before collapsing back onto her pillow. What kept her going through all the adversity and hopelessness, through all the inconclusive medical tests, was her belief that one day she would lick this thing and be back where she belonged, on millions of TV screens.

Johnny was sitting on the chair beside her bed as her finger listlessly pushed the remote-control unit's button. She settled on "Wide World of Entertainment," which was just beginning. A video fan-magazine, the popular syndicated show featured gossipy stories about film and television personalities and projects. Johnny was glad about her choice, which might provide an appropriate means for leading up to what he could finally no longer put off telling her.

The show's producers had heard rumors of Annette's withdrawal from "I Love Luba" and replacement by Sally Foster. In return for keeping the story absolutely confidential until Thursday, two days from now, allowing Johnny time to break the news personally to Annette, they had been granted an exclusive to report it, with taped interviews of Sally and Johnny.

"Tonight," one of the show's hosts announced in the opening tease intended to induce viewers to stick with the show, "the exclusive story behind why one of television's brightest and most beloved stars, Annette Valletta, will not appear in 'I Love Luba' this year and her best friend, Sally Foster, will."

"What?" Annette cried out like a woman being roasted on a spit.

"It's a sad and touching story, so stay tuned."

"Sally will replace me in 'Luba'! That can't be true."

"We kept it from you," Johnny confessed, "hoping you'd get better and could come back onto the show. But you haven't."

"Double-crossed! Betrayed!"

"Look, FBS didn't want the show to die."

"So who jumped in? My husband and my best friend. Now I really have nothing to live for."

"It wasn't like that."

"Get out!" she screamed. "Get out and let me die in peace! I never want to see you or Sally again!"

Johnny tried to placate her, but finding that impossible, threw some clothing into a suitcase and drove over to Sally's. Actually, he was due there later anyway, after Annette fell asleep.

Biff Stanfield was due to go onstage soon. He sipped his Pepsi at the bar, listening above the muted patter from the adjacent nightclub to his bartender friend, who was needling him that Biff still had to work at this grim, third-rate nightclub despite all the excitement about his pilot film a few months back. The week before, Biff had inadvertently provoked a customer who drew a knife on him and threatened to cut off his balls.

"As soon as I get word the show's been picked up," Biff declared, "I'm out of here. You'll never see me performing like a monkey for these assholes again."

"The governor just turned down your pardon," a woman's voice remarked.

Lily was standing behind him. He had not expected her. She had told him she was going home to relax tonight, do her nails, watch TV, and catch up on a briefcase full of legal briefs.

"What's that supposed to mean?" he wanted to know.

"Guess what I just heard on 'Wide World of Entertainment.' "

"That the kid on 'Wonder Years' grows up to be a date rapist on 'thirtysomething.' "

"That Annette Valletta is sick, and our dear, loyal friend and partner, Sally Foster, has taken over for her in 'I Love Luba'—permanently."

Biff was stunned. "You've got to be kidding. We have a deal with FBS."

"Not if they don't put your show on. It looks like they don't even know you're alive. You told me you called Sally Foster. Has she gotten back to you?"

"No. But I can't believe they would do something like this."

"I'd say the one to talk to is Marian Marcus. But I expect she hasn't been answering your calls either."

Biff jumped up. "I've got to see her in person and find out where I stand."

"You're about as welcome at FBS right now as that Defense secretary they've been trashing on the news. You won't even be able to get past the guards in the building."

"I'll think of a way," he growled.

"Hey, Bonzo," the bartender called playfully over to Biff, "you're on next. Want to take a banana with you?"

FBS rented a corporate jet to fly Chris and a crew to Maine first thing in the morning. While they were in the air, the company's lawyers obtained a federal court order to enter the missile base and videotape it, providing the tape was shown first to the judge and not put on television without his approval. Federal marshals were sent to verify the base's location.

The caravan found nothing. The access road was there, but where the guarded entrance should have stood were only woods.

Chris was dumbfounded. The group hiked all across what should have been the base. No buildings. Not even any clearings. The land appeared to be virgin forest. She felt they had entered some sort of time warp in a science-fiction story and had regressed to a date before the base was built.

"This is impossible," Chris cried out. "There were people here. Trucks entered and brought in supplies."

The group walked back to the vehicles they had parked on the access road. A large truck rumbled toward them. Chris rushed to halt it. She seemed to remember seeing the truck on the road before.

"I'm up here most every week," the driver confirmed. "I pick up lumber at the mill, about ten miles farther on."

"Do you remember the military base that was here? Soldiers? A fence? It was back a little bit from the road, so you might not have noticed it right away."

The man eyed all the people awaiting his answer and shook his head. "Can't say that I do."

He hurriedly continued on his way.

Several people in town corroborated her recollection that soldiers occasionally appeared in town. But no one could agree on where the soldiers had come from. And memory seemed to differ too much to be accurate on just where the base out of town had been located.

"There were guards and a fence," she prodded one man.

He wasn't sure.

"Wasn't that a lot farther south?" another remembered.

She flew back to New York City in a deep melancholy.

Meanwhile, the researcher trying to track down the Craig brothers was also having little luck. Neither man could be located, and no one in the military would discuss them. Finally, she was able to establish that their home was Columbus, Ohio, and to reach their mother at work. The woman, a telephone-sales representative, was bitter at the television network for bringing such trouble to her family. The only thing she had heard—and that was strictly rumor—was that both her sons were being held in a military prison somewhere and charged with treason.

Within an hour FBS's lawyers served subpoenas on the Defense Department to question the Craig brothers. Less than an hour after that, the answer came back that the whereabouts of both men was unknown and they were the objects of a manhunt.

Biff carefully printed "FBS NEWS" on a white card using a black marking pen and taped the card to the home video camera he had borrowed from a friend. Then he added sunglasses and a baseball cap to his outfit of jeans, a T-shirt, and sneakers. He then drove to the FBS Television Studios.

A guard stopped his car at the entrance.

Biff's accent roughened into working class. "Hi, how ya doing?" he greeted the guard, who nodded. "Hey, have the rest of the crew left in the remote van yet? We were supposed to go out on assignment."

Biff lifted the camera to display the white card on the side.

"Your credentials," the guard demanded.

Biff patted his T-shirt pocket. "Oh, jeez, I must have left them on my jacket. All that stuff is in the van. I've got to get to a phone and locate that van fast. Thanks."

Biff gunned the accelerator and sped past the guard into the lot and down into the office building's basement parking garage.

Camera on his shoulder, Biff nodded familiarly at every security guard he passed as he worked his way up into the building until he was at the floor on which he had met with Marian Marcus.

A secretary stood up to bar his progress into Marian's office.

"I've been sent up to tape an interview with Ms. Marcus," he announced with gruff amiability, appearing to chew gum as he spoke.

"You mean, for the affiliates?"

"Right," he quickly agreed.

"I thought that was supposed to be this afternoon."

"They told me I had to get it right now." He appeared to check his wristwatch. "I get a break in fifteen minutes. Union rules. We better do it now."

"She's on the phone, but she won't mind if you set up."

The young woman opened the door for Biff, mouthing the words "morning show" to Marian, who glanced up from her phone call as they entered. Marian nodded and turned back to the phone.

Biff closed the door behind him and pretended to set up the camera. A couple of minutes went by before Marian hung up the receiver.

"Where do you want me to sit?" she asked.

"On my lap, sweetheart," Biff said in flawless imitation of James Cagney.

Marian laughed, then did a double take.

"Biff?"

He lifted off his sunglasses.

"Why the disguise?" she asked.

"I have to talk to you."

"You could have called."

"I did. Twice."

"Oops." She quickly shuffled through the deck of pink messages before her. "One. Two. Sorry. This has been a hellish week, getting

373

the new shows and promos ready. I swear I would have called you back by tonight."

"You didn't call when Sally Foster was taken out of 'Adam and Eve' and put into 'I Love Luba.' "

"I must have. Or Fred did."

Marian snapped her fingers, recalling with embarrassment that her subordinate in charge of dramatic development had not attended the meeting with Sally Foster. "And Sally didn't tell you."

"Sally didn't tell anyone. I finally reached John and Marti Rosenthal last night to let them know. They're in New Mexico doing a movie of the week for you."

Marian remembered. "Oh, right. There was all that secrecy so Annette wouldn't find out what we were doing. Damn, I wonder if anyone has told *her* yet."

"I've been sitting on pins and needles for months waiting for word. And all the time, my show had already been knocked out of the box."

"Look, I'm sorry," she apologized. "It's just that 'Adam and Eve' never seemed to have the right chemistry, so I didn't mind pulling Sally out of it. The guy and gal were supposed to be buddies and potential lovers, but never really clicked together. They should have been more like, you know, those cops in *Lethal Weapon*."

"That's what they were originally supposed to be like: two guys, one white, one black, working together undercover. Really menacing situations, but a lot of humor. And I wanted them to be TV reporters with hidden cameras. You'd never see their real faces on the news. But Danny thought they should be cops and Sally talked me into changing the black's part so she could do it."

"It would work a lot better your way."

"Now I find out." Biff shook his head sadly. He kept to himself that his original concept featured a single lead, not buddies.

"Did you ever mention it to John and Marti?"

"A couple of times. They liked the idea, but we were already shooting the version with Sally."

"Can you put something on paper, just a page or two and get it here this afternoon?" Marian asked, her enthusiasm growing. "We'll fax it to them. I've got a couple of hour series that might not make it. I'd feel a lot more comfortable with a backup hour show in development."

If she had asked for it in thirty seconds, Biff would have agreed.

She was deep in thought. "Chad Laidlaw and who?" she muttered, flipping through possible black actors in her mind. "Somebody who can pull off the little ploys and disguises with a light kind of charm. You know, like you just did bluffing your way in here."

"There must be a lot of guys—"

374

Marian suddenly jumped up.

"You!" she screamed. "You've got the style, the humor. You sure understand the part."

"I don't want to be an actor. I'm a writer."

"Are you really crazy enough not to take the part?"

Biff deliberated for the barest instant before lifting a pen from her desk to serve as a mike. "And for the role of Lance in 'Daye and Knight,' Biff Stanfield. The envelope please."

"If the show works on paper like I think it's going to, you really solved a big problem for me."

Biff wanted to dance and sing and shout for joy. "Just glad I could help," he said coolly.

"What was the title again?"

" 'Daye and Knight.' But—"

"I like it."

"Dynamite, isn't it?"

Within days after Ev Carver resigned from FBS, he announced the formation with Basil Markham of a new company seeking to acquire media corporations. The announcement, at least initially, had an adverse effect on their plans. Guessing that the first company they would seek to acquire was FBS, around which Markham had for months been rumored to be buzzing, investors began buying into the broadcaster, and the price of the stock rose a point and a half.

Greg had already hired lawyers and investment bankers to devise defenses against hostile takeovers. Now they had a possible enemy to keep in their gunsights.

Barnett began showing up at his office each day at FBS and meeting with key executives. Greg knew the Chairman was developing strategies for attacking his policies when the directors convened in November. Both men devoted a significant amount of time to cultivating their relationships with the directors. Several whom Greg knew had lunched with Barnett found reasons not to have lunch with him. A few others lectured him about the scandal in which he and Chris had embroiled the company and expressed their impatience about the lack of a counterattack against the Defense secretary.

Yet, none expressed dissatisfaction with his progress in lowering expenses, the company's small, but perceptible rise in the ratings, and consequently, the higher income that scatter sales were earning. Even those most closely aligned with Barnett and most repelled by the notoriety seemed to be holding off on judging his performance as CEO until they saw the results of the new season.

*   *   *

"I can't believe it," Chris said sullenly as she gazed into the twilight from Greg's living-room window. "Ten years have passed, and even though more Americans probably know about our love affair than can name the President, we still can't go out in public for a simple dinner or movie together. It's worse than it was back then. We can't even live together. I have to sneak in and out of your apartment through the garage just so we can have a little time alone. So much for success."

Greg stepped up behind her and putting his arms around her, kissed her neck. "We can still make love."

She pulled away. "That's the last thing on my mind right now. I haven't eaten all day, and that Chinese restaurant said the food would be here half an hour ago."

"They did say maybe longer, they're backed up."

"For God's sake, don't defend them. And don't defend the video rental place we called that didn't have any of the movies we wanted. Or the manicurist who was too busy to leave the shop to come here to fix my broken nail even though she knows perfectly well I can't go to her. No matter how unreasonable I sound or how cranky I get, I want you to defend *me*. . . . I want you to tell me how abused and mistreated *I* am. Just say I'm right. Okay?"

"Okay."

"This is one of those times I envy smokers. What I wouldn't give for two or three minutes of even insubstantial comfort."

"I offered sex."

She frowned. "The truth is that you feel as distracted and unsexy as I do right now. Nothing is going right for us." She began to count the setbacks on her fingers. "The Defense Department has blocked us at every turn. Actually, they're kicking our butts. Those poor brothers are probably locked up somewhere so deep underground it would take an archaeologist to find them."

A second finger went up. "I'm a pariah. 'An immoral example to young people' is what they call me in those mimeographed letters and petitions from religious groups. I haven't appeared on the broadcast in over a week, and they still haven't let up on you or the sponsors to get me off the air. How many sponsors have canceled?"

"A couple." One had frantically pulled out after receiving a single letter.

She lifted a third finger. "And you're hanging on as CEO by a thread."

Greg was about to speak when she interrupted. "Oh, and there's one more: That bitch Hedy Anderson. Our own Edward R. Murrow with cleavage."

"You want me to tell you again that it's all worth it because I love you?"

"What's lovable about me is shrinking fast. On top of no longer having a professional life, I have no private life. Because I'm on television and come into their homes, everybody out there thinks they own me and can step all over me."

"You're a star. Comes with the territory. You know that. With the high salary and all the glory. Then, after you get to be a star because people like you on the tube, they get bored and look for reasons not to anymore."

"I used to think success came because I had something to contribute."

"Congratulations, you just lost your virginity."

The intercom buzzed to inform them that the delivery man had arrived from the Chinese restaurant. Chris felt as if she and Greg were holed up in the bunker during the last days of the Third Reich.

Ken Chandler tried to continue campaigning after the scandal broke about Chris's affair. The summer was a good time to hit the resort areas and city beaches, to get on TV during the seasonal dearth of news. But he soon perceived in the voters he met either pity or disdain. Common sense caused him to cancel active campaigning for the time being after that.

In a variation of the "Rose Garden strategy" incumbent presidents often utilized when campaigning, Ken buried himself in Washington, claiming that his legislative duties demanded he be there, despite the fact that Congress was in summer recess. He managed to get on TV from there once in a while, but not enough to rebuild his image. He could not avoid the truth: His career was in tatters. The allegation of his wife's dishonesty as a reporter, more than of her infidelity toward him, had virtually destroyed his public reputation. In the voters' minds he, too, was now considered untrustworthy.

At night, he thought of little but Chris, missing her desperately. Before the scandal occurred, he could still count on spending some time with her and even hope for a reconciliation. Although she was doubtless lost to him forever, he felt as sorry for her as for himself. Chris's downfall had been triggered by her finest quality: her honesty. When she saw a government lie, she reported it. When she fell in love with another man, she slept with him and asked for a separation. Ken had to believe that in the missile-base controversy, too, she had told the truth. Moreover, the fates of their careers were now linked. If her integrity as a reporter was not vindicated in her clash with the Defense secretary, neither would his be as a senator.

He obtained the approval of the Armed Services Committee chairman to set up a subcommittee to investigate the charges and countercharges. Money was allocated to hire a small staff and begin to probe. In his years in Washington, Ken had made a lot of contacts and earned a lot of favors. Now was the time to call in the chits.

Two days later, Iraq invaded Kuwait. Most of Ken's Defense Department contacts suddenly had more urgent business to attend to.

"Dollink," Sally crooned to Luba's husband, "I love hotfurters."

The audience roared with laughter and broke into applause.

The director waited until he had enough applause on the sound track to fade under the closing theme music and then called out over the PA system from the control room, "That's it, kiddies. A wrap. Fabulous, Sally."

The season's first episode of "I Love Luba" was in the can. Sally bounded over to the glass-sided booth at the side of the stage. A batch of nervous network executives was packed inside. They all had a lot riding on her success as Annette's replacement. Some had been anxious about the audience's accepting a different female lead. Some about her ability to do broad comedy. She had not dared to sneak a peak at the booth during the entire taping.

Marian was out of the booth and into her arms before Sally reached the door.

"You were incredible," the programming chief cried out, "dazzling, adorable. We loved Natasha."

"You mean it?"

"We've got too much at stake on this show for me to lie to you."

The other executives crowded around her.

One rhapsodized, "You make 'hotfurter' sound like the most torrid word in the English language."

"But clean," Marian added. "Sultry, but innocent, that's what we were saying in there."

The lesser executive quickly corrected himself. "Right, innocent-sultry, clean-sultry."

One called her a comic genius. Another, one of America's most brilliant comediennes. Sally appraised the level of Hollywood hyperbole and found herself satisfied. If not pleased, they would merely have called her "great" or "terrific." Johnny, who had been in the booth with them, stood smiling at their rear, nodding to confirm what their reaction had been.

Sally was jubilant. She was back. Better than back. She was on top. Higher and bigger than she had ever been. Every setback and humiliation she had ever endured was now worth it because each had served to bring her to this moment. She, Sally Foster, a baton twirler from a little town in Alabama, was America's new superstar.

* * *

In early September, the brain trust that had gathered several afternoons a week since the scandal rimmed the News Division's rectangular conference table: Chris at one end, Greg at the other; between them were, on one side, Alan Howe, Manny Ramirez, Hannah Rafael, and a senior producer; and on the other, the company's public-relations chief, general counsel, and outside lawyer, clocking three hundred dollars an hour. The network's Pentagon correspondent in Washington often joined them by speakerphone. Afterward most of the group would remain to discuss coverage of the crisis in the Middle East. A huge American military force had rushed to the Persian Gulf and to Saudi Arabia to defend the region from the threat of further Iraqi aggression and to enforce an embargo on trade with Iraq.

The room was large and through a wide picture window, overlooked the newsroom one floor below. Chris peered down at the anchor desk, where Hedy was editing news copy she would read during the broadcast. Chris was still managing editor, and the two women maintained a curt civility, but the hurt of watching someone forceably placed into her job, someone whose perfidy she believed had betrayed her, cut her deeply.

"The audience is falling off," Chris observed. "Every night we lose more. All the other anchors have been to the Middle East. We're in full retreat."

"It's not just Hedy," Greg rejoined. "It would have happened if you had stayed on."

"There's a heartwarming show of support!" Chris observed tartly.

"Our viewers are losing faith in us. They stayed with us a few days waiting for us to refute the charges. When we didn't, they began to drift away. No proof, and with a possible war brewing you still stayed off the air. A double whammy to the ratings."

Greg was asserting what no one else had had the heart to depress Chris further by saying: that although a trial would take many months to decide the issue, by deserting the broadcast for anchors who were now themselves in the potential war zone, the public was demonstrating its own conviction that the Defense secretary—now a heroic figure seen commanding his generals and consulting with foreign rulers—was in the right. Whatever the final judgement, she and FBS News may already have been mortally wounded.

The outside lawyer asked whether FBS's reporters and investigators had uncovered any additional evidence to refute the Defense Department's charges against Chris. Heads slowly shook.

"We might just have to face the fact that you were wrong about that base," he asserted to Chris, "and try to minimize the damage."

"More steadfast support!" she snapped.

"Part of my job is to protect the network—and you—from having to pay damages."

"How would we do that?" Howe asked.

"Try to show that Chris's reporting was an honest mistake and she hadn't purposely lied about the guy. Absent actual malice—you know, purposely lying—the press can say anything it wants about a public official."

"That's something to consider," Greg agreed.

"Fuck you!" Chris exploded. "Fuck you all!"

Chris and Greg's relationship had been strained to the tearing point by the new circumstances; they had borne too much raw emotion for too long. On edge, grown anxious, both were beginning to blame each other for some of their misfortunes—or at least were beginning to believe the other was casting that blame. Now the strain was also apparent to their colleagues, who fidgeted in embarrassment.

"Cool it," Greg told her.

"So you can save your ass and leave my reputation slime."

"Nobody's abandoning you," Greg retorted heatedly. "Stop thinking of yourself as some sort of scapegoat. We all made the decision together to run the story. We're all on the line. But we should at least protect ourselves legally, just in case."

"I don't think like that," she said, standing up.

She stepped away from her chair, turning back to the lawyer. "Do whatever you need to do to protect us. I appreciate it. But don't say that I made a mistake. I told the truth in that report. I did my job as a journalist. That should be enough." She glanced at Greg. "Enough for everyone."

He stood up, too.

Chris shook her head. "I need to get away from this for a while. I'm going home."

"I'll give you a lift," he called after her, and followed her out of the room. He wanted to forestall a rift; he could foresee her growing sullen and self-righteous in the mistaken belief that he was not totally supportive.

Greg provided most of the conversation in the back of the limousine heading uptown. Thinking his motive for accompanying her had been to induce her to spend the night with him, Chris allowed her irritation to show.

"By this time you ought to realize that we react to worry differently. I don't want to be around people. I just want to get away by myself and think."

"And when I'm worried?"

"You want me there just to be sure I'm there. It makes you feel safe."

"I want you with me because I love you."

"That, too," Chris allowed. More out of politeness than interest she asked, "What are you going to do tonight?"

Long experience had taught her that Greg grew restless and fidgety alone; he needed company. If he was not working late on an evening when she could not be with him, he would often seek out friends for dinner or attend a sporting event.

"I'll think of something," he grumbled.

His tone was so surly that Chris spun around. Then she remembered.

"Oh, Greg, I'm so sorry. I forgot. The new lineup premieres tonight. We were going to watch the shows together at your apartment."

"Look, if you're not in the mood or you're doing it to—"

"Of course, I want to be with you tonight." She hugged his arm and pressed her cheek to his.

He smiled at her and kissed her lightly. But there was no mistaking the chill loneliness that had surrounded him for an instant like sudden winter fog, penetrating down to his bones. No matter how old he became, it always waited to return, laughing at his delusions of hope.

26

~~~~~~~~~~~~~~~~~~~

The FBS network had expended tens of millions of dollars in commercial time to promote the new lineup, the "star time, good time" it would bring the viewer. Advertising was bought in *TV Guide,* as well as on the TV page of newspapers across the country. TV critics were asked to preview the shows in hopes of good reviews that would attract the public. Actors in the series were put on FBS talk shows and offered for interviews to virtually every reputable newspaper and magazine that might be interested.

Because of Labor Day, FBS had decided to wait until Wednesday of that week to start rolling out the new shows. Most shows on other networks figured still to be in repeats.

Having already seen its pilot shows, Greg anticipated that this first night of FBS's premiere period would be something of an anticlimax for him. The tension would peak the next morning, when the overnight Nielsens were examined to determine whether viewers had been drawn to the lineup. Next week would be even more crucial: Viewers would already have sampled or heard about FBS's shows. Did they like them enough to return? In effect the climax was a rolling one that would occur over a number of tense weeks and culminate in November, sweeps month and also the month that Greg's fate would be determined by the board.

Although she had provided an ear for Greg's and Marian's cheers and gripes during the period of development, tonight was the first time Chris had seen any of the pilots. Greg observed and grilled her as if she were all the Nielsen families wrapped into one.

Half a dozen phone calls linked Greg and Marian during the evening, some to convey sudden ideas, some to relay Chris's spontaneous reaction to a new show.

" 'My Kind of Place' is a little broad and silly for her, but she thinks some of it's funny."

"That's the first time she's seen 'A Funny Marriage,' she says. She's enjoying it."

Chris laughed with pleasure at "What's the World Coming To?"—a show she had seen before. But "Lowdown" often had her roaring and clapping her hands in delight.

"It isn't just because I'm in news and know some despicable characters like those, really it isn't. They are just so funny."

"She loves it, Marian," Greg cried out. "What does Derek think?"

Marian reminded him that the West Coast would broadcast the program later. She was still at her office and Derek still on one of the FBS sound stages shooting an episode of "Miss Grimsby." The two-hour movie that would kick off the series would be shown on Friday, starting at eight and replacing this week's showing of "Luba." Sally Foster's first show would air the following Friday.

"You really liked Derek's work in it, Greg?" Marian asked.

"Terrific. The early reaction we're getting on him is great. He's going to be a major star."

"Wonderful," she said quietly, and swiftly ended the conversation.

Having been notified that Derek's last shot was being set up, Marian hurried over to the sound stage to pick him up. They usually drove here and back together. Marian maintained that it gave them more time together. Actually, she worried about the nubile nymphs populating "Miss Grimsby" 's boarding school. Her only defense was eternal vigilance.

At ten o'clock FBS presented a new hour-long drama series that quickly propelled Chris to the kitchen for a snack. By the second half she was consciously forcing herself not to scan the magazines on the coffee table to escape the depression that wanted to sneak back to its accustomed seat on her chest. This was Greg's night; she wanted it to be splendid for him.

"She's bored with the show, and so am I," Greg groused to Marian when he reached her at home. "It never gets off the ground. We've got to be curing insomnia all over the Eastern seaboard at this moment. The lead—what's his name? . . . Right. Well, he's got all the appeal of a side of beef. No wonder he's always got his shirt off. His pecs do all the acting." He sighed, recalling the show's title. " 'High Impact.' Why did we ever think the story of a crime-solving aerobics instructor would make it? Did we really believe people at home would want to exercise along with him, especially at this hour?"

"It was the only series we had to counterprogram the competition with."

"The competition should pay us to put it on against them."

They discussed ways to improve the show in upcoming episodes.

Neither of them had much hope for resuscitation. Greg asked what they had in the pipeline with which to replace it.

" 'Daye and Knight.' Remember? Undercover white TV reporter and black cameraman using disguises to uncover big stories? They shot that five-minute segment for us with Chad Laidlaw and Biff Stanfield. It tested through the roof. I'd like to order six episodes."

"Who's producing?"

"The Rosenthals. You liked their movie of the week."

"I never asked: How did a black guy get a name like Biff?"

Marian began to laugh in recollection. "He tells people his mother was hoping for a blond, blue-eyed white boy . . . who could slam-dunk."

Greg was laughing, too. "Sounds a hell of a lot more promising than this. Order the six and be ready to pull this other thing fast."

"It will take me ten minutes to convince Biff I'm not kidding."

"Phone me in the office when you get up tomorrow. I'll have the overnights by then."

He hung up. Chris was perched on her knees beside him on the sofa. She held two open beer bottles and handed him one.

"Here's to you, Greg Lyall," she announced, holding her bottle aloft. "I think you really came through. A lot of fun in those half hours. Some quality. Except for 'High Impact,' a lot better Wednesday night than FBS has seen in a long time. Six more nights to go, but definitely a promising start."

Greg was touched. Chris parted with compliments sparingly, having been raised in a part of the country where compliments were rarely given to a child for fear of breeding conceit.

"How did it feel watching shows you picked?" she asked. "Was it anything like steering the world? That's what you once said you wanted to do."

"The truth?"

"Of course, the truth. This is me here."

A smile slowly widened across his face as he recalled the feeling. "It was incredible! I felt unbelievably powerful, as if a little push from my pinky could level a mountain. And somehow separated from other people, elevated. No wonder people get addicted to power. It's like a drug. I imagine you must feel like that sometimes on the air."

All of Chris's concentration was on Greg and what he meant to her. Remembering her own plight would dishearten her and break the mood. "You're my dearest addiction, Greg. You're the sweet poison I can never resist."

She leaned forward and kissed him. "You know that no one reaches me the way you do. No one makes me feel so alive. Are you ever sorry you gambled on our getting involved again?"

He shook his head. "I was dead for a decade—opulently embalmed, for sure—but dead. You brought me back to life. We're like two halves of a single engine. Put us together and we race at ten thousand RPMs."

She smiled seductively, putting her arms around his neck. "You're the piston. I'm the cylinder."

"Oh, yes."

Arms encircling her, he drew her toward him so she reclined across his lap. He began to unbutton her blouse, gazing down at her.

"Oh, yes."

The phone rang a few minutes after Greg arrived at his office early the next morning to peruse the overnights.

"I couldn't sleep," Marian said the instant Greg answered. "How'd we do?"

Greg started at the top. "They went for high-concept comedy at eight, just as you thought they would. 'My Kind of Place' drew a thirteen-point-three rating, a twenty-one share."

That meant more than 13 percent of all U.S. households possessing TV sets and 21 percent of all those with their sets actually on were tuned to FBS.

"Twenty-one is terrific for a new show! If we can keep it from getting so dumb the audience's brains freeze, maybe we can hook them."

"We slipped a little at eight-thirty, but not much. After the number of times we moved 'A Funny Marriage' this summer, it's probably a victory." He gave her the figures.

"Hooray! The producer will have a heart attack."

"That's about it," Greg joked.

Marian was too tense to notice the comic tone. "Uh-oh! You're trying to hide the rest of the night from me. 'World' and 'Lowdown' must have done terribly. How bad was it?"

Greg was chuckling at her mistaken despair. "We swamped everything on the air. By the time 'Lowdown' ended we were up to a thirty-six share."

Marian was screaming and babbling comments nonstop. She finally stopped to ask if ten o'clock was as bad as they had guessed last night it would be.

"Worse." Greg was no longer joking. "We opened with a thirty-one share on the strength of 'Lowdown' 's lead-in and dropped to a twenty-two by ten-thirty. By eleven we were at eighteen. Think about it: Over forty percent of the audience wouldn't stick around long enough to find out who done it."

"*We* done it, Greg. We won a lot more than we lost. We got off to the running start we were hoping for."

"By next week, we could be crying in our beer."

"By tomorrow night," she reminded him pessimistically. "We'll be up against NBC's Thursday-night lineup, starting with 'Cosby.' No chance. We're just trying for respectability. Even that's a stretch."

"That's what I love about this business. Being a genius lasts all of about a day."

As soon as she hung up, Marian raced back into the bedroom, flipping on the overhead light in passing, diving on top of Derek, and planting kisses all over his face. He struggled to wake up.

"A quake?" he mumbled. "Is it a quake?"

"My sweet baby, the whole world is shaking. So far, so good."

He sat up and looked at the clock. He would have to be up in a couple of minutes anyway.

"Do you want me to have Rosa make us something for dinner tonight?" she asked.

"I won't be eating home tonight. I'll be out late."

"You've got plans?"

"Last-minute thing. The girls on the show decided to throw Ginny Lansing a surprise birthday party tonight."

"No escorts?"

He shook his head as he started toward the bathroom. "All girls. Except for me."

Marian stiffened. "Why only you?"

"You're not going to believe this. They asked me to jump out of the cake."

"I believe it all right."

When Derek joined her in the kitchen a few minutes later, she casually remarked, "I'm glad you're getting along so well with everyone on the show. I get the feeling Ginny is a lot of fun."

"Jesus, she's wild. Just like she is on-screen."

Marian knew Derek hated when she was possessive, but she could not help herself. "I just remembered. I may have a business dinner tonight. I can drop you off at the party and pick you up afterward."

"I'll take my car."

Annette Valletta had never been more miserable in her life. Her illness, she had begun to admit, was terminal. Barely able to lift her hand to ring for the full-time nurse, she felt death taking more of her body away each day. Sally had replaced her as if she had never existed: on "Luba" and in Johnny's bed. On top of all her other calamities, Annette had caught a dreadful cold. Her nose dripped, and her head ached and was so stuffed up she felt the pillow was inside it, not behind it.

"I need an antihistamine!" she called out to the nurse.

"I think we ought to phone the doctor first," the nervous woman replied.

"So he can charge me another two hundred for a consultation? If I'm going to die, I intend to do it with a dry nose."

At that moment Annette sneezed. The effort so racked her body that the nurse rushed to her patient's medicine cabinet to find the bottle of antihistamines. Annette took a double dose.

The nurse suggested washing Annette and putting a little makeup on her. Annette shook her head and let it fall back onto the pillow. She was too far gone, she decided, to hang on to meaningless vanities. She waved the nurse from the room.

When life turns on you, it really turns, she observed. She had been blessed with stardom and a loving husband. Suddenly struck down by illness, she had seen them ripped away by a treacherous friend.

She lay there for a long while grieving over her obliterated fortunes and the betrayals visited on her. She did that every day, but today the nose cold had taken away her last ounce of combativeness. She no longer had the strength to fight back. She was done for, defeated, replaced in every way, a dry hulk of a woman waiting for death to claim the shell.

As time passed, she began to grow angry at the thought of how badly her kindheartedness had been abused. Finally, she grew so angry that she jumped out of bed and began stalking the room. She was halfway to the curtain-drawn windows before she realized that she was feeling better and stronger than she had in months. She stopped in midstride. She extended one foot. No problem at all. She extended the other. Okay. Then her arms. A little bit sore, but no more than she would feel after a long workout.

A miracle! God had sent her a miracle! She dropped to her knees in the center of the room, as she had done as a child with her devout Italian grandmother, who had rarely let an hour slip by with her chest uncrossed. Annette had prayed to St. Jude each night for intercession with God—both son and father, just to be sure—and to the Virgin Mother to save her. Her prayers had been answered.

"Thank you, God," she whispered in utter gratitude. "Both of you. Thank you, Holy Mother. Thank you all for returning my health and letting me live."

Contributions! She must make them, she decided. Danny Thomas's hospital would get a big one, of course. And the Church. Which church in particular? She had not been inside a church since leaving home—if you didn't count that church set in a film she had made a couple of years back. She would just have her accountant send the check directly to the Pope and let him figure it out. Annette peered up at the ceiling and wondered if that was enough to show her gratitude.

At that moment her rationality took over. What had been different this morning? she tried to deduce. Well, the nose cold. But the antihistamine had whisked away the symptoms, so it couldn't—

That was it! The antihistamine! She had taken an antihistamine. The pills would have suppressed any allergy she might have had. Highly allergic, she was susceptible to asthma from air-blown pollutants, was made miserable by trees and grasses in the spring, and had suffered from hives until she spotted lemon as the culprit and eliminated it from her diet. She knew all too well how dangerous and yet how relievable by medication were allergy symptoms.

But what could this possibly have been an allergy to? She tried to list all the substances to which she might have been exposed that could have caused an allergic reaction. Perhaps it was something she had skipped this morning, so there was less of it in her system than usual.

This particular morning she had eaten her usual breakfast. And unlike most days, she had not bathed or put on makeup and perfume.

The perfume!

She had started to wear a new perfume a couple of months ago. She thought back to the day she had bought it and then to when she had first opened its box and removed the stopper to put it on. She remembered perfectly. That had been the day she had first felt a little shaky.

She must be allergic to the perfume! She had put none on today, and the antihistamine had blotted out its reduced symptoms.

The door opened. Seeing her patient on her knees in the middle of the room, the nurse cried out for the maid's assistance and rushed forward.

"You shouldn't have tried to go to the bathroom on your own," the nurse admonished Annette worriedly, dropping down beside her.

A moment later the maid was also on her knees, on Annette's other side. Each grasped an elbow to lift the patient, who stared at the women in turn.

"The only one missing now is Billy Graham," Annette observed.

That's when she was sure she was all right.

By nightfall she was back in "Luba" and Sally was unemployed. Johnny convinced her he had hung around the production only to be sure nothing would stand in the way of her return to the show once she recovered. How wrong she had been about him, Annette decided. That bitch, Sally Foster!

* * *

388

By October no doubt remained that "Lowdown" was a runaway hit. But Stew Graushner could derive little pleasure from his success. He was so depressed that on his day off he could barely drag himself to Rodeo Drive to pursue his new hobby of shopping.

He became sick to his stomach when his lawyer phoned to let him know that Patty had just pulled off "the slickest maneuver" the lawyer had ever seen to advance the divorce case on the calendar. It would be coming up for trial in a matter of weeks.

"Some Wrath of God!" Stew groused sorrowfully to Susan. "He's more like a dishrag. Patty wipes the floor with him."

Stew grabbed for the computer keyboard and began to write an episode for "Lowdown" in which the naive professor is hunted by his ex-wife, a lawyer, whom he imagines to be a vampire trying to suck out his last drop of blood.

"It's the best script you've ever done," Susan later commented with delight.

Chris had become so obsessed with the investigation, so desperate to prove her innocence, that she sometimes seemed close to madness. That she was unable to report on the Middle East confrontation while the American public flocked to other networks' newscasts aggravated her agitation. She knew how near her mental edge she was skirting, but retreat seemed the greater madness, presenting the greater danger of a life much like death—without purpose because she would be barred from the profession that gave her life purpose, permanently dishonored because certified dishonorable by a court of law. She ceaselessly drove herself and the people working under her in the search for the means to break through the now vastly popular Defense secretary's seemingly impregnable fortifications. Days had stretched into weeks. Weeks into a month and then two. Even with a military crisis facing America and the world in the Middle East, she had not been on television since July.

Chris slept very little now and was often in Washington or Maine, pursuing leads that invariably wound nowhere. Yet, much of her time was diverted from the investigation by opposing lawyers, who spent days on end examining her before a court stenographer. She had to spend additional days preparing.

She and Greg spoke on the phone every day, but except for periodic conferences to assess the status of the investigation and the lawsuit, she avoided seeing him in person for long stretches because she knew that her obsession with the investigation made her dreadful company and that he was consumed by his own obsession: the upcoming board-of-directors meeting.

389

Greg worked from earliest morning to late at night now: with Marian to fine-tune the schedule, with his vice presidents to complete the corporate restructuring and make one last attempt to cut expenses, with the sales staff to monitor daily sales and to pep-talk and push the people to discover every penny of advertising income for the coming year, with the Finance v.p. on his own quarterly projections, with lawyers and investment bankers to fend off potential takeover interest, and with the company's directors to gain their support before the showdown.

Many at FBS who wrote him off as a courteous windup toy when he was first named CEO longed now for a return of some of that graciousness. Demanding in the extreme, he often gave orders with peremptory abrasiveness. He had no time for those who could not move as fast as he. Ted Woodruff had been fired the day after Ev Carver left. Two other people since then had been abruptly terminated when Greg surmised during meetings that they were incapable of carrying out his policies effectively. No one still considered Greg Lyall a lightweight. No one doubted that he was the boss.

The new season had opened better for FBS than it had in years. Although several new shows were languishing in the cellar, that was to be expected—the attrition among new shows was always high, especially when a network had few strong lead-in shows to haul new ones along. In general, though, and despite the other networks' premieres, FBS's ratings had been showing increasing strength in several key time slots as the weeks progressed.

Monday night had been strengthened by the ascent in the ratings in recent months of the revamped "Hot Time" and the unexpected success of "Play Pen," an ensemble comedy about a theater company composed of funny characters trying to succeed in a shabby playhouse in a small city.

The Wednesday night combination of "What's the World Coming To?" and "Lowdown" were flipped in the schedule and now gave promise of growing into a blockbuster hour that might someday dominate that night. "Luba" had come back strong on Friday nights. Annette had been using her small patches of free time in between the accelerated rehearsal and taping sessions to appear on network talk shows to discuss her near-fatal illness and gain sympathetic viewers for her series. Much of the audience watching "Luba" was staying on to catch "Miss Grimsby's School for Young Ladies." Problems still existed on that one, but with some tinkering, it was expected eventually to catch on. The drama at ten was proving weak. On Thursday "Castaways" was getting critical acclaim but no audience and might be moved to Friday at ten to follow "Miss Grimsby."

Except to Marian personally, Derek was definitely not one of "Miss Grimsby"'s problems. TV critics had lauded his work. Fan letters were arriving by the thousands every week. Magazines were fighting for interviews. *TV Guide* was rushing to put him on the cover of an issue. Discovering that he was living with Marian, important hosts and hostesses were inviting them out as a couple. To many events he was now the one invited, who brought her along.

For Derek this was all new and exciting. For Marian it was torturous. No matter how assiduously she tried to stick by his side, desirable women would swoop in at first sight of him. Why not? she thought. One look at her, and they knew she was no competition. When she finally forced herself to move away to forestall his annoyance, they flocked around him like caged animals at feeding time. Marian was desolate.

Coming up was the November sweeps-month effort to boost the ratings, with all sorts of special offerings added to the regular schedule. FBS's directors were also scheduled to meet during that month, when enough of the sweeps' ratings were in for next year's income to be fairly well estimated.

Because Barnett had never formally introduced a motion to terminate him and was rounding up the backing surreptitiously, Greg could discuss the matter openly with only a small number of directors he could be sure were on his side. In subtle ways, however, he could try to convince the others of the value of retaining him as head of the company at year-end, when his present contract expired.

Greg recognized that what he had been able to accomplish in the course of a year was only a start, but he felt it had been formidable enough to go a long way with the directors to offset both the scandals that had rocked the company and the force of Barnett Roderick's crusade to displace him.

In late October Chris's investigation suffered a grave setback. An Air Force officer she was convinced had knowledge of the clandestine missile base and was about to open up to her was suddenly transferred abroad. The only possible conclusion was that the Pentagon had gotten wind of their contact and taking no chances, had quickly acted to remove him. Chris had no viable leads left. She dragged herself home that night in a state of utter hopelessness.

As much as by her failure to gain the proof to acquit herself and condemn the Defense secretary, her determination was being drained by the personal abuse his actions had caused to be heaped on her. Her entire life, planned and worked at with such care, had slithered down into a sewer overnight. She had gone from being one of the most respected newspeople in America to a butt of Johnny Carson's monologues, this year's Tammy Faye Bakker.

She went into the kitchen. The maid had prepared supper, but she could not eat. She put the dinner into a plastic container and placed it in the freezer for another time.

She thought about reading, but unable to free herself from the morass of depression, ended up pacing the living room, brooding over her predicament.

"Chris, are you home?" Ken's voice called out.

Lost in coils of thought, Chris had failed to hear the front door open.

"I'm in the living room," she called back.

He appeared in the wide entranceway.

"We agreed," she said a little testily, "that you would phone first if you wanted to use the apartment."

"I couldn't phone. You'll understand why in a minute. I just managed to catch the shuttle as it was."

"If you're hungry," she relented, "there's some chicken. It's in the freezer. You can heat it in the microwave."

"Thanks." He remained in the entranceway. "You don't look good."

She chuckled grimly. Ken offered her an exuberant smile in exchange. She considered his pleasure at her misery inappropriate.

"I always thought," he said, "that the main reason you left me was you were getting a little bored because I wasn't the dynamic hero type, like your friend Greg."

"We've been over this ground a hundred times," she replied brusquely. She wanted to cut off the pleas and recriminations before they began to flow.

"No, but admit it, you did."

"Did you come all this way just to tell me that?"

"A lot more. A lot more." He was grinning. "I just want you to recognize your misconceptions about me."

Chris started to leave the room. Ken held up a hand, then put his finger to his lips in a secretive manner. He surveyed his surroundings for a moment. His eyes fell on the telephone, which he unplugged and placed in the foyer closet.

Returning to the living room, he drew two pieces of paper from his breast pocket. He handed her the first. Chris's initial thought was that he might have become unhinged. Now, she was annoyed.

"Just tell me what it says, Ken. I really don't have the energy right now to read one of your speeches."

Once again he put a cautionary finger to his lips.

"Read it to yourself," he whispered.

Chris exhaled a long-suffering sigh and shifted her gaze to the sheet of paper. An instant later her expression changed.

"My Lord!" she breathed.

In her hands was a photocopy of the original top-secret Defense Department memo that authorized the construction and manning of several U.S. nuclear-missile bases. It acknowledged their illegality and asserted the need to keep them absolutely unknown to the outside world.

Chris glanced at Ken in shock before taking the second paper from him, which was quite recent. It ordered, first, immediate demolition of the base in Maine in a manner that would make it appear no development had ever existed there; second, the incarceration of all of the base's military personnel who may have had contact with FBS; and third, "stonewalling" when inquiries were made about the matter. After pointing out that the incriminating photos of Chris leaked to the press had proven valuable in undermining her credibility, it went on to order wiretaps of the FBS Building and Chris's and Greg's residences, in the hope of coming upon more such derogatory material.

Both memos were restricted to the eyes of only a small handful of top people in the Pentagon and were signed by the secretary of Defense.

"I guess you can understand now," Ken whispered with a huge smile, "why I couldn't phone first."

She was smiling, too, eyes wide as blue morning glories, as she whispered back, "I guess you're pretty satisfied with yourself."

"The way I look at it, I just may have saved a few very exposed asses, mine included."

"Senator Ken, you may have done just that."

He turned on the stereo, tuning in a loud rock station to block reception on microphones that may have been hidden in the room.

"Okay, Miss Reporter, as one of my Western colleagues sometimes says, you and I have some horse-trading to do. What I'm offering are these documents and access to highly placed people who've been put in extreme jeopardy by giving them to me, so you can assure yourself they're accurate. What I want from you in exchange is your help as a newscaster in clearing my name while you clear yours. Fair enough?"

"I owe you my life."

The network's logo dissolved to the sleek graphics announcing "This Is FBS News Tonight," which cut to Chris's face in close-up speaking directly into the camera.

"Good evening, everyone. FBS News has learned that United States Senator Kenneth V. Chandler has obtained and will release to the public highly confidential Pentagon documents signed by Defense Secretary Phillip Grant that first ordered the secret construction of illegal nuclear-missile bases and then, in an elaborate cover-up, concealed the matter. Grant's earliest document ordered that three bases be constructed on American soil in admitted violation of this nation's treaty with the Soviet Union to dismantle and eliminate such bases. One was to be built at a site in Maine, as was first reported in July on 'This Is FBS News Tonight.' "

A taped report then rolled that showed some of FBS's previous footage in Maine and highlighted key passages of the initial memo. The graphic then displayed highlighted phrases of the second document and other appropriate shots under Chris's narration.

"In a second memo, which was issued only this last August, just after FBS's report was broadcast, Secretary Grant ordered the Maine base to be dismantled and the land made to look as if nothing had ever been built there. In addition he ordered that wiretaps be placed on this network's phones and on the home telephone lines of two of its employees, including this reporter. The memo admits as well that the secretary released compromising photos of this reporter in order to deflect attention from the truth of FBS's charges."

No doubt could remain of the secretary's total deceit.

In the next piece the Pentagon reporter described the disappearance of the Craig brothers, who were believed to have illegally been jailed and kept incommunicado in accordance with the secretary's directive.

The final piece in the sequence featured sound bites of various members of Congress to whom Ken had shown the documents. They all called for congressional hearings and several for a special prosecutor to determine whether criminal charges should be brought against the secretary. Some suggestion was made that the President himself might even be subpoenaed for questioning, although all indications so far were that the secretary had acted totally on his own.

Greg had alerted the company's directors to watch the broadcast. Videocassettes and transcripts, with a covering letter from Greg, would go out by air express to all of them within the hour. He would have phoned them himself were he not concerned about Chris. Instead of jubilation, what he saw on her face was the stunned relief of someone who had just been saved from certain death. She looked battered and exhausted.

He wrapped an arm about her and led her from the newsroom and out of the building. He took her back to his apartment.

She did most of the talking as they sat in his dining room, barely eating. Despite her exoneration, she still seemed enmeshed in the tangles of Grant's net, picking at the knots. She reminded Greg of someone in deep grief who continually reexamines every detail of a morbid event in order to free herself from it.

Remorse, too, would not leave her. Although her report would aid her husband's standing with voters, she could not unburden herself of the guilt she felt at his being implicated at all. A good man who loved her, he had not deserved to be dragged through public disgrace for her infidelity. Would his newly heroic image be enough to restore his credibility less than a week before the election?

A vote to be held two days after that one had her concerned about her own survival. "Greg, if you lose at the directors meeting, Barnett will try to force me off the air again, won't he?"

"He'll try, but you have a contract."

"He'll make it difficult for me, though. You once said he might pay me and keep me off the air anyway."

"A lot will depend on whether your ratings bounce back."

"People will remember those photos."

"People are basically fair. They'll give you a chance. You were responsible for breaking the biggest story in years. It's still unwinding. And election-night coverage is coming up next week. That'll help, too."

She smiled wanly. "I can't even take a vacation, can I? Now's when I have to get out and hustle to win back viewers."

"Yes."

"It won't be the same, though. The audience used to love me. I could almost feel it looking at them through the TV camera. Now they know in their heads that I'm honest, but in their hearts they'll always think of me as a slut."

She lost herself in thought for a moment before speaking again. "I wonder if work will ever be fun again, if I'll ever feel . . ."

"What?"

"I guess, just innocent and worthwhile; you know, so that viewers will believe me when I condemn other people's actions."

"Sure you will."

Greg started to get up from the table.

She stopped him. "Your mind's somewhere else now."

He nodded.

"The directors meeting?"

He nodded again.

"Everyone says you've begun to turn the network around. The directors have to be grateful for what you've done."

"I keep telling myself that, but I just don't think it will be enough. Barnett appointed them. He's a giant to them. When the chips are down, most of them will side with him."

"You can't give up without a fight."

"I won't. I'll struggle for every last vote till the very last second. I tell myself that I'm still in it, that I've got a chance to win out over Barnett. But down deep I really don't believe the votes will be there for me."

Normally stoic, Greg allowed his sadness to show on his face. "I'm going to miss that job, Chris. Millions of people watching entertainment I helped create or getting news I believe they should know. Like tonight. You were bringing them the story, but I was somewhere in the background, the general who planned the campaign that won the war. Next to the President, I've got the most powerful job in America. Even better than I dreamed it would be. But soon I'm going to lose it. That's all I can think about right now."

"Those photos!" she exclaimed. "Those damned photos destroyed so much. Even after I left Ken, I still felt carefree and young. I don't anymore." Her mouth pinched. "When you and I make love, I see all the people out there in the dark who used to admire me staring at us, just like we were in those photos."

The TV sound was off, but the screen was vivid with news footage smuggled out of Kuwait. Soldiers were moving down a sunny street, rifles in hand. Civilians were scrambling to take cover. Greg stared at the screen.

"When I was a kid," he said reflectively, "what I loved best on TV were the game shows and the sitcoms. The problems were small embarrassments, the resolutions fast and sweet. When the half hour was up, all the problems had been solved. Remember?"

"And real life isn't like that. Is that what you're saying?"

"Real life is messy and incomplete. It never turns out as you hoped it would." He shrugged in resignation. "You always lose what you love, like the job."

"Or what you loved about it. Everything seems to come with a price you have to pay in the end."

He nodded sadly. "There's always a struggle, and no matter the outcome—even with the best outcome—you're always left with regret."

Seeing Christine Paskins on his TV set that night for the first time in months, Jonathan Dearey rushed uptown in the van with P.J. Jonathan had winnowed his disciples down to the toughest and most fanatically loyal. Furious at having received little media coverage for his antiabortion demonstrations, he had determined to kidnap Christine Paskins, an act that no news organization could ignore. Everyone would then have to listen to God's message. He would become this century's John Brown, and New York would be his Harpers Ferry. His righteousness would wake America from its moral slumber, even if God willed that he and his followers must die in the process.

They had parked in front of the FBS Building, waiting for her to emerge. But when she did, the street was full of other people, a man was with her whom they could not see well in the dark from their angle and a large chauffeur opened a limousine door for them.

Jonathan and P.J. stayed in the van and trailed them. The limousine entered the entrance to a garage under an East Side residential building. Less than a minute later, the limousine emerged without its passengers and drove off. Jonathan figured that she would leave the building alone later that night and try to find a taxi. But as the hour grew later, it gradually came to him that she had no intention of leaving, that the man she was with was probably Greg Lyall.

"Damned whore!" he cursed.

"Should we wait?" P.J. asked.

At that moment Jonathan recognized the drawbacks to his original plan. Kidnapping Christine Paskins might prove no more effective in alerting America to God's message than bombing abortion clinics might be.

In the distance he could see midtown's office towers lit like Christmas candy canes. Among them was FBS's. Suddenly, he was overcome by an awesome idea. But he knew he would have to plan it out with absolute precision if it was to succeed.

"Let's go," he growled.

P.J.'s head swung around at the sharpness of the tone. His prophet was peering into the night, burning holes through it to God.

27

O n a Friday afternoon in the beginning of November, Ev
Carver sat alone in his cavernous office at the hub of
corridors through which scurried employees hired for his
Evcar Communications. Laid out for his inspection under a single light
bulb were several weeks' ratings, including last night's overnights. This
was the first of the four sweeps weeks. He was evaluating not merely
the raw figures, but the underlying trends.

To his trained eye, the trends were clear. If you discounted the
two-night miniseries a rival network threw on to hypo its ratings this
week, you could discern a strengthening all along FBS's schedule. He
would not have given ten cents for the lineup's chances before the
season started, but no genius was needed to see that many of the shows
were finding audiences. Annette Valletta's recovery from illness had
drawn sympathy and viewers, lifting "I Love Luba" into third in the
overall ratings. The new show "Lowdown" was eleventh, just behind
what he still thought of as that weird sci-fi comedy that followed it in the
schedule. But just as significantly, in several other time slots in which
FBS had run a poor last the previous year, the network was now a solid
second. Because the spring upfront buying by advertisers left a lot of
scatter-sale spots available, those avails—and the holdbacks to cover
possible ratings' guarantees—could be sold at higher rates.

The most glaring exception to the network's upward direction was its
nightly news broadcast. Chris Paskins's rating since coming back on the
air had not resumed its prior level. The bloom was off the rose, Ev
deduced. She was no longer the nation's sweetheart—the girl next door
had been caught in a vice scandal. Offended, the viewers were reproachful.

Evcar's financial people had projected out the network's numbers for
next year. The red ink would turn to black. Not vast profits yet, but

certainly respectable and indicating an upturn and better years ahead. A few months from now, after the financial community became alerted to what was happening, the stock's price would certainly climb sharply.

Armed with his figures, Ev took the elevator up one flight to Basil Markham's office. Markham had proven to be an excellent partner, a bit cautious perhaps, but that was understandable—the man had provided the $100 million with which Evcar had quietly been purchasing FBS stock in recent weeks. Buying had stopped just before the point at which the law would have required Evcar to disclose the size of its stake.

"I agree," Markham said when Ev finished analyzing the latest ratings for him. "The value is there and building."

"I think we ought to make a bid for the company in the next few days. But we should do it privately and get the directors to back our offer."

Markham's bushy, graying eyebrows lifted. Born of middle-class English parents, his boarding-school education had formed a patina of upper-class manners over his hungers.

"One of the directors is a friend," Ev explained. "He's always felt I could do better than present management to maximize earnings."

Markham's expression remained impassive. He took it for granted that the director in question would expect some sort of favor after the takeover. "But I gather he isn't your only ally."

Ev smiled in a way that reminded Markham of a lizard about to flick its tongue at a fly.

"Greg Lyall," Ev said, and leaned forward.

"Maybe I'm wrong, but I had the distinct impression that you and this Lyall chap didn't get along well."

Ev's features fleetingly disclosed a hatred so ardent that Markham perceived it might well have been a form of love. "But we understand each other. I can read Lyall's mind like a brain surgeon who's got the top of his skull off. He's got to be very worried right now. He dumped Roderick's daughter and made a spectacle of himself with the anchorwoman. The old man is raving mad. He wants Lyall fired and is moving heaven and earth to do it."

"Does he have the votes?"

"Probably. So Lyall has a right to be worried. I doubt if he has two pennies of his own to pinch together. Everything depends on his contract getting renewed at the end of this year."

"But you don't think that seems likely."

"He's produced good figures, no doubt about that. But Roderick is a god in that company. What I propose is that I make our buy-out offer Monday morning directly to Lyall. I lay out the offer and promise him a sweet severance package, a million outright and five years of salary, if he takes our side with the directors. Four million dollars. That gives Lyall a soft cushion when he's fired—and us an ally at the top for our offer."

"And if he turns you down?"

"He still has to bring the offer to the directors, where we'll have support. But if they don't buy our deal, we play hardball and go directly to the stockholders."

"How much a share do you want to offer?"

"Thirty-five dollars. It's selling at twenty-seven and change right now on the stock exchange."

"The company's worth?"

"Fifty now. Maybe sixty in a year."

"Is all the financing in place?"

"The last of the banks came aboard this morning," Ev confirmed.

"Get hold of Lyall and make the offer."

Mickey Blinder was walking on air these days. "Lowdown" looked like the year's big winner, worth hundreds of millions to Monumental.

"Of all the shows to make it!" he said to himself with a disbelief he could still not quite shake.

"Mr. Small wants to see you as soon as you come in," his secretary told him as he strolled into his office.

She handed him the message. Mickey lifted it in a carefree salute and reversed direction.

Tiny Small was the big guy, the CEO, the force at Monumental. Until lately Mickey had dreaded this summons; now he was delighted. He had sent "Lowdown" 's sunny projections and all the backup material to Tiny's office yesterday. Now, he was being summoned to be praised, rewarded, and stroked. There would be just a thin edge of fear in the big guy's voice, the fear that Mickey might not be happy enough with the largesse showered over him to stay at Monumental.

Mickey ignored the elevator and took the stairs to the next floor two at a time. Only slightly out of breath, he entered the CEO's office.

Less than five feet tall, Richard Small had chosen to be called Tiny, rather than Dick Small, his acquaintances assumed for obvious reasons. In all other respects, he reveled in his difference from other men and considered himself blessed by his conspicuous smallness.

"All a man needs in life is to be noticed," he often squealed in his forceful mezzo-soprano. "Once he's noticed, it's up to him to show what he can do. I sure showed 'em."

"You sure did," several vice presidents in earshot would usually manage to chime in unison.

None were in Tiny's office as Mickey entered. The CEO was sitting high atop his elevated desk chair perusing some papers.

"That my report on 'Lowdown'?" Mickey asked ebulliently.

Tiny nodded.

"Like what you see?"

"Over the next ten years, between this and 'Luba,' our TV syndication is a gold mine—we're talking hundreds of millions of dollars." Tiny grinned at Mickey with satisfaction. "The board is insisting I take an extra half-million-dollar bonus this year and another block of stock options because of how well it worked out with Annette and of course, with 'Lowdown' doing so well."

"That's really great, Tiny." Mickey immediately doubled in his mind the figures that Monumental would bestow on him.

"I wish you could hear for yourself how happy the directors are with the show, Mickey, but you won't be with us that long."

"I won't."

"No, you're fired."

Mickey's knees buckled. He grabbed the arm of a nearby chair to keep from collapsing.

"Fired?"

"As of this moment," Tiny said, pitching his voice all the way down to alto to show his concern. "Actually, I signed the memo half an hour ago."

"Why?" Mickey whimpered. "We have the most successful new show in years."

Tiny stood up, which actually lowered his height somewhat, and scampered around the desk to emphasize just how compassionate he felt about Mickey's plight.

"You don't know how this hurts, Mickey. You *can't* possibly know."

"Trust me, I know. But just tell me, why?"

"Well, it was the success of that new show which forced my hand. If you hadn't had a good year, I still intended to give you another year to prove yourself. But how can I ignore the man who's really responsible for the most successful new show in television?"

"The man responsible?" Mickey was floored. Who the hell was he talking about? That dizzy Stew Graushner? "Look, you don't know him like I do."

"Don't know him? I've known him fifteen years. Everybody in the business knows him. He's an outstanding talent. Frankly, I was wondering how you came up with a show as imaginative as 'Lowdown.' It's so different from your usual predictable style. But then, last night at home, when I was reading all the financial material on the show and came across his name, I knew in a flash who was really the creative force behind the show."

"You can't be serious."

"Raoul Clampton, of course."

"Raoul Clampton!"

"Frankly, I couldn't understand why he gave up his job as head of programming for FBS, but last night, when I discovered he was executive producer of 'Lowdown,' I understood."

"Executive producer? Look, that was all—"

"You have to admire a guy who believes so much in a show that he'd give up a network job to make sure it succeeds. I checked with our payroll people, and sure enough, we've been paying the guy a bundle to be executive producer on the show."

Mickey started to protest, to explain that Tiny misunderstood. Paying Raoul Clampton as executive producer on "Lowdown" was just a way to cover up a little under-the-table deal the two had been caught at. But then he recognized that anything he said would reveal his own complicity in a scheme that could have landed them both in jail. Tiny was always happy to see the loot roll in if one of Mickey's shady schemes paid off for the studio, but he never wanted to know the details. Mickey could not reveal anything.

Tiny was striding back and forth in front of Mickey now, his hand waving grandly. Ankle deep in the plush carpet, he appeared to be trekking through a bog.

"When I realized that we had a genius like Raoul Clampton in-house, the man whose vision has already revolutionized television comedy in the nineties, I jumped immediately. No grass grows under these little feet, you know. I went right up to his office myself."

"All the way up to the top of sound stage A?" Mickey inquired weakly.

"The very top. Once I got up there, I could instantly tell the man was a genius. No phones."

The guy had no one to call, Mickey grumbled inwardly.

"No flunkies running in and out to disturb him," Tiny continued.

People barely knew he was alive up there, Mickey wanted to scream.

Tiny jabbed at his temple. "Just pure thought."

Mickey could conceal his scorn no longer. "They call him the Phantom of the Upper A."

"Perfect name for him. A kind of sublime wizard who can see farther than other men. And *we* have him."

Tiny reached up and pumped Mickey's hand good-bye. "Don't worry, you'll get the usual two weeks, and oh, this year it will be a Christmas *chicken*—the new cost-cutting program, you know. Be careful not to slam the door on your way out."

The rest of the morning the executive suite of the Television Division of Monumental Production Corp. busied itself with Mickey's departure and then Raoul's arrival and then the latter's long consultation with the interior decorators, who promised to have his office completely redone by Monday. By then lunchtime had rolled around, and Raoul left for the studio commissary on another part of the lot.

As he stepped out of the office building, he ran right into Sally Foster. Effusively apologetic, he helped her up from the sidewalk. Actually, Sally had been waiting there quite a while in the hope that Raoul Clampton would run into her.

"Raoul, how terrific to see you! I've been meaning to call you. What a raw deal those bastards at FBS gave you. I've always admired you so. How are things going?"

"As a matter of fact, things are going pretty well," he admitted. "I've just replaced Mickey Blinder."

"No! What a spectacular surprise! You don't know how happy I am for you."

Actually, Sally had heard the news through a girlfriend whose decorator had confided that he had to cancel an appointment with her that morning because of an emergency meeting at Monumental to redecorate Mickey Blinder's office for Raoul Clampton. Sally knew she did not have a second to lose.

She immediately jumped into her car—doubly good timing, as it turned out, because the loan-company collector was just pulling up to repossess it. After a ninety-mile-an-hour chase on the freeway, she managed to lose the repo man with a fast turn onto an off-ramp and arrived outside of Raoul's office building in plenty of time to run into him—by purest chance—when he went out for lunch.

"Raoul," she cooed, taking his arm and making sure that her breast nuzzled up against it, "I've missed you so, all those good times. Why don't we do something wild and crazy tonight to celebrate your new job, just you and I?"

"You said it was important that we meet right away," Greg began as he slipped into the dimly lit banquette across from Ev.

Ev had chosen the bar and the table with care. No one was likely to see them. Even if someone did, the thought would probably be that two former colleagues were catching up with each other.

Ev pulled an envelope from his inside jacket pocket and handed it to Greg. Inside was a letter to him as FBS's chief executive officer and to the directors offering to buy all of the company's stock for thirty-five dollars a share. The letter expressed the hope that the directors would recommend to FBS stockholders that they accept the offer. Although unsurprised by the letter's contents, Greg found himself enraged by the grab for the company, *his* company. He fought to maintain an unreadable expression.

"We bid so high because we want this to be a friendly transaction," Ev said in a lowered volume that made his words sound more ominous. "It's a great price."

"If the directors turn you down, I suppose you'll make a public offer and launch a hostile takeover fight."

"The lawyers tell me I can't say that."

"But that's what you'll do."

Ev smiled, his voice a soft hiss now. "We're holding all the cards, Greg. Believe it. Our financing's locked up. A lot of stockholders thought they'd be stuck with the lousy stock forever. They'll beg us to buy it at the price we're offering. We're ready to fight as dirty as you want to get."

"It would be a mistake, Ev."

"Exactly what I've been thinking. You don't want to lose the company back to the old man and be left with nothing for your troubles. You've done a good job, but that won't mean shit in a few days. Roderick has the votes to bounce you. I'm willing to make your leaving worthwhile."

Greg struggled not to lash back and to keep uppermost in his mind that winning the war was more important than winning a skirmish. He kept to himself that the mistake was Ev's and not his own.

"A golden handshake?"

"If you back our offer, you'll get a very pretty severance package." Ev outlined it. Noticing the frown on Greg's face, he added, "But I'm so eager to make this an amicable experience for all concerned—and we're such old friends—that I'm willing to raise the initial million to two. With your salary that's five million dollars over five years."

"Lot of money. Used to be only thirty pieces of silver."

Ev's eyes narrowed. His mouth curled insolently. "Don't get dramatic on me, Lyall. Either way you're out. This isn't my contribution to the needy. I'm buying you."

Greg used to think that Ev Carver merely wore his ambition more prominently than other men. Now, though, sensing the terrible passion that fueled Ev's ruthlessness, he understood that Ev Carver was truly an evil man. An aggressive, immoral urgency propelled his every action: the accumulation and exercise of power for the pure pleasure of dominating others. He was evil because his rapacity was limitless, respecting no boundaries, no point of satiation. Many years before, Ev had told him that they were alike. In Ev's black, glittering eyes, Greg saw his own lust reflected, and the resemblance disturbed him.

"I'll think about it," Greg said. His anger at Ev's attempt to usurp his domain aside, the offer was advantageous in several ways. It might afford him the means to hold off Barnett, at least temporarily, while the directors studied it or maybe even to stay on during the battle if they decided to oppose it. And if he lost out to Barnett—or to Ev—the severance package would let him walk safely away and start over somewhere else.

Greg rose from the table. "I'm required by law to submit the offer to the directors. You know that. In the meantime I'll think about how I want to handle it."

"Don't do anything dumb, Lyall. I told you, I'm holding all the cards."

Are you really? Greg conjectured as he walked away. I have you by the balls, only you won't know it until I squeeze. I can send your offer down in flames by firing a single bullet. But do I want to? Will that help me? What do I want to do?

Greg worked late on Monday night. He had spent the day signing off on as many decisions as possible that would lock FBS into future policies; he wanted to make it difficult for Barnett—or Ev, regardless of what he decided about Ev's offer—to undo his changes and erase his vision. Firm orders were given for several midseason shows and for pilots for next year. Contracts he had pressed the lawyers to conclude were signed for foreign deals and for arrangements with cable networks and systems. All the while, a contrary impulse counseled him that, instead, he should be arranging to pull down the temple around him in revenge, like Samson, if he was disposed of.

Greg's second major task that day was alerting the directors by phone to Ev's offer to buy all the FBS stock, which also gave Greg an opportunity to intimate that now was not the time to rock the corporate boat with a change at the helm. The directors meeting would take place in three days.

FBS's investment bankers were also working late, evaluating Ev's offer in order to apprise the directors of their opinion as to whether it was adequate and thus, should be accepted. Their instinct was always to turn down any offer and then seek large fees to repel the resulting takeover effort or alternatively, to find a more acceptable buyer, a so-called white knight, again earning large fees. They now sought a sense of which way Greg was leaning on the offer. Investment bankers were known to have very flexible consciences about valuation.

"Let's wait and see how things look by the time of the meeting," Greg told them. He thought of the private offer Ev had made to him.

Perhaps by then, his own conscience would be flexible enough to side with Ev.

He would not be seeing Chris tonight. She needed a long night's sleep. Tomorrow night she would do the news as usual and then would anchor the election coverage into the early-morning hours. This would be her first turn at the job, and a lot of eyes would be on her. The stamina of anchors at live events had become an important attribute after Walter Cronkite was lauded for his endurance; anchors who followed had to live up to that standard. Questions about a woman's innate biological vigor, purportedly laid to rest almost a year ago, were suddenly resurrected.

By the time he had made his last call to a director in a later time zone and then rose to stretch and put on his jacket to go home, Greg was no more optimistic than before about his candidacy. Barnett's supporters remained loyal, none wavering. In many of their voices he could detect an undertone sometimes of reproach, sometimes of outrage for the disgrace he had brought upon the company. Many had known Diane since she was a child and, Greg sensed, felt called upon to exact retribution for the wrong done to her.

Let our keen-eyed network news analysts forecast that particular election, Greg muttered to himself as he moved toward the door.

He suddenly halted and turned around, announcing aloud to the empty room, "With less than one percent of the vote counted, FBS News declares Barnett Roderick the winner of the CEO race. Yes, folks, the old gray fox came out of retirement to win back his seat and fling the feeble, scandal-smeared incumbent, Gregory Lyall, out on his ass."

He tried to memorize the desk, its chair, the sofa and club chairs, the credenza with the TV screens, even the progression of portrait photos on the wall.

"I loved it too much," he confessed.

Then he turned out the light and left.

In the lobby he signed out at the security desk and said good-bye to the guards. Mac MacNamara was usually on during the day, but in the holiday season, he was glad to work double shifts for the overtime pay. A new guard was on duty with him. In all the years he had gone in and out of this building, Greg still had not learned Mac's first name. Superstitiously, he decided that the man's loyal presence before the revolving doors might be a kind of good-luck charm for him. Only if by some incredible fluke he won the vote, Greg promised himself, would he inquire about the man's first name.

He buttoned his coat and turned up his collar against the cold as he stepped onto the pavement. He had long since sent his driver home. He looked for an empty cab. None came along the almost deserted canyon walled with office buildings. After a while he began to walk uptown.

The dinner had been arranged on short notice, slipped in before their scheduled departure on a late flight to New York. Marian picked up Derek at the sound stage, and they drove to The Palm. His final scene of the day had been a complicated bit of farce, and he was still unwinding, so he was glad not to talk much. Marian, too, was quiet, thinking ahead. Raoul Clampton would be bringing Sally Foster. One look at Derek, and Sally would go after him like a leopard after a lamb.

Tiny Small would be bringing his current wife, his fourth. As his career advanced, the wives he chose got bigger and younger. This one was well over six feet, as buxom and airbrushed as a centerfold, and fussed adoringly over him as she might have over a Chihuahua.

"Why this dinner?" Derek asked Marian as they approached the restaurant. The last few months had taught him that not even the most casual-seeming appointment or conversation among those at the apex of the entertainment industry was purely social; the ultimate purpose was always to make a deal.

"Raoul fired me from FBS. Then Greg fired him and gave me his job. Raoul was making private deals for himself, lying—stealing from FBS in effect. The works. It was nasty."

"Then why are we having dinner with them?"

"They claim it's to celebrate the success of 'Lowdown.' "

"But it's not."

"Derek," she patiently explained, "there are only a few major networks. Unless they have access to me, Monumental's new projects are closed out at one of them. They need a peace powwow."

"But how can you even deal with a man like that?"

Marian heard echoes of her own ingenuousness a scant year ago. Again, she answered patiently. "Monumental is a big supplier. We don't want to be cut off from their projects."

"I also thought Sally Foster hated you for dropping her from 'Luba' and some other show."

Marian nodded glumly.

Derek groaned. "A fun evening."

At the restaurant Marian and Sally fell into each other's arms like long-lost sisters. After complimenting him on his performance in his series, the men paid little attention to Derek; they seemed hardly aware of his presence. Marian kept a wary eye on Sally, but the actress was almost primly demure.

Derek picked at his oversize steak, chatted sporadically with Tiny's wife, and listened to the others converse. The men fawned over

Marian. They enthused over her observations. When she made a humorous remark, Tiny nearly fell off the phone book in laughter. Derek hated every moment of the meal and by the end, was abysmally glum.

As they all shook hands at the door, Raoul said he was sending Marian an important project that Sally would star in. Sally beamed modestly. Marian replied that she was just delighted. And Derek felt Tiny's wife slip her phone number into his pocket.

28

~~~~~~~~~~~~

Marian was miserable throughout the United Airlines flight. This was the first time Derek had joined her on one of her frequent trips to New York. His shooting schedule had been arranged to give him two days off for publicity appearances, among them a party FBS was giving tonight in connection with its election-night broadcast.

She tried to engage him in conversation, but he barely looked at her. Finally, she went to sleep. She awoke during the night to discover that Derek's seat was empty. She spotted him at the front of their first-class cabin in a laughing discussion with two women flight attendants, who appeared enthralled. She could not sleep after that and continued to observe him under lowered eyelids.

Marian and Derek had just time enough to wash up and change in their suite at the Plaza before going down to the lobby for a breakfast meeting with Greg and a European distributor eager to make a long-term coproduction deal for the network's self-produced projects. The men were enthusiastic over Marian's plans for next season. They talked with her about subsidies, quotas, and fees, about scripts and casting. Derek ate quickly and excused himself, claiming to need to return to the suite for several interviews FBS had set up for him. Actually, they were not for an hour, but he could not bear sitting there beside her for another minute.

"Do you have the list of stores I gave you?" Marian asked him. She thought he might like to go shopping this morning after the interviews.

She privately worried that, instead, he would be spending his free time learning personally from his new friends at United the aptness of the airline's name.

* * *

Strangely, Marian and Chris realized, despite the long months Marian had pined for Derek at UCLA and the recent months of living together, Chris had never met him. Lunch for the three of them was arranged for one o'clock at Chris's table at Symphony Cafe. Derek arrived on time, carrying several packages from men's stores. Marian's relief was transitory. He seemed entranced by Chris and kept asking questions about Greg Lyall.

When Derek excused himself to use the men's room, Chris commented to her friend, "He's as beautiful as you always said he was."

Marian fought back her tears. "I'm going to lose him, Chris. Women kill for him. The second I turn away, he's with one of them. He's getting impatient to leave me."

"You don't know that for sure."

"I try everything I can think of to hold on to him. But my desperation probably makes him more eager to leave. Now that he no longer needs me, it's only a matter of time."

Chris sometimes felt that, like Marian, she loved too possessively, too fearfully. Often, when the strains on them grew excessive, she felt like screaming out to Greg that she did not want to be selfless and forbearing and understanding, that she wanted them to get their divorces and marry each other that very minute, so she wouldn't risk losing him. But she was afraid that might prove as self-destructive as what Marian was doing.

The women noticed Derek making his way back to the table.

Marian quietly asked, "Why would someone who looks like him stay with someone who looks like me?"

"Maybe because he loves you."

"Ha!"

"We've identified key precincts in each state and placed polltakers there to interview voters as soon they leave the polls. We're able to project those samples into accurate voter counts. Now we even factor in possible bias by, say, whites who claim they voted for a black but didn't."

With a few minutes to go before the broadcast commenced at nine, Sam Mathias was providing Greg's nearly two hundred guests, squeezed into the open side of the large studio serving as the election-coverage center, with a behind-the-scenes look at the network's election coverage. That and a handful of FBS stars were the attraction to draw the press, advertisers, bankers, and some of the company's directors. Also present were some members of the affiliate board. They had met earlier in the day, but were staying on for this party Greg hoped would generate favorable news stories and goodwill for the new prime-time lineup and for the continuing rehabilitation of Chris's reputation.

An ex-college lineman nearing fifty and tending to paunch, Sam Mathias had been in charge of Special Projects at FBS since before Greg's appointment as CEO and had held down most of the other top news jobs at FBS. Anytime FBS News undertook coverage of an event outside the normal time slot for the nightly news, Special Projects and Sam were in charge.

"But why do you ruin the fun for everyone?" asked Gail Dawson, the actress starring in "A Funny Marriage." "I get into a comfortable nightgown, make some popcorn, settle down in front of the TV for a suspenseful night, and you guys have already told us who won."

"Well, for one thing, in presidential election years, we hold off until after the polls have closed in the continental U.S. For another—"

Chris was just walking by to take her place at the newly constructed anchor desk, a winged object in light gray trimmed in red and blue. She wore a bright red suit, hoping that the arresting color would help to grab and hold viewers zapping their way around the dial.

Greg interrupted. "Sam, since Chris is the one directly responsible for ruining Gail's evening of popcorn and suspense, why don't we ask her why networks race to be first to predict the winner, which I think is what she's really asking."

Chris directed her answer to the entire group. "Because all of you want it. Next day, the press always writes about which network won the 'race' to name the winner. But that's all in the past. Beginning tonight, all the news networks are chipping in to share the same organization for voter projections."

A gadfly reporter who covered broadcasting for a large metropolitan newspaper spoke up. He had his notepad out. "How do you feel reporting on election results that concern your estranged husband?"

"I'll try to do a professional job, but leave analysis of his race to someone else."

"But you've got to be conflicted. Your affair with Mr. Lyall here may be the reason he loses."

Chris's anger flared. "If anybody was responsible for the bad publicity that rubbed off on Ken, it was the secretary of Defense. Have you asked how *he* feels?"

"Let's be realistic. Doesn't the public have a right to know about the private behavior of someone who broadcasts into their living room, especially if she's a candidate's wife?"

"Are *you* having an affair?" Chris shot back.

"What kind of a—"

411

"You're a newsperson for a major newspaper. Don't the people have a right to know about you?"

The reporter struggled to formulate an answer. She had waited weeks to embarrass a hypocritical questioner with an interrogation of her own.

"Are we supposed to take your silence to mean that you're concealing an illicit love affair?" she pressed him. "How will that affect your performance?"

"Which performance?" Marian quipped.

Everyone laughed. Marian had defused the awkward moment. Whatever the outcome of the directors meeting, Greg assured himself, he would never regret having chosen her to head Programming.

Next, Alan Howe informed the group about the operation of the tabulation board and at the side window of the control room, how the director and his assistants would orchestrate the procession of various elements into the program that went out over the air.

Every studio contained its own control room, although picture and sound could be operated from any other control room in the building. An engineer in the Master Control Room, where the commercials were added, then directed the signal by internal wires and telephone lines to an "uplink" dish that beamed it to a satellite for distribution to the affiliates. Master Control sent a separate feed of the signal to the World Trade Center antenna for broadcast to the New York City metropolitan area.

As nine o'clock loomed, the guests retreated to the open end of the studio to watch the broadcast for a while.

The night shift at FBS was usually a slow time for Security—mostly news staffs and technicians going in and out. Tonight, election night, would be a little busier than usual. Mac MacNamara was still tutoring a new man, Bobby Williams, on the details of the job. Bobby was a young, light-skinned black, thin and open-faced, who had taken the job while studying criminal justice at college during the day. He hoped to be a policeman after graduation. Mac had spent three nights training a previous guard, and the guy had quit at the end of last night's shift, deciding he hated New York's cold weather this time of year and was returning to Florida.

Mac explained that every half hour they had to phone downstairs to Security Central, where a supervisor monitored closed-circuit TV screens, including one that displayed the lobby. In an emergency they needed only to push the button under the desk to signal Security Central directly.

A man of steadfast loyalties, after his family and the church, Mac MacNamara placed FBS and its people at the apex of his priorities. As a result, today, for the first time in his life, the ruddy-complexioned Irish-American had voted Republican, for Chris Paskins's husband. She worked at FBS, and he liked her; sunny and smiling, she often stopped for a word or two when passing the desk on the way in or out. Compared to those factors, her public disfavor and marital estrangement were irrelevant to him.

Most offices and many public areas in the building contained a television monitor. The lobby had a large one set on a pedestal in a corner. Noticing the red, white, and blue graphics announce that election-night coverage with Christine Paskins was about to commence, Mac turned up the sound.

Jonathan Dearey watched the numbers on his digital watch change into "9:00 P.M." He nodded to the other men, and they emerged from the van. P.J. placed a sign in the windshield that read "FBS."

Jonathan's gaze swung up the FBS tower, its silver mullions and reflective glass lit by spotlights, to its letters at the very top.

"We come in Your name," he declared to the darkness beyond it. "We are here to do Your work, Lord. Please bless our effort. Amen."

"Amen," the others echoed him.

Jonathan was filled with such intense exaltation that he knew God was with him. All else in his life had served as prelude to this moment.

He began to walk toward the building's entrance. Except for the two security guards in gray uniforms behind the reception desk, the brightly lit lobby was empty. The other men fell into step around Jonathan. They entered the lobby.

Mac observed them with a practiced eye. All six wore jackets and ties and loose overcoats. Mac's impression was that the smaller man might be someone in government the others were guarding. That aroused his wariness, rather than allayed it: No one had called down to alert them to expect the group. And if the bodyguards were Secret Service, they would have been wearing a little identifying button on their lapels.

The group walked up to the security desk's high counter.

"May I help you?" Mac inquired.

The small, balding man in the center spoke. "I have an appointment with Christine Paskins."

"She's on the air right now."

"Yes, I know. She's supposed to interview me."

413

"You'll have to sign in—all of you—and I'll phone up. What are your names?"

Jonathan nodded to Ted, at eighteen the youngest of his followers. Hands deep in his coat pockets, Ted had moved to the end of the desk to gain a full view of the guards behind it. Now he was pointing a pistol at them.

"Look, if this is a stickup," Mac said levelly, "we don't keep any cash here. My money is in my locker, with my street clothes."

His immediate impulse was to push the alarm button to alert Security Central, but Bobby Williams was in his way. He could not reach past him without alerting the intruders. Downstairs, Harry was supposed to be watching the screens, but there was no way to be sure that he was.

"If you do as you're told," Jonathan said, "you won't be harmed. Simply tell us where the newsroom is."

Mac's expression hardened into bulldog resolve not to answer. Jonathan shifted his gaze to Bobby.

"Man, I'm new here," the latter spoke up. "This is my first night."

Jonathan turned back to Mac. "You have exactly five seconds to tell us where the news is doing the election results. One. Two. Three. Four—"

Mac dove in front of Bobby for the alarm button under the desk. He heard the gunshot before he felt the concussion in his back, even as it occurred to him that the two should have been simultaneous. He did not reach the button before he fell to the floor.

"Keep your hands away from there!" the shooter ordered.

Bobby lifted his hands. Mac was groaning at his feet. Three other men had pistols out now.

Jonathan spoke again to the young security guard. "Now, *you* have five seconds."

"It should be on this list here," Bobby said carefully, raising the list to keep his hands in full view. A note had been paper-clipped to it. " 'Election Center. Fourth floor,' " he read. "The elevators are over there."

Much had been planned out, but Jonathan had left room in the plan for divine inspiration. He could feel a higher power guiding him now. He motioned to a sandy-haired young man about the same height as Bobby.

"Get into his uniform and put the two of them into the supply closet over there. Fast."

"He needs a doctor," Bobby pleaded.

The sandy-haired young man moved behind the desk, trying to button the uniform jacket over his broad chest. He noticed the visitors' passes and ran to the elevators to hand his associates the clip-on plastic cards.

Harry returned from the bathroom and poured himself a fresh cup of coffee from the coffee machine. Then he dropped back into the seat and scanned the surveillance monitors on the wall before him.

Everything looked okay. Why wouldn't it be? Very little ever happened. But as long as the company paid, he was glad to sit here and take their money.

He had not seen the new man in person, but noticed nothing unusual in the long shot of the desk taken from behind him. Harry guessed that Mac had gone off on a short break. The correct procedure would have been for Mac to call in when he was about to leave his post. When they phoned in again at ten, he'd find out where Mac had gone and write it in the log. He picked up the *Newsday* he had purchased on the way to work and began to read about the Giants' upcoming football game against the Rams.

"With the Democrats making a strong early showing throughout the country, if the pattern continues, they could gain additional strength in Congress."

Chris shifted to her left and directed her next comments at the second camera. A man and a woman sat together at one end of the desk. "With me is Todd Rudolph"—Chris's eyes shifted to the man— "who's been keeping track of the House races for us, and Anne Nelson, who's been covering the Senate. Todd, how would a Democratic landslide in the House affect President Bush's program?"

With the first camera moving in on him, Rudolph began to answer the question, and Greg began to herd his guests toward the door. The party would resume upstairs, where the band, buffet, and drinks were waiting.

Marian looked around for Derek and caught sight of him chatting with Hedy Anderson at the desk from which she would be reporting on gubernatorial races. Marian quickly joined them.

"We've got to go," Marian informed Derek in a whisper.

Derek coolly turned back to Hedy to finish what he was saying. Chris was absolutely right about her! Marian grumbled inwardly. The woman's a barracuda. But look at Derek. He no longer even knows I'm alive. Why go on tearing my heart out and humiliating myself running after him? Better just to recognize reality and try to start my life over again without him.

Head down, hiding the tears about to burst from her, Marian rushed after the others who were leaving.

Ted, invariably the quickest of God's Warriors to be helpful, jumped forward and broke the electric eye to keep the elevator doors from closing. The five men stepped from the lobby into the car. Ted pressed the button for the fourth floor.

A few seconds later the doors opened on that floor. A huge, noisy throng blocked egress.

P.J. glanced worriedly at his leader, but the problem was solved by one of the partygoers who called out to the others, "Let them off!" and kept the elevator door from closing prematurely.

Derek was the last person out of Studio 4C. P.J. sprinted to catch the studio doors before they closed. He was too late. The latch clicked shut, locking them.

"The keys," P.J. remembered. "We forgot to take them from the guards." He pulled out the walkie-talkie hanging on a halter inside his coat. "We can have Rick bring them up from the lobby."

"Put that away!" Jonathan ordered. "Rick is needed where he is. We'll wait here. People are going in and out all the time."

Greg emerged from the elevator on the seventh floor and fell into step beside Abel Hastings. Only a few years older than Greg, Abel was a company director who had risen by dint of talent to the top of a Fortune 500 company. Barnett had recruited him and several other newcomers to the board in recent years in an effort to boost the value of FBS's stock on Wall Street. He and two other directors on the Finance Committee had spent hours that day with the investment bankers examining Ev's offer.

Of medium height with wavy black hair and eyebrows, he spoke in quick bursts. "Carver's offered a good price—if you don't see too far into the future. An outside threat like that . . . it might convince the board to put aside discussing your contract for the time being."

"Will that help in the long run?"

Abel shrugged with what Greg took to be resignation. "Although a couple of directors claim the other networks had more weak new shows than usual . . . and more aging ones trying to hold on for an extra year, no one quibbles with the job you did. Your personal life is the issue. And Barnett Roderick's resentment. It's as if you'd spat on the flag. I get an odd feeling from that bunch. They think by getting rid of you they're going to wipe out everything they detest in the world, all the new developments that drive them crazy."

The men entered the large room where the party was being held and soon separated, with Abel moving off to get a drink. Greg stopped to check one of the TV screens placed around the room. Marian appeared to be staring at the set.

"How's Ken doing?" he asked.

Marian had been lost in her grief. She tried to piece together the question and answer it. "The same, I think. Neck and neck. Nobody willing to forecast a winner."

Greg chuckled. "ABC has to be tearing their hair out that the election falls during November sweeps."

"We'll pick up four or five rating points tonight without 'Roseanne' against us." Her voice was strained, her eyes reddened and puffy.

"You all right?" Greg asked.

"I'm fine."

She was peering across the room. He followed her gaze to Derek and Gail Dawson, who were drinking wine together in a corner. Having just broken up with her latest boyfriend, Gail had come east alone for the party and to do publicity for "A Funny Marriage." Gail Dawson, Marian knew, was not the type to sleep alone for long.

Marian excused herself from Greg and tried as casually as she could to stroll by the couple.

"Hi. How's it going?" she asked Derek, adding in what she hoped would sound to Gail like a proprietary tone, "Derek, I'm sorry I can't spend more time with you, but this party should end pretty early."

"You don't object to my talking to Gail, do you?" His own tone was cruel in its directness.

"No, of course not," she said. "I hope you're enjoying yourself. You, too, Gail."

Derek did not bother to reply.

One of the double doors to Studio 4C suddenly swung open. A young woman with a single pale-blond braid, a pencil stuck behind her ear, and a sheaf of papers in her hand went rushing out, so intent on what she was reading that she paid little attention to the five men standing there.

Ted grabbed the door. Jonathan led the others into the studio. For several seconds they stood quietly to one side, becoming acclimated to their surroundings. Men and women were seated at desks around most of the room. One colorful wall contained the names of candidates with numbers beside each. Christine Paskins's face gazed at him from several television screens.

He located her, seated at a wide desk placed well to the front of the wall. Two cameras pointed at her. Overhead lights illuminated her. Like a false priestess, Jonathan thought, deluding a vast populace with graven images. Yet, this place was the spring from which all of God's people could finally have their thirst slaked, their sins washed away. I am come, saith the Lord! Jonathan uttered silently. Hallelujah!

Nodding to his Warriors, he walked quickly to the center of the room. As planned, Ted stood by the entrance, blocking it. P.J. rushed ahead of his leader, circling the desk as he drew his gun. Intent on what she was saying into the camera, Chris never noticed him coming.

P.J. pressed the pistol against her temple. A moment later, Jonathan was on her other side.

"Put the camera on me," Jonathan's deep voice boomed. "God has something to tell America."

"Oh, Jesus!" the cameraman exclaimed into his headset. "What the hell should I do?"

Sam Mathias grabbed the mike in the control room. "For now, do as he says. Don't let anything happen to her."

His next words over the closed line were directed to the technical people and the director. "Kill the signal we're sending out of here, but keep it going on the monitors in the studio so this guy won't know."

Sam was following the rules for dealing with terrorist situations laid out a couple of years earlier. The technicians upstairs in the Master Control Room would keep the signal from going out of the building and would quickly get the local station's news staff on the air from a different studio. The terrorists would never know the difference.

"Lock the control room door," Sam ordered. The window was made of bulletproof glass. "Get the police on the phone—"

One of the gunmen appeared in the control room's doorway, his gun pointed at Sam. Sam slowly stepped back from the microphone.

Greg had been watching the monitors. For a moment after he saw a gun materialize in the close-up beside Chris's head, he was too stunned to understand what was happening. Then as the camera pulled back and he saw the powerfully built man holding the gun and the small man on the other side, he realized that terrorists had taken over the broadcast. The men who had emerged from an elevator as he and others were entering!

Greg raced to the wall phone near the door. A young woman was speaking to someone. Greg pulled the receiver out of her hand and punched in the number for the lobby security desk.

"This is Greg Lyall. Armed terrorists have taken over Studio Four-C. Get the police here right away. Are any of our security people armed?"

"No, sir," the voice replied to him.

"Then just stay put. When the police get here, lead them up to Studio Four-C."

"Yes, sir."

Rick, in the lobby, hung up the phone. Everything was going according to plan. But when he turned back to the television screen, the picture from the election-center studio had been replaced by a sign that read the network was experiencing technical difficulties. The same picture was on the little Watchman TV he had brought and set up behind the desk. He reached into a drawer where he had stuffed his overcoat. The walkie-talkie was in one of the pockets.

"What happened to the signal?" Greg cried out.

Alan Howe remembered. "They automatically cut it off. I think the FBI asked us to do it, you know, to keep terrorists from thinking they can get access to airtime."

"Nobody told the terrorists."

Howe immediately phoned Master Control and learned that the signal from Studio 4C was now limited to the monitors there. He ordered that the signal be sent to the building's other monitors as well. An instant later, the picture from Studio 4C reappeared.

"I have a message for America," the round-faced, balding man beside Chris was saying on the screen. His eyes shone with a brilliant light. "I am the prophet Jonathan, God's spokesman on earth. He has sent me here to tell America that this is your last chance to repent from your wickedness."

P.J.'s walkie-talkie began to beep. He switched the pistol to the other hand and began fishing inside his coat for the device. Jonathan tried to ignore the sound.

"You have sinned and blasphemed. You take the lives of His innocent unborn babes. You whore in private and cheat in business. You—" Flushed with anger at the beeping, he cut off his sermon and yelled at P.J., "Answer it! Rip it out! Something!"

P.J. already had the walkie-talkie to his ear. "Rick says they've cut off what you're saying to the outside. It's only being heard inside the building. His little portable TV is getting some other newsroom that's going out over the air."

Jonathan's anger became ferocious. Eyes popping, teeth gritted, he grabbed Chris by the hair.

"Get me on the air!" he screamed at her.

Chris looked to the control room. "Sam," she said carefully, "I think what Mr. Dearey has to say is important. Please get him back on the air."

Sam's voice sounded throughout the studio over the open public-address line. "I can't, Chris. In these situations Master Control needs a v.p. or higher to approve our getting the signal back."

Jonathan stared into the camera. "In exactly five minutes, unless this starts going out to America, she dies."

29

~~~~~ ~ ~~~~~~~~

Bobby Williams had lowered Mac into a sitting position among the pails and boxes inside the narrow closet. He had loosened the older man's clothing, stuffing his handkerchief into the back wound to halt the blood loss. The closet was totally dark, and Mac had not answered any whispered inquiries about his condition. He was still breathing, but the breaths were getting fainter. Bobby assumed he was unconscious.

At one point Bobby had heard a phone ring and then, quite clearly, the gunman speaking to someone. But then Mac's low moans drowned out the words.

Bobby felt around, but found no knob to open the locked door from the inside. The door's hinges, too, were on the outside. There was no way to escape until someone let them out.

Mac moaned again and then asked where he was. Bobby crouched down and tried to explain. He got only two sentences out before the tension left Mac's body and unconsciousness returned.

Greg took the elevator to the sixth floor, where the newsroom for WFBS-TV, the network's New York station, was located. At the newsroom's far end, one of the local anchormen was on camera, reporting on the crisis two floors below. As Greg dashed toward the control room, he passed the young woman with the single blond braid. Still trembling, she realized she had left the network's election center only seconds before the terrorists took command.

"Has anyone called the police?" she asked aloud to a writer quickly pounding out some copy for the anchor.

"Someone must have," he replied over his shoulder.

That did not seem very certain to the young woman. She did not want to look foolish, but it was better to be safe than sorry, she told herself, and dialed 911.

"Hello, police? Has anyone called to report a hostage situation at FBS?"

Greg burst into the local station's news control room and ordered the technicians to patch him into the PA system in Studio 4C. He could see Chris on one of the monitors speaking to Dearey, trying to establish some semblance of a relationship that would give him pause about taking her life. Greg leaned into the microphone on the counter.

"Mr. Dearey, I'm Greg Lyall, the chief executive officer here at FBS." Greg could see from the facial reactions in the monitor that he was being heard. "I promise you that if you give up your guns and let everyone go safely, we will read your statement over the air."

"Mr. Lyall," Jonathan replied into a camera, his anger not one scintilla diminished, "I know who you are. You are a liar. You lied to your wife and committed adultery. You cannot be trusted."

"I swear that you will be heard."

"You swear! To what do you swear? To fornication. To adultery. To deceit."

"I control what goes out over the airwaves. If you want to be heard, you'll have to trust me."

Jonathan laughed in a rich baritone. "You control nothing anymore, Mr. Lyall. Nothing! Are you prepared to let your mistress here die? If not, Mr. Lyall, then you do not control your precious airwaves. I do."

Greg feared for Chris and for the other lives in that studio. But irrationally, he too was filled with a rage, a rage paradoxically caused by the same sort of powerlessness that Jonathan Dearey had felt for years. Greg considered this network his possession. He had struggled all his life to win it. And it would remain his until the moment the directors wrestled it from him. In his most secret of hearts, he believed that his power to control the information and entertainment upon which millions of Americans depended each day made him as close to being God as a man could get. His desires and convictions could change the world. That gave him a rare kind of immortality. Now, another man, with no right to that authority, only his own insane assertion of divine inspiration, was trying to extort that power from him by force. All the efforts over the last months to take the network from him—by Barnett, by Ev—merged into his rage at this last violent grab. He would grapple with the madman with whatever weapons he had.

"You won't harm her," Greg dueled. "I know you won't. You'd die, too, and I'm sure you don't want to die."

"I have no doubt that I *will* die tonight. And be blessed with life eternal and sit at God's right hand. That certainty makes me fearless and invincible."

"But there are people in that room who have nothing to do with any of this," Greg said. He hoped to begin a negotiation leading toward the release of some of the hostages. "You've talked about God. God tells us not to kill. Some of those people might get killed accidentally. Why not let some of them—"

Jonathan's eyes darted to the wall clock. He interrupted Greg. "You have exactly two minutes left to get my face and voice on the air before she dies! Until you do, we'll kill another person every five minutes."

Greg was shaken. He stared at the man's image on the monitor—round face and features, mushy mouth, jowly cheeks—and fumed that only someone so unprepossessing could delude himself with the fantasy that God was speaking through him. But the man was clearly willing to die to be heard.

Chris's frightened face stared into the camera, beseeching Greg to protect her. Her and the others' safety was his priority now. The evenness of the madman's voice when he threatened to kill had unnerved Greg. The man meant it. Greg would have to yield, even as some part of his psyche boiled over with bitterness that so marginal a creature had bested him.

"All right," Greg conceded. He turned to the technicians in the control room. "Get me a line to whoever controls what goes over the air. We're switching the guy back on."

As time had dragged on, Rick, guarding the front door, had become increasingly nervous. Prophet Jonathan should have made his speech on television and been back down by now and in the van, with them all making their escape. Cutting off the television signal had blocked their plans. The longer it took, the greater the chance of the police storming the building while they were still inside.

The elevator doors opened. Rick spun around. He had not stopped the two people who had entered the building so far, but to his surprise, none had yet left. A young woman was walking from the elevators and into the lobby. She nodded good-night at the desk. Sizing her up, Rick decided she was unaware of the attack. He nodded back at her and let her pass out through the revolving doors and into the night.

A moment later a siren wailed very close and then another. A squad car came to a screeching halt outside the entrance. Two police officers, a man and a woman, ran into the lobby, guns drawn.

"We got a report of hostages being taken," the woman said.

"Must be a prank," Rick answered calmly. "Everything's quiet."

"Where's Studio Four-C?" the male officer asked.

"It's locked up for the night."

"You haven't heard anything?"

Rick shook his head.

The female officer glanced at her partner in disgust. "The second false alarm tonight." She turned back to Rick. "Okay. Sorry we bothered you."

They were just starting to lower their revolvers when a loud banging issued from the closet.

"He's one of the terrorists!" a voice yelled from inside the closet. "He's got a gun!"

Rick's gun was only halfway up when both officers shouted at him, "Drop it!"

Other squad cars were pulling up now, and more officers were running toward the entrance. The woman officer ran to the closet with the keys she found sitting on the desk. The third key fit.

"Get a doctor fast!" Bobby exclaimed as soon as the door opened.

He grasped Mac's inert form and pulled him into the light, quickly relating what had happened as he did.

The phone was ringing. One of the police officers grabbed it.

"Are the police here yet?" a voice yelled from the receiver.

"Who's this?" the officer asked.

Greg identified himself and then said, "Get up to the fourth floor. I'll meet you at the elevator."

Bobby pointed at the pudgy face on the TV screen. "That's the guy who went to Four-C," he told the police, "the one who's speaking."

". . . And unless you turn from your wicked ways, God will smite America as surely as He smote Sodom and Gomorrah. He punished the people of Japan and Germany and then he raised them up again. Is it any wonder that we have become the world's largest debtor? We beg our former enemies to buy our debt, to fund our military ventures, to keep sending us their oil, to buy our once-mighty companies—our Columbia Pictures and our Radio City—so as to stave off for a little while longer our day of certain reckoning. Now God has freed the Communist countries. We rush to help them grow strong and dominate us. Make no mistake, they, too, will rise up and beggar us and shove our faces in the dirt and make us their economic slaves.

"Why? I tell you again it is because we are sinners. We have turned from God. We fornicate and then we murder the infants of that lust and call it 'freedom of choice.' We steal and hurt people to get money to buy the drugs that will blind our minds to those crimes. We ban God from our schools." Jonathan's voice was ringing with the splendor and glory

424

radiating in his breast. "God has sent me to save you and this nation. . . ."

In a hall located at the rear of the studio, Harry located the passkey on his ring that would unlock the back door. He had seen the lobby commotion on the security monitor and joined the police. Greg and eleven police officers were massed around him. They spoke in whispers. The police sergeant, now holding the little Watchman TV, took the key from him, but was in a quandary as to what to do next. Several people who had watched the drama unfold on television thought they saw one of the intruders standing guard toward the rear of the studio, near this door. It would be difficult to surprise the terrorists.

One of the officers suggested waiting for the department's trained attack force to arrive.

Greg disagreed. "The leader told me he's prepared to die tonight. I believe him. I'm afraid that once he's through with his speech, he'll have no reason to let the people in there live."

"Will we have a clear area in front of us if we break in?"

"Some extra equipment back here," Alan Howe remembered.

Greg spoke up. "The best bet is for me to talk my way in through the front and then distract them somehow. If their attention seems to wander for an instant, break in from both entrances. Keep watching the TV set and stay in touch with each other by walkie-talkie. You won't get more than a second or so—if that."

The people in the newsroom had been ordered to place their hands palm-down on their desks. Nervous, sweating, they all appeared to be keeping the desks from rising up and out of sight.

A knock sounded on the double doors at the studio's entrance. The Warriors of God snapped into attack postures. P.J. thrust the gun hard against Chris's temple.

The knock sounded again and then a man's voice called out, "It's Greg Lyall. You don't want my people, you want me."

"If he's alone, let him in," Jonathan ordered. "Then check him for weapons."

Ted, who was guarding the door, opened it a crack and then swung it back, his pistol at the ready. Greg stood alone in the doorway, weaponless.

"Satan's emissary has arrived," Jonathan crowed. "All you Americans out there, I want you to see for yourself the fornicator and adulterer in charge of purveying this network's lies and filth."

Greg stopped in front of Jonathan.

"Pull back," the latter commanded the nearest cameraman. He kept an eye on the monitor overhead. When he and Greg were both in the picture, his hard gaze descended again to the camera. "This, Americans, is the man who keeps the message off your television that God commands me to bring you."

"We try to report the news honestly in the time we have available," Greg answered carefully. "If you feel we slighted you, I'm sorry."

Jonathan leaped forward, his face glaring up at Greg. "You slighted *God!*"

Jonathan was struck by what seemed to him a small but significant revelation. "You know, I truly believe you do not do it on purpose or out of malice. The reason is more insidious and thus, far more evil. You are all *objective.*" He spat the word as if it were a curse. "You strain God and morality out of the news and give everything the same weight: a fire, a drug raid, a new movie, the fall of a Communist dictatorship, the weather, a new diet fad. You condemn nothing. You are guiding America toward degeneration and ruin."

Chris's anger spiked above her fear. "How dare you call yourself an American!"

Jonathan spun around, but her voice continued to ring with her fervor.

"You have no respect for America's true values. What built this country was reason and tolerance for other people's opinions and beliefs."

"Quiet!" Jonathan roared. "I didn't come here to listen to alibis . . . for your *objectivity.*"

"What you really want is to impose your own tyranny. You're just one more petty dictator without a country."

Jonathan grabbed Chris's arm and yanked her upright.

Greg decided the time was right to act. He suddenly addressed himself to the entire room.

"All right, let's settle this the democratic way: by a voice vote. All those who believe that Americans should have the right to the facts and then make up their own minds say aye."

"Quiet!" Jonathan bellowed at him.

"Well, come on," Greg implored the room.

He suddenly directed himself to P.J. "You, there, do you really want to leave all the decisions to somebody who says he speaks for God? Come on, how can you be sure he does?"

P.J. appeared confused.

"Shut him up!" Jonathan yelled at P.J.

"Hedy! Dan! Eli!" Greg shouted at the captives, his stare attempting

426

to convey to them the urgency of following his lead. "All those who agree with me, say aye. *Now!*"

"Aye," they shouted.

At that instant a torrent of blue uniforms charged through the back door.

"Drop your guns!" some of the officers yelled.

"Police!" others were screaming.

The double doors in front suddenly gave way, and more dark blue poured into the large room. Ted fired into the torrent surging at him and was cut down by half a dozen shots.

Chris threw herself to the floor. P.J. did not know whether to keep his gun trained on her or to fire at the police. A bullet caught him in the shoulder. He dropped the gun and grabbed for the shoulder, looking more surprised than wounded.

Greg seized Jonathan around his neck with one arm and his torso and arms with the other in case he, too, carried a gun.

"You little bastard!" he screamed at him. He wanted to rip his head off.

The terrorist in the control room doorway realized as he was about to fire at Greg that he could kill his leader. The shot went astray. Several police fired at him. He shot back, into a group seated at news desks. The next bullet caught him in the chest, and he went down.

A moment later the siege was over.

The cameras had followed all the action. The director had been sending it all over the air. Greg ran to Chris. She reached up and hugged him for one relieved instant. Then she pushed herself back up to her feet to resume her seat at the anchor desk, even as she did so beginning to describe to viewers what had just happened.

The rest of the room was still in chaos. Noticing several people crouched around Hedy and a young man near her, Greg rushed over to them. A bullet had creased her along an arm. The young man, an associate producer, had caught that same bullet in his abdomen. He was bleeding profusely. Two police officers decided time would be saved if he were immediately moved downstairs, ready for the ambulance's arrival. Hedy refused to leave for the hospital, stanching the wound with a borrowed handkerchief while awaiting a bandage from a first-aid kit.

Two terrorists were dead: Ted, near the front doors, and the gunman in the control-room doorway. P.J.'s collarbone was shattered. One policeman had been hit, but a bulletproof vest had saved him.

A number of people were in shock. Many others would not regain an even keel for days and some not feel totally secure for months.

Greg glanced up at a monitor. Totally poised, the professional engaged in her trade, Chris was moving among her fellow newspeople with a hand mike to get their reactions to what they had just undergone. They themselves were now the story, and many were already back to work reporting it.

Marian and several other FBS executives and directors quickly arrived to see if they could help. With them were reporters who had also been at the party and were eager to cover the big story they had been lucky enough to be close to. All the while, staff members were phoning home to assure loved ones they were all right or were taking brief calls from worried friends and relatives.

One of the desk assistants located Greg beside the associate producer who was being placed on a stretcher.

"Mr. Lyall, a woman on line five is asking whether you're all right. She says she's your mother."

Greg regarded the shiny-faced young man before him, but what he saw was a woman's dark-haired countenance framed by the living-room window through which he had glimpsed her for the last time. The sight was more than a quarter century old, but it appeared sharper to his eye than this young man's features.

"Tell her that I'm all right." He paused for a moment, deciding. "And that I'll call her soon, when all this quiets down."

As the young man turned to go, Greg caught his arm. "Be sure you tell her that."

Soon afterward, Greg left for Roosevelt Hospital, where the wounded had been brought. Alan Howe remained in the newsroom to help organize the coverage and the cleanup. Other newspeople were descending on the building, such as Manny Ramirez, to help out as well. Even Carl Green, the agent for Chris and several others there, arrived to show his concern for their ordeal—and assured them the publicity would be fabulous for their careers.

Marian and Abel Hastings went with Greg. They all stayed with the associate producer's wife and her parents during the long hours he was on the operating table.

Mac MacNamara's wife and daughter arrived at the hospital from Staten Island frantic with worry, only to learn that he had died in the ambulance. The group from FBS tried as best they could to comfort them. Greg finally sent the family back home with his car and driver. The death certificate called for the security guard's correct name: It was Aloysius.

Well past midnight, the surgeon came out to the waiting room with the news that although still in critical condition, the associate producer was expected to survive.

428

Chris remained on the air until the last major election result became known. It involved Ken.

Although his popularity had risen sharply since the Defense secretary's disgrace, pollsters had labeled him the underdog in a close race. For most of the evening, he was behind, but around midnight, the vote difference started to narrow. Three hours later, he finally passed his opponent. An hour after that the networks declared him the winner.

Without consulting Sam Mathias, the FBS field producer at Ken's campaign headquarters thought it would make great television if he could get Ken on camera for an interview with Chris. But Ken had the good taste and the shrewdness to decline. If he waited until after seven to make his victory speech, the morning TV-newsmagazine programs would be on the air and the audience much larger.

Slumping from fatigue and despair, Marian shuffled through the Plaza's brightly lit lobby. She had already accommodated herself to her certainty that Derek would be gone. She had no idea what hotel Gail Dawson was staying at, but Marian had no inclination to break into the woman's room and make a scene. If Gail had not provided the inducement for him to leave tonight, someone else would have been the pretext tomorrow or the next day. Why prolong the misery?

At the front desk, Marian observed that several keys still remained in the compartment for her suite. That told her no more than she already knew, but confirmed her intuition. She took the elevator upstairs.

"Where the hell have you been all night?" Derek cried out the instant she entered the suite.

"Me? What did you come back here for, your toothbrush?"

He was standing in the middle of the living room with his arms crossed, as if he had been pacing the room, waiting for her. "Don't try to avoid this thing by trying to blame me. You're the one who disappeared all night. I checked. Greg Lyall was gone and so were you. He's some smooth operator. Your buddy Christine fell for him. Why not you? You're in New York seeing him all the time."

Marian was aghast at Derek's audacity. "You practically told me to get lost. You were all over Gail Dawson."

"You knew I was doing that to make you jealous. I couldn't get a rise out of you. You know I'm not the type to look at another woman."

"What possible reason would you have to want to make me jealous?"

His eyes dropped. "Because *I'm* so jealous. You're brilliant . . . and incredible at what you do. I didn't know that before because we never went out much, but now I see how the men you meet with look at you.

429

They're powerful, incredible men and they're awed by you. They want you. Half the time I can't even follow the conversation. Who am I compared to them?"

His face reflected his agony. "I've been hoping that if I could make you jealous, you'd think I was worth sticking with. But you're too smart to fool like that." His shoulders drooped. "Why in the world would you get jealous over someone like me?"

Slowly, Marian's arms opened wide and she walked toward him. "Oh, baby! You know Mama loves you. You don't have to make me jealous. Even though all those other men are crazy about me, you're the one Mama loves. Come to Mama, baby. Come to Mama!"

Greg slept until noon and then hurried back to his office. The morning newspapers were on his desk. Chris's photo dominated the front page of every one. *The New York Post*, in its usual punchy style, seemed to sum up public reaction to what had occurred the night before: Under the banner headline "Terrorists Seized at FBS" was a smaller headline that read, "Heroine Chris Tells Them Off."

Greg scanned the overnight ratings. The hostage-taking had sent FBS's prime-time ratings through the roof.

30

~~~~~~~~~~~~~~~~~~

S tew Graushner parked his car in a lot and walked to the court building with Susan. He halted before the entrance, his feet cemented to the pavement. As a reporter, he had covered a host of trials, even a couple of sensational divorce trials. In one a young woman claimed her older and hugely wealthy husband was having an affair with another woman. The city's population was jubilant when the sweet young thing won a multimillion-dollar award. Two days after she received the check, she disappeared. The following month she was discovered in Europe, with her husband's lawyer. Now, Stew was the poor sap on the slaughtering block.

Susan tugged at his arm. "No one likes these things, but Hal says you have a chance to keep the division of property reasonable."

Stew shook his head dejectedly. "You better try to get along with her, Susan. She's our partner for life."

Susan finally coaxed Stew forward into the building.

Several wizened spectators were talking together outside the court-room doors. He remembered that trial-watching was a form of enter-tainment for the retired and unemployed.

"What's the judge like?" he asked them.

"Depends on the case," one answered.

"Divorce."

"Yours?"

Stew nodded. The man groaned in reply.

"What? What?" Stew cried out.

"He's a very old-fashioned guy," one man explained. "Believes men should take care of their women. Wives try their best to get him to hear their cases. If he thinks you've got another woman, then he really goes nuts."

Only Susan's hanging tightly to his arm prevented Stew from fleeing out the building and onto a plane for Katmandu. She led him into the courtroom. Hal Diamond, his lawyer, was waiting for them in the front row. He looked worried.

"I've had investigators tailing her off and on for weeks—you'll get their bill in a day or two—but she's clean as a whistle. She's just too shrewd to misbehave so close to the trial date." He frowned. "It's a shame she knows all about you and Susan."

Just then, Patty arrived.

"Our TV show seems to be doing well," she remarked pleasantly upon greeting Stew and Susan. She then fixed on Hal with a sly smile. "I hear you had a wild night with that redheaded cocktail waitress at the Beverly Wilshire."

Hal appeared flustered. Patty proceeded to the plaintiff's table to await the opening bell.

"Jesus," Stew groaned. "After weeks of surveillance we have nothing on her, but she knows who my lawyer was boffing last night. We're dead."

He curled up on a chair at the defense table. Over and over, he silently chanted the Twenty-third Psalm. But no matter how many times he repeated that the Lord was his shepherd so he need fear no evil as he walked through the valley of the shadow of death, he knew in his heart that God's rod and staff were doing their comforting one table over.

"All rise," the clerk intoned.

A tall, austere man in his late fifties swept in through the door behind the bench. His cheeks were hollow, his head totally bald, his eyes dark and unforgiving. The case of *Graushner* v. *Graushner* was about to be heard.

After the opening statements, Patty put herself on the stand. As she recited the history of the marriage, the judge appeared increasingly sympathetic. When Hal objected to one statement as hearsay, the judge sternly admonished him "to let the woman speak."

"My dear," the judge said, turning back to her, "you just tell me in your own words about your terrible experiences."

For forty-five minutes Patty recited all the cruelties inflicted on her. The judge's glances at Stew grew so hateful that only Susan's restraint again kept him from fleeing.

"What do you think?" Stew whispered to Hal.

The lawyer averted his eyes and shook his head as sorrowfully as a doctor telling the family that the patient would not last out the hour. Stew's only solace at that instant was the recollection that he had taken all his money from the bank and stashed it where his wife would never find it.

"That brings us up to the time when I learned he was writing and producing a TV series," Patty said brightly, simultaneously batting her eyelashes and smiling at the judge, bending forward to expose her cleavage down to the navel, and hiking up her skirt as she crossed her legs.

Not an easy bit of coordination to master, Stew acknowledged with some admiration.

"What's this about a series, my dear?" the judge asked.

"A new network television series he stands to make millions from called 'Lowdown.' "

The judge suddenly straightened and turned directly toward Stew.

Patty raised her arm and pointed at Susan. "And that woman there, the one he's living with, she writes and produces it with him."

"Is that right?" the judge exclaimed.

"In nearly every episode there's a very sinister woman character, the professor's shrewish wife, who makes his life miserable. She's a lawyer and is clearly based on me. Everything she does is taken directly from something that has occurred between my husband and me."

"Is that right?" the judge repeated with a chuckle. "You're the one on the show who they call God's Curse?"

"Yes, Your Honor."

"I never miss that show."

"My friends and professional colleagues all recognize that the character is me. Her portrayal is a vicious attempt to mock and humiliate me and destroy my professional and personal reputation."

Patty bowed her head as if too enfeebled by the calumny heaped on it to keep it high. But when she did look up again, the judge was laughing uncontrollably.

"Did you get him to sign that separation agreement"—he guffawed—"and then kick him out just like Curse did on the show . . . just before he got fired?"

"Yes, Your Honor, but it was more complicated than—"

The judge howled with laughter. "The guy was really broke, right? I remember. The professor's wife—you . . . were making a great income at a law firm. But you forced this guy who was absolutely broke to pay your kid's tuition?"

"Well, yes, but—"

The judge could barely get the words out now, he was laughing so hard. "Did you come back into his life . . . you know, like Curse did on the show . . . only after he'd finally hit it big?"

Patty nodded glumly.

The judge pounded the bench in hysterics. "And then you told him . . . you told him . . . that the question of whether he deserted you . . . was something for the court to decide."

"Yes, but I swear to you I wasn't dressed in a vampire outfit at the time, Your Honor. It was a little Yves St.—"

"So, you're Curse, and he's the professor." The judge was rolling around on his chair, nearly falling out of it. "That's the funniest thing I ever heard."

He managed to tilt himself upright long enough to grab the gavel and slam it down.

"Divorce granted without alimony." He pointed the gavel at Patty. "Get out of here before I make you pay the poor slob damages for harassment."

Whoops of laughter convulsed him.

Stew and Susan jumped up and hugged each other. They ran over to the bench and pumped the judge's hand, inviting him to play the part of the judge when they shot an episode about the professor and Curse's divorce trial.

As they left the courtroom, Hal told Stew, "I'll send you a bill for court time."

"But I gave you twenty-five thousand dollars."

Hal's tone was incredulous at such naïveté. "That barely got us through pretrial motions. There was all the research I did, all the preparation." He gave a little wave and veered toward another courtroom where another case awaited him. "See you."

Susan threw her arms around Stew. "You're a free man. Let's drive right to Las Vegas and get married."

"This is the happiest day of my life: the divorce. Getting rid of Patty. Marrying you."

The two skipped out of the building like children, all the way to the parking lot.

His parking space was vacant.

"My new Mercedes!" Stew screamed. "It's been stolen!"

He collapsed cross-legged onto the ground, holding his head in his hands.

"It's leased—and insured," Susan reminded him. "You have nothing to worry about."

"You don't understand."

She had never seen him so distraught. "Stew, we'll call for a taxi."

"My last fifteen thousand dollars!" he wailed. "I hid it from Patty in the trunk!"

He could hear God laughing at him all the way to the bank.

The night before the directors meeting, Greg took Chris to dinner at the Madison Grille, in the east sixties. They asked for a table in the rear. He was deeply gloomy and spoke little. She tried hard to sympathize with

434

what he seemed certain was his imminent plunge to oblivion, but her elation kept bubbling up out of her uncontrollably.

Just twenty-four hours earlier, she had been sure she was about to die. Every moment of life granted to her after that became a miraculous gift.

And the first miracle had spawned a second. The ordeal had drawn public sentiment back to her in great loving waves. All day, newspaper and TV reporters and talk-show producers had phoned for interviews and appearances. Diners, spotting her now, felt compelled to make the pilgrimage back to her table to congratulate her on her narrow escape and praise her spunk. A few, recognizing Greg, included him as well in their goodwill, but she was the object of their admiration—admiration of a different sort from what it had been before the scandal.

Her new image seemed more valid and long-lasting, based to a far greater degree on the qualities that made her a good broadcast journalist—integrity, intelligence, the ability to communicate well, even under duress—and no longer on the happenstance of sweet, fresh beauty. Even their affair seemed to be viewed much more positively, as a product not of a promiscuous nature, but of the same honesty and courage she had shown as a reporter. Her ratings would doubtless swiftly climb to reflect the prodigal daughter's return to favor. Any CEO replacing Greg would find it difficult to remove her from the air; but if one did, Chris would be able to write her own ticket anywhere.

Greg was happy for her for all those reasons. She would thrive. She would find fulfillment. She would wield her influence to inform the public like a charmed sword. She would track deep footprints across time. His own survival would be in body only, a body empty of purpose, empty of spirit, slumped behind her, obscured by her shadow.

"You're just feeling sorry for yourself. Nothing will be changed between us," Chris assured him. "It's just that you've always been my boss when we worked together, and your once-secure male superiority isn't sure how to handle the comedown."

"If I just knew what I'd be doing afterward, it would be fine. But running a network is the only thing I ever wanted to do."

"Greg, let's be realistic. My salary will support us in high style"—she noticed his grimace at the prospect of being supported again, but went on to complete her thought—"and give you time to find something you'd like to do. You might enjoy doing something new."

"How'd you feel if I asked you to give up newscasting and take up, say, writing magazine articles about people who are still broadcasting the news?"

"Sorry."

"Maybe I'll try to raise the money to buy a TV station somewhere."

"That's a terrific idea." She knew he would hate filling a schedule with a network's lineup and syndicated fare after having once developed the programming himself.

"It's something to think about . . . if things go against me with the directors tomorrow."

Buying a station would be tough with no cash of his own, Greg knew. Ev's five million dollars could be a big help.

Greg had told Judy, his secretary, to cut off his calls. He wanted time to prepare his thoughts in the hour before the board met. He was annoyed when she buzzed him.

"Your wife is here to see you, Mr. Lyall," she said nervously.

Greg stood as Diane diffidently entered. The chestnut hair was pulled back on the sides, away from her face, which was drawn and anxious. Greg had not seen or spoken with her since the night they separated. All communications had been transmitted through their lawyers.

"I was worried about you . . . with the terrorists," she said. "I was watching."

"I'm fine."

"I can see that. You look good. These last months I had pictured you not eating right, not getting enough sleep. I guess she takes good care of you."

"It isn't like that with her. We worry about each other differently from how you and I did."

Her eyes dropped. "Are you still happy with her?"

"Usually. You didn't come here just to ask that, did you?"

"Yes, in a way." Her eyes lifted. A light flickered in them. "I saw Doctor Bascomb yesterday."

"Is something wrong?" Bascomb was her gynecologist, Greg recalled, *society's* gynecologist.

She smiled uncertainly. "He told me that I'm pregnant."

For a moment Greg could not comprehend the significance of the words. "You and I are going to have a baby?"

She nodded. He was sure that in order to lure him back, she had counted on his desire for a family and had become pregnant. Although she loved children, she had avoided having them out of fear of the medical consequences.

"How could you decide to have a child just to hold on to me?"

"I didn't know then there was another woman," she said, her voice catching. "We were still together. Please believe me. I wanted this child for my own sake. That finally became more important to me than my fears."

Her gaze was clear, her voice earnest and direct. Greg could not judge her truthfulness.

"I would have regretted all my life not having a child—our child—to love," she said. "If I die the same way my mother did, at least I'll leave behind something of you and me. She knew the danger, but decided having me was more important to her than her life. I don't want to spend the rest of my own life regretting my cowardice. And I want our child to have a family."

Diane had spent yesterday and this morning thinking through her thoughts and feelings—and what approach might induce Greg to return to her. Her words tumbled out.

"I'm as responsible as you for what happened to our marriage, maybe more—I was so much more inflexible. I love you, Greg. I've been miserable without you." Her eyes were turning liquid. "Please, let's start again. I'll try harder at this than anything I've ever done."

She paused, looking away to regain her composure.

"Greg, you've done a wonderful job with the company. You deserve to stay on."

"You ought to tell that to your father."

"He doesn't know I'm here or that I'm pregnant." She forced her gaze back. "Between the shares of this company I inherited from my mother and what he kept buying for me or transferring over the years for tax purposes, I'm the largest stockholder in FBS. I own eighteen percent of the company."

"And Barnett owns thirteen percent. That total of thirty-one percent gives him working control of the company."

"There's never been any reason before now for me to vote differently from him. He was always watching things for me. But now . . . now I think . . . you should stay on. If you decide to put up a slate of your own directors . . . you know, in a proxy fight to win control from him at the next shareholders meeting, I'll vote my shares for you."

For a moment Greg was astonished by her offer, but then he snorted. He knew her deftness at manipulation so well. "But in order to obtain your support, I'll have to leave Chris and go back to you."

"Yes."

"I get to keep my job," he repeated, so there would be no mistake, "you get to keep me."

Family was paramount to Barnett. Greg did not doubt that he loved his daughter enough to swallow his rage and deny personal ambition if Greg chose to return to her. Directors supporting him would change their votes if he asked them to. How could they condemn Greg's adultery if his wife and father-in-law did not?

"But I wouldn't want that to be your reason for coming back to me, no matter how much I want you." Tears overflowed Diane's eye and ran down her cheeks. "It will be different this time, I promise. A child will change things between us. We'll be a family, what you always wanted. But even if you don't come back, I want this child."

Just how dangerous pregnancy could be for Diane had gradually begun to pervade Greg's awareness. Regardless of her motive, he realized, her decision to have a baby was an act of great bravery, perhaps even of foolhardiness. The gestation diabetes that had stricken her mother in childbirth was probably hereditary. Her own life might be at risk. In the face of such jeopardy, her intention to have a child suddenly overwhelmed him. He was both awed and frightened for her.

"Will you think about it, Greg?" she implored. "Really think about it?"

What if this woman who had always fought for dominance had indeed changed, Greg conjectured, softened by a humility totally new to her. She seemed unsure without the false self-esteem her pride lent her, a bit awkward, he noticed, but appealingly so, like a schoolgirl at her first adult party. If she truly had changed, perhaps it *could* be different. They might accommodate better to each other. Their lives together might at last grow content, satisfying. He did not delude himself that she would ever be scintillating like Chris, that she would ever ignite the fire in his skin.

Greg's eyes shifted to the wall of his office and the portraits of FBS's on-air talent. Most of those stars would flicker for their brief time, then sputter out, to be replaced by newer ones. Only a rare few would possess the appeal, the luck, and the relentless determination that made for lasting success. A single photo had retained its place since his arrival here.

Chris's blue eyes focused on his, although he stood well to one side of the picture. The photographer had managed to capture in the eyes and smile some of her bright vivacity. She was a woman who lit up the very air around her. He loved her so much. A decade before, he had chosen Diane over Chris and never ceased to regret it. The years without her had taught him how essential she was to his happiness.

Now some divine, bizarre grace had granted him the opportunity to erase his terrible mistake by rejecting the enticement Diane offered that was so precious to him: control of FBS. He was being granted that rarest opportunity in life, a second chance to stare temptation in the eye and renounce it, to choose Chris and love.

In recent weeks he had steeled himself to relinquishing the power and status he had finally won in exchange for spending the rest of his life with Chris. But that had been far easier to do when he saw no chance to retain them, when Barnett possessed the votes of a majority of

438

directors and shareholders and might well have tried to retake the top job even if Greg had never left his daughter.

But now Diane had presented Greg with her vote, a weapon that, joined with the votes of enough other backers, could mow down the opposition like ragtag recruits. He had the edge now, not Barnett. All she wanted in return was Greg.

And that they be a family to the child she was giving him. The anguish of growing up in a fractured household rose up around him like the walls of a jail cell, making the sacrifice of his unborn child's future happiness feel unendurable.

"It's too much," he muttered, swiping at the tears. "It's just too much."

At that instant Greg feared that by choosing Chris, he would be sacrificing far more than his deepest ambition for power, he would be repudiating an integrity at the center of his being purer and more insistent even than his love for her: the obligation to one's child his mother had reneged on, and on which he had waited all his life since to make good. Deserting his child would be the ultimate sin.

"I hope you realize how much I'm offering you," Diane declared.

Greg stiffened.

"I didn't mean it that way," she protested. "I love you. Greg, please. please promise me you'll think it over."

She quickly drew a pen from the holder on his desk and scrawled a note on a piece of paper. "Here. In case anyone doubts you have the right to vote my shares."

"On condition that I go back to you."

"You're an honorable man," she said quietly. "You won't use that piece of paper unless you're coming back. My shares can win it for you. Running the network means too much to you just to give it up."

He grew angry. "I'm not giving it up. You and your father are taking it away from me."

"The choice is yours, Greg," she retorted. "Don't try to put the blame on me."

"Just once in your life, can't you do something unselfish, something that buys you nothing? You've said that I did a good job running FBS, that I deserve to stay on."

She nodded.

"Then support me against your father even though it won't buy me back."

Slowly, she shook her head, tracks of tears sparkling like icicles on her cheekbones. "Then I would lose both of you."

Diane waited for Greg to speak again. When he kept silent, she started to leave, but then she halted.

"Please come home. I need you. But whatever you decide, I hope our baby is a boy. You probably want a boy."

"If it's a girl," he asked, "would you do me a favor? Would you name her Margaret . . . Meggy?"

"Yes," she said, and then left the office.

Excited, Greg quickly began to calculate the number of shares he would need to control the board. He then made several critical business phone calls. Most of FBS's stock was held by financial institutions, mainly mutual and pension funds. Greg had spent a lot of time during the past year keeping the money managers informed and cultivating their support. All of them he spoke to now offered to vote their shares for him in a proxy fight. A rough calculation showed that adding their shares to Diane's 18 percent gave him close to 37 percent of the votes. Diane's stock was the key. It represented the balance of power between him and her father.

The intercom buzzed.

"Mr. Lyall," Judy's voice sounded. "The directors meeting is about to start."

"I'll be there in a minute."

Greg took out his wallet. In its small pocket was the message with her phone number his mother had left. He laid it on his desk. Later, after all this was over, he would call her—and keep calling until he reached her. It was time. He wanted her to know she was going to be a grandmother. A child should have a grandmother.

Greg picked up the second piece of paper on his desk, the note Diane had given him, and slipped it carefully into his shirt pocket.

31

~~~~~~~~~~~~~~~~~~~~~

J udging by the degree of formality with which they greeted him as they all entered the vast wood-paneled chamber and took places around the oval table in the center, Greg was certain he could discern which directors were favorable, which unfavorable, and which still sitting on the fence, even without the count Abel Hastings had given him. Of the twenty-three directors, Abel believed eight would side strongly with Barnett, who also had a vote, come hell or high water. That block of nine was comprised primarily of older, conservative men, old friends of Barnett's.

More narrowly focused on the company's bottom line and less on Greg's notoriety were the newer board members who supported him because of his success in reversing the company's decline. Five appeared to be solidly on Greg's side of the ledger: Abel and another young corporate CEO; Tom Blake, a commercial banker who held a lot of the company's debt; an investment banker whose clients owned a substantial amount of FBS stock; and the lone economist and woman on the board. Counting himself, that gave Greg six votes.

Eight directors were undecided. Barnett needed only three of those to oust Greg. Neither Abel nor Greg held out much hope for a rebellion among the undecided contingent, sensing the prevalent feeling among them was that this was Barnett Roderick's company and that Greg's immoral behavior had sullied both it and the Roderick family.

Abel was first on the agenda, presenting the Finance Committee's evaluation of the Carver-Markham offer to buy FBS. He hoped that concern over the takeover threat would forestall consideration of Barnett's expected move to terminate Greg's contract.

"So," Abel concluded, "the Finance Committee recommends that we neither accept nor decline the offer at this moment, but enter into discussions with Evcar while we study it further. In short, show a solid front while we carefully think it through."

Jay Dickenson, whom Greg knew to be Ev's ally, had been fidgeting in his seat throughout the report. Thick-waisted, with graying sideburns and predatory good looks, he was a smoothly efficient politician who had served two terms in Congress and was a friend of the President. Presently vice chairman of a medium-sized life insurance company, he chafed for a wider and more lucrative range for his talents. As soon as Abel sat down, Dickenson called for the floor.

"That's nonsense, Abel. What the hell are we waiting around for? These people are offering fifty percent more than the stock was selling for on the stock market before the offer. If we don't grab it, the stockholders will sue the pants off us for acting against their best interests. You've talked about the profit FBS is projected to earn next year. That's nowhere near enough to outweigh this offer. I say we recommend the stockholders take it. I'm sure a lot of others here agree with me."

Greg glimpsed a hint of alarm in Barnett's eyes. Perhaps the old man would be willing to join with him now to beat back the takeover. Greg waited for Barnett to speak up to denounce Evcar's bid, but the latter kept silent as one after another director spoke in favor of it. Then Greg realized the problem. Barnett was aware of something he himself was not: Dickenson had done a lot of legwork in the past three days to line up directors behind the offer.

Greg interrupted. "Can we take a break for a minute? I'd like to discuss this privately with the chairman."

He glanced at Barnett, who considered for a moment and then stood up.

"Ten minutes," Barnett pronounced, and slammed down the gavel.

They stood alone outside the closed door.

"The way things are going," Greg began, "we'll both lose this company—to Ev Carver and Basil Markham. You know that, don't you?"

"There's a strong possibility, yes."

"I'll be out as CEO. You'll be out as chairman."

"What are you getting at?"

"I can stop Carver, dead in his tracks. I have the ammunition. I'm willing to do it if you and I can come to an arrangement."

Barnett's expression twisted into the vindictive anger he had displayed the evening Greg left Diane. "For what? So you can stay on as CEO? I'd rather let the company go than leave it in your filthy hands." Months of brooding resentment turned Barnett's voice into a snarl. "You're a despicable fortune hunter, a snake who used my daughter and then callously discarded her when your lust fastened on someone else. I would rather see FBS blotted off the face of the earth than leave it with you."

Greg stood up. "That's your last word?"

"That's final."

Greg reluctantly opened the door to the boardroom and led the way back in.

"Pretty quick," one of the directors noted.

Greg's gaze fixed on Jay Dickenson, who was caucusing to one side with some of the uncommitted. Dickenson would do well if the takeover occurred, Greg assumed. Big fees funneled to him in some way. Maybe the chairmanship and stock options. All Greg himself had to do to pick up $2 million outright plus five years' salary—another $3 million—was come out in favor of the offer. He knew FBS's worth and future prospects better than anyone. If he spoke in favor of the offer, the majority of the directors might well follow. Then, before he publicly advocated that the stockholders take Evcar's offer, he and Ev would sign his contract. It made very good sense.

Then why did accepting an offer that would secure his financial safety rankle so? he asked himself. He was being discarded. Why did he care what happened? But Greg could not evade the knowledge that he cared deeply. He knew Ev Carver inside and out and was appalled that so corrupt a man was grabbing for the worth he himself had begun to build into the company and for the newly bright future he had fashioned for it. Ev would rape and cripple FBS. Ev understood money and power, but had little feel for the nuances of a changing, worldwide communications industry. He would cut costs by slashing into the bone and muscle of staffing and would cater to what he conceived of as the public's simplistic news and entertainment tastes, which were really a reflection of his own condescension. Inevitably, the company would slide backward into ruin.

No matter how Greg tried, as if it were a bad meal, his conscience could not keep that down. He took the floor when the meeting recommenced.

"I had hoped you would decline Evcar's offer without my having to reveal what I'm about to. But momentum seems to be building for acceptance. I have to tell you, there isn't the faintest possibility that Ev Carver can ever acquire this company."

Dickenson exploded. "The man has every bit of financing he needs and more."

"I'm not talking about financing. I'm talking about character."

"Oh, jeez!" Dickenson moaned.

"You may not be interested in character as a qualification for buying

443

into a broadcasting company, Jay, but the Federal Communications Commission will be. I've had investigators dig into his past. To begin with, Ev Carver's real name is E. V. Carvalho. As a young man, he was convicted of securities fraud and barred for life from dealing in stocks. He changed his name by lying on a Social Security application. Lawyers I've consulted are convinced the FCC will forbid any company in which he has a substantial interest from buying a stake in FBS because his original crime, fraud, demonstrated his dishonest character."

Dickenson was shaken, but too much was on the line for him to retreat now. "That had to be ages ago. He was probably just a kid. The man has become an upstanding citizen."

Greg shook his head. "He concealed his real identity for over twenty years and continued to lie about it to us and to the FCC whenever he testified before them. That's their proof that the dishonesty is still deep in his character."

Charles Morrison spoke up. He was one of Barnett's oldest friends and a distinguished lawyer who had recently retired as a partner at a large Wall Street law firm. "He's right, Jay. The FCC's policy statement on the character of applicants they license for ownership would clearly bar a man who's been concealing his identity and a criminal past."

Like a draft from a suddenly opened window, Greg could feel the bias against the offer sweeping through the room. During his very first interview with Ev at KFBS-TV, to decide whether he should become executive producer of local news, Ev had belittled the FCC and the importance of laws and rules. He had declared that the only thing that mattered in television was ratings because they meant income. That was very nearly true, Greg had quickly learned. Very nearly, but not completely. A decade later, perhaps unfairly, the rules had just jumped up out of the grass and fatally bitten Ev Carver.

Barnett slammed down the gavel.

"Next item on the agenda is new business. Greg's employment contract as CEO will be ending next month. We have to decide whether to extend it."

Greg detected contempt in the old man's glance at him. Despite Greg's having held the winning hole card, Barnett had faced him down during the short recess, refusing to yield and thus, had raised the stakes. The way he saw it, Greg's nerve had failed him and caused him to throw in the winning hand.

As chairman Barnett had the right to pick the order of speakers and the length of time they could hold the floor. Barnett had his backers all lined up and ready to speak against Greg, one after another. And they did.

"FBS has become a laughingstock during his administration, the butt of dirty jokes."

"The man's life-style reflected badly on him and on this company. That's not the sort of regard in which I expect a CEO to be held."

"Things were about to turn for the network when he took over. Raoul Clampton did a hell of a job putting all the pieces in place, so Greg here could reap the praise. Did any of you know that Clampton was the real brains behind 'Lowdown'? Monumental, which produces the show, sure knows. That's why he's now running their TV operation. So, let's not give more credit to Greg here than is really coming to him."

Greg was sure that the sustained criticism had to be swaying uncommitted board members. When, grudgingly and with distaste, Barnett finally called on Abel Hastings, Greg wondered if they could still keep an open mind.

Abel zeroed in on the revival in the company's fortunes over the past year. He quoted hard figures as evidence. Expenses had been sharply cut and revenues dramatically raised. Instead of losses, there would be profits next year. The company was pervaded by a new optimism, a new belief in its destiny. That was all Greg Lyall's doing.

Abel reminded the other directors that Greg's employment agreement permitted a single valid reason for not renewing it: failure to lead the company into profits. But by any measure, profits would be strong next year and on an upward swing. Therefore, he concluded, no grounds existed to dismiss Greg, and the directors had no choice but to renew his contract for five more years.

Morrison, the lawyer, raised his hand and was called upon. He read from a piece of paper containing a carefully researched legal opinion. Its conclusion: that the clause in the contract requiring Greg "to continue to be of good character" gave the board an absolute right to dismiss him now on moral grounds.

Barnett smiled like a big cat after a full meal. "You see, Greg, the issue of character cuts both ways. Many of us on this board believe it important that the person who heads this company be above reproach."

The CEO of a large manufacturing company, one of the undecideds, declared, "Now that I know we don't have to go strictly by the financials, I want you to know my feelings here. FBS can't afford to have someone in charge who's brought so much bad publicity to himself and the company that he can't function effectively. I just hope that Barnett is willing to step back in again and take over."

The unsolicited endorsement brought spontaneous applause from Barnett's group.

All he needs are two more directors, Greg silently counted, and he'll have a majority; just a couple more and the deed will be done. The mood of the meeting provided little hope. Firing Greg was the easiest course. Too much controversy had arisen during his tenure. His personal life was too great an embarrassment to them all. They owed it to Barnett to punish his misdeeds.

Greg's supporters spoke vehemently for him, but the main reason to keep him on—what seemed to Greg the essential one—seemed to fade in importance: that having saved a dying company, he embodied its hope for the future. Greg guessed that he would be out of a job within half an hour. Gone would be the seductive, heady power to influence America's attitudes and help form its goals. One year. Such a very short time.

He gazed at Barnett. The Chairman was smiling now, sure of his victory, ready to end the debate and ask for a vote.

Greg recalled how, many years earlier, he had conceived of Barnett as some sort of demonic tempter, a human Mephistopheles offering him unimaginable wealth and infinite power, the satisfier of all his desires. All Greg had had to surrender in return back then was the love that comprised the essence of his soul. Now, however, the conviction overcame him that he had misunderstood then and all the time since: Blaming Barnett had simply rationalized the shift of guilt off his own shoulders. His own ambition had been the faceless devil that tempted him. Other people—Barnett, Ev—were merely its surrogates, its reifications. But that ambition was now lifting his sword arm and exhorting him not to accept defeat without calling out Barnett from behind the enemy ramparts for one final, perhaps futile battle.

Greg drew Diane's note from his shirt pocket. He unfolded it and read her words silently, to himself.

I hereby nominate Gregory Lyall to vote all of my shares of stock in the Federal Broadcasting System, Inc. at his sole discretion.

Diane Roderick Lyall

She seemed so sure that having a child would resolve all of their conflicts, he recalled, would harmonize all of their differences. But she had said something that disturbed him. What was it? Oh, yes. She had said, "I hope you realize how much I'm offering you." Her tone spoke not to his heart, but to his self-interest, demanding that he recognize the monetary worth she had placed on the negotiating table. If they had still been together, he would have replied with equal sharpness.

That thought flung him back some thirty years, into the bed in the little room he and Meggy had shared. He remembered clutching futilely at the fear clawing his intestines as his mother castigated his father, and then the months of resentment that chilled the house until she left both for California. He finally understood why not even the love of her children could keep his mother in that house.

He and Diane had been ill-matched from the beginning. Self-protective in the extreme, she had always measured so much of her commitment to him monetarily and held so much of herself back. He had tried to love her and never could. His resentment and despair would only increase as time passed. And guilt would always remain—for putting Chris through the torment of his rejection a second time. Each day he would miss Chris and hate himself even more.

Resuming his marriage to Diane—no matter what he stood to gain from it—would destroy the joy he took in life. The marriage would fail just as surely as it had before. What they wanted from each other always turned out to be just what the other could not bear to give up. Their child would suffer more because of their animosity than if they were apart from the start.

The price he would have to pay for Diane's vote was too great. In the end you are always your own devil, he realized; you grab for goodies with fingers already powdered with the evil that will poison you. An immutable law of nature dictates that every blessing carries a curse. There is always some sacrifice, some loss. Nothing is ever free.

I promise you this, he pledged silently to his unborn child. Your parents may not live together, but you'll always know that I love you very much—Diane would, too, he knew—and I'll always be there when you need me and even when you don't. That's the best I can give you, but it's the most important. I know.

Very deliberately, Greg ripped in half Diane's note giving him the right to vote her shares and then ripped it in half again and then once again. He dropped the pieces into an ashtray.

"Would someone move for a vote?" Barnett called out.

"Not yet," Greg responded before anyone else could. He stood up. "You've all had your say. Now it's my turn. There's only one person I want to speak to here." His gaze was fixed on Barnett's.

"A little while ago, your daughter told me she was pregnant with my child. My best wishes to you, Barnett. You're going to be a grandfather."

The Chairman's expression did not change.

"She also told me," Greg continued, "that I could vote her shares for my own slate of directors. She owns eighteen percent of the company. I phoned several money managers who control large mutual and pension funds. They say I'll have their proxies, too, and they'll round up others."

Greg looked across the table at the investment banker whose clients

447

held a significant number of the company's shares. "Would I have yours, David?"

The latter nodded. He had supported Greg from the beginning.

"That would give me the votes of over forty percent of the shares," Greg informed the group.

Tom Blake, president of the bank that was FBS's prime lender, decided the moment called for his voice as well. "A lot of the company's debt comes up for refinancing this year. We and the other bondholders have developed a lot of confidence in Greg. If he was no longer running FBS, we might think twice about rolling it over."

Greg returned his full attention to Barnett.

"You're the only director on your side with a substantial stake in the company, about thirteen percent. The others are friends of yours, advisers. But in the end a company is run by the shareholders who elect the directors. Ours have seen FBS's prospects brighten this last year and the value of their stock rise. I'd need only ten percent more of them for a majority. You'd need—what?—thirty-seven percent more. Which of us do you think would win?"

The question carried its own answer and floated above the table like an advertising blimp.

Barnett's rage could not contain itself. "You turned my daughter against me."

"No, she came to me with the offer. It would give me control. The problem is I won't accept her terms, what she wants in exchange. So, Barnett, you still have her vote—if you really want it. What should concern you, though, is that she was right to side with me—for your sake as well as for the company's."

"Let me be the judge of what's right for me."

"Stop fooling yourself. You had a very bad heart attack a year ago. You're lucky to be alive. Now that you're feeling better, don't delude yourself that it's still the seventies, that FBS is still on top of the ratings, and that you're still young and healthy. Those days are gone. Reviving this company is going to take endless thirteen- and fourteen-hour, rough-and-tumble days. You're too sick and you're too old. It will kill you."

Silence had seized the throat of every listener in the room, but Greg's eyes never left Barnett's. "And your ideas are too old. You know that as well as I do. Everything has changed. And keeps changing every day. This is a new industry, about to burst into a new century. Cable. Satellites. Direct broadcast. International programming. Maybe even interactive technology—TV and computers combined."

"Are you asking me to throw in the towel," Barnett exclaimed, "just go out to pasture?"

"I'm asking you—for your own sake and FBS's—not to try to reclaim the power you once had because that can destroy everything you built."

What surprised the listeners most, they later said, was that Greg's voice conveyed, not the resolute anger they expected, but respect and a sad sympathy.

"You built this television network from an idea only you believed in or understood. You envisioned its greatness before it possessed a single station or even a camera to put in one. But it's no longer your private empire. It belongs to thousands of shareholders and employees, to hundreds of affiliates and their employees, to millions of viewers. I can't take back what happened between Chris Paskins and me—and wouldn't if I could. But don't destroy what you created because you're angry at me or because you miss the power."

Abel Hastings spoke up. "For God's sake, Barnett, think of what's best for the company."

Greg's voice was a gentle entreaty, almost a whisper. "Which of us do you really want protecting this legacy you created? You or me? Which of us do you want watching over your investment in it—your grandchild's inheritance—building it? You or me? Barnett, the time has come for you to step down and look elsewhere for fulfillment. Have the good sense to walk away with honor and dignity and your place in history assured."

Greg's gaze now widened to take in the others around the table. "I think it's time we voted on renewing my contract."

Greg sat down.

Deep in anguished thought, Barnett suddenly looked old, spent. No one spoke. It did not seem proper before Barnett. When he finally did, his voice was weak.

"I move we renew your contract as CEO."

The vote was unanimous.

For only the merest instant Greg experienced the elation of absolute consummation. Against all expectations he had triumphed. Power was his once more. And enormous wealth. Every dream he had had as a boy. And then his glance fell on the reproach and defeat in Barnett's eyes. Would that someday be he? Would another, younger man someday wrest the power away and leave him with little of ultimate value to fill his days until death?

Barnett roused his energy to speak once more. Spite underlay the words. "You're so concerned about the welfare of this company. Scandal has racked it for months. Christine Paskins should take time off now, say a four-month leave of absence. Give this whole mess with my daughter and you and the Defense Department a chance to blow over. You talked about honor and dignity. Leave us and FBS some."

Directors eager not to hurt Barnett more than they already had jumped in to make similar requests.

"Granted she's popular," the manufacturing CEO said, "but there's no need to rub your love affair in the public's face. Turn down the fire under this thing for a while. You owe Barnett and your wife that much."

Even Abel jumped in to support the suggestion. "Chris'll probably be pleased at the chance to recuperate a bit after the strain she's been under. God, she came so close to getting killed! It really is better for the network—for all concerned—if we let things settle down."

"Aren't any of you thinking?" Greg asked incredulously. "She's the hottest news talent in America right now. Do you know what that will mean in ratings? But even if she weren't, that isn't how you pay back her kind of guts and loyalty."

His gaze slowly circled the table. "I want there to be no mistake. If she goes, I go."

"At least talk it over with her," implored the manufacturing CEO.

Greg eyed the Chairman. "Barnett, this meeting is over."

A crack of the gavel. Barnett left immediately. The other directors flocked to congratulate Greg on his victory, those who had opposed him being particularly eager to demonstrate their loyalty. Ideas were thrown out for the company's future.

As soon as he could break away, Greg rushed downstairs to tell Chris the good news.

"What about the piece on that toxic dump that's burning in Nevada?" Chris asked the newswriter distractedly. She was standing behind her anchor desk in the center of the newsroom, too nervous to sit. He had just handed her a rewrite of an intro for the evening's script.

"I already told you, Chris. We haven't seen the piece yet."

"We were told the piece was definitely ready to screen."

"They said by three it would be ready, Chris. I told you that."

"Sorry, my concentration's somewhere else today."

It was upstairs in the boardroom, she knew, and had been all day. She had no idea what was happening up there, but she was worried. Not that she had any real hope for Greg's survival. His defeat would probably mean bad news in some way for her own job, too. Well, she would struggle against them every step of the way.

She noticed someone signaling her and looked up. It was Manny. He was pointing across the room.

Chris shifted her gaze to that side. Greg was leaning casually against the door buck. An immense smile stretched across his face.

She raced around the desks and chairs on her way to him like a punt returner and leaped into his arms.

450

"You won, right? You won!"

He barely got out the confirming "Yes" before she covered his mouth with kisses.

"I knew you would figure out some way to do it. I knew you'd win in the end."

"I won," he managed to say. "CEO. Numero uno."

"You wiped up the floor with them."

Everyone in the newsroom had stopped to watch and was smiling.

"Hey, I think we need a little privacy," he said.

He put an arm around her and led her back to her office, quickly recounting what had happened. They sat down together on the sofa.

"So, in a strange way," he concluded, "what Diane did helped me to beat Barnett."

"And caused virtue to triumph over the machinations of evil."

"Something like that," Greg said, chuckling. "The threat that his daughter would vote against him, the coming of a new generation . . . they made Barnett feel mortal."

Chris was exuberant. "Congratulations on becoming a daddy. But Diane would have had to fight me to the death for you. You're mine, and I'm not about to give you up without a fight."

He smiled. "Feeling pretty cocky, huh?"

"And proud. As proud of you as I can be."

"After all the agony, it really did happen like we hoped it would . . . I mean, my asking you to wait until the board voted at end of the year."

"Destiny. Like Romeo and Juliet . . . and Tristram and Isolde . . . and Abelard and Heloise—"

"Hey!" Greg chuckled. "Those guys didn't end up in the best of shape."

She kissed him again. "But *we* will."

"Chris, I want you to move in with me just as soon as you can throw your things into suitcases. And to marry me as soon as our divorces come through."

"Is this a proposal? You're sure?"

"The minute our divorces are final."

She sighed happily. "I can't wait."

"Let's get away for a few days. Right now. We need time alone . . you know, to recover from all we've been through, to get used to living together again. Some warm island somewhere. Just a bathing suit and sunscreen."

"Sounds heavenly." She went to her desk to check her appointment book. "But I've got a satellite interview tomorrow morning with the head of the FBI. Domestic terrorism. And I'm booked solid into next week on morning talk shows. You know how important guest appearances are for building ratings back up. Tonight's Ted Koppel. '20/20' tomorrow night—can you believe that? 'Confidentially Speaking' competes with them and they want me? Letterman is Monday night. I'm trying to squeeze in time to do Carson in L.A., before the broadcast goes to Washington on Thursday."

"How about a long weekend somewhere for a start?"

"I've already committed to 'Sunday Morning' for CBS."

Greg's face was clouded. "You're running on overload and wound tight as a drum. Maybe the directors were right."

"What's this about the directors?"

"Some of them wanted you to take some time off," he admitted. "But for a different reason: to let things settle down. I refused, but a little time off right now wouldn't hurt either of us."

"Exactly how long did they want this vacation to be?"

"Four months."

Steam began to rise into the blueness of her eyes as if from heat vents on an ocean floor. "If you turned them down when there was nothing in it for you, that would be a first. In fact I can just see you tossing them a little bone. 'Pull Chris Paskins off the air? No problem, guys. Leave it to me. The chick's putty in my hands.' "

"You really believe I'd do that to you?"

"You always have in the past." Her hands were on her hips now, self-righteous indignation fueling her words. "Right after we exposed those memos from the secretary of Defense—how many days ago was it?—you told me I couldn't take any time off—remember?—that I had to take advantage of being cleared and rebuild my stature with the audience. Now you're talking four months."

"That's what the board said, not me."

"Being off the air after breaking that missile-base story was like being buried alive. I'm lucky to have made it back on. And you want me to take myself off willingly? No way."

"Just a short vacation. We both need it."

"The next few weeks are crucial to rebuilding my career," she shot back, "not to mention we're taking the broadcast to South America for the President's meetings down there and then following him to Japan. Every network anchor will be in Japan. I sure don't intend to be conspicuous by my absence."

She began to pace the room. "The real reason the board wants me off the air is to show America that the lovebirds aren't getting off scot-free, that we're being punished for our illicit pleasure. So, just like always, they want the victim to be the woman. Pin the old scarlet letter on my chest. Make me pay. Well, no way!"

"I've already told them I'd resign if they insisted on it. Don't turn this into a crusade. I had forgotten all about Japan." He was also reminded that this was still sweeps month. "Maybe we can manage some time away after that."

A thought struck her. "And just who did you intend to have sub for me—Hedy Anderson?"

"Probably."

"Hedy Anderson!" Chris was furious. "The Hedy Anderson who's been parading around here with a bandage over that scratch on her arm big enough to enclose a mummy! All she needs is a piper on one side and a drummer on the other to make it into the Smithsonian. You don't have a chance in hell of my letting her try to squeeze those wide hips of hers into my anchor chair."

"If she bothers you so much, I'll think of someone else."

"It's not just Hedy. It's your attitude."

"You're not thinking very clearly."

"My thinking was never clearer. You claim you didn't knuckle under to the board. Fine. But that was in the heat of battle, when you wanted to show them they couldn't push you around. The crisis is over for you now. You've won. You're safe. You've got your five-year contract. So, you want to reward yourself with a vacation and take me there for company."

"Judging by how wrought up you are, I think you need a vacation a lot more than I do."

"What you really think is, 'I want a normal life and don't like going away alone.' Losing a few viewers isn't as important as when you were fighting to hold on to your job and every tenth of a rating point was precious to you and you were demanding we fire people I needed to put out a top news broadcast."

"Let's drop it."

Chris was too worked up to stop. "You still think you can have everything and give up nothing, make no sacrifices. You married Diane for the luxury and the advancement—"

"Don't start that again. I paid for that ten times over."

"Once you'd gotten all that, you wanted me back again. Everything neatly back in place. No sacrifices—just wait it out until the end of the year. Now, miraculously, you have everything else, and the glamorous anchorwoman is just supposed to get fitted into it, as if I were some appendage of yours with no career of my own—except, of course, when you get worried about ratings."

"Chris, stop this. Maybe I didn't think it through, but I just wanted us to go off somewhere alone together. I hate it when you're not with me. My life's awful without you. That's why I went through all this."

453

"But not awful enough for you to compromise an inch for me and my career if yours might be affected."

His own temper was rising. "That may be true, but I've never seen much in the way of concern for my career when it happened to get in the way of yours, have you? Only when it costs us nothing, when our ambitions don't clash. That's the trouble: We each want to come first. A mathematical impossibility. Don't kid yourself, your career comes first for you, too."

"Well, I sure can't trust *you* to watch out for me."

Greg threw up his hands. "Is this what I want with my life, to be married to the same woman I butt heads with at work?"

Chris suddenly sat down. She was silent for a moment. Then her voice grew reflective. "Ten years have passed and the argument hasn't changed, just the details."

"It hasn't, has it?"

"This could be our little apartment in L.A. and that damned consultants' report."

"Or your piece on toilets."

"Or having to do one nincompoop interview too many."

"There won't be an end to it either." His voice, like hers, was quiet, almost sad. "We're both locked into FBS. We'll be butting heads forever."

"And we'll both be on the run, making appointments to meet in airports, neither one able to compromise for the other. That won't stop."

"Not the old-fashioned idea of marriage, is it? It might not even work out—you know, between you and me—no matter how much we love each other. Neither of us seems willing to pay for our love by yielding a single ounce of our ambition."

"I think the problem is we're scared," she said.

"Of what?"

"Greg, this should have been the happiest moment of my life, but two minutes after you asked me to marry you, I was picking a fight."

"And I jumped right in to slug it out with you," he admitted.

"We've always had some barrier before, some reason for keeping our love affair secret. Now we don't."

"And that scared you?"

She nodded. "I tried to find some way to put the barrier back up. I think we both did. I think we're both scared of being asked to give up too much."

"Or that finally getting each other—what we always thought we wanted—might not measure up to the dream." He smiled ruefully.

454

"They say you're punished in hell forever with too much of what you always wanted."

"I love you, Greg, I'm sure of that."

"I love you, too, you know that."

Now they were both silent. Greg spoke first.

"Chris, this marriage thing has probably put too much pressure on us. No need to think about marriage now. It will be months before those divorces come through."

Chris, too, was relieved to back off. "And we both have so many other things to worry about. Winning back the audience really is a giant priority for me right now. I'll have to work very hard at it."

"And FBS is only a very small way toward where I want to take it." He paused. "It just occurred to me: Since you can't get away right now, I'd like to go out to see my mother. Spend a little while getting to know her again."

"And you've got a child on the way. That's going to be another call on your emotions you're going to have to get used to."

Greg eyed Chris anxiously. "Are you saying you don't want to try making a go of living together? That you want to split up?"

"Oh, no!" She threw her arms around him and kissed him. Then she looked at him before saying gently, "But we have to be realistic. Loving each other might not be enough."

"Damn it! This is crazy! I thought I finally had everything in the world a man could want—this company, wealth, the most desirable, exciting woman I ever knew. I had even made *that* right again after all the regrets." He and Chris should be dancing in the streets. The world was spinning on their fingers.

"I always believed that once I was in full control of my life," she said, "as soon as I had made it, everything would automatically be wonderful."

"It wasn't supposed to be like this . . . unsure, unsettled. Just before the final credits, we're all supposed to smile and hug each other and feel reassured because everything turned out right."

"Until the next episode," she reminded him.

He pulled her against him. "I just always thought that when you got all your wishes, you lived happily ever after."

"And you're sure we won't?"

"It seems to me that what you get is just more wishes."

"And we'll have to compromise and give up a lot and work our tails off to make *those* come true."

"I guess no matter how angry and painful living together might get, we just have to keep remembering that it was worse being apart."

She hugged him tenaciously, but her voice was forlorn again, tentative. "That's not very much to start with, is it? That it hurts more to be apart?"

"Not much at all."

"And not very romantic."

Greg's voice grew stronger. "But I'll be damned if it isn't something! It won't be easy, but it certainly is something."

"Maybe it's as much as you ever get."

"Maybe," he said. "Maybe in real life that's all there is."